Building a Pack is Ruff – Part 2

Galadreal Simmons

<u>Dedication:</u>

To everyone who is hanging on by a thread...
Fingers crossed that shit gets better.

<u>**Music that inspired this story and these characters:**</u>

Dirty Little Secret – The All-American Rejects

Chop Suey – System of Down

Scar Tissue – Red Hot Chili Peppers

Hallelujah – Rufus Wainwright

Famous Last Words – My Chemical Romance

I Hate Everything About You – Three Days Grace

Adam's Song – Blink 182

A Long December – Counting Crows

Wake Me Up When September Ends – Green Day

Undone (The Sweater Song) – Weezer

Dance, Dance – Fall Out Boy

Numb – Linkin Park

Heart Shaped Box – Nirvana

Jumper (1998) – Third Eye Blind

Sweet Child O' Mine – Guns N' Roses

Lose Yourself – Eminem

Fake It – Seether

Val Kilmer – Bowling for Soup

What Makes You Beautiful – One Direction

Contents

This book is intended for mature audiences, 18+, and while I like to think it is a mostly light read, there are some events that might be triggering for some readers, including but not limited to: physical and mental abuse by family members (past and current), threats of sexual assault (past and current), family drama, death, anxiety, depression, illness, hospital visits, pet injury, mentions of attempted suicide (past). If you feel you need help, please reach out to the a mental health and suicide hotline, or dial 988 for the National Health Crisis and Suicide Prevention hotline.

This book also contains a fair amount of explicit content including excessive use of profanity, obsessive behavior, size difference, biting, knotting, nesting, sword crossing, sharing is caring (double penetration). If you think this book might not be for you, be sure to check reviews. If you still have questions, I can probably answer them, feel free to email me at galadreal.simmons.author@hotmail.com

Errors:

Lots of people have looked over this book, but we are human (and human with a spellchecker). If you see an error or a misspelling, please drop me a line. I am on Facebook as Galadreal Simmons, or you can email me at galadreal.simmons.author@hotmail.com

Garret

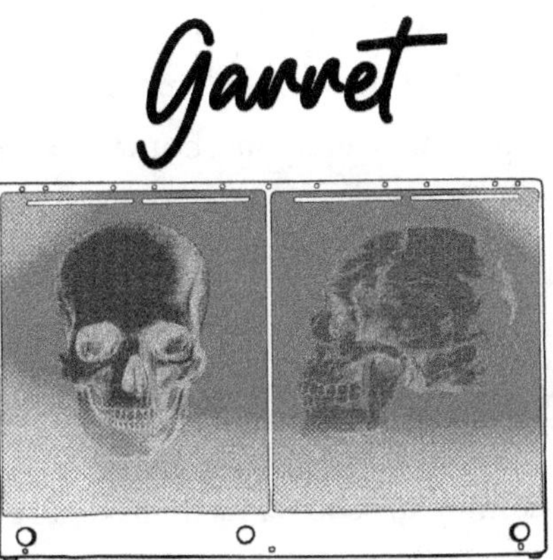

In which we fast forward through the week

Honestly, watching the two of them floundering in the snow while Sam tries to teach Steve how to install windows is probably the highlight of my week. My brother has never been the most graceful of creatures, and since he's basically neglected his body for most of the last ten years, it's a complete comedy of errors. Of course, then Kelly steps in and offers to help, so *I* have to offer to help. Before long everyone but Teddy clusters around the windows learning how to install the stupid things, while Sam does all the actual work and Kelly just holds them in place. So, I get to watch Steve make a fool of himself, and spend time with my sweet beta. It's a win-win.

Moreover, Sam and Teddy have been taking turns cooking, and both spending time with my brother, teaching him the basics. He seems fascinated by it. Which also leaves ample time for me to get to know Kelly better. She's more than I ever imagined, sweet and caring. Kind to everyone, but with a fiery temper. But I also kind of want to wrap her in bubble wrap because she is the most accident-prone individual I've ever met. I have a feeling my medical training is going to be fully utilized with this pack.

Sam insists on taking her to her doctor's appointment on Friday, even though there's still some snow on the ground. With Teddy's heat coming up, she wants to make sure her birth control is fully active. She says it'll take about a week, according to the doctor, but we're following her lead on this.

The snow finishes melting over the weekend, and today Steve and I are going with Teddy and Sam to turn in revised paperwork at the courthouse. Thank goodness he has a club cab in that truck of his. We haven't driven the SUV since we talked to Dad, and I keep expecting someone to show up for it at any time. So, it's easier for us all to just use the truck.

Not that we would've been able to talk to him again. He seems to have made good on his threat on our phones as well. That one surprised me a bit, as I expected Mom would still want to be able to reach out, but it doesn't feel like a huge loss if she decides not to.

Chapter 1

Garret

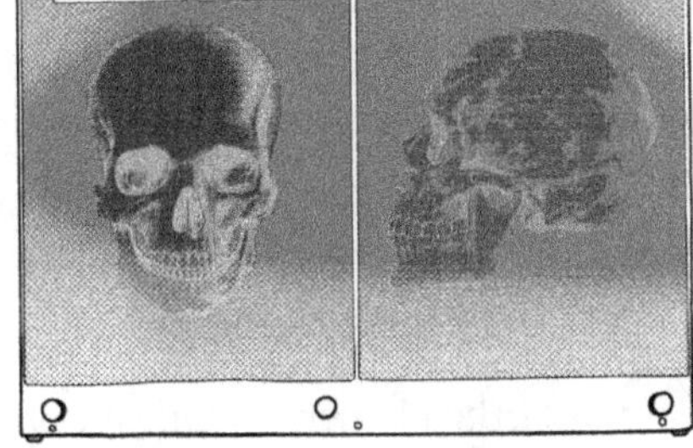

Kelly gives me a quick kiss on the lips before she leans down to give Jake a peck on his snout. She's running late, but can't seem to leave the house without giving him due attention. I'm pretty sure the big baby wouldn't let her anyway. He'd probably lie down behind her car and refuse to move until she got out to pet him. She has him spoiled rotten.

Snagging Jake's collar, I give Kelly a minute to get out the door and to her car before I let him loose. He stops yanking immediately and turns a dirty look my way. "Yeah, buddy, I hate that she has to leave too, especially since she has to get back to classes after work. It just means we need to get all the cuddles we can when she gets home." I ruffle his ears before heading back to the nest to collect Steve and Sam while Teddy finishes cleaning up breakfast.

"Come on boys, we gotta go if we're gonna have a chance to make it to pick up flooring and paint after we hit the courthouse. I wanna be home before dark," Sam's voice calls loudly from down the hall as he stomps out, already covered in dust despite the early hour. Steve walks a few paces back. The knees of his black jeans are nearly white from where he was crawling across the floor checking measurements on the nest this morning. These two are determined to get it finished this week so that when they take Teddy back to the omega center to get his stuff, he has a proper place to set it up.

Teddy comes out of the kitchen, a cloth shopping bag slung over his wrist by the handles and four to-go mugs divided between his two hands. "Ok, guys. I got breakfast burritos all around, coffee, coffee, a spiced chai latte"—he looks pointedly at me—"and...ugh...orange spice tea for me. Remind me to pick up more decaf at the store. The paperwork for the courthouse is already filled out in the truck. Does anybody need to use the bathroom before we leave?" I never imagined that Teddy would go all mother hen on Steve, but that seems to be the case. He and Sam both treat my brother and our beta like omegas. Even when Steve is being a catty little shit about having to share them with her.

My twin leans into Sam, kissing him on the cheek before practically prancing to meet Teddy and taking one of the mugs from him. "Thank you, Bear. I think we're good. Oh, do you have the names of those paint colors you wanted to look at? Garret, do you have your ID?" It's been less than a week, but Steve already looks so much better. His face is filling back out—I didn't even realize how gaunt he was looking until suddenly he wasn't anymore.

"What are you, my mother?" I pause before swallowing thickly, realizing what I just said, my eyes flicking quickly between my soon-to-be-pack before I let out a mumbled, "Sorry."

Sam's big hand comes down on the back of my neck, his size and surly exterior belying his gentle nature. "Nervous? It's not every day you join a pack." We basically already have, not the bonding part, but all of this just feels like a formality.

Sam passes out coats, just in case, and we all head out, letting Jake loose to run around before we climb into the truck. The weather around here is going to take some getting used to. Plus, once we figure out how, we need to try to get back to Los Angeles to see if our apartment manager locked us out and what happened to all our stuff. I have no doubt that Dad followed through on his threats, or at least some of them, if the phone situation is any indication.

I really miss wearing my own pants. I only brought a couple of changes of clothes with me, and no real pajamas since we were in a rush. With five adults in the house, we're washing a load of laundry every day. Sam says we need to set up a chore chart, so everybody chips in, and I'm fine with that. Just point me in the right direction and tell me what to do. As long as they don't try to make me cook again, everything's golden.

I take the back seat with Steve, letting Teddy sit up front with Sam. Despite their frantic reunion on the couch, they're taking their time getting to know each other again, and learning how much has changed...and what hasn't. A lot has happened in ten years, and I'm not sure if my brother understands yet just how different things are.

Sam rolls his window down, and yells to Jake. "Be good, guard the house. We'll be back soon!" The big dog wags its tail and flops down on the porch, stretching out in the warm sunshine as we back up and get turned around. I take another look at the SUV we haven't touched since we unpacked it last week. I wonder briefly what the hell is going on with our parents, before everyone starts arguing over who gets to control the radio.

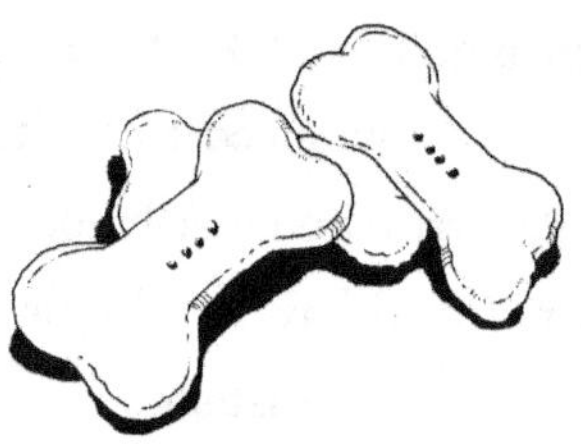

Sam

The courthouse is almost empty this early in the morning. Technically, they haven't opened yet, not for another ten minutes, but no one else is waiting outside, so hopefully we can get in and out and then make it to Springfield to get what we need before lunch. I can't believe that it's only been a week since I was here with Teddy.

A few other groups show up before the doors are unlocked, but Steve practically bolts up the steps to be first in line when they open the door to the clerk's office. He's already holding his ID and the new paperwork we filled out. But, clearly Ruth is having another Monday, because she doesn't seem excited to see us. Maybe she's just not a morning person.

Steve bounces up to the counter, dragging Garret with him. Ruth takes one look, heaves a sigh and repeats, "Marriage licenses are down the hall, second door on the left. Next!" Dismissing the overwhelming enthusiasm before turning to Teddy and me. "Oh, Mr. Carpenter, how can I help you this morning?" She gives Teddy a bright smile, so maybe she's just not fond of bouncy alphas first thing.

Teddy speaks up, since she seems to dislike him the least here. "I'm so sorry, Ruth. We screwed up. Is there any way we can adjust our paperwork from last week to include Steven and Garret Carson here? We didn't think they were going to be able to join us due to a previous commitment, but they showed up out of the blue right before the snowstorm. If not, then we already have the new forms filled out. We'll just need Kelly to come back and show her identification again at lunch." I can't be the only one staring blankly at my omega. He sounds so polite and professional; his voice has even taken on a sweeter tone than his usual grumpy growl. It feels like we're doing an invasion of the body snatchers moment.

Ruth smiles at him, reaching across the counter to take his hand. "Of course not, honey. That snow got so bad I didn't get a chance to get it filed. It's no trouble at all, young man." She pats his hand a couple of times before pulling back. Her smile drops as she turns to the twins, but there's no way she could know what happened between them and Teddy, so I have no idea what's up.

"So, you boys are gonna be a part of Pack Carpenter? Hmm, ok. I have some forms for you to fill out, and I'll need a copy of your identifications, please." She shuffles papers around on her desk until she pulls out the paperwork we came in and signed last week to hand over. Garret fills it out first, and Steve is practically vibrating by the time it gets to him. I get that he's excited, but I think it's a bit much since when he hands it back, Ruth gives him a hard glare followed by, "Sir, your handwriting is terrible. Oh well. Sign here and here, please."

She passes them back their IDs, and looks at all of us again before pointedly looking at Teddy and me and saying, "Congratulations again, Mr. Carpenters...er...Misters Carpenter." Steve offers her the new paperwork we did last night—it's already wrinkled from being clenched too tight in his hand. She looks at it for a moment, her eyes flicking up briefly to meet his. "Sir, this would have been very helpful before...You know what? That's ok. I'll just take this too. We can staple them together to avoid confusion. Have a good day, Misters Carpenter."

Effectively dismissed, we make our way back out to the truck, and drive the few blocks over to the garage to let Kelly know she doesn't need to make any stops before she goes to classes. It hasn't been long enough to justify taking her lunch, but my mind flicks over ideas on what I can do for her the entire way over, what she might need help with, or what she might like for a random gift. I really thought that a beta would be easier to take care of than an omega, but Teddy is so straightforward with what he needs: food, shelter, cuddles, a knot...and the alpha in the backseat who is acting like a hyper puppy.

But Kelly...I can feed her and give her cuddles, but everything after that is a mystery. She's less about the visceral reactions than Teddy, and while a lot of Teddy is personal preferences—like his love of heavy metal, dark fabrics, and artisanal cheese boards—it's harder to use alpha instincts to prove myself to her.

We pull up at the garage and Garret scrambles out the back door before I've even got it into park. This kid practically vibrates any time he's not around her. It's like somebody transplanted Jake's brain into a human. I swear to fuck, he practically wags every time she walks into a room. And I can't even blame the kid, I'm just...not jealous. I want her to know that I'm happy to see her too, and want to support her in whatever she does. I'm just not great at showing enthusiasm the way these two do.

Kelly's behind the desk talking to Sal when we walk in. She still gets that adorable blush when she meets my eyes, and Sal grins at all of us. "Yeah, just lemme know if you need anything else, or if any assholes call for a tow truck." She smiles at Steve and Garret before ducking out into the garage and throwing a wave at Gabe and Xan. Teddy walks up to the counter and leans over, leaving a loud smacking kiss on Kelly's cheek, causing her blush to get darker—before Steve pulls him back. Garret saunters over next, trying to look cool. He pulls her hand across the desktop and places a kiss on the inside of her wrist before glancing at me and stepping away.

Guess that's my cue, so I step around the counter and lean down to give her a quick peck on the lips. "Hey, Sugar. We already finished up with the paperwork and were about to head over to Springfield to get the flooring and paint. Do you need us to grab anything else while we're out, or do you want me to make anything special for dinner after you get home from class this evenin'?" Her arms reach up to wind behind my neck and my purr starts up automatically when she snuggles into my chest.

Her voice is muffled against me. "No, sorry. I'm just a bit worn out from getting dropped back into life after a week off. I can barely keep my eyes open today. It might also be the hormones from the shot doc gave me on Friday. Hopefully, the coffee will kick in soon." Her warm cheek presses against me as she turns her head up to look at me. "I might be kind of a zombie by suppertime."

"You need to go get some rest, Sugar. We can drop you at the house before we head out if you're feelin' under the weather." She shakes her head against my chest, taking in a big breath of my scent.

"No. I have work I need to get done here, and I can't miss class. I'm so close to finishing. But I'll call you if I have any trouble, or if I don't feel safe to drive, alright?"

Not wanting to argue with the pretty beta, I just nod my reply, squeezing her tighter against me before letting her go and returning to the proper side of the counter right as Gabe walks in. He puts some paperwork on the desk beside Kelly before turning to me, his face serious. "Hey, Sam. I...I don't want to step on your toes, but since you're here, I wanted to tell you. You should probably call your brother. We...uh...we saw him at the hospital this weekend when we took Candice in. She was feeling kind of off, so Jacks insisted on a trip to the ER. She's fine, but Joseph was there with Brice. I don't know if either of them saw us, 'cause Brice was lookin' pretty bad—pale—and your brother was completely focused on him..."

Gabe tapers off, scratching the back of his head, and my stomach gives an uncomfortable twist of concern, but also at the idea of inviting more anger and drama into my life. "Thanks, man. I...I appreciate it. I'll take care of it soon." When I turn around, Teddy is staring intently at both of us. I don't immediately remember that he's Brice's cousin, but yeah, he might be worried too. Shit.

Chapter 2

Teddy

Vee's tugging at my arm, trying to distract me from Kelly, but I can only focus on one thing at a time. Gabe and Sam are talking, but I'm not really registering the conversation—Kelly's staring at me intently. I look at the two big alphas, trying to figure out what's going on. "Thanks, man. I…I appreciate it. I'll take care of it soon." Sam looks back at me, his body tense and that little crease is back between his brows, the one that he's had for most of the last week.

Vee lets out a pathetic little whine as I pull my arm free of his, approaching our dominant alpha. My inner omega wants me to go back and soothe him, but I need to find out what's going on, why Sam looks so upset, why Kelly looks shell-shocked. Garret leans close. His hand comes up and wraps around the wrist she's brought near to her face, his thumb skating over the tender skin on the inside. Now they're all looking at me.

Shit, what did I do?

A whine slips loose before I can bite it back.

Too much fucking attention.

I can handle the attention at home, or with just my pack, but out in public, not so much. Gabe isn't a complete stranger, but I still feel the need to hide. Which is fucking ridiculous. I'm not some frail little creature that needs to cower around big, strong alphas.

Fuck me.

Why do I feel so fucking off kilter lately?

There should still be two weeks till my heat, it's not exact, but fuck.

Take some deep breaths, plenty of time.

Stop freaking the fuck out.

Still, why the hell is everyone staring at me?

Sam's big arms come around my shoulders, pulling me in for a hug. "You can call him if you want to, whatever you need to do to feel better." Now I'm even more confused, so I just nod stupidly, hoping like hell I'll catch up to the conversation. Vee wedges himself against both of us. His voice is a low mumble against my side, blending and melding with Sam's soothing purr. Have I heard Vee purr at all since he's been here?

"Sugar, if you're alright right now, we're headed out. Send me a message if you need anything, otherwise I'll have dinner ready when you get home."

Kelly doesn't say anything, just stares while Gabe grabs another set of keys off the wall before heading back to the garage. My head feels all static-y, like I missed something important, but I don't know what. Once I figure it out, everything's going to go sideways.

Sam and Vee keep me sandwiched between them all the way back to the truck. The twins climb into the backseat while Sam pulls me against his side as soon as I slide into the front. His purr rumbling through me feels like my bones are melting, and I just want to curl against him and sleep. I fucking hate biology—there's no logical reason for me to be on edge, and no real sense behind me wanting to sink into Sam and have him fix all my fucking problems. Other than my impending heat and no nest, I don't even know what the fuck my problems are. Ok, there's the whole Vee situation, but that's more of a frustration and confusion thing than an actual problem.

My phone chimes and I pull it out of my back pocket before sliding back to my own side of the cab and buckling in. Sam's hand reaches across the seat, the offer there if I just want to hold it, but I'm too focused on checking my email to do much of anything else right now. It's from Ms. Kimberly, my dorm supervisor at the omega center. I emailed her last week about picking everything up and getting transferred to online classes.

Dear Mr. Darnell,

First off, congratulations on finding and preparing to join a pack. I am happy to hear that your spring break went well.

I am CCing Ms. Jerrika Clarkson, your academic advisor, she should be able to assist you with discussing online options for classes for the remainder of the year.

There should be no problem retaining your nest for the next two weeks until your pack is able to arrange for transportation of your belongings. However, I would be remiss if I did not remind you that we do not allow unbonded alphas in the dorms, so please plan accordingly if you will be picking everything up.

If this will take longer than the allotted two weeks, please be aware that we may need to have housekeeping pack your things for storage, or charge you for an additional month of rent.

If you have any questions or concerns, please feel free to reach out to me or the office of admissions for further clarification on what paperwork will need to be filed for your release to your new pack.

Sincerely,

Kimberly Ross

Dorm F Supervisor

Reading over the email again, my stomach clenches. I didn't expect to need to have everything so soon. But that's ok. I completely spaced on needing paperwork to be able to fucking leave, though. This was never a problem when I was supposed to be an alpha, and it's not something Sarah and I ever really talked about, probably because neither of us ever thought we would go anywhere other than back to our parents' houses after graduation.

I do a quick search on the school's website and pull up the office of the registrar as well as admissions to search on what I might need. I'll call them if I can't find it on my own. But it'll probably just be faster to find it myself. Plus, it gives me something to occupy my time and distract my mind while we drive to Springfield to pick up flooring and paint. I picked out a dark black-stained cork flooring. Sam really wanted me to go with a mahogany. He says it's the most durable option if I don't want to do stone tile. But I liked the cork, it's softer than wood, moisture resistant, and it makes me feel good knowing that I'm not chopping down half a fucking forest to walk around on.

If we have enough time, I also want to look at mattress options, but Sam says he wants to finish the bed frame before we go too wild with that. Hopefully, Kelly won't need stairs for this one. I constantly worry about her falling already. We don't need her rolling out of the nest and having to make a trip to the emergency room during my heat. My poor pixie would probably insist on driving herself so she didn't interrupt everybody.

At least scrolling through my phone keeps me distracted, so I don't have to pay attention to the looks my pack is throwing my way for the entire trip. I should probably just give up and ask what the hell's going on, but I'm not sure if I can deal with anything else right now.

Back at the center, I read an article about something called fork theory, and I can completely relate right now. Each problem is represented by a fork you've been stabbed with. So, family drama is a fork, my nest not being finished is a fork, transferring schools is a fork, my upcoming heat is a fork, and Vee might as well be a damned trident. I just can't handle any more forks right now without bleeding out.

So, I try my best to ignore it, until it becomes painfully obvious that Sam won't let me. We pull into the mall parking lot first and he rushes around to my side, offering his hand down—which doesn't even make sense since I'm not much shorter than him—and then wrapping me in a warm hug and purring. "Don't worry, Love, whatever happens, I'm right here."

Ok.

Well, I wasn't freaked out before, but now I am.

Shit.

Pulling away from Sam—he doesn't want to let me go, and his purr stutters like a candle flame before going out—but now I'm worried about what'll stab me next. No point beating around the bush. "Sam, I've got to be real honest, I have no idea what's going on here. I mean…I was talking to Vee, and suddenly everybody was looking at me. What the hell did I do?"

Sam swallows a few times, that crease back in his forehead. Before he can say anything, I reach up and try to smooth it out. That at least brings a hint of a smile to his face. "It's…Shit. Gabe said he saw Joseph and Brice in the ER this weekend when they took Candice in for some pain. She's fine, but apparently it was bad enough that neither of them even noticed Gabe's pack in the room. I don't know if you want to give him a call, or if you'd rather I just get in touch with Joseph. I know this isn't the best time, but even though I'm pissed at the lot of 'em, Brice is still your family. If you wanna check in with him, that's fine."

Oh.

Brice.

Yeah…no, I should probably…

Fuck.

Leaning back into Sam, I wrap my arms around him and squeeze, pressing my face against his neck. "I appreciate it, Alpha. Once we get home, I'll call Mom. They're still on vacation this week, but she's probably checking her voicemail, and if it's anything serious, she'll know." I'm thankful that he would deal with his asshole brother for me, but I'm not too worried. For as long as I can remember, Brice has been smaller and weaker—it goes with being an omega. Still, Aunt Sandra will have called Mom even if it's nothing, so she'll have the scoop, and I can avoid any more drama.

"Alright, sweet boy, but I'm here if you need me, ok? Just say the word, whatever you need." Sam gives me another tight squeeze before letting me go to step away. The alarm on the truck beeps and I look back to see Vee and Garret just standing there. I think they need their personalities reset, because this zombie thing isn't really working for me.

I grab Sam's hand, dragging him towards the mall. "So, what are we gonna get for Kelly, and is there any other reason we're stopping here?"

Chapter 3
Steve

I'm missing my business ethics class for this. Ok, it's not like I could go anyway with what happened last week. The school probably already dropped me as a student. I hate the mall. At least we're not staying long. We don't even go shopping for Teddy. They all just want to go to the bookstore to look at something for Kelly.

Ugh, what's the point? I wander over and look through some books on photography and cooking before circling back to the manga section where my pack is standing. Dear lord, she probably reads some sort of shōjo shit. All the skinny little waiflike girls that are built like her, getting the handsome guy that everyone else wants.

Nobody likes the scrawny look.

Staring down at my own emaciated body, I scoff. Now that I have my bear back, I feel more like my old self. I can get back into a shape that he finds attractive. Unless, somehow, he does like her shape and I need to actually lose more weight. Shit, maybe I should stop eating as much. I don't think I can learn to cook without gaining weight. Fuck.

Sam takes the stack of books they've picked out to the checkout. I don't know why she's getting presents. It's not like she really contributes anything. I was hoping that Teddy and Sam would start getting tired of her soon, but it looks like I might be out of luck there. It's ok, I can wait. Besides, this trip is for him. If he wants to do something for her, that's fine. As long as it makes him happy.

Shit, why am I acting like such a jealous bitch?

Teddy wants us to be able to share.

Kelly doesn't have a problem with it.

Of course not, she has a uterus...and tits.

Even if they are on the small side.

She's prettier than me, too.

Fuck.

Once we get the nest sorted out, I need to get myself some cookbooks, but until then I can always take in some videos online, learn how to make a proper pancake. I need to do something to be useful, because clearly, I've fucked everything up. Sam is an amazing cook, and I'm sure he'll teach me if I ask, but there's just something about learning to do it myself—of being able to take care of Sam and Teddy on my own—that makes me happy.

We haven't actually tested out our debit cards, and at least if it's declined here, I don't have to see these people again. I pick up a copy of the newest volume of My Hero Academia and carry it up to the front, standing in line behind my pack to see if this rings up so I can go grab some cookbooks I looked at earlier. It's a long shot. The dads have probably already canceled all our cards, but I won't know if I don't try. Hell, if this works, maybe I should hit the ATM and see what else I can pull out. My mind swirls with possibilities, lost in the dream of being able to access our accounts and withdraw enough money to finish out the nest for my bear.

There's no telling how long I'd daydream if Teddy didn't pull the book out of my hand to look at the cover. When he speaks, my mind blanks completely. "Oh, nice...but I think we already grabbed that one. Let me check with Sam." He takes my manga over to our pack leader and they sort through issues before he brings it back.

"Yeah, no, we got that one already, but I really appreciate your help. Did you see something else she might like? We could grab it as a gift from you?"

Choking back my retort, I snatch the book from his hand. "This is for me. You...you don't remember?" But his puzzled expression is explanation enough. Taking a deep breath, I let it out in a sigh. "No, why would you? Fuck, it's been so long. No, this is for me. I'm hoping to get my collection back from the apartment, but we still need to call our landlord and see if we can get in to clean it out. I'm sure he'd prefer not to have to deal with it himself."

Teddy studies me for a minute before opening his arms, and I want to step in to them...fuck do I want to. Instead, I pull back and he lets them drop, his expression slightly puzzled. He turns back to Sam and Garret. I need to fix this—and just leaning on him and Sam and letting them take care of everything, and then acting like a catty asshole every time I see Kelly isn't going to do that. Shit.

They finish checking out in front of me and I step up to the counter with my book. The scanner beeps and I push my card in the slot. It takes a few minutes to run, but eventually it goes through with no problems. Jackpot. Now I can try to pay for the flooring and paint for Teddy's nest. I had planned on grabbing books for myself, but I can order those online. For now, we'd better get to the hardware store before Dad sees my card being used and cancels it out from under me.

Walking out of the store, I see Garret carrying three bags of books and scrolling through his phone quickly. His head is bent low between Sam and Teddy as they look over whatever he wants to show them. Teddy points to the screen a few times and Sam murmurs out some numbers but I don't have any idea what they're talking about. Sam sees me coming and wraps his arm around me, pulling me against his big chest. "What's on your mind, Steve?" I lean in against him, letting his rumbling purr ease some of the tension in my shoulders.

He isn't that much taller than Garret or me. Heck, we're not that much taller than Teddy, but Sam just feels larger than life. It's like he's so vibrant that everything else just bends around him. That sounds poetic and illogical, and I don't know why it goes through my mind, but even though we're both alphas, I just feel safe and protected and small next to him. My inner alpha rebels at the thought that I need anyone to take care of and protect me, but I'm still really enjoying the sensation.

My voice sounds hesitant to make the offer that I know would help them out, but I need to. "Hey, Sam. I want to see if our bank cards still work enough to buy nesting supplies if that's ok. Or at least, what we need to finish building the nest." I feel Teddy's arms wrap around my other side before he sinks against me, leaving Garret alone with his phone.

Teddy grabs his sleeve and drags him with us over to a bench to sit down. What the hell is he so focused on? After about ten minutes, he looks up. His grin is huge. "Ok, I ordered the black cork flooring tiles and dark sapphire paint for the nest. I did get an extra can, just in case, and for any repairs. They had the charcoal bamboo that you three thought would look good in the downstairs bedrooms, and some of that pale wintergreen paint for her room. Plus, a shitload of moisture barrier so we can start the install. Probably not enough to do the whole house, but it should be enough to get started, at least. Checkout says it should be ready in about an hour, but they'll send me a text. Payment went through fine...so...want to go grab some lunch while we wait?"

Shit, he beat me to it...and he didn't make a big fucking deal out of it.

Just saw what needed done and did it.

Why the fuck didn't I do that?

While I'm tempted to march right back into the bookstore and binge shop for myself, I let Sam pull me towards the food court. I know I can't fix this, but I need to try to make things better. What kind of gift says, 'I'm sorry I was an asshole for almost ten years, please forgive me, I suck. Also, I don't want to replace your beta, but I'm scared shitless you've already replaced me and don't want to deal with my shit anymore.'?

Fuck.

Oh, hey, pizza!

Chapter 4

Kelly

Cripes, when will this class end? I just want to go home and cuddle up with Teddy. Seriously, having the whole week off was too good and now I don't want to do anything. My eyelids are too heavy, if I can just close them for a minute while I listen to this lecture...

Nodding off over the table, my head thuds painfully against the desktop.

Ouch, too hard, what the what?

Bringing my hand up, I rub what's probably gonna be a red spot on my forehead.

Maybe I should hit the coffee shop before I leave campus.

Maybe I could bring one for everybody, a sweet coffee treat.

I still have another class after this one, but I like A&P. Business Composition is just...boring. Why do I even need this class? *Ugh.* My hands come up, rubbing my face and I debate slapping myself a few times to try to get the blood going. But a few people are already staring at me for my graceless face-plant earlier, and I don't want to give them any more reason to think I'm weird.

Today has been strange enough, people moving out of my way on the sidewalk, a few loud sniffs when I walked by. *Did I forget to put on deodorant this morning?* Zoning out is the only real way to stay awake, and I let my mind wander to the last week. Things started out pretty tense, but I like to think we've gotten into a good groove. I wonder what kind of coffee Steve likes—I can't make him like me, but I can at least try to be nice and hope he stops seeing me as a threat, and splurging on getting everybody a drink is a good start.

Pulling out my phone, I send off a quick text to Teddy asking what everybody wants from the coffee shop. He'll have a good idea or be able to get everybody's information, and it's easier than trying to use the group chat, which always goes off the rails. I don't want to have to sort through a bunch of replies that have nothing to do with coffee. If I can order it online, then I can just pick it up on the way to my car before I leave campus.

Teddy replies asking me for the name of the place so he can look up their website. It's just the big chain that they have on campus. So, I send him a quick link and then turn my phone face down on the desk. This is the first time all year I've even had a reason to have it out of my bag in class, but I don't want to be rude to the professor. Instead, I go back to staring intently at the clock, willing time to move faster.

People shuffling around me draw my attention away from where I've mentally drifted off, my mind finally registering that class is over. I snag my phone, flipping it over to see a reply from Teddy, but when I go to swipe it open, a low growly voice sounds right behind me. "Hey, Kelly...Kelly Girl...who's Teddy?" My whole body jerks in response and I tilt my head back to look up.

Looming over me is Spencer, aka Spence—big, alpha, super sweet but not the brightest bulb in the box—who is currently trying to stare a hole in my phone. Noticing my reaction, his face turns down so he's meeting my eyes. Blushing, he takes a step back. "Sorry. Just...how was your vacation?" He's rubbing the back of his neck with one big hand. Spence is big, like, as tall as Dr. Leo, but also wide. The guy looks like a darned grizzly bear, but he's also kind of a big marshmallow. He's in school on a football scholarship, but I don't know what he's actually studying.

"Oh, vacation, yeah, no, it was...it was good. Crazy. So crazy, but good." I close the screen on my phone, thinking I can order coffee before I leave my last class.

His eyes watch my hand, following the movement as I push it into my back pocket. "So...um...Teddy, is he a friend of yours? You've just...uh, you've never mentioned him before. Not that we're great friends or anything, but...shit—er...shoot...um, sorry, I know you don't like cussin'. You smell really pretty today." His voice trails off, and he looks at me hopefully.

Ah crud.

Deflect! Deflect!

"Oh, no, Spence, talk however you want. I just don't cuss 'cause Mom would skin me alive if she heard it. And yeah, I know, I'm an adult, but...uh. How was your break?" Stuffing my notebook into my bag, I try to return his smile with one of my own, something to get him talking about himself. The man really is a golden retriever, even if he's built more like some kind of mastiff. Ugh...he actually reminds me a lot of Jake, and that thought makes my smile more genuine.

His own grin gets wider as he follows me out of the classroom and down the hall. "So, um...Teddy?"

Deflection fail!

"Oh, uh...Teddy's my...well, he's my omega. We met at the start of break." That's a gross oversimplification, but I don't want to go into it. Spence is an alpha, and an amazing person, so I doubt he has any problems with it. Still, I had to deal with some negativity when I was dating Sal, and I couldn't handle it.

That's not why our relationship didn't work, but it didn't help the situation either.

Spence isn't following me anymore, and I feel silly talking to myself. Turning around, I notice him stopped in the hallway, staring at me. His nose has gotten kind of red and he kinda looks like he needs to sneeze. I turn around and head back. There's a few more minutes before the bell, and I'm doing great in A&P, so if I'm late, it's not a big deal. "Hey, are you feelin' ok? You look a little flushed all of a sudden. Did you get dizzy or...?" The question hangs in the air, waiting for him to fill it.

I step into his personal space. His face has dropped and he's staring at the floor. Part of me wants to reach out and feel his forehead, make sure he's not running a fever or anything. We've never been super close, but I worry about him, anyway. He's the kind of guy who'd give you his coat in a snowstorm to keep you warm. Oh, I hope he didn't get sick with that storm we just had.

"No, I'm...I'm ok. Thanks. Uh, Teddy's a guy's name, right? It's not short for like Theresa or something like that, huh?" His eyes are almost pleading with me.

"No, sorry. Teddy's a guy. I kind of got an entire pack last week along with him, but he's the biggest snuggler. That's probably why I smell like him. Sorry, Spence."

He shakes his big head. "Nah, no, Kelly. No, don't be sorry. Congratulations. I'm happy for you. Now, let me buy you a coffee and you can tell me all about it. How did you guys meet?" His eyes are a bit watery, but his voice has stopped being shaky by the time he finishes talking.

Shoot.

"That sounds great, but I gotta get to A&P, you know. We're so close to the end I don't want to mess up now."

He goes pale. "Oh, no. No, you go to class, I'll…I'll see you afterwards." He waves his hand in my general direction before turning and trotting off down the hall.

Now to hope I still remember all the bones in the human foot for this stupid test. Who gives a test right as you're coming off a break? That's just mean.

Teddy

If the coffee shop on campus wasn't a national chain, I probably wouldn't be here. Instead, it seems like a good place to ambush Kelly for post class snuggles. We haven't been separated this much since we met, and it sucks. My arms ache to wrap around her, pull her into my lap, and bury my face in her hair. Purring until she melts against me.

We all go, because apparently, we all want cuddles. Well, except for Vee—he tries to squeeze in next to me and Sam no matter what we do. How do I tell him to back the fuck off because he's suffocating me? I don't want to be cruel, but after the last week, I'm exhausted. I appreciate him standing up to his dad, but I still can't fully trust him.

We arrive at the coffee shop, and I wander up to the counter to ask about an online order for Kelly. The barista's just finishing up my caramel ribbon crunch frappe, and we each collect our drink, plus hers, and go find a table to wait for our beta. Vee, once again, tries to wedge himself in between Sam and me, and earns a loud rumbling growl from our alpha. Vee looks between us before going and sitting on the other side of the table, next to his brother. Meanwhile, Sam pulls me across the bench and into his side, nuzzling into my hair. "You ok, Omega? How're you holdin' up?"

Before I have time to really ponder that question though, in walks Kelly followed by a huge fucking alpha with a dopey grin on his face. Three loud growls break out around our table, and it still surprises me when I realize one of them is coming from me. Her voice is friendly as they carry on some sort of conversation. "—told you, I need to pick up coffee for my pack, then I'm heading home. You don't have to walk me to my car, Spence. I promise I'll be fine."

The big idiot looks flustered, but tries to argue. "I just...I worry about you, ok. For my sake, please?"

She lets out a resigned sigh. "Fine, but it's a waste of time. Nobody bothers betas, you know that. But if it'll make you feel better, then yes, you can walk me to my car."

The gormless guy just continues to smile as he trails her to the counter. "Besides, I still need to pick your brain about how you met your omega and your pack. I thought we knew all the locals." Kelly's only half listening as she searches the counter before calling over the barista, who points at our table.

Kelly turns, and you can see the rage flaring in her eyes before she recognizes us. Then a smile blooms, and it's like the sun has come out from behind the clouds and all is right with the world. She grabs the big alpha's arm—causing another wave of low growls to erupt—and drags him behind her. I look down to see my hands tracing the edges of my cuffs and try to stop myself. It's an annoying habit I do whenever I get stressed, and the big alpha, at least, notices. My fingers twitch as I pull them away, trying not to fidget.

"Spence, this is my pack. That's Teddy, Sam, Garret, and Steven. Guys, this is Spencer. He's in my Business Composition class." She points at each of us in turn and the big alpha nods, eventually holding his ham sized hand out to Sam first, then me, Garret, and Vee last. "Now, you have seen me safely back to my pack, thank you for your chivalry, kind sir." Kelly tries to do a curtsy and her feet get tangled, even in jeans—almost face planting against the table, before I catch her and pull her into my lap.

Spencer looks back and forth between us, then down at my arms, one circling Kelly's waist, the other reaching for my drink. "Oh, hey, nice cards, do they have special meaning for ya?"

Blinking quickly, I draw my hand back and drop it under the table, hiding my tattoos and cuffs.

Everyone at the table stares at the big alpha, causing him to blush. His hand comes up, rubbing the back of his neck, and he stares intently at the floor. "Sorry, I don't always have a filter. My little sis used to try to read the tarot cards, and I can't even tell you how many times she attempted to do mine. They kinda got stuck in my head after a while...I could probably read 'em better'n her by now." He raises his head, trying to plaster on a smile, but it looks unsure.

I raise my wrist back up and turn it towards him so he can see the lady and the lion on my right forearm. Only the bottom inch or so is covered by the leather cuff, and he looks intently at it for a moment before his eyes flick back to my other arm. I bring that wrist up, letting Kelly balance on my thigh. The three of swords—a heart with three swords running through it. It's slightly different from the original design. This one needed to cover a bit bigger area, so I had a roman column put in behind it. With the number VII on a small plaque at the top.

The big alpha's eyes stare intently at my forearms for a long moment before his eyes flip up to my face. The concern written there is a shock, to say the least. I subtly shake my head no, and he gives a slight nod in response. "So...strength and betrayal, huh? Well, I'm glad Kelly here found you, she'll stick by you no matter what. So, you can relax now."

He smiles his big stupid smile at me again before continuing. "Oh, but it looks like you got the number wrong on the strength card. It should be a number eight, not seven, but at least that's an easy fix."

He nods at me again. "Anyway, I just wanted to make sure Kelly Girl was safe. She smells really good today, and I didn't want anybody trying to be stupid at her. I know she can take care of herself, but she's my friend...so...yeah. It was nice meeting y'all!" With a booming voice and an exuberant wave, he leaves the shop, and I take another moment to pull Kelly tight against me and breathe in her light lilac scent before we make our own exit.

Chapter 5

Kelly

The truck is parked right next to my little car. Not that the parking lot here is huge, but they should have parked closer to the main campus...then I could have hitched a ride with them instead of having to walk so far. Still, at least I don't have to carry all the drinks now. When we get to the lot I'm in, Sam, Teddy, and Steve all pile into the truck. Steve tries to get in the front seat, but there isn't enough room for three big guys without being squished.

My attention is drawn from their attempts at circus clowning the truck by a loud thunk. When I turn around, I see Garret has dropped his forehead on the top of my car. "Hey, Kelly, can I ride home with you? I just kind of need some space from...that."

With his face still pressed against the roof, he waves his hand vaguely in the direction of the truck.

Reaching across, I run my fingers through his short hair until his face tilts up to mine. "I understand needing to get away more than you know. Hop on in, sorry the ceiling's so low." His warm smile in reply makes my chest flutter a little. But I still laugh when he sits down, and his head has to tilt to the side just to fit in. Once he buckles his seatbelt, I fire up my tiny beast and we're off.

One of the major downsides of living in Oak Flats is how tiny everything there is. Even the college I go to is almost thirty miles away, and it's not much bigger than a vocational school. Which means every bump in the road on the long ride home has me apologizing for my car being so short. Garret just smiles and slides as far down as the seatbelt will let him. His knees are now pressed up against the dashboard, and I'm worried I might need a rope to drag him out when we get home, but at least he won't have a headache.

The silence is almost deafening, but I'm at a loss for what to say. So, in the interest of preserving my sanity I start talking, well, more like babbling, but I'm a nervous talker. "So, how did it go today? I know you guys were headed to Springfield. Were you able to get everything you needed? Did you remember to eat lunch, I worry about y'all not eating...which is really silly now that I think about it, I'm sure Sam wouldn't let anybody go hungry. Oh, did you go by the mall, they have the coolest soap and candle store that you can make your own scents at.

A few years ago Jacks went and got a whole bunch of candles there for Candice before she joined their pack, one for each of 'em. Though, apparently, he didn't read the instructions well, or they aren't really meant to burn for a long time, because he almost set the nest on fire last year when they finally got around to lighting the things. I guess it's lucky they work at the fire department, huh?"

Why can't I stop talking?

Nervous rambling is an understatement right now.

And I'm not even nervous around Garret, he's sweet.

Ok, well, a little nervous, our one-on-one relationship is closer to what I expected.

Though the purring, growling, and knot all still require a learning curve.

Shoot, did I say that out loud?

Why is he staring?

Please Kelly, stop talking.

My voice babbles on, and I'm not even sure what I just said. But he has a tiny smile, and his eyes are darned near twinkling. He looks like he's trying not to laugh and failing miserably.

I hate when I talk so much that I forget what's coming out.

Crap. Crap. Crap.

Biting my lip to stop the verbal flood, he finally laughs. "Sorry, I was starting to worry you were going to hyperventilate. Do you need a paper bag or anything? Do we need to pull over and you can try to put your head between your knees? Maybe you can bend over in this car, but I think I might need help to get out." His smile is warm, and that funny fluttery feeling is back in my chest. "To answer your...many questions. Today went fine. We did go to Springfield and picked up everything we needed. Sam took us to the mall to visit the bookstore, and we had lunch at the food court there. Pizza."

My head swings towards him before paying attention to the road again. I really need to find time to get over there. His smile gets bigger when I give him more attention. "We did not go by the candle shop, though I'm sure it's lovely. And yes, it's very lucky that Jacks's pack works for the fire department. Though from what I've seen of them I'm pretty sure that Gabe could glare at a fire and have it go out just to escape." This last bit sounds kind of silly, partly 'cause Gabe's a teddy bear, but maybe it's some of that sophisticated humor I don't get. Still, at least my hysterical ramblings have quieted down, so I'll count it as a win.

He doesn't offer up anything else on his own, and I turn on the radio. True to form, I can't get any signal out there on FM, and I don't feel like listening to someone ramble on about conspiracy theories on an AM station, so I turn it off again after a few minutes.

I'm about to start rambling again just to break the silence when I hear a low murmur. Looking around to make sure the car's not going to explode, I notice that Garret's eyes are closed, his lips moving slightly. Apparently he's singing quietly. So softly that I can't make out the words. The tone is sweet and melodic, and I want to lean closer to hear more of it.

Unfortunately, when I try to get closer his eyes snap open and the singing stops. Shoot. His blush is so cute as he notices me leaning way too far over while I should be driving. One of his big hands comes out and pushes gently against my arm, straightening me out in my seat. "Sorry, Sweetness, you need to pay attention to the road right now. If you want me to sing to you later…well, I'm not very good, but I can try. For now, just be safe." His eyes close again without waiting for a response, and I once again get angry at this stupid commute, since it won't allow me to curl up against him for a nap.

Dang-it coffee, why aren't you working?

I yawn so hard my jaw cracks. Today wasn't too crazy, but being back after a week off from everything because of the storm and break has worn me down. I can't even roll my shoulders because of this darned seat belt. And it's too cold to put down the window. My jaw cracks again on the next yawn and I pull over on the shoulder, determined to wake myself before I have an accident. I suddenly feel betrayed by my caramel mocha and want to throw it at something.

Checking for traffic, I get out of the car, moving around behind it to stretch my spine and legs. I feel too heavy today. Oh crud. What day is it? Pulling my phone out, I check the calendar.

Oh, look, fun times.
Shark week is almost here.

Feeling entirely too whiny, I pat my cheeks aggressively and get back in the car. Garret has apparently fallen completely asleep. A tiny spiteful part of me is tempted to wake him up and make him go into the next gas station we pass to buy me chocolate. I shoot the idea down in my own mind. I'm sure he would, Garret is super sweet. But I am already dragging, and I need to get home for a hot shower, warm food...and go by Mom and Dad's house to get my heating pad, more books, and clean out the bathroom cabinet, 'cause Tuck sure doesn't need pads.

At least now I know why I feel like sludge. Still, knowing and being able to handle it are two separate things. I get back in the car and get situated before pulling back out to head home. The guys are already gonna beat me there. Part of me wants to call now and ask them to stop for chocolate on the way home. But I feel bad making them take an extra trip for me. I hate feeling so whiny and off-kilter.

I shoot a quick text off to Teddy and Sam about impending doom and that they might want to trade me Teddy's bed, or be prepared to be used as heating pads for the foreseeable future. With that done, I slide my car back onto the road, heading towards my parents' house. Then I can hurry home to my cuddly omega.

I need a hug.

Chapter 6

It's not exactly on the way home, but I make a quick detour and pull into the grocery store. Teddy read the text from Kelly too, and while neither of us has a lot of experience living with beta women, I think we can figure this out. He's already got a search pulled up on his phone for what she might need. Steve gets out of the truck and follows us in. I doubt he knows what we need to get either, but I can send him to grab some candy while Teddy and I try to figure this out.

The store here is pretty small. It has a little bit of everything, but not much variety on anything. Except condoms, apparently. I chuckle a little at the memory of our beta's shopping trip on our first night together. At least it makes shopping for feminine hygiene products easier. I peer over Teddy's shoulder where he's pulled up a questionnaire designed to help pick out the perfect products for your period.

Do they have to sound so damned upbeat about this?

Eventually, Steve wanders back, and in the spirit of getting us the hell out of here, pulls up his own search engine. "What's Kelly's age, approximately? Uh, she's *so* not a virgin. Do you think she needs something for overnights? Probably better to grab those, too, just in case." He scrolls down his screen before handing me a giant bag of gummy bears and a package of chocolate bars, then stacks some truffles on top before reaching over to grab some slim tampons, a box of pantyliners, light overnight pads, and regular flow, passing them all off to Teddy. He walks farther down the aisle and picks up a bottle that says Menstrual Pain Relief and a bright pink bottle that says Midol, reading the back of both before putting the generic looking one back.

"Ok, that...looks like everything," he says, still scrolling through his phone before looking between us. "Did you want to make her some sort of comfort food? According to this site, it might help with the PMS...but it might not. Oh, we should probably get some hot cocoa and marshmallows, that's always good. She probably already has a heating pad though..." He trails off, looking thoughtful before shoving us to the freezer section to pick out some cartons of ice cream. "She isn't lactose intolerant, is she? No...she's been eating that soup...hmmm. Fuck it, everybody loves chocolate."

All three of us are now thoroughly loaded down as we make our way to the front. Billy is working again this afternoon, and he looks from me to Teddy to Steve before he shrugs and starts ringing us up. "Afternoon Mr. McKinnley, is Kelly feeling ok?"

My eyes squint before I nod. "Sorry, it's Carpenter now, but you know you should just call me Sam—unless your manager's around."

He gives me a big grin. "He's not, but he gets upset if I use first names, it's just easier to remember this way. Also, I saw your friend there"—he nods towards Steve—"and another guy chasing after her last week, and I was keeping an eye on her when your truck pulled up. Sorry, I didn't mean nothin' by it." His ears are red as he stares down at his hands, scanning our items.

"Well, Billy, I appreciate it. Thanks for keepin' an eye on our beta. This here's Steve—he was with his brother Garret—and Teddy, our omega." Billy's eyes flip up to Teddy for a brief moment before they swing back to me. He finishes ringing us up in silence, and I press my debit card to the reader. We each grab a couple of bags before he pipes up again. "Congratulations, Sam...Mr. Carpenter...Carpenters...not sure how that works. But tell Kelly I said congrats too. Have a nice evening."

I nod in return as we file out and start loading stuff into the truck bed. Teddy's staring intently at Steve as we all settle in. "Ok, Vee, I appreciate your helping back there, but I didn't think you liked Kelly. I mean, I thought you actively disliked her. What gives?"

Steve looks between the two of us. He's chewing his lip and looks like he's trying to decide on an answer. "That's...fair. I don't like her. I don't hate her, but...I'm jealous? You all seem to have such a good relationship. She makes it look easy. I didn't think I'd ever have a pack, and now I do, and they're falling all over themselves for a skinny little beta girl. It's...frustrating." This last word is spoken almost like a question. "Besides, whether I like her or not, I don't want her to feel bad—if she feels bad, you two will spend all your free time trying to make her feel better."

Teddy is staring intently at him from the front seat. "So all this"—he waves his finger around towards the bed of the truck where we stowed all our purchases—"is just so we won't give her attention?" Teddy sounds skeptical, and I can't blame him. What Steve says doesn't make a lot of sense for a long-term plan.

The alpha throws up his hands. "Ok, fine, I don't hate her as much as I thought I would...just because I don't want to fuck her doesn't mean I want her to be uncomfortable. I don't want to fuck Garret either, but he's a miserable bastard when he doesn't feel good. It's just...better for people to not hurt. Alright?"

Teddy reaches through the seats and pulls Steve into a tight hug. "Thank you, Alpha. I appreciate your help. Now buckle up and let's get home and get dinner started." Steve pulls back. His smile is as big as I've seen it yet.

Three seatbelts click as I start the truck, then Teddy pipes up. "You know, with all of us at the house, it would probably make more sense to plan out meals, at least by a week, so we don't have to go to the store as much. I know you mentioned the chore chart too, but you've been doing all the cooking, and most of the cleaning. We've all been washing our own laundry. Let's be honest, I was under the assumption we are going to bond. It seems kind of silly to keep everything separate at this point."

I nod along. It's a good point. We'll talk about it more after we get his nest finished, and the twins settled. For now, let's just get home and get warm food and cuddle our pretty beta.

Steve

Helping Sam in the kitchen is a lot more enjoyable than I would have ever thought. He's a good teacher, and every time he gives me a compliment, I want to melt. He said we don't have time to make a proper slow cooker chili which, in his opinion, is the best comfort food. I completely disagree, but I've never had his chili, so maybe I'm wrong.

Instead, we're making breakfast for dinner. Which seems kind of counterproductive to me since it's meant to wake you up. However, as he kneads the dough for biscuits, I'm starting to realize this isn't a quick cup of coffee and quinoa bowl type of breakfast. Teddy stands behind me cooking sausage in a skillet and looking over a recipe for country gravy on his phone.

Sam's voice draws my attention back to him. "Steve, can you please get in the fridge and get out the buttermilk? I need a touch more, and my hands are sticky." I grab the green bottle he points out and pour into the bowl until he says, "Stop," then put it away and go back to watching his big hands knead the dough. He's explained to me that if he works it too much, he ends up with hockey pucks instead of biscuits, so he's trying to get it done right as fast as he can. He rolls the whole thing out onto the stone countertop and starts pushing it flat before nodding at a drawer. "Rolling pin, please."

Cook used to use one of these when making croissants, but I never got up early enough to watch her make breakfast other than pancakes, and I'm kicking myself now, because this is fascinating. I want to learn to do this, to cook and take care of the people I care about...and Kelly, because they care about her.

Passing the rolling pin over to Sam, I watch as he flattens out the dough, kneeling down to check the height of it before grabbing a glass out of the cabinet and cutting out rounds of dough, then kneading it together and rolling it again. I'm so engrossed in this strange repetitive behavior that I jump when Teddy touches my shoulder. "Sorry to interrupt, but can you get in the pantry and hand me the cornstarch? I forgot it, and I need to keep whisking."

It's still both amazing and freaky to walk into Sam's pantry. Sometimes I feel OCD, but this shit is next level. It does make it easier though when I locate the shelf full of baking supplies. I grab the clear bin marked 'cornstarch' in his neat block letters and take it to Teddy, who gives me a quick peck on the cheek and goes back to stirring.

Sam is just closing the oven door when I return to his side. He takes a timer that's shaped like a bell pepper off the back of the stove and turns it to twenty minutes, then bends over to reach under the cabinet where he keeps pots and pans. I am apparently a fucking thirsty bitch, because all I can do is stare at his ass while he shuffles around, occasionally grunting, before standing up with a...wok? Well, it's not something I would expect for breakfast, but if he wants to make a stir fry, who am I to complain?

My internal musings about Sam's delectable ass are cut short by a low "wuff" and Jake scrambling out from under the dining room table and flailing into the living room. I guess that means Garret and Kelly are home. It took longer for them to get here than I thought it would, especially since we also stopped at the store.

A moment later, Garret walks in, arms full of a box of books, trying to block Jake from running out the door and knocking Kelly over. She follows soon after with several pieces of clothing still on hangers draped over her arm. She startles when she sees me. "Sorry, Steve, we...I needed to stop at my parents' place to grab a few things, and so they could meet Garret. Now the back of the car's full. I hope y'all weren't waitin' on us for food. That took a lot longer than it was supposed to."

Garret returns from down the hall, sans a box, and takes the clothes out of her arms to carry upstairs. He doesn't even acknowledge that I'm here, which isn't overly strange. We often have that freaky twin relationship where we just move around each other without ever talking. And most of the time, I'm fine with that. But right now, for some strange reason, I need him to acknowledge me. Maybe it's because he's been with her for the last hour and a half or so, but I need him to acknowledge that we still have a good relationship.

What the fucking hell is going on with my mind?

I never needed validation from Garret.

Is it just an insecurity thing because other than going to class, we're always together?

Is it because it's Kelly?

Would I feel this frustrated if he was with Sam or Teddy?

Ok, yeah, probably, then it would totally be jealousy.

I step in his path as he comes down the stairs, and his head jerks up, eyes meeting mine. His filled with a question while I just stare, annoyed. "Everything ok there, bro? Sorry it took so long. Kelly's parents wanted to ask what my intentions were towards their daughter and tell her, repeatedly, that she could come home anytime she needed to." He looks annoyed at that last part, but at least it explains some of the tension in his shoulders and his lack of speaking.

Really, I should be elated for my brother. He's never wanted anyone like this and the fact that she's reciprocating his feelings, even hesitantly, is wonderful for him. Unfortunately, like with everything else in our life, I'm waiting for the other shoe to drop. Something great happened, we found our pack...now what kind of horrible disaster is going to occur? Seriously, if Kelly's over-protective family is the worst we have to worry about, I'm going to count it as a win.

Speaking of the devil, Kelly walks over and leans against Garret, burying her face in his chest. Her voice is muffled as she talks. "Is there time for me to grab a shower? I feel crusty and gross from work and school, and I really want to de-funk and put on pajamas."

Garret drops a kiss to the top of her head. "I'm sure that's fine. Just go get comfortable."

Her arms tighten around his waist in a quick hug, but instead of replying to him, her face tips to me. "Sorry, Steve, but...you would have a better idea. About how long till dinner? I don't want anybody having to wait for me, but I feel wrung out."

Oh...ok, well, we don't really talk.

I mean, we talk just...shit.

"Um, Sam set a timer for twenty minutes on the oven right before you guys got here, so you probably have time, I'm guessing."

She rubs her cheek absently against Garret, cuddling closer, her eyes closing. "Thank you, yeah. A shower sounds really good. Sorry, I'm just so tired. Lemme...Lemme go get cleaned up and then I'll be happy to eat. Thank you guys for making dinner." It seems strange that I'm included in her show of appreciation, since I'm still learning, but I still preen at the thought of taking care of my pack.

She stumbles a bit towards the bathroom before pulling up short. There's a mumbled, "Need a towel." Then she swings towards the stairs. Garret follows her up, arms outstretched to catch her in case she falls, before joining me in the living room. Teddy pops out of the door to the kitchen before I'm able to make it back to check in.

"Hey, gravy's all done, and Sam doesn't need any help with the eggs. You want to help me set the table, Vee?" I nod once, and his attention turns to Garret. "You ok, man? What took so long?"

Garret stares at him. My brother does look a little shell-shocked right now. "Kelly wanted to stop by her house to grab a few things and her parents insisted on talking to me while she packed some stuff up. They also want to meet Steve, even though I tried to tell them he wasn't in a relationship with her."

They both turn towards me as I snort laughter. "Yes, we can all agree her virtue is safe with me. Come on." I grab Teddy by the arm and drag him towards the dining room to start setting the table. Before long, Sam comes out, loading down the center with a big platter of steaming biscuits, the pot that Teddy made gravy in, and the wok filled with scrambled eggs.

Huh, weird.

I guess it works when you have to cook for this many.

Teddy follows him into the kitchen and returns with a pitcher of water and a jug of orange juice, while Sam returns with jelly and butter. He looks between the two of us. "In case y'all don't like gravy on your biscuits." Oh, makes sense.

Before I can reply, Jake comes scrambling into the room and slides into his place under the table, his tail thumping against the chair legs. A moment later, my brother comes in, leading a sleepy-looking Kelly. Her hair is damp from the shower, and she's rubbing her eyes with the hand not holding my brother's.

Why does she have cartoon boobs drawn on her shirt?

Shit, I know that design.

Chapter 7

Kelly

Steve is staring at my chest and snickering, and I know it's not 'cause he likes how it looks. *What the heck?*

I look down, not realizing that I put on my One Punch Man pajamas. I just grabbed something with soft, fleecy pants out of the closet where Garret hung my stuff. These are a size too big, but they are so comfortable, plus they have Saitama and Genos fighting all across the bottoms, and Oppai written across the front over...oh, right, boobs.

Tuck, of course, thinks they're amazing, but he's a teenage boy, anything with tits is hilarious to him. I picked them up at the mall a couple of years ago, and this was the only size they had left, but they're some of my favorites. Even though I have to tighten the drawstring on them to keep them from falling off.

Garret, Sam, and Teddy are looking between Steve and me, but Teddy's the first to speak. "Vee, Honey, I know you find boobs funny, but this seems a bit excessive." Steve is leaning against the wall, bent over and wheezing, but he can't seem to stop giggling. He doesn't stop laughing until Teddy steps over and touches his back. "You ok?" is all our omega gets out before Steve stands up, wiping the tears off his face. He doesn't look entirely happy, though.

"Fuck me...a full fucking house. The person I have the most in common with is the beta. Seriously?" The glare he throws at Teddy makes him take a step back. His gaze swings back to me, and I'm fully awake now, wondering what spite he's going to throw at me this time.

"No, seriously, Kelly, I love those pajamas. Totally jealous, in fact, just a bit frustrated at the moment. Sit down, let's eat, then we can get some rest. Today was too fucking long." The others all exchange a long look while Steve plops down and starts filling a plate. Not to be delayed when it comes to food, I let Garret move around me to their side of the table so I can sit down as well.

Sam shakes his head before looking us all over. "The kettle's ready if anybody wants tea with dinner, er...breakfast dinner. And Steve picked up cocoa for later." He nods at the alpha in question, who barely acknowledges it. "I know you're tired, Kelly Girl, but we need to sit down and discuss our plans for the next week after dinner. You ok with that?"

I nod muzzily, tucking into my biscuits and gravy. "Sorry, yeah, sorry. Let me just...um. Hopefully food will wake me up at least a bit, ok?" He just nods in reply, but no one else says anything while we eat.

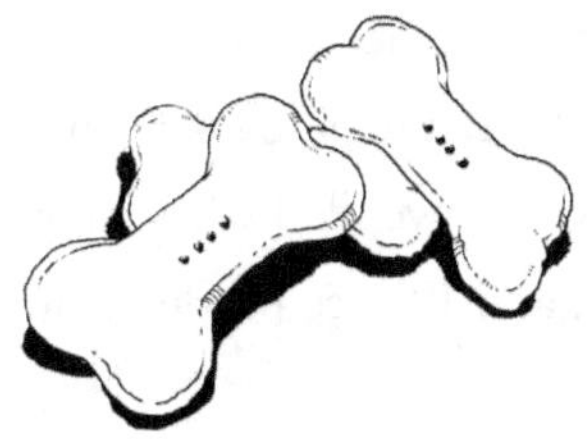

As usual, everything Sam makes is delicious. Thankfully, I'm a bit more awake now, though I think that has more to do with the orange juice than the food. My whole body is warm and cozy as I snuggle into Sam's lap on the couch.

Gosh, but I hope one of the things we're talking about is getting more furniture.

I don't want to sound ungrateful.

For the three of us and Jake this was good and cozy.

Now we have alphas spread across the floor, with Jake trying to crawl in their laps.

Funny, but not super helpful.

All eyes go to Teddy as he starts the conversation. "Ok, so, the biggest elephant in the room is my heat...it'll be starting in a couple weeks now if everything stays consistent." Two growling purrs fill the air. "Yeah, so. Sam almost has the nest done. I think his plan was to paint tomorrow." It's more a question than a statement as he looks towards our pack leader, who nods in response.

"Then we can do the floor and get the room set up for the actual event. I'm still waiting for my delivery from Nest-n-Stuff." He looks at his phone. "It was delayed due to weather, but should be here by Friday. So, the room may be ready by then. Unfortunately, I will need to go back to the courthouse and get a copy of the paperwork we filed with the notarization on it to take to the college, and I'll need at least one alpha to go with me."

His gaze turns to the twins, making Sam pout adorably, but Garret speaks next. "We need to head back to Los Angeles anyway to try to get any of our stuff that...Marc didn't have thrown away." He looks almost in pain as he bites out the name instead of saying Dad. "We can take the car, since it's still here, then pick up a moving truck for all our combined stuff and drive it back. If that works for everybody. I know it won't be cheap, but it seems like the best option. Plus, if we *are* able to get our furniture, we'll have something else to sit on." He smirks as he looks over the three of us on the couch.

Teddy nods his head. "So, we're looking at least a five to six-day trip. Cost of gas, cost of truck rental, maybe motels, and hope like hell you can get your stuff. I don't think we should rely on that though. Marc's a douche. We *will* need at least a pickup though to clean out my dorm...and a trailer if we don't have a moving truck." All eyes turn to Teddy, but he's staring intently at the wall, his mind spinning out ideas.

"Ok...I know it'll delay the nest being finished. But how about Sam and Steve come with me back to Los Angeles? They can't exactly help me clean out my dorm, but they can try to get the apartment taken care of while I pack up."

Garret snarls in annoyance. "Ugh, the apartment's in my name, Steve isn't on the lease. I'll need to go." He's looking longingly at me.

"Sorry, y'all, I need to stay here. I don't want to leave the guys in the garage in a lurch, and I really need to make sure I don't fall behind in school." Garret and Sam nod, Teddy just looks sad, and Steve looks...annoyed.

He opens his mouth, no doubt to say something snarky. "Ugh, fine, you three go." He waves his finger at the other two alphas and our omega. "I'll stay here, I can paint the nest...and maybe Sam can show me how to do the floor before you all have to leave. Kelly won't have to miss work or class. Sam is the lead alpha, so he really should be there, and he can help Garret move furniture if needed. Plus, that way he can drive his truck down so that if we don't need a full moving van, we don't have to waste the money."

He huffs an annoyed sigh when he sees Teddy's smile. "Besides, Kelly needs someone here in case any of our sperm donors show up looking for me or Garret, or in case Jake knocks her over and lays on her." He throws me a smug little smirk before Jake launches himself into Steve's lap. Any mention of his name is a reason for puppy cuddles.

Sam takes Teddy's hand. "So, Omega, why do you need a trailer?"

Teddy blushes and it's adorable. "Um...I...kind of have a motorcycle. Sarah helped me rebuild it. I only drive it around town. I'm not comfortable taking it halfway across the country."

Sam's growl is slightly menacing. "Please tell me you at least wear a helmet?" Teddy nods dumbly. "Fine, we'll see if we need a trailer."

Teddy's purr kicks up and I nuzzle deeper against Sam's chest, causing him to start laughing. "Come on, two against one is hardly fair." But his arms come around both our shoulders, pulling us tighter against him. I'm pretty sure he couldn't say no to anything Teddy wanted regardless, but I'd still rather have happy Sam than grumpy/stressed Sam.

Garret and Steve look up at us from the floor, Garret staring at me intently. "So, that's the plan? Fair enough. When do you guys want to leave?" Through much discussion and online research about filing pack paperwork, the guys decide to plan to leave tomorrow or Wednesday. Depending on when they can get the forms to officially transfer Teddy.

I start to doze off to the soft rumble of Sam's chest, and Teddy's hands stroking gently over my feet. And I don't remember anything else until I wake up in a dark room, surrounded by big purring bodies, and an urgent need to get to the bathroom.

Chapter 8

Teddy

Shit, I forgot to call Mom! Fuck a duck. Snapping awake, I sit up from my toasty alpha sandwich. I'm wedged between Vee and Sam, who has his arms around Kelly's back, while Garret cuddles into her front. So far, it seems to be the best way for everyone to get cuddles. I can still reach over Sam and touch her, and Garret isn't pressed up to anybody's dick, but still gets to cuddle Kelly. Plus, he doesn't have any chest-hair, and that was starting to be a problem for Sam. After the last week, he was starting to notice thin patches in his front pelt.

It's not easy to wiggle down the bed and escape without waking everyone up, but the light coming in through the curtain is barely a faint blush on the horizon. It's not like I can call Mom now. At the same time I feel like an asshole that I forgot yesterday. I can't really ask Brice if he's ok right now, but since Gabe says they saw him at the hospital, it worries me. Still, I can only handle one thing at a time.

Tiptoeing across the room, I open the door and nearly wipe out on Jake laying in the hallway. He snuffles briefly at my foot before letting out a loud huff and rolling over on his side. His eyes gleaming in the dim morning light. I fucking hate being awake this early, but now that my brain is running, there's no way to get back to sleep.

Holding on to the rail with a death-grip, I creep down the stairs and into the kitchen. The wind blasts me with a frigid gust when I open the backdoor to let Jake out. Fuck, I'll be glad to get the rest of my laundry and stuff from the omega center. My coat is pretty ratty since I haven't needed it for several years, but it's better to have something.

Sam showed me how to set up his coffee maker. It's not hard, but there are a lot of buttons on it. I get a fresh pot brewing for them and fill the kettle for myself before I let Jake back inside. He nearly knocks the door out of my hand trying to get in out of the brisk morning. Then he goes and turns in a circle a few times before laying in front of the stove and glaring at me. Huh, I guess Sam does normally have him fed before the rest of us are up.

"Sorry, bud, I have no idea where your kibble is. How about we just wait for a bit until your dad gets up and he can show me, huh?" He makes a loud grumbling noise, but after a minute lays his chin on his paws and closes his eyes. It probably won't be long before Sam's up, anyway. That man seems to rise with the roosters. I really need to look through that catalog on blackout blinds for the nest and get some ordered.

Not that I'm a night owl either, but the closer we get to my heat, the more of a whiny bitch I'm going to be. Also, if they don't give me proper snuggles as we get closer, I'll need to drag Kelly in there beforehand and lock everyone else out so I can have proper beta cuddles. I love having Sam and Vee wrapped around me, but I also kind of miss waking up with my nose full of Kelly's sweet lilac. It just starts the day out calm and relaxed.

Plus, Vee and Garret have made the sleeping situation so much more complicated. Vee doesn't want to accidentally touch Kelly in his sleep. Maybe he's afraid he'll get girl cooties, or some shit. Garret only wants to touch her. It's a pain in the ass. The layout from last night seems to work best, or Sam and I can switch places, so he's spooning me and I'm spooning Kelly. Otherwise, there's whining and drama and I don't have the patience for that at night.

The kettle starts making little, short whistling bursts, causing Jake's floppy ears to perk up. He grumbles at me again before getting up and leaving, heading towards the living room. I don't know if he'll crash on the couch, or head back up to try to trip the next person out of the bedroom door. If I hear a scream or a crash, I can check.

Turning off the kettle before it gets loud, I rifle through Sam's tea box, looking for some more of that orange spice I had on the first day. It's not as good as coffee by a long shot, but the citrus helps wake me up. We all did our packing last night before bed, so hopefully we can be at the courthouse when they open and then be on the road for a fucking twenty-seven plus hour trip.

Fuck, I don't want to do this.

Better to just get it over and done with.

I'm just pouring water over my tea-bag, having found the orange spice, when I hear a loud thud and, "Gosh darn-it, Jake, you big log. You tryin' to kill me this morning?" No one else is in the room, so I don't try to hide my smirk—even after Kelly enters, followed by her fuzzy admirer. I nod towards the coffee pot as she stares blearily around. She walks up to me and just leans her whole weight against my chest, face first. "You are a gift from the coffee gods, Teddy. I love you."

My heart feels like it just skipped a beat. I don't know if she realizes what she just said, but it swirls in my mind, making my whole-body light up in elation. I doubt she means it that way, the way I think of her. She's probably still half asleep and talking through the brain cotton.

But I'll take it. Any sort of affection she wants to give me, I'm more than happy to have. Not that she's not affectionate, but we only had a couple of days with just the three of us, before we were pulled in different directions, and I miss the simplicity of just us, of Sam and me holding her to fall asleep. Of not having to worry about who I'm making jealous when I touch her. I didn't think being in a pack would be this stressful, and sometimes, it sucks.

"Hey Pixie, do you have any idea where Sam keeps the dog food? Jake's not a happy guy right now." Jake's ears perk up at our conversation and he starts wagging in full-body circles around us as Kelly continues to lean against me. She takes a deep breath before letting it out.

"Yeah...yeah, let me just..." Her voice trails off before she squats down and starts rummaging through cabinets. The position automatically throwing me back to the day we first met and how she was squatted down in the front yard petting Jake, her dress riding up. I can't bite back the little whine that creeps up my throat at the memory, and of what I want to do to her while she's on her knees down there.

It might be a few days before I see her again, and suddenly my inner omega is going nuts, thrashing at my control, needing to make sure no one else touches her while I'm not here. I need to make sure she smells like me, like *us*, before we leave. My jaw aches from clenching down, and with the need to sink my teeth into her pretty neck and make her mine forever.

It's well documented that bonding bites are strongest during an omega's heat, but I don't care right now. I can't count on Vee to keep an eye on her, and I don't know that big alpha she was with at school. What if he tries to lure her away while we're gone? Kelly wouldn't go willingly, but she's so tiny by comparison. Shit, Vee will be the only one here. What if her car breaks down? It's kind of a piece of shit. No, no, Xan and Gabe would never let that happen, and she'd be smart enough to call them if it did.

My mind whirls with all the possibilities of what could go wrong while I'm not around to protect her. The entire time she's going from cabinet to cabinet looking for goddamned kibble. Can't she see I'm having a nervous breakdown over here? *Fuck.*

A triumphant, "Ahah!" heralds her success, and she stands up, pulling the waist of her pants up and her shirt down, and dragging a huge plastic tub out from under the cabinet by the fridge. I lean over and grab it with one hand, yanking it the rest of the way out before I scoop her up and carry her out of the room. Much to Jake's consternation, as his eyes flip between me carrying her out of the room, and the unopened bin of his breakfast.

Chapter 9

Kelly

Teddy scoops me up, just as I was feeling accomplished. I manage to stifle my surprised squeal, since I don't want to wake up the rest of the house. He marches purposefully to the hall, and into what has been his room from that first day, closing and locking the door behind us. Honestly, it's the first alone time we've had in a week, and I can already feel my body warming up at the thought of having him all to myself.

He's been helping Sam try to stretch me out with those toys, which doesn't feel bad, but it does feel like every time we're together we have to have an end goal. Right now, this isn't an exercise or a practice anything—I just want him. I want my omega holding me, filling me. I want to bury my face in his cookie scented neck and lick him like a lollipop.

"Kelly, Pixie, I...I need..." He trails off, burying his face in my shoulder, his tongue tracing a long, hot line up my neck before he nips lightly against my skin. "Kelly. I need to mark you. Please. It won't be permanent, but I won't see you and...Fuck."

His teeth bite down harder, and I can't stop the pained whimper that slips free. "Shit! I'm sorry. Kelly. I just...fuck. How can I keep you safe when I'm not here? If you're marked, then no one will bother you." He grinds his hard length against me, his forehead dropping to the area his teeth were just on.

In truth, no one bothered me before. I talked to people, but no one really harassed me. Heck, I'm pretty sure that the only reason Spence even noticed me yesterday was because of Teddy's scent on me. He's always been friendly, but that was the longest conversation we've really had. He's sweet, but usually super quiet and reserved. Even during the few times I've helped him with homework.

Grabbing Teddy's jaw, I lift his face till his eyes can meet mine. "No biting. You can leave a hickey or something, but that hurt. Remember, I'm not an alpha or an omega. I'm not opposed to a little bit of sting, but we gotta work up to that, Teddy." His eyebrows draw down, and I don't remember if he's been with us during any of the times Sam has gotten more spanky. My cheeks heat at the thought, and I feel the tips of my ears getting red.

A low growl comes rumbling from his chest. The vibrations make me want to melt against him. "Fuck, Pixie, you smell so damned good. But I need you to smell like me. I know it won't last, but at least today. Please." His hips tilt and swivel against me, slowly building the warmth in my core. Dragging his lips to mine, I kiss him, cutting off his words. This I can do, smell like my cookie omega for a day or two.

He pulls back, trying to catch his breath. We're both panting, but he hasn't stopped moving his hips, and I am so glad I haven't changed out of my pajamas yet. These are gonna be soaked by the time he's done. His big hand comes up, pulling my collar farther down my shoulder. It's oversized already, but now my stupid boob is about to spill out.

Oh, I guess that was the plan.

Derp.

His mouth is so hot against me as he kisses over my collarbone and down to my nipple. He laves his tongue over it, and my whole body twitches, little bolts of pleasure shooting through me all the way down to my clit. He's far enough down my body that he's no longer pressing against where I need him, and my hips roll and surge on their own, trying to get some of the friction back.

His chuckle is dark and tickles my skin, right before he sucks my tip between his lips, and I cry out, then slap my hand over my mouth. Shoot, I forgot I'm trying not to wake the rest of the house up. I want this time alone with him. He laughs harder this time. "Oh, that was fun, Pixie...now I need to see if I can make you scream loud enough to wake everyone else. Let them know exactly how good I make you feel."

His free hand comes up, pushing the other side of my shirt higher. His thumb circling my stiff nipple before he rolls it between his fingers, teasing and tugging gently. My back arches, and I moan against my own hand when his teeth come down on my other side, biting lightly, his tongue flicking over my fevered skin. He moans into me as I writhe.

"Teddy, Teddy...please. I left some of the...um...my shot won't be fully effective until this weekend...please."

He raises up, and his mouth comes off me with a loud popping noise. "Where are they, Pixie? I need to feel you."

My arm flails towards the bathroom and he grumbles loudly as he leaves me feeling like a cold puddle on the bed. "Sorry...there's only the bed in here. I didn't know where else to put them."

He grumbles to himself as he comes out carrying a long strip of condoms.

Reaching behind his head, he pulls his shirt off in one smooth motion. It doesn't make sense that he's so self-conscious of his body. Our omega is so sexy. Sure, he's not as ripped as Sam, but he's solid with wide shoulders and a broad chest. So, what if he has a little bit of extra padding? But he's still blushing when he looks at me. Poor boy, I don't know how he hasn't figured out how much I want him yet.

"Ok, Pixie, strip. Time to get you out of those...really attractive pajamas." He snorts at the last bit, not able to hold in his humor at my One Punch Man sleepwear.

"If you want me to wear something frilly and cute, you're gonna have to get it for me. This is what I have." His eyes go dark as he looks over at me.

"Hmmm...you say that, but would you? Wear something I got you? Maybe something in white lace, something just as sweet as you are?" He looks like he's picturing it now instead of my frumpy jammies, and he likes what he sees.

"Or maybe we should go the other direction, something in latex or leather? Would you rather wear a collar or hold the leash, Pixie?" His voice is a low thrumming growl again that I can feel in my bones.

I slide my top off, and his eyes are drawn to my chest. It's a little cold down here, but I don't think that's why my high beams are on right now. Half of me wants to cross my arms and hide from his intense stare, the other half wants to sprawl out and let him do whatever he wants to with me.

He hasn't failed to make me feel good yet. It's only been a little over a week, but Teddy and Sam are very attentive in and out of the bedroom. Garret seems to be afraid he's going to break me, so we need to work on that.

Taking the third option, I scoot up the bed, letting my too big pants slide off my hips as I go. Teddy's eyes follow me, getting darker the farther away I get. "You trying to make an escape, Pixie? Not that you can get far without these." He tugs my pant leg, and the whole thing pulls the rest of the way off, before he bunches it up in a ball and tosses it towards the door. I wasn't planning on escaping, but if that's the game he wants to play...

I roll towards the side farthest from him and start to scramble off the bed. But this isn't the big master bedroom, and while it's not a bad size, by the time my toes touch the carpet, he's already upon me. Ducking under his outstretched arm, I spin to the side, smacking him on the butt as I pass. The expression turned towards me is puzzled. One eyebrow raised in question.

"If you want to play, you have to catch me first." Smiling at him, I wave my wrist in a 'come on' motion. The low growl that rattles out of his chest would be scary if he wasn't smiling so widely. I back up, but it's only a few more steps before I'm trapped by the door. Spinning, I try to run but immediately trip over my own pajama pants laying on the floor. My arms come out to catch myself, but big hands circle my waist before I can slam into the door.

"Maybe chase isn't such a good idea, Pixie. Isn't this how we met?" He pulls me up and against his chest, turning back towards the bed.

Looking up at his very kissable lips, I say the first thing to pop into my head. "Sorry, Teddy, if you weren't so handsome, I wouldn't keep falling for you."

He snorts laughter before dropping me onto the bed. "Shit, Pixie...that was awful. You and the dad jokes, I swear. Are you trying to make me lose my hard-on or what? That was just...terrible." Now we're both giggling as he lies down on the bed beside me. I'm sprawled out where he dropped me, giggling at him. It wasn't even a funny joke, but sometimes when someone else starts laughing, and you start laughing, then it's not even about the original pun.

We lie there giggling together, my eyes squeezed shut against the tears from laughing too hard at the absurdity of the situation. But his hand landing on my thigh shocks the last of the laughter out of me. My lids pop open at the ticklish sensation running over my hip. I look down to see Teddy's rolled over, his nose tracing along the sensitive skin there. "Fuck, you smell good, Kelly...are you sure I can't mark you? Just a little bite to make sure no one else tries to while we're gone?"

Reaching down to touch his face, I draw him back up my body. "No, no biting. Seriously...what is with this weird possessive thing you have going on? We've been together for a week and this is the first I've heard about trying to leave marks." His face nuzzles into my hand, and he inhales deeply before leaning over and giving me a quick peck on the lips.

"We *have* been together for a week. In that time, how often have we been separated? There was last Monday where you went back to work, then we all got snowed in. Then we've been housebound since...plus you brought home two more alphas. A guy could get a complex if you bring anybody else home."

I try to look affronted but end up laughing, "Ok, point of order, but *you* brought home two new alphas. *I* was just trying to work and grocery shop." His eyebrow goes up, giving me an 'oh, really?' look and I concede, "Ok, so we each brought home a new alpha...ugh, poor Sam."

Suddenly, he rolls over, covering me completely. He kisses me again quickly on the lips. "Ok, enough about the alphas. I want this to be time for the beta and the omega...before the alphas all wake up and I have to share you again." He tilts his head to the side, and we hear a few muffled thumps that could be either Jake or someone else getting up.

Chapter 10

Kelly

“Gotta seize the moment, Pixie.” And then he’s kissing me again, not soft and sweet like the small, gentle things before, but hard and hungry. His tongue traces along the seam of my lips. I open for him with a gasp as his hands roam over me, down my shoulders—his thumb tracing the edge of my nipple as they quickly make their way lower.

His fingers dig into my hips, holding me still as he grinds against me. The rough fabric of his sleep shorts chafes against the sensitive skin between my legs, and I let out an undignified little squeak, trying to wiggle away. He moans into my mouth at the friction but lets me push him away. “Shorts, Teddy, lose the darned shorts. That hurt.”

A quickly mumbled, "Shit," is his only reply before he shoves them down his thighs and kicks them away. Then he's on me again. His mouth going to my neck, licking and sucking the skin there.

I am definitely gonna have a hickey after this.
But at least he isn't using his teeth.

My own shuddering moan bursts free as he grinds against my sensitive clit. I want him; I want to feel him inside me again, not having to worry about the stretching and training—just the two of us. His fingers slide around my hip, where his hot length is already thrusting against me, and he pulls his hips back to give himself room.

"Need to make you come first, Pixie. I don't know if I can last with how you already feel against me. I need to make sure you feel good first." His face is buried in my neck, voice muffled. His fingers stroke over my sensitive flesh, tracing along the edge of my core and spreading the moisture around.

I don't make slick like an omega, so sometimes it takes a while to work up enough self-lubricant. Especially with my hormones being crazy. I should probably just be thankful that it was a giggling fit earlier and not being angry or weepy. I never know what my body's going to do when I have PMS.

"You still with me, Kelly?" His fingers are barely tracing around my lower lips now. He's still laying gentle kisses along my neck and shoulder.

Ugh, I spaced out.

I push on him again, rolling him off of me and following along to straddle his thighs while taking in his puzzled expression. "Sorry, Teddy. I just need to be in control for a bit." And hopefully gravity will help with my lack of moisture. Maybe.

I don't know; I'm still fairly new at this.

Most of it has been self-exploratory.

And I'm usually on my back.

Teddy doesn't seem to mind the change of angle. His hands slide up my waist, pulling my hips down and grinding me over his hard shaft.

Oh, that feels good.

I put my hands on his chest to help center myself and roll my hips against him, causing him to let out a low whine, and his whole-body shivers. "Fuck Kelly, you're beautiful." His eyes shine up at me. One hand tracing up my ribs to cup my breast, his fingers flicking across my nipple, squeezing and rolling the whole mound.

Now it's my turn to shudder. I bear down harder, rolling my hips against him, building up to a slow rhythm. Grinding against the hot bar of his cock that's trapped between us. His breathing grows faster the longer I move, but I'm already so close. I need to finish and then feel him inside me. I want that so bad.

Both of his hands clamp down on my hips, holding me against him as he thrusts up against my core. Personal lubrication is no longer even a tiny problem, and the squelching noises that are coming from between us are starting to get embarrassing.

"Fuck, Kelly, I can't—" is the only warning I get before I'm tipped over sideways and sprawled back across the bed again. "Can't last that way, feels too good," he mumbles against my nipple, right before he sucks it into his hot mouth. His fingers fly down my body, diving straight for my already sensitive and saturated core.

It takes just a moment for him to find my clit. It's so swollen that the first stroke of his thumb causes a deep burning ache. My hips rise involuntarily off the bed, and then he sets a tight pace, circling and stroking my hard nub with his thumb while two of his big fingers slide inside me. If I thought the sounds were embarrassing before, it's got nothing on this.

Biting back the start of another giggle at just how we sound together, it quickly turns into a muffled moan as he sucks hard on my nipple. His free hand grabs my other breast, his elbow braced on the bed beside me. His big palm covers me completely, and he raises his head to look into my eyes. "Come for me, Pixie. Come now."

I don't know if it's timing, the onslaught of sensations, or his raspy demand, but I do. My eyes squeeze shut, and it feels like I shatter, my nerves lighting up. Lightning racing under my skin as I feel his heavy body pinning my legs, his hot breath panting across my chest, the soft blanket under my back. Everything goes white and I can't stop the cry that erupts from my lips.

"Shit. Fucking...Goddamnit!" His muffled shout brings me back. He looks around frantically. My eyes trace down his body, and his erection looks a painful red. He's leaking profusely all over the bed. "Shit!" He gets up and starts stomping back to the bathroom before stopping and picking up the long strip of condoms that he dropped on the floor earlier.

His voice is nothing but frustrated mumbles as he fumbles to tear one off and open it without ripping the rest of the packaging. I reach for him, ready to help him as he tries to roll it on, but he gently pushes my hand away. "Sorry, Kelly. I'm about two seconds away from blowing my load all over your stomach...if you touch me right now, I'm gonna lose it. Just gimme a second, Love."

My mind sparks briefly at his use of the word love, but he probably just means it as another term of endearment, like when he calls me Pixie. Just a heat of the moment thing. I don't know how much alphas and omegas worry about love when scent is involved. I'd like to think it's important to them, but that's a question for another time, as he finally gets the condom rolled on. His penis is now covered in a bright banana-yellow rubber, and I have to stifle another giggle at the sight.

"Ugh, well, having your girl laugh at your junk is one way to stave off finishing early...so...thanks for that. I guess." Teddy lets out a loud sigh, and I capture his lips with mine.

"Sorry, I didn't realize I got one that was gonna make you look like fruit. I can't help it."

His head drops to my shoulder, snickering against my skin. "So help me, Kelly, if you get me laughing again…" His teeth nip at the skin of my shoulder, and this time, it jolts a little moan out of me. "Much better," he says, his hands coming down on either side of my head as he grinds his hips against me.

His head and shoulders drop until he can whisper in my ear. "I'm going to fuck you now, Kelly Girl. I'm going to try to hold on until you can come again, because that is the hottest fucking thing I've ever seen in my life. But I need you now. You good with that?"

My head goes up and down dumbly at his words, my entire focus now on the huge omega caging me in. His voice is a low growl that sends new shivers down my body. It must be reply enough, because he stares into my eyes as his hand reaches down, lining us up. I'm still so wet that he slides in with one long smooth thrust of his hips. There's a slight stretch as he gets to the end, but then his pelvic bone is rubbing against my clit. My legs lift, wrapping around him and holding him close.

My hips try to rise to meet him. "Oh, fuck…Kelly." He plants his hands and knees on the mattress and then all I can do is hang on as he pounds into me. The room is filled with his growling and grunting, the hard wet slap of our bodies together. I hear myself whimpering each time he thrusts against me. My hands circling under his arms to hold him close as he moves. My skin feels on fire with all the sensations. His chest is smooth, not like Sam, and our sweat soaked skin slides against each other.

Good thing we both still need a shower this morning.

Soon his movements grow frantic, the thrust of his hips becoming erratic. My name falls from his lips, a mumbled chant. His deep thrusts grind against my overstimulated clit until my whole body lights up as I'm suddenly pushed over the edge of my own release.

Fists clenching, I try to pull away so that I don't scratch him. I don't want to hurt Teddy. His body shudders above me as he finds his own end. My name mixed with a long groan as he bucks against me once, twice. He shudders, his big shoulders twitching, and breath coming in harsh pants as he locks his body to keep from falling on top of me.

"You ok, Love?" There's that word again. My mind drifts, chasing answers I don't have.

"Shit, Kelly, did I hurt you?" His words are gruff as he pushes up on his elbows.

I grab his face and pull it back to mine. "No, no. That was..." I roll my hips, stretching my back, and he shudders above me from where we're still joined. "That was really good. Sorry, my brain went offline for a little bit."

His smug smile is adorable as he wraps his arms around me, rolling us both to the side so that my leg is still draped over his hip. He slowly withdraws, causing my body to twitch at the suddenly empty feeling. The concern in his eyes comes back with a vengeance, but I put my fingers over his lips to keep him from apologizing again. "You're fine, it's just...it feels weird. Going from that full to empty so fast."

He ducks his head away from my fingers and leans towards me for a kiss. His arms around my shoulders hold me tightly against him. The two of us must fall into a light doze, because we both startle when a soft knock sounds at the door.

Chapter 11

Sam

As annoying as it was to wake up with just the twins, I can't help but smile at the sounds coming out of Teddy's room downstairs. I'm also jealous as shit, but they need some time alone. Do I wish I was in there with them? Fuck yes! But ever since Steve and Garret got here, these two have barely gotten a moment to themselves.

Teddy at least grew up with them, but Kelly's been pretty overwhelmed. She almost seemed relieved to go to work yesterday just to get some time to herself. 'Course, that being said, if Steve doesn't pull his head out of his ass soon and stop being a petty little shit, we're gonna have another set of problems.

Running my hands down my face, I try my best to ignore those tempting moans and force my feet into the kitchen. Jake's standing by the stove casting annoyed glances between the door I walk in, and the large bin of his food. At least he's not prancing at the back door to be let out. Grabbing out a scoop of his food, I pour it into his bowl and stand back before I get trampled. He acts like he's starving, but Stephanie already warned me once that he's prone to overeating and put him on a diet.

The coffee pot is already full, and little clouds of steam are escaping from the spout on the kettle. I'll have to thank them for getting that taken care of. While I would love that to be in the form of a big breakfast, Kelly's gonna be late for work if they don't finish soon.

Not that I'd interrupt them for that, but it means I can fix her something quick to go. I still have some biscuits from the batch I made last night, so I can toss together a couple of breakfast sandwiches that she can carry out the door if she needs to. It's less effort than I want to put in, but logically it makes the most sense so she doesn't have to rush or drive unsafely on the way to work.

While her eggs are frying, I pull out stuff to make a sandwich to pack for her lunch. As soon as I'm able to order an insulated lunch bag, she can start taking soup or something warmer. Not that the weather is going to be cold for much longer—at least, I hope not.

Decking out her sandwich with more vegetables than she wants—she keeps turning down my offer of lettuce and tomato—I put it and some carrot sticks in a plastic storage box and wrap the whole thing in an oversized handkerchief so she can carry it. Her breakfast is done, and the sandwiches are ready and wrapped in parchment paper for the road.

The clock says it's five till seven, and as much as I don't want to break up their fun, she'll be frazzled if she's late. The hallway is quiet when I enter, which means I'll probably be interrupting snuggle time. It's still a shame, but hopefully less embarrassing for them. Knocking gently on the door, I wait for someone to call out or open it.

There's a muffled squeak that's probably Kelly, and then Teddy opens the door a crack. When he sees it's me, he blushes adorably and opens it the rest of the way. Kelly is curled up on top of the bed. She blinks owlishly at me over her shoulder before smiling. "Sorry, Sam, good mornin'. I woke up early, and we weren't sure if y'all were leaving today or not."

She rolls over, stretching like a cat, and I have to bite back the groan at how sexy she is. Especially considering the time crunch. If we do leave today, it's gonna be even more disappointing that I have to wait at least another five or six days to touch her again.

Fuck my life.

I stalk over to the bed, startling another little squeak out of her when she sees me so close after her stretch. "Kelly Girl, you are trying every bit of control I have this morning." She looks up at me sheepishly, her mouth popping open to apologize, but I cut her off. "Nope. It's just about seven now, if you're gettin' a shower, you better get it done, 'cause you still gotta get dressed. Your breakfast and lunch are already packed to go."

Despite my words to make her hurry, I lean over the bed, trapping her between my arms. She looks up at me with those big brown eyes, and I'm lost when she sits up enough to kiss me. My restraint snaps at the taste of them mixed together on her lips. My arms lock around her, pulling her up and against my chest to deepen the kiss. Her lips part against mine, and I have to fight to keep my control from shattering completely.

My voice is a low growl when I manage to pull away. "Dammit, girl, I don't want to make you late for work...Fuck."

She practically purrs against me. "Sorry, Teddy wanted to make sure I was marked enough and smelled like him before y'all left. He says he wants to make sure nobody bothers me while it's just me 'n Steve here for a few days."

The marking I can get behind, but her smelling like our omega is just gonna draw in more alphas. Which Teddy must have forgotten since they don't usually bother him, but sending her out into the world like that is just gonna make it worse.

Shit.

Taking a deep breath and letting it out slowly, I say, "Ok, Sugar, go take a shower real quick and get cleaned up. We can get this taken care of before we take off for today. Just...lemme talk to Teddy real quick while you get ready." The two of them exchange a look as she slides off the bed and pads out the door.

Teddy glares at me, crossing his arms, but he softens when I wrap my arms around him. "It wasn't a bad idea, Love. I don't like the idea of her being here without us either. But, do you really think her goin' to school smelling like an omega and not wearing a bonding mark is the best idea? I saw what you did to her neck, but it's not quite the same thing and you know it." He sniffs against my shoulder, his small whine muffled where he's pressed against me.

"Nope, no, none of that. Don't worry. I understand, and once we're all bonded properly, then she can smell like you all day long, and I won't worry. Though truth be told, I'd rather her smell like both of us." I can feel his mouth curve into a smile, and his low chuckle eases some of the tension in my shoulders.

"Until then...how 'bout you help me gather up all her shirts, we can go throw them at Garret and Steve and make them roll around in the bed on 'em so they smell like the whole pack? The more alphas, the better in this case." His laugh is much louder this time.

He pulls away and looks up at me. "Vee is gonna hate her smelling like she belongs to him...and I am so fucking here for it. Serves him right. Let's go before she gets out of the shower, so that's all she has to wear today." I don't even try to stop my laugh. Yeah, neither Steve nor Kelly are real happy about our current situation, but shit, maybe it'll be good for them to get some time alone without him constantly feeling jealous. Maybe they'll find some common ground.

Or at least not strangle each other for the next few days that we're gone.

Chapter 12

Garret

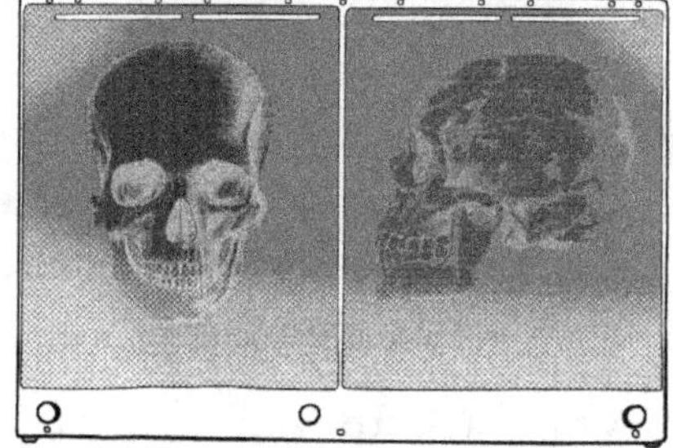

There are worse ways to be woken up than getting smacked in the head with my beta's clothes. I'd have rather it been her naked body, but beggars can't be choosers. Also, they can't really blame me for stuffing her sleep shirt into my duffel bag before we leave...especially if they don't see it. But I need her, and I need to be close to her, even if this is the only way.

It wasn't a bad idea for her clothes to smell like us while we're gone. Maybe it'll keep that great hulking beast away from her at school.

That's unfair.

He didn't actually seem like a bad sort.

But my inner alpha is obnoxiously protective and possessive of our little beta.

Plus, she's so small.

Betas aren't as weak as omegas, generally speaking.

I should have gotten her a taser while we were out yesterday.

A can of mace.

Something.

Her eyebrows draw down as she looks at the clothes Sam and Steve are rehanging when she comes out of the shower. "Why is everything I own now wrinkled? Guys come on, I need to get to work, I don't have time to iron anything...and I don't iron. *Ugh*, forget it." She huffs, snatching a polo shirt from the pile on the bed and slipping it over her head. "Whoa, guys...no worries about anybody getting close now. Wouldn't it have been easier for me to just borrow one of Sam's jackets? Dang!"

Sam and Teddy just look smug, while Steve picks up one of her T-shirts with a pirate flag wearing a straw hat on the front and steps into the bathroom. I'm now unsure if this is a jealousy thing because of their scent, or if he just wants to steal her clothes. He's lucky he's still so underweight, and she likes baggy shirts.

She lets out an exasperated sigh before quickly kissing Sam and Teddy, and then coming over to wrap me in a tight hug. "Gimme a call or stop by the shop before y'all head out, or whenever you find out if you gotta wait till tomorrow. I gotta get gone, but *please*...if you do leave, please be safe." She throws a mildly annoyed look at my brother as he comes out of the bathroom wearing her T-shirt under his over-shirt. Then she turns and walks off, thumping down the stairs while Sam and I finish packing our bags.

Teddy follows her out, and I hear the soft susurration of their voices before the front door opens and closes again. It didn't escape my notice that he smells like lilacs and sex, but that, at least, would be an excuse to get me out of bed early any day. Of course, the three alphas were up late painting the nest last night to make sure it had time to air out before we got back. So, it's not a huge shock that those two woke up before us.

Steve looks down at his stolen shirt before turning to Sam. "So, do you have time to show me how to install the floor in the nest so I can take care of that while you're gone? I'd like to have it ready when you get back."

Sam pulls him into a quick hug. "Sure thing. It'll still need the baseboards, but if you do get the flooring down, I sure would appreciate it. But take Kelly's shirt off first. She doesn't have many, and I don't want it gettin' ruined. I got a few work shirts up here that'll be fine for you to use when shit's messy."

He leans into the closet and grabs an old worn flannel shirt covered in paint splatters and tosses it over to my brother. Steve holds it up to his nose for a deep inhale before carrying it back to the bathroom to change out of my beta's top and snuggle into Sam's shirt. When he comes back, he looks like a kid dressing in his dad's clothes. Sam smiles a bit, watching him roll the sleeves up so they don't hang off over his hands.

Teddy walks back in, his eyes darting between the two of them before he walks over to give them each a kiss. "Mmmm, you smell like my two favorite alphas, Vee." He nuzzles into my brother's chest.

Undeterred by the lingering scent of Kelly, Steve grabs his face and tugs him in for a deep kiss before pulling back and meeting Teddy's eyes. "I don't want you to go...I know you have to, but I just got you back. You'll be safe? Sam, you promise?" His gaze flicks over to Sam, who smiles at them both and nods in reply.

The big alpha's hands come down on each of my pack mates' shoulders. "Now, let's get everybody fed." He looks over at me, nodding to make sure I know I'm included. "And I'll show Steve how to install flooring while we wait for the clerk's office to open. If we do leave this morning, he can stay here and work on that while we head over there, then hit the road."

They both nod, leaning against his bigger frame, and I'm once again left feeling like the odd man out. I don't want Sam or Teddy, not like that. But the ease with which they've come together still stings, especially with Kelly already gone to work. My hand tightens on the handle of my bag where I stashed her shirt. I don't know if my clothes will start to smell like her, or if her shirt will smell like me by the time we arrive, but at least it's something.

Not waiting for the cuddly trio, I carry my stuff downstairs. I'm taking pretty much everything I own with me, since I barely brought anything to start with. I do leave one of my button-downs hanging in the closet, in case Kelly needs it while I'm gone. She didn't ask, and there's no way to be sure, especially since she'll have most of Sam's and a few of Teddy's things here too, but I don't want her to feel abandoned either.

I snag my phone from the charger in the kitchen. There's no point in keeping it on hand since the damned thing doesn't work right now. I should have looked into that yesterday too, but I was so focused on getting the house stuff and getting home, I completely spaced. It's not like I have a way to pay for service anyway right now.

Teddy walks in and sees me staring at my stupid screensaver. At least I can use the damned thing to log onto Sam's Wi-Fi—or the one at the mall yesterday—but it'll be pretty much a useless brick when we're out on the road. Maybe Teddy will let us borrow his for the trip, so if we get separated, we can still get in contact.

Heaving a sigh, I set my phone down on the counter and go about fixing myself something for breakfast. Sam said he would make breakfast, but really, what kind of alpha am I if I can't even feed myself? Honestly, I'm only even going on this trip because we don't have any other options if we want to try to get into our old place.

I'm not quite ready to give up everything I own if there's a slim chance of getting things we can use here, like my clothes or the furniture. Shit, even things that we can sell to help out until we can find work. Though I don't know who in their right mind would hire someone with only the start of a residency. I'll need to get in touch with the school as well to see about getting copies of all my records.

Fuck me.

I couldn't even work on it last week, because everything was shut down for spring break.

Should have called yesterday.

I am so fucking useless sometimes.

Sam stomps into the kitchen, pulling me out of my spiral before it gets too deep. "Nope, no, nada. I remember the soup. You, outta the kitchen. Go…fix a cup of coffee or something." I leave the room as he grumbles to himself, pulling leftovers from last night together and a big box of eggs out of the fridge.

Chapter 13

Steve

Garret almost plows me over on his way out of the kitchen. Sam and Teddy have already started on breakfast, so maybe my brother is just feeling useless. He might also be worried since he's about to leave Kelly behind in the possibly vain attempt to retrieve our belongings. I'd gladly trade him places.

Sam turns and wipes his hands on a dishtowel before nudging Teddy and nodding to me. Teddy drops the tea bag in his hand and turns, stalking towards me, and taking my arm to lead me out of the kitchen. He leads me into the living room and positions me beside Garret on the couch.

"So, Sam, he's not good at...well, fuck. Here, see if they fit your phones." He tosses us a couple of flat pieces of plastic. "If that doesn't work, we can grab some cheap flip phones or something until we can get everybody upgraded." I look down at the credit card sized item in my lap, and it has a smaller card to push out...oh.

"Anyway, he stopped at his service provider in the mall yesterday and put us all on his plan. I gave Kelly hers last night, so she should be good to go too. Your old numbers are registered, so you should be set once we see if these work." Damn, I thought Sam was just taking a really long time to figure out his lunch. That was...sweet.

Garret already has the side slot of his phone popped open and is swapping out his old red card for the new green one. Is it really that simple? Once he slides it back together, he restarts his phone, then takes mine out of my lap and does the same again. Then I notice that the card in my lap has an S drawn on it in black marker. Ah, so they knew whose number goes where—gotcha.

Teddy stares down at both of us, scrubbing his hand over the back of his hair. "So...yeah. I'm gonna go help him out." He turns and stalks out of the room, and I hear quiet voices from the kitchen a few minutes later.

Garret hands me back my phone, which is booting up. Out of the corner of my eye, I see his fingers flying over his contacts before he puts it up to his ear. It rings several times and no one answers. Fuck, time zones. I slap his arm. "It's barely after 5 a.m. there." He pales, hanging up just as the voicemail clicks over.

He covers his face with his palms. "Sorry, I'm just scattered this morning. Fuck...well, hopefully that doesn't push Mr. Wazowski over into not letting us get our stuff. Shit." Patting him on the knee, I stand and follow after my omega towards the kitchen. He and Sam move around each other, Sam seems to be doing the cooking, and Teddy follows close behind, cleaning and putting things away as he goes.

Not knowing what else to say, I wave my phone at them. "It works...uh...thank you." Sam grunts, but Teddy at least smiles and comes over to give me a hug. His breath is hot against my neck. "I don't like having to leave either of you behind, but I have to do this. Like, legally, I should already be back at the center. The longer I delay, the more problems it could cause. I don't want anybody to try to use this as an excuse for us to not be together."

He looks over his shoulder at Sam, who's staring at him tenderly. The big alpha finally leaves off cooking and makes his way over to wrap his arms around Teddy—trapping him between us and squeezing tightly. He lets go with a sigh. "Breakfast should be ready in a minute. I made up some scramble bowls...so, little of everything. Can you go get your brother to the table? I wanna get this show on the road, and I still need to show you how to do the floors in the nest."

Garret comes walking into the room before I even have a chance to turn around. "Thanks, I...I heard." My brother looks lost again, but I don't know what to do to help him. Shit, some days I feel like I'm barely hanging on myself. Waking up this morning without Teddy and Sam nearly sent me into a fucking panic. The only reason it didn't was because I saw Garret, and my brother and I didn't sleep in the same bed until we came here.

I turn to grab plates, but Teddy's already bringing out the coffee, and Sam has each plate already made up...filled with fried potatoes and a bunch of other stuff, an egg on top of each one. If carpentry fails, the man at least has a career as a short-order cook.

Breakfast is, as usual, really good. I still want him to teach me. Shit, part of me wonders if I could go back to school and learn to cook that way. Dad would shit a brick but fuck it. If I'm not having to do a business degree for him, I might as well do what I want. And right now, that involves me taking care of my new pack. Even the beta.

Kelly

It's almost nine when Sam walks into the office, followed by Teddy and Garret. Teddy and Sam walk behind the counter and wrap me in a big hug, squeezing me between the two of them. When they pull back, Garret is there. He looks like he's just about had his guts ripped out, and I wish I knew how to help him feel better.

Wrapping my arms around his neck, I pull up against him, giving him a quick kiss on the lips, and he melts against me. My name is nothing more than a soft sigh as his arms tighten around me. He slowly lets go, stepping back, as his eyes meet and hold mine. "Promise me. Promise me that you'll stay safe. Steve may not like it, but if anything seems unusual, take him with you. He's probably not much of a fighter, but I'll feel better if he's at least close by if something happens."

His forehead drops to mine as his eyes close. "I just found you...and you probably think it's stupid, but I love you. You mean more to me than anything. I hate being away from you at all, but since we don't know what's going on with our dads...just...be safe. And call, call for any reason, even if you just want to hear my voice." He pulls back enough to kiss me on the forehead before turning and abruptly stalking out of the shop.

Teddy and Sam both look stunned, so I can only guess they weren't expecting the declaration of love either. It's just kind of a shock. No one's ever told me that, other than my parents. Sam comes back to the counter. "Well, this is awkward trying to go after that. But the kid's right, if anything feels off, make sure you take Steve with you. He'll bitch about it, probably a lot. But he can just fuckin' deal. We already picked up a notarized copy of the pack registration from the courthouse, so we're headed out. You have your phone?"

I nod my head, and he continues, "Alright, Honey. Just...be careful. Call us if you need anything. I can get somebody out there to help you. And please call me tonight when you get in from school, just to let us know you're safe, yeah?"

I smile at Sam and Teddy. "Y'all realize my parents are just down the street, right? I've lived here my whole life. I can even call Xan or Gabe if Momma doesn't answer her phone. Go, I promise I'll call tonight. You be safe, you're the ones with the stupidly long drive, and dealing with a bunch'a new people."

My eyes meet Sam's, and he still looks worried. Teddy gives me one more hug before pulling Sam out the door. I barely hear him as the door closes. "The sooner we get there, the sooner we get back. Let's go."

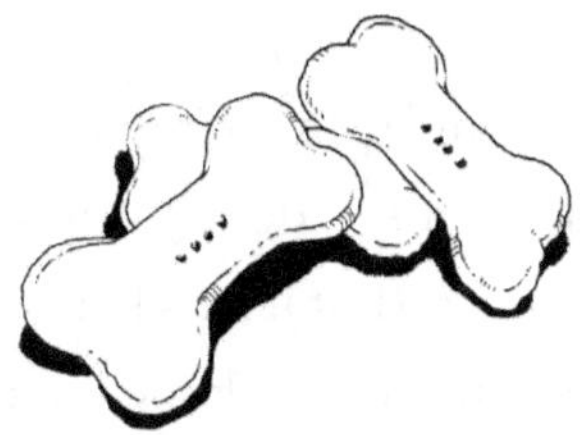

Work finishes with no problems, and while Spencer insists on following me around campus to make sure I stay safe, the rest of the day goes by fairly quickly. He saw me walking in from the far parking lot and asked how Teddy was doing, so I told him they were heading back to the center to pack up his room.

He looks confused for a minute but then smiles widely. "Hey, do you think he knows any other omegas there, like…anybody who might not want to live in a big town?" Poor Spence, the closest omega center to Oak Flats is still about four hours away. We've never talked about if he has a pack or not, but I'd guess the courting process for that distance isn't really plausible with full-time school and work.

"Well, I'm sure he knows lots of omegas, though I don't know if any of 'em would want to move here. I even sort of met his friend Sarah on the phone last week. She was pretty…um…exuberant." I'm not sure what all else to add to that. She's his best friend, but she was also super loud.

Spence looks crestfallen for a few moments before grinning again. "Ah well, Kelly, it'll all work out. Don't stress out about it." Unsure of why I would stress about Spence meeting an omega, I shrug it off.

He walks me to class and then meets me after each one to walk me to the next, and soon I'm done for the day. He insists on walking me back to my car, but it feels kind of awkward to have him just following me around. "Ok, well, I'm headed home. Ya think I should pick up takeout…or we can just do sandwiches. I don't have Steve's number to ask, but I guess we can just do sandwiches if his pancakes are anything to go by." Spence grins at me again, not getting the reference, but happy for me anyway.

"Bye, Kelly! Give your omega phone hugs when you talk to him tonight! I'm sure he'll need it!" His big arm waves over his head as I pull out. Seriously, you'd think we were best friends and I'm going away for a year instead of just heading home for the night. Still, Spencer is sweet, and I hope he finds his own pack and omega soon.

Steve is still working in the nest when I get home, and the floor looks amazing. I didn't doubt that he'd be able to do it. But between the painting last night and this, you can barely tell it's the same room.

Standing in the doorway, I watch as he sweeps up every bit of dust on the new floor, before using a damp mop to pick up any stragglers. He's so focused, I don't really want to interrupt him. Unfortunately, that means when he finally looks up and sees me, he lets out a screech that makes me jump in response. Now we're both standing here, glaring at each other and hoping not to drop dead of a heart attack.

After a few deep breaths, I try to ask what I came in here for. "So, did you have any idea what you might want for dinner? It looks like you've been working your butt off, I thought I might take you out to the diner if you feel up to it." One eyebrow goes up, and I don't know why he's so suspicious of me. "I mean, if you'd rather, I can see what Momma and Daddy are doin', and we could go over there. Otherwise, I can fix sandwiches." I don't want to mention pancakes since I worry he'll think it's a jab.

He stretches his shoulders, looking thoughtful for a minute. "Yeah…yeah, let me just go get cleaned up. Scooting around on the floor all day, I'm pretty stinky now." I will neither confirm nor deny this statement, so I just turn around to let Jake back in and feed him, then shoot a quick message off to Sam that I made it home, and we're about to go grab food.

A short time later Steve meets me downstairs—and he's wearing my shirt. It's fine, it's one of my older ones, but still, it makes me wonder about this guy who seems to hate me half the time stealing my clothes.

Chapter 14

Steve

S he looks skeptical that I'm wearing her clothes, but she doesn't say anything. This isn't meant to be a power move; I just like her shirts. Also, I don't particularly feel like dressing like I usually do. I'm fully aware that the T-shirt leaves my arms exposed, and all the black ink that covers them, but it feels good not to look like I'm headed for a funeral for once. I grab one of Sam's flannel shirts out of the closet to wear as a coverup. My courage only goes so far.

"You ready?" I slip my wallet into my back pocket, and my phone in the other.

She nods and calls out, "Jakey, we're gonna go grab some food. Do you want to stay inside or outside?" The big dog comes lumbering out of the kitchen, still crunching away at a bite of kibble, and walks to the front door before looking back at us.

Kelly lets him out, rubbing his ears a little before she closes the door. "Stay here and protect the house, Jake. Sam's gone for a few days, so we need you to protect us, ok my baby?" I swear to shit the dog sits up straighter, like it fucking understands her. It's both cute and also kind of freaky.

"Ok, Steve, sorry...um...my car's kind of short. I just...yeah, Garret bumped his head, so just...ya'know. You've been warned." She won't meet my eyes, and her cheeks are a deep pink as she stares at the ground. When I don't say anything in response, she finally looks up at me, her eyes flicking down to her shirt again. "So...um, are you more into the manga or the anime?"

Oh, we're doing small talk.

Fun. Fun.

Fuck.

Well, if I don't reply, I'll be an asshole. "Both? I prefer the manga. But I'll watch it too sometimes, mostly dubbed though. I'm not a huge fan of subtitles."

She's smiling at me now, her eyes bright and excited. "Oh...after dinner, do you wanna stop by my folk's house? You can look through what I have there and see if there's anything you'd like to read...I mean, we picked up a bunch last night, but there's still more...if you want to." The offer is surprisingly sweet, and it takes me aback, because I don't feel comfortable sharing with her yet, despite my current attire.

"Let's see how dinner goes first. I'm already kinda sore from working on the nest today." Her face falls, and she looks horrified for a moment. "Oh...Oh, gosh, I'm so sorry Steve. I completely spaced. I just...Let's get you some warm food, then home to stretch out. I might have an extra heating pad around if you need one for your back." Her hand comes down and rubs across her lower stomach—I forgot that just last night we were at the store picking up supplies for her. She's probably not feeling great either.

Trying to be more agreeable, I lower myself into her tiny car, and she was right—I am totally gonna get a concussion the first pothole she hits, unless I'm slouching down. It's still a surprise that the car dips even lower as she gets in. Will this thing even have an undercarriage left by the time we get to the diner?

It soon becomes apparent that the bottom of her car is the least of my worries. This girl acts like her little rust bucket is a race car—sliding around curves in the dirt road, flying over the gravel so fast that I don't even know if we hit most of the potholes. By the time we finally reach pavement, I'm surprised I haven't yanked the O-shit handle off her damned car.

She must hear my sharp intake of breath, because she slows her drift as we pull onto the blacktop, and then it's only another couple of miles to the diner. She's grinning like a maniac and I wonder briefly if she normally drives like this or if she just wants to torture me. Why the hell didn't Garret warn me?

"You ok?" is all she says as we pull into a parking space a few minutes later, and it takes me a moment to get my tongue unstuck from the roof of my mouth enough to answer.

"That was...what was that again? Do you normally drive as if being chased by all the demons of hell, or am I just special?"

Her giggle would be adorable if I didn't feel like leaning out of the car to vomit all over the sidewalk. Maybe that's her plan, she wants me to be too nauseated to eat. "No, silly. I don't get to cut loose often. First it was Mom and Dad, and now Sam and Teddy and Garret. Any of them would flip their lid if I drove like that with them. Heck, I've barely gotten to drive at all since I met the guys. Sometimes you just need to turn the music up really loud and go, ya'know?"

I look briefly at her little radio. It doesn't appear to have a bluetooth, or a CD player. There isn't even a front plug in for a phone connection. Dear lord, does she only have FM? Her laugh is high and clear as she watches me staring at the dashboard. "Come on, Steve, let's get some food. Then maybe some books, a heating pad, and home." She bounces out of the car like some kind of highly caffeinated squirrel.

Dear god, what have I gotten myself into?

My legs are still unsteady as I climb up and out of the car. She giggles again when I lock her door, and the engine makes a low ticking sound as I circle the hood to walk inside. It's odd that I even notice that, but then again, there are barely any sounds, even right in the middle of town. None of the constant hum of traffic I'm used to, or the people passing on the sidewalk. Just the birds settling in for the night in a tree beside the building, and the low hum of the streetlights kicking on for the evening. It would be peaceful if it wasn't so creepy.

The bell jingles over the door as we walk in, and Kelly looks around, seeing the server. "Oh, Hope. I didn't know you worked here."

A younger woman waves back at us. "Yeah, for a while now. Just sit wherever you want. I'll be there in a few." Kelly grabs a couple of menus off the counter and leads me back towards the far wall, stopping in front of the last booth.

"This ok?" she asks, and I nod briefly before sitting down with my back to the wall.

She stands there fidgeting and staring at me. "Do you mind? I...I don't like my back exposed. I just...Can you scoot over so I can sit next to you?"

That's fair. I don't like people walking up behind me either, so I scoot closer to the corner and she slides in next to me. We're both so scrawny that we could probably fit another one of us in the space that's left. When I go to pluck one of the menus from her hand, her grip is tight, and I tug a couple of times before she finally relaxes enough to let go.

"Sorry, Steve. I don't...I don't always deal well with people. It's easy enough with Sam and Teddy. They feel like my family, like they're mine, ya'know? But...I've never had a lot of friends, or really any serious relationships before. I just can't...Cripes, this is embarrassing." The tips of her ears are bright red as she searches for the right words.

Instinctively I reach out, touching the back of her hand, and she flinches briefly before relaxing and letting me touch her freely. The waitress, Hope, chooses that moment to make it to our table. She takes in our joined hands and smirks at Kelly. "Another alpha, Kelly, really? Well, I guess now that Pack Asher's officially bonded, you had to find somebody else to chase after." The bitch tries to sound offhanded, but I see the sparkle of malice in her eyes, and Kelly sinks down into the seat beside me.

That doesn't work for me.
I mean, I might not like her, but no.
Besides, even if she's not mine, she's Teddy's.
And Sam's.
And Garret's.
Fuck.

I summon my best stereotypical flamboyant gay best friend voice. "Oh, honey no. Kelly's my beta-in-law. She's getting mated to my brother...and my omega, and my alpha. But I don't like pussy. Speaking of which, if you could stop being such a cunt and bring us a couple of cheeseburgers and chocolate shakes, that would be just *fabulous*." I smile sweetly and bat my eyes at the stupefied waitress.

Kelly and Hope both stare at me open-mouthed—Kelly's ears turning redder by the second, and I worry I've taken it too far. But before our beta can either laugh or cry—I'm not sure which one I'm waiting for right now—Hope huffs and walks off. Thank fuck another older waitress is behind the counter, so at least if we have problems, like something disgusting in our food, we have someone to actually take it up with.

I turn back to Kelly in time to see a tear slide down her cheek. "Oh, Kelly, no. No, I didn't mean to embarrass you. I just...She was being such a bitch, and I reacted. I'm so—" My apology is cut off by a loud snort and then she's laughing so hard more tears run down her face. Wrapping my arm around her to keep from falling out of the booth, I wait until everything has tapered off before handing her a napkin.

She wipes her face with it before turning to me. "Sorry, Steve, the voice just kind of surprised me."

She lets out another little giggle. "And I went to high school with Hope. She's always been mean. First, about the fact that I had a job at the garage, which is supposed to be a man's job." Her fingers make air quotes on this last part before she huffs out, "Tell that to Sal."

I've heard a bit about the female alpha who works at the shop with Kelly, but I've only met her the one time, when we first got to town. In truth, it was enough to make me jealous—hearing Bear say she's pretty. That's all it takes, apparently.

Fuck, I really am a petty bitch.

Shit.

Kelly waves her hands in the air like she's wiping away the conversation. "Anyway, thank you. I appreciate you standing up for me. I'm...I'm not used to people doing that. Mom and Dad, yeah. But...I don't have a lot of people. Mostly the guys at the garage, and they're closer to family. I have a few that I talk to at school, but not even that, really. Spencer started following me around this week, and I think that has more to do with trying to get Teddy to introduce him to another omega." She sniffs again, her eyes still leaking a little, but I don't think it's still from the laughter.

Oh great, common ground.

Just what I don't need.

What would Sam do...or Bear?

Fuck, I'd channel my twin if it would help her stop crying.

Well, ok, I won't kiss her, that's for damn sure.

Ew, gross.

But hugs, I can do hugs.

I wrap my arm around her. She really is petite. Not as small as an omega, but I can see why Bear calls her Pixie. Pulling her against my side, it doesn't feel like the intrusion I thought it would, having her in my space. Maybe it's because her clothes still smell like the rest of the pack, maybe it's shared trauma. Regardless, she shouldn't be sad right now. I hold her and rock gently back and forth until the older waitress comes to our table with the food.

"Sorry for the wait, folks. Hope had to go on break but just call me if you need anything else." She waits patiently while I inspect the burgers and push one of the milkshakes into Kelly's hands. Then she nods and walks back to the front counter. It's too much to hope that Hope gets fired, but as long as we don't have to deal with her again, it'll make my night.

It takes a bit, but I finally manage to pull Kelly out of her funk by asking her a million questions about her favorite manga, and the town, and what else she does for fun. She's regaling me with a story about her bosses' pack meeting their omega when the waitress brings over our check. "Everything ok tonight? You can just take care of it up front when you're ready." It seems more like a polite way of asking us to leave, and I'm fine with that. Kelly did say everything closes early around here.

"Come on, Pixie. Is it too late to stop and meet your parents and get some books? I'm not sure if I'll be able to find any baseboards tomorrow out in the shop, and it's going to be super boring at the house otherwise." She smiles up at me, and yeah, I think I should try to make this work. Not a relationship like with any of the rest of our pack, but friends. She really can be my beta-in-law, maybe?

She jabs me lightly in the ribs before handing her debit card over to the waitress, who's now working the register. "Well, you could always use more practice on the kart racing. Maybe then you could actually beat me next time." Her smile is huge as she takes her card back and we walk out into the parking lot.

I have an overwhelming urge to ruffle her hair. Instead, I snark back, "Oh, har har, very funny. I happen to know for a fact that you only won because Garret would blue shell my ass every time I passed you for first place."

Her fake gasp of shock brings a smile to my face now. "Steve, are you insinuating that I used my feminine wiles to cheat? 'Cause let's be honest here, I don't personally see that as being even remotely possible. If Garret was waiting for you to get in first place to shoot, it's because he's your brother. Come on, you'll understand when you meet Tuck."

Thankfully, the ride to her parents' house is much more sedate.

Chapter 15

Kelly

"Mom, Dad...Tuck, this is Steve. You met his brother Garret last night." My parents stand in the living room staring at us. Tuck is playing his Switch on the couch, but at least he can still form sentences.

"Jeeze, Sis...how many alphas are you going to collect? Good on you for building up a harem there, but I think you might have broken Dad this time."

Steve looks between me and my family. His gaze swings over to Tuck, who isn't even looking back. A look of understanding passes over his face. "Oh god, no. Nope, not a thing. Don't even go there, tiny dude. Think of me more as a replacement for you than any sort of romantic relationship. Strictly platonic, possibly one day bordering on familial or sibling affection. I don't...um...the whole...female thing. Not my cup of tea."

Dad does a slow blink as Tuck starts laughing on the couch. "Oh, so you're there for Teddy? That's cool, the whole alpha and omega thing we have to learn about in school. Yeah...I don't care. Whatever makes y'all happy, I guess." My brother never looks up from the screen on his game, despite his words.

Mom blinks this time before pulling Steve into a tight hug. "Oh, Steve, it's so nice to meet another one of Kelly's friends...isn't that her shirt?" I laugh as Dad finally shakes some sense back into himself.

"Yeah, looks like we're going to be clothing buddies, at least until he gets his luggage from Los Angeles, anyway." I stare pointedly at Steve, who just returns his own smirk.

"Anyway, we were at the diner, and wanted to stop in and grab some more of my books before we head back to the house. And get Steve to meet you, so now you know the whole pack."

Dad nods along, only losing his rhythm when I say the word 'pack'. Finally, he reaches out and offers his hand for Steve to shake. "Well, uh...Steve, it's nice to meet you." He's still processing, and honestly, he's handling this better than he could. I mean, just look at Steve and Garret's dad.

I don't like that man.

It's not just that he caused Teddy to get hurt.

But Garret and Steve too.

Ugh, I don't even want to like Steve.

He's like one of those tiny yappy dogs.

The kind that are super loud and obnoxious, and try to bite anytime you get close.

I wanna get along with him, 'cause I like being friendly.

But how do you make friends with that?

I must have zoned out because the next thing I know, Mom's touching my shoulder. "Are you ok, Kelly? You look so tired."

Leaning into her, I just absorb her warmth. "Yeah, sorry Mom. It's...um...impending doom?"

It takes her a moment to reply, her face puzzled. "Oh, yeah. Ok, let's make sure you have everything you need then. Living in a house with a bunch of men can be challenging. I swear, your father would never keep chocolate in the house before we met. And forget ice cream or a heating pad. That being said"—her eyes scan over my dad for a moment—"well, he's still quite the looker."

Oh god, I don't need to hear this.

The PMS wasn't bad enough.

Now my parents are flirting.

Ew.

Tuck hops off the couch. "Yeah, no, I'm out." He turns to me at the bottom of the stairs. "So, this is a permanent deal, right? You guys are all gonna do that freaky biting each other thing? 'Cause I don't wanna learn everybody's name if you're just gonna break up in a few weeks."

Steve looks between the two of us as I choke back the urge to throttle my brother. "Yes...I think. I mean...ok, I need to look into that, 'cause I don't actually know how it works. But I'm pretty sure Steve and I aren't biting each other."

There's an emphatic shake of the head from the alpha. "Yeah, no bonding for Steve, but you can still remember his name. I think we'll both get bitten by Teddy and Sam, and he's Garret's brother, so that's another no...and then Garret isn't with Sam or Teddy, so no biting there."

Tuck's holding up his hands and shaking his head at us. "You know what? Forget I asked. That sounds a bit too kinky for my young virgin ears. All this talk about bonding, you might have scarred me for life, Sis."

He looks deep in thought for a moment. "Well, I can't guilt you into taking over my chores for the month, but fifty bucks would probably go a long way towards helping me forget this conversation."

The little butt-head actually smirks at me. "I'm not giving you money, Tuck!" He cackles all the way up the stairs, and I turn around to lead Steve up to my room so we can get books—only to be accosted by my parents kissing, right there in the living room.

Snatching his hand, I drag Steve up the stairs. Not stopping until we're secure in my room with the door closed and I'm leaning against it. Mom and Dad have always been super affectionate. That's how I ended up with a brother eight years younger than me. Plus, it's super sweet that they still love each other so much, but I still don't want to see it.

When I look up, Steve's made himself at home, sitting on my bed with a stack of old Fruits Baskets manga in a pile in front of him. He meets my eyes with a wide grin. "Ha! I knew you read shōjo!" My face heats as I try to make excuses. But that's a fair assessment. It was the first anime I ever saw, and it got me interested in manga. Once I started collecting those, I realized how many other types there were, and I've been hooked ever since.

Besides, it doesn't escape my notice that despite his words, he sprawls across my tiny bed, reading the first issue. "Ugh, I can't get into this. She's just too sweet. So perfect in every way. How can you read this?" He sounds outraged, but he's still turning pages. I leave him to it while I pull milk crates out of my closet filled with books.

By the time I have enough bins to fill up the back of the car, he's already on the second book. Either he's skimming, he reads super-fast, or he's just looking at the pictures. Any option is fine, really, as long as he's enjoying them. I nudge the bed with my foot to get his attention. "While I'm glad you're enjoying all the romance and gooey books, I need help carrying these down to the car."

He blushes a pretty pink-rose color, even on his ears. His skin is so pale that it should look weird on him, but it seems to work. He stands up, putting one of the boxes on the bed, and stacking all the books he was reading on top of it. It looks fairly precarious now, but he can still haul it. I packed these things so

I could lift them, but there's no way I'd be able to carry the one he just added so much to.

He looks disdainfully down at the rest of the crates. "Um, don't you want to fill them the rest of the way up? It's gonna take a lot more trips at this rate." It's my turn to blush now, and he stares at me intently.

"In case you haven't noticed, I'm not exactly graceful, or as strong as an alpha. So...I'll take what my noodly little beta arms can, and if you wanna add more to boxes that you're carrying down, be my guest." He looks from me to the closet a few times before shrugging and walking over to it, grabbing handfuls of books and stacking them on top of the boxes I already filled till they look ready to overflow.

My teeth grind with the need to tell him not to damage my books, but he must see the reaction. "I can get them down the stairs, then we'll balance them out between boxes so nothing gets torn up and you don't go ass over teakettle down the steps." He grins for a moment like he finds that mental image amusing, and I playfully swing my leg out to pretend to kick at him.

Fortunately, I'm still standing next to the bed because my center of gravity is more off than usual holding the load of books, and while the box lands on the floor with a loud thump, I manage to faceplant into the soft mattress. Embarrassing, yes, but at least I didn't get hurt this time.

Unfortunately, the loud thump brings my mom to the door. She swings it wide, Dad standing behind her, and she sees me face-down on the bed with my butt in the air. Steve stands there with his own crate looking between us as she laughs and Dad mumbles something awkward before shuffling down the hall.

To top off my mortification, I hear, "Really, Kelly, throwing yourself at me like that! And in your parents' house no less. What would Sam think? And your poor parents." Then he turns and marches out of the room. His cackling starts about halfway down the stairs, but by then, Mom has already come over and helped me up, both of us now blushing profusely.

Chapter 16

Kelly

The bed feels too empty! Thankfully, everyone's pillows are here, so I feel around until I find Teddy's. My big cuddly omega always smells like cookies, and there are lingering traces of Sam's fresh cut cedar mixed in. It makes me feel warm and cozy and safe, even if they aren't here with me. I miss Sam, Teddy, and Garret, and not just because they make amazing living heating pads.

Seriously, sometimes I have to escape. It gets too hot when we're all wedged in here.

A warm weight presses against my back, arms circling tight around me. A masculine voice whispers against my neck. "Missed you so much." Teeth scrape over the tender skin of my throat and big hands run up my stomach.

The hard body undulates against my spine, a stiff rod pressed against my butt as he grips my hips, pulling me against him. "My Bear." It's nothing more than a sleepy murmur against the back of my hair. A heavy palm slides up my waist and stops at my chest, thumb brushing against the underside of one breast.

Then a sniff...followed by another. "The fuck?"

Mumbles followed by another deep inhale and then the hands fly off me. Steve goes scrambling off the side of the bed, rubbing his palms up and down his sleep pants, and making gagging noises.

"What are you, dude, twelve? I don't have cooties."

He stares at me, a full-body shudder running across his shoulders. "I know you don't have cooties, dammit! It just felt too much like I was feeling up Garret or something. It was nasty. Not that you feel like Garret, but it was that same mentally slimy feeling. It's not something I wanted to wake up to after dreaming of Bear."

That's fair.

I don't even wanna think about how it would feel to wake up in that position with Tuck.

Ew, now I wanna throw up.

Taking a deep breath, I try to clear my mind. Get away from any thoughts of my brother in a compromising position and back to the issue at hand. "Ok, I get why feeling me up in my sleep wouldn't exactly be appealing. I do lack the essential penis. But why would it make you think of your brother? I mean, I'm with both him and Teddy. Wouldn't that make Teddy off limits by extension?" He swallows convulsively, looking affronted by my logic.

"No, it's not the same…dear lord woman, how can you even think that? I grew up with Teddy. We were as close as siblings." I raise my eyebrow in silent question of that statement, and he blurts, "Well, it's not like we're actually related."

My hand waves down my own body, indicating that we are, in fact, also not related. Not that I want him to touch me like that, ick! He's right, it does feel squidgy. I'm just trying to figure out how he's thinking about this.

Shaking himself all over, he gives me an irritated glare before marching into the bathroom and slamming the door.

Well, good freaking morning to you too.

Ugh!

I wonder how the guys are doing?

Have they gotten to Los Angeles yet?

Pulling out my phone, I check for new texts, but nothing has come in since last night when they stopped at a hotel to rest.

Jake greets me when I open the door, full-body wagging around my legs, before trotting down the stairs. He stares at me expectantly after I follow him all the way to the back door. "Sorry Jakey, it's too early for me to go play with you. How 'bout I get your breakfast ready while you do your business?" He huffs in what I take to be acceptance and bounces down the stairs before sprinting off into the yard.

I feel awful this morning. I just wanna take some Midol and crawl back into bed. But then what would be the point of me staying home while the guys took that long trip? Plus, as smart as Xan is, the office seems to hate him, and I don't want to deal with going in tomorrow and having anything broken or on fire.

Breakfast at my parents' house has always been cold cereal, unless it's a weekend. Tuck and I get up, grab a bowl, and get ready for school. Dad snags one before heading out to work. I don't really know what Mom does—I always just assumed she had cereal too, but maybe she fixes something after everybody's gone. And of course, that means it wouldn't occur to me that Sam doesn't have cereal.

Looking through the pantry, there's nothing quick to fix in here. This might be a problem. After scanning the shelves for a few minutes, I give up and get some food out for Jake before letting him back in. He prances into the kitchen and makes a beeline straight for his bowl, hoovering up the kibble like it'll disappear on him.

No point in wasting more time on food. I can grab an apple for breakfast and then pick up some stuff on the way home from school today. For now, the shower is calling, and there's no way to ignore it if I want to get to work on time.

It takes a few minutes for the water to heat up, so it's as good a time as any to brush my teeth and pull my hair back into a braid. I need to perk myself up, because otherwise I'm gonna be crampy and unpleasant to everyone I come across today.

It also seems like a good time to pull out my peppermint body wash. I don't use it often, 'cause it was stupidly expensive, but some days you just need to pamper yourself. Without the chance for snuggles, I could use the indulgence, and the bubbles tingling against my skin.

Unfortunately, even if I wanted to stay in here longer, it seems like Steve used up all the hot water. Which is frustrating and does nothing to improve my state of mind. My special fancy soap doesn't help like I had hoped when I have to rinse it off in a lukewarm spray. Grumbling, I leave the bathroom wrapped in my towel, stalking back upstairs to grab some clean clothes and a pad.

Steve appears to be in a better mood when I walk in, but that just makes me madder. Of course he's in a better mood, he used up all the dang hot water. Brushing past him, I dig through the closet, but all my work shirts are wrinkled from where the guys were rolling around on them. I forgot to toss them into the dryer to fix it.

Crap.

"Girl, what crawled up your ass and died this morning? I thought you were one of those perky morning people."

Steve draws back at my glare before huffing to himself, doing a remarkable impersonation of the dog downstairs. Jake, at least, would give me cuddles if I asked. Instead, I get to deal with a snippy alpha and then rush off to work.

I would maim someone for one of Jacks's double chocolate muffins this morning. But it's rare that the guys bring food in from home. And with four alphas and a pregnant omega, it's not surprising. Heck, just the groceries for that house probably cost a fortune. Thinking of money, though, I should probably start contributing here some more, so Sam doesn't have to suddenly take on the cost of four people. The shop doesn't pay a lot, but at least I can help by buying groceries. I'll get some easy breakfast options today.

And of course, I stuck all my pantyliners and stuff downstairs in that bathroom...where I don't keep clean undies. Because why could I possibly make sense and put stuff where it, logically, needs to go? The need for Midol and cuddles slams back into me, and I start crying. Why not? Steve already hates me. Now he gets to gloat when I start crying like a small child.

I'm never gonna hear the end of this.

I sniffle loudly, turning back towards the closet so my leaky face won't be obvious. But he can't give me a moment to just deal. He has to mess with me this morning. "Ok, what is all...this?" Even though I can't see him, he's probably waving his arm at my disheveled appearance and shaking shoulders.

"Seriously, I don't even know what's going on with you. One minute you're perky and upbeat and happy, and then next...BAM! Ugly crying, slouching. And if I can be completely honest, kind of a bitch. Is the perky thing just so Sam and Teddy like you? Because that would be pretty messed up."

Turning a hard glare on him, I guess we're doing this now. "Steve...I'm tired...I didn't sleep well last night because I'm worried about the guys. I'm also hungry because there is nothing easy in this house to eat. Someone used all the hot water this morning, so my shower was freezing after the first five minutes. My hormones are insane, and it feels like someone is trying to put my uterus through a juicer. Do not test me right now, I will cry on you! Move!"

Steve looks affronted for a second, before he opens his mouth and makes it worse. "Oh...the period. Yeah, I forgot about that. You were in such a good mood yesterday. Hm..." He looks deep in thought for a moment. "I know. Come with me."

Not waiting for me to follow, he grabs my arm and leads me downstairs to what is officially my room, even though it's mostly unfinished. There, in the corner, sit several bags from the grocery store.

What the heck?

Steve points at them with a flourish. "We went shopping...ok, well, Sam and Teddy went shopping...I just stood there, not helping." The way he says it seems so random that I stare at him for a minute before I cross the room. In the bags are several boxes of different sized pads and tampons—but at least a few in sizes I need—Midol, a huge bag of gummy bears, and four different types of chocolate.

Well, at least I won't go hungry. Though I don't think any of these would be a good idea for breakfast, I still really appreciate the thought. Steve is watching me carefully when I turn around. "Yeah, Sam looked up some stuff online at the store, and they thought this stuff would be the best option. I don't know, just...don't get all weepy on me anymore, ok. It's not a good look." With that insulting statement, he turns and stomps out of the room.

That conversation feels off in so many ways. Not that Sam wouldn't do nice things for me, but we've been living together for over a week, and I've never seen the man look anything up on his phone. He has a laptop with a fold-out keyboard he uses for email and stuff. Maybe he meant Teddy looked it up online. It seems like something he would do.

There's no time to think about that confusing conversation though, so I grab a chocolate bar and a handful of supplies to put in my bag for school and head for the door. Jake is sitting beside it, waiting for me to try to leave so he can follow me out. There's no sign of Steve and a tiny part of me wonders if I upset him, and if I care right now.

The drive into work is quick, and I'm really glad the weather is warming back up from that crazy storm last week. Unfortunately, warmer weather means that we're swamped trying to do catch up from everything that was supposed to get done then, as well as all the stuff from the schedule for this week. So, it's all hands on deck with Gabe, Xan, Sal, Ray, and Lenny all working today.

Gabe and Xan are already in when I arrive at my usual time. Xan is rolling up the bay doors while Gabe glares at the computer. The bell jingles when I enter the office, and he looks up. "Hey, can you get that damned coffee maker working this morning? It looks like we're gonna need it."

I nod an affirmative before heading back to the erstwhile office. They've moved out the big desk that was rarely used, and turned it into a break room. Which is nice, except they still haven't updated the coffee maker, and that thing might be older than I am.

It takes me just a few minutes to get the thing started, and get back to the front, where Gabe is glaring daggers at the printer. "Kelly, do you mind? This thing hates me." Nodding again, I go to wiggle the cord on the back and start printing out work orders for the appointments we have today. I tried telling him last year that he just needed a new cable. But Gabe said he'd have Jacks come look at it. Which is fine, but then they learned Candice was pregnant, and he never leaves her side.

Of course, to completely start my day off right, my stomach makes a loud rumbling noise when I step out into the garage to bring the orders to Xan. He and Gabe both stare intently at me, but Gabe's the one who speaks first. "Isn't Sam feeding you, do I need to have a word with him?" There's no stopping my laughter, and by the time I finally get it under control, Gabe looks murderous.

"He is, seriously. I've never eaten as well as I have since I moved in there. But Sam, Teddy, and Garret all had to drive back to L.A. to pick up stuff from the omega center and clear out the twins' apartment. I didn't realize Sam didn't have any cereal or anything at the house and didn't get up early enough to fix something. So, no. This is on me."

They both look intense for a moment, then Xan reaches into his pocket and pulls out a couple of twenty-dollar bills, handing them to me. "I know it's not part of your job, but can you run down to the diner real quick and see if they have any breakfast pastries or burritos, or some kinda hand food you can bring back for the breakroom? Preferably something that will go with coffee if you got that damned thing to work already." Then he turns his back to me, not giving me a chance to reply.

Gabe looks between the two of us. "Uh, yeah. If you'd rather, there's also the grocery store, if bagels or something would work better...for the breakroom. We'll...uh...Sal can watch the front office till you get back. 'Cause, you know...we're gonna be busy. Better to have food on hand in case anybody needs it." He rubs the back of his head and shuffles a bit before turning and walking off.

Well, I guess I'll go grab some breakfast...for the breakroom. My eyes tear up a bit at their attempts to make things better in an inconspicuous way. They obviously failed horribly, but I really appreciate it anyway. Plus, maybe I'll luck out and the diner really will have some good Danishes that I can bring back for everyone.

Cherry and cheese would be heavenly right now.

Chapter 17
Steve

That could have gone better.

Why can't I talk to her without being an asshole?

I don't hate her.

As fucked up as it is, the two of us seem to have the most in common here.

Garret never plays video games with me, because he knows I'll win.

Bear would never read manga, he just can't get into it.

I'd like to learn how to cook and build like Sam, but I don't know if I can.

Heck, I can even borrow her clothes right now.

Hopefully not for much longer, though.

Once she leaves for work, I go out to the shop. Sam said something about baseboards, and so I looked up some tutorials online for how to do those. If I can get that done, then the rest of the nest will just be furniture and decorations, maybe blinds. I could probably order some, they have guides to measure and stuff. Teddy loves black, but does he want that on the windows?

Correction, Teddy, used to love black.

I have no idea what he loves now.

Other than her and Sam.

The walls are a dark blue; the floor is almost black, the few bags of blankets and stuff I've found lying around are dark, but not black.

Jake follows me out to the shop, and then inside. The big room smells like Sam, and I don't know if it's because he spends so much time here, or because of all the sawdust. Jake runs straight to a big cushion in the corner and starts scooting it around with his nose before flopping down on top and yawning. He shouldn't be tired—he doesn't do anything. Though I suppose jumping around like an oversized jackrabbit could take a lot of energy.

If I was a baseboard, where would I be?

He has to keep them around here somewhere...if he has any.

It's ok, even if I can't find them, Sam can do it when he gets back.

But it would help, right?

Isn't that the whole point?

Jake's ears perk up and he lets out a long baying bark, bolting up from the cushion and running out of the shop. That can't be good. Chasing after him, I run out the door and see a large box truck pulling up in the empty parking area. Jake's still bouncing around in circles, and I call his name, trying to get him away from the truck before his stupid ass gets run over. The truck shudders to a stop and he immediately runs towards the driver's side, sliding across the loose gravel and hopping away.

A man gets out of the truck, older, a bit heavyset. Jake runs over and starts trying to lick the guy. This dog has no sense of boundaries or self-preservation. Thankfully, the man just laughs. "Hey, Jake! Is your dad home?"

Stepping forward, I make sure he can see me before calling out, "Sam's not here right now, he had to go pick up some stuff with our omega." There, that's vague enough to explain without opening the house up to strangers.

He looks surprised for a minute at seeing me but then smiles; it looks relaxed and easygoing, but if he's working for the dads, who knows? "That makes a bit more sense then. Name's Shaun, I do some specialty deliveries around here. Stuff that don't normally fit with FedEx or the post office. I've got a big shipment here from Nest-n-Stuff for one..." He lifts up a small electronic scanner with a screen. "Kelly Parker. Wait, Kelly's a beta, her parents live on the other side of town...though I guess it's not an uncommon name. *Anyway,* does a Kelly Parker, who may or may not be a beta, live here?"

A small, spiteful part of me wants to say no. Kelly doesn't live here. But she does, and that would be fucked up. "Yeah, I think it might officially be Kelly Carpenter now, but yeah. She's out too. Can I help you?"

He looks at me and nods his head. "This is still Sam's place, right? I mean, I know you said he was just out, but I been makin' deliveries out here for years, and I've never met you. Never seen anybody here other than him and Jake." His smile is still there, but his stare is hard, like he thinks maybe I shouldn't be here.

Rolling my eyes, I call to the big idiot. "Come on Jake, get over here, show the nice man that we live here now, yeah?" The big dog comes wiggling over and leans against my legs with a groan, reveling in the ear scratches I offer.

"Yeah, that don't mean nothin'. Jake's never met a stranger he wasn't friends with right off." Shaun eyes me with open skepticism now.

I throw up my hands before marching across the yard so we're separated by a few feet. "Fine. Hi, my name's Steven, Steve to my friends, Vee to my Teddy Bear. You can just call me Steven. My brother and I joined Sam's pack last week. That being said, you probably didn't even know he had a pack, because it seems to leave everyone in this town in shock. He had only started it with our omega, Teddy, and Kelly, who is a beta, a few days before. Yes, it's the same Kelly from across town, with the mom and the dad, and the little brother she calls Tuck...I don't actually know what his real name is, but for his sake I hope that's a nickname. They live in a two-story blue house about fifteen minutes' drive away. Except when she's behind the wheel, then it's probably less than ten."

Shaun's openly laughing at me now. "Yup, that sounds like Kelly alright." He wipes his eyes. "So, Sam left you here all alone with just Jake, huh? Fair enough, I'm gonna need you to sign for this, and then I can either leave it all in a huge pile in the yard, or you can help me carry it up to the front steps. Gentleman's choice."

He rolls up the back of the truck, and I step up behind him. There are so many boxes, all with the big Nest-n-Stuff logo on the side. What the hell did that girl order?

Shaun climbs up onto the tailgate and grabs a box. It's big enough to require two hands to lift. He eyes me speculatively for a moment before tossing it in my direction. I'm not proud of the girlish shriek that erupts from my throat at having a large box flying at my head, but then my arms come up and it's incredibly light…less than ten pounds definitely. What the ever-loving hell did Kelly order?

Unloading takes quite some time, but he does indeed help me carry them up to the porch, and then hands them to me one at a time so I can set them safely inside. At first Jake prances back and forth, following us to the porch and back, but once it becomes obvious he won't be getting more ear scratches, he lays down and watches us work, yawning periodically.

Once everything's in the house, Shaun holds his hand out. "Well, Steven, it's nice to meet part of Sam's pack. I hope I'll be seein' you around. Oak Flats is pretty nice, as long as you don't mind quiet, and a little bit crazy." Well, he certainly has that part right. So far, these people are nuts. We should probably fit right in.

I shake his hand before pulling away. Jake comes over to lean against me again—now that all the manual labor is done, it must be time for more ear scratches. "Thanks Shaun, I look forward to it. And you can call me Steve."

He smiles and nods at me again, giving the dog a rough pat on the head and ruffling his ears, before waving, getting in his truck, and pulling away.

Now what the hell do I do with all these damned boxes, and where the fuck does Sam keep his baseboards?

Kelly

Spence has decided to sit beside me for Business Composition now, apparently. I'm not sure if this is going to be a permanent addition—until the end of the semester—or just while my guys are out of town. He seems to have gone into overprotective alpha mode, which is sweet, but also really awkward, since he's not one of my alphas. Still, the thought is appreciated.

It's taken me a lot less time to get used to being around alpha guys than I thought it would. Not that Spence is possessive or anything. He's been incredibly respectful of my personal space. He just growls at anyone else who gets too close. I actually worry a little for any omega who ends up with him if he's this protective with a beta who's not even in his pack. He's gonna drive the poor girl or guy crazy.

Of course, other people aren't helping. I've gotten a few ugly glares from some girls in my class with him following me around. They're the same ones who were butt-heads when they found out I was dating Sal. There's no point in trying to explain that Spencer is just my friend. They probably wouldn't believe me; they just want to be mean. Besides, I *am* living with three alphas and an omega now. They'd probably faint if they knew about that.

A tiny part of me chuckles at the idea. The thought of asking Teddy to come to class with me. Having him here would make me feel good—but I don't want to make him uncomfortable, and being around that many strangers surely would.

I really hope they're doing ok.
Surely they've already gotten to L.A.
Maybe they're too busy to text.

The bell finally rings, and Spence follows me out of class. "Hey, um, Kelly? Are you headed over to the union today? I thought you normally go to the workout center after your

A&P class, but you didn't on Monday. You feelin' ok?" He's walking beside me towards my next class, when I'm pretty sure he should be running across campus to get to the sports complex for football practice.

"No, sorry Spence. I appreciate it, but I'm not feeling up to it today. I think I'm just gonna head home and curl up with a book tonight. Aren't you gonna be late?"

He blushes and stares down at his feet. "Oh, Coach won't mind, and I can head home right after practice, so if I need to stay late and make up any work, it'll be fine."

Neither of us speaks for the rest of the walk, and it's easy. Some people have to talk. There has to be a conversation for comfort. Spence isn't like that, and it's surprisingly relaxing to be around him. Waving at him as he runs off, I turn and find my desk. Just one more class for the day, then I can stop and get a few groceries before I get home. Hopefully, one of the guys will answer the phone when I call.

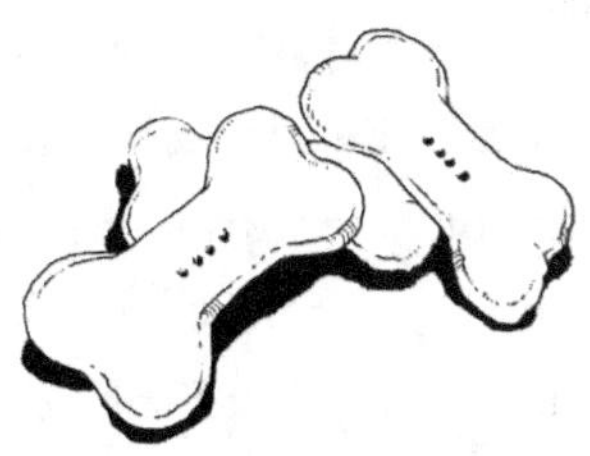

The grocery store is usually pretty dead, and tonight is no exception. As far as I can tell, it's just me and Billy at the front. I sent a text to Steve to ask what he might like for dinner, but he never replied, so I'm just going to grab some chunky soup and call it good. It doesn't seem like he really cooks, so he can eat what I get or starve. I snag up a couple boxes of cereal for breakfast, two frozen pizzas for dinner tomorrow, and a carton of chocolate chip cookie dough ice cream.

Billy asks how I'm doing, looking me over with a critical eye, and making me wonder if I sprung a leak or something. Do I have blood somewhere? Is he gonna call the cops, 'cause that would be super awkward.

"What's wrong, Billy? You keep starin' at me like you expect me to start crying. Seriously, what's up?" He sets his jaw, but he doesn't look angry with me, just concerned.

"Those alphas. Now, I know Sam's a good guy. But they were in here yesterday, all except the blond, buying a whole bunch of feminine hygiene products...and I just...I worry. Spencer said he met 'em all on Monday at the college and he was worried about your omega. I didn't want to say anything yesterday when they were in...but are you ok? Is he? Nobody's hurt?"

What can only be described as a guffaw bursts forth before I even try to stop it, and now Billy looks bashful. A blush staining his cheeks as he tries not to meet my eyes. "Yes, oh god. Billy, you know betas have a regular once a month cycle. I have no idea why they got me so many, but I shouldn't be back in here to restock for another six months or so." My eyes are watering, and I can't stop the giggles.

"Ok, Kelly. I didn't mean any offense. Shit...with the scars and everything. All the stuff to absorb blood...I was worried. I don't know. It's probably dumb. Just, if you ever need anything or y'all don't feel safe, we're here, aright?"

My laughter tapers off at the talk of scars and blood...and Spence. I must look as confused as I feel right now, because Billy keeps talking. "Listen, I know, sometimes life gets to be too much. It's all so overwhelming. I've been there, but I had people to help me—so it never got as bad as it could've. Sometimes you need help and you don't know who to turn to. I just want you to know I'm here, for you or him. Just someone to talk to."

He shrugs like he's embarrassed now, rubbing his wrists in the same way Teddy does when he gets nervous. I'm still confused. Gathering myself, I try to shake off the thoughts whirling through my head. "Thanks, Billy, I...Thanks. Really." He nods and shuffles his feet, still refusing to meet my eyes. When Teddy gets home, I'll need to ask him what scars Billy's talking about. And how did I miss that?

Chapter 18

Teddy

We didn't make it as far as I wanted to on Tuesday.

It looks like Wednesday's going to be a bust too.

Fuck.

I'm glad Kelly and Steve are doing ok, at least if her message last night is any indication.

I mean, she could have stabbed him overnight and had Jake help her bury him in the backyard.

I want a hug.

Nothing against Sam.

He gives great hugs.

But I like hugging Kelly because I feel like an alpha with how small she is against me.

And she smells good.

I'm pretty sure I love her too, not that I've told her yet.
She makes everything so much brighter.

Long car trips suck even worse on the second day. The company is fine, but all I want to do is curl up and sleep. Because between the hum of the engine and the movement, I was blinking like crazy before we'd even been on the road for an hour. It's probably worse for Garret since he's riding alone. I wish Vee and Kelly had both been able to come. Not that any of the alphas will be able to help pack up my nest, and I wouldn't let Kelly lift heavy boxes. But she should totally meet Sarah.

Oh, shit...Sarah.
She'll have my fucking head when she meets Garret.
Then she's going to have his head.
Or some other body part.
It's probably a good thing Vee didn't make the trip.
But she'd have loved to meet Kelly.

Sam hums beside me for a few minutes, probably thinking I've already dozed off. He's not completely wrong. My eyes ache, desperate to stay closed, and I hear the faint strings of some old music that seems to be a cross between rock and country...maybe The Eagles, maybe Skynyrd.

Before my mind can finish 'name that tune,' the ringing of a phone jolts me fully awake. Sam reaches up to the dash where his cell is docked and answers the call. Garret comes over the line. "Hey, I ran out of coffee about four hours ago. My GPS shows a spot about ten miles down the road. I'll need to make a pit stop there, if you want to join me to stop and stretch. Otherwise, I'll catch up to you on the road."

Sam looks over at me, and I nod. A bit of a flex does sound good, and it'll be nice to hit the bathroom and get something cold to drink. I'm not supposed to have much caffeine, but I can order a decaf frappe, or some sort of smoothie. Just something to help my eyes open up. If I can't have the caffeine, I'll take the damned sugar fix.

Sam turns off the radio as I sit up and try to shake the sleep from my eyes. "You know, if you need to catch a nap, that's fine. It's been a while since our last stop, and we still have a long-damned way to go." He's right. It's starting to get dark. We've been driving for almost ten hours already just today, but I know we were hoping to make this damned trip in two days, not three.

Pulling out my phone, I check the GPS. Right now, it's set to the omega center since I don't even know where Garret and Vee's place is. When we stopped for lunch, Garret said he would call his landlord once he got back on the road, and I'm curious if we'll be heading over there tonight when we arrive. It's not a terrible plan, but it does mean this trip is going to take longer if he and Sam have to spend the day loading up furniture.

A few minutes later, we follow Garret into a little shopping center on the side of the highway. There's a Starbees there and my body jerks at the thought of all the caffeinated goodness I'm not supposed to have. Maybe I can order online and then Sam won't know. But then I'd get the added bonus of guilt along with my caffeine buzz.

Shit.

Fine, whatever. I'm at least getting half-caf.

Anybody who doesn't like it can fuck off.

Not that that's really an issue with any of my pack. Sam doesn't have a problem with me drinking coffee. He won't be happy about it because it's not good for me, but he wouldn't actually say anything to me. He's the most mother-hen alpha I've ever met. And I appreciate that, I do. Sometimes it's just...I don't want to be taken care of. I'm supposed to be the one taking care of them. They're my pack, and I don't think this is an omega thing.

Wait?

Is it?

Is that why I want to make sure Sam, Kelly, and Vee have everything they need?

Garret to a lesser extent, he isn't really mine except that he's Kelly's.

Maybe it's because she's mine, and he's hers, so by extension...

Fuck, I need caffeine.

Scrubbing my hands down my face to dislodge any remaining sleepiness, I step down from the truck when we park beside Garret. Sam's voice comes from closer to the building. "Ok, let's try to get back on the road in the next fifteen minutes. Get yourself stretched, bathroomed, and caffeinated, then let's get the fuck outta here. We still got a long way to go, and I don't really relish the idea of sleepin' in the cab of my truck tonight. I'd like to try to make it to L.A. so we can crash at y'all's apartment instead of another damned motel room."

He sounds surly and irritated, and I'm not surprised when people step out of his way so he can pull open the door. It does make me wonder briefly if I did something to upset him, but my thoughts scatter when Garret puts his hand on my shoulder and gently nudges me towards the entrance.

Sam is already at the counter, grumbling under his breath when we walk in. So at least his mood isn't directed at me specifically. His voice gets louder as we near the counter. "Listen, I don't care what it is, just gimme the biggest coffee you have." The beta barista behind the counter looks from him to Garret and me as we step up behind our alpha, and I put my hand on Sam's shoulder.

Garret touches his other shoulder for a moment. "Sam, go take care of what you need to. We got this."

The beta huffs a bit as our big alpha turns and heads down the hallway marked with the bathroom sign, and Garret steps up to the counter. "Ok, we will have..." He looks towards the hallway Sam disappeared down. "One trenta vanilla sweet cream cold brew, with an extra shot."

At my raised eyebrow, he turns to me. "He needs the sugar right now as much as the caffeine. He looks like hell." He's not wrong. I didn't notice it in the darkening truck interior, but Sam doesn't look good right now. I wonder if he just doesn't like car trips or if he's worried about something, like his brother.

He refuses to call and ask if everything's ok, and the message I left for Mom hasn't been returned yet.

Garret's voice pulls me from my thoughts. "Also, one trenta salted caramel cream cold brew...and, what did you want Teddy?" Stepping up to the counter I scan for anything new, but nothing really springs out at me, so I just go with something I know I'll like. "Yeah, a venti mocha frappuccino."

Now it's Garret's turn to eyebrow *me*. "Ugh, fine...decaf. Happy?" He nods at me with a little hum of approval and hands the barista his debit card. Tapping his shoulder, I point towards the hallway that Sam disappeared down, and he nods again before going to stand by the end of the counter to wait for our drinks.

Sam must still be in the bathroom, and instead of wandering around, I decide to just wait for him to come back. Soon a warm body steps up behind me, and it's strange that our drinks were ready that fast...or that Garret is standing so close to me. Then the scent hits and it's none of my pack. Whoever presses themselves against my back smells like rotten fruit, and I have to swallow back the bile that rises in my throat.

I'm not small, but I'm not an alpha either, and when a hot sweaty hand lands on my neck, I snarl at the asshole who's too far into my personal fucking space. Unfortunately, we're down a hallway, and the only doors lead to bathrooms or what I'm guessing is a locked door since it's marked as 'Staff Only'.

"Now, now, Omega. Don't you know you shouldn't be out here alone? But I guess omegas usually have a sweet tooth. Did you sneak off on your own to get a treat, boy? I might have something sweet for ya." Internally I cringe, externally I try to shrug the hand off before turning to face the putrid smelling fuck behind me.

His hand comes back to my shoulder, pinning me against the 'Staff Only' door. "Don't be like that, Omega. You look like a sturdy fella, someone we wouldn't have to worry about breaking nearly as easy..." His words trail off, the threat left unsaid.

Shit.

I fucking hate being an omega.

Fucking red-neck asshole.

Pushing my shoulders out, I try to dislodge him without actually having to come in contact with any more of his nauseating smell that's probably already clinging to my shirt. But he hangs on, pressing me harder against the door, pulling himself up taller.

He's not much bigger than Vee and Garret height-wise, but they're still bigger than I am. Still, he's wider than them, with broader shoulders and a bigger stomach. He's the first alpha I've seen to actually have a beer gut, and he's putting off dominance like crazy, trying to get me to submit. It doesn't feel the same as when Sam does it, and my skin crawls with the need to bow my head to this fucker.

The door opening behind him causes his head to swivel around, but it's just another barista, a small beta coming out of the women's room. She looks shocked to see us back here, but scurries away when he growls at her. His attention returns to me. "Where were we, omega? You gonna play nice and come join my pack's table out there. I'll get you a treat. And then you can give us one." He's squeezing my shoulder hard now as he stares down at me.

I almost melt in relief when I hear Garret coming down the hallway.. "—an you check your phone? I haven't heard from Steve or Kelly yet, and I'm starting to worry." He's staring at his phone, his thumb running over the screen, a cardboard drink carrier in the other hand.

His head finally comes up as he registers my lack of answer, and his eyes turn hard immediately. "Sir, I'll ask you once to step away from my omega." The asshole standing between us squeezes my shoulder hard enough to hurt before turning towards my pack mate.

"He's not yours." His head lifts in the air, taking in the scent of our surroundings. "He don't smell like you, and he ain't marked. So scurry on out of here, little alpha, before you have more trouble than you can handle."

Garret looks between the two of us for a minute before he opens his mouth and shouts, "Sam, hurry the fuck up man, we need to go!"

The asshole holding me smirks, turning back to face me, and dismissing Garret, who he must think plans on abandoning me. The door directly beside me opens. "Sorry, I'm tryin' to send a text and my fingers are too—" Sam looks up from his phone, and I never clocked how tiny it looks in his big hands. Yeah, texting probably is a problem with a normal qwerty keyboard. I make a mental note to get my pack lead a stylus next time we go shopping.

The growl that rips out of Sam sounds like someone's let a tiger loose in the hallway. His nostrils flare as he takes in the scene we make. Me trapped against this door by this asshole, his hand wrapped around my shoulder, thumb tracing the edge of my shirt collar, and Garret standing behind him with his phone now pressed to the side of his head, his face set in angry lines. "Get your fucking hand off my omega before I remove it for you. Permanently."

The asshole squeezes my shoulder tighter, and a small whimper of pain slips free as he turns his face to my alpha. "We were just having a friendly little chat. He was gonna come play with my pack for a bit, but then you can have him back. No real harm done." He smiles again, his yellow teeth and rotten breath making me nauseous.

Chapter 19

Sam

All I see is red as rage washes over me. I want to break every one of this motherfucker's fingers. Fuck that, I want to tear his goddamned arms off and beat him to death with the damned things. How dare he fucking touch my omega—hurt *my* omega! Teddy's pained whimper draws my gaze to him, and I can practically hear the tendons in my neck creaking as I turn. He looks shaken, not exactly scared, but unnerved at least.

There's no decision, no 'I'm going to do this' moment before my hand snaps out, grabbing the wrist that's hurting him and squeezing. The bones grind under my fingers, and the hand attached to it spasms, letting Teddy slip loose to circle behind me into the bathroom. The alpha tries to jerk back, but I can't let go. Even if I wanted to, the muscles in my hand don't seem to be taking orders from me right now as they tighten, drawing a high yelp of pain from him.

I step forward and he retreats until he's the one now trapped against the closed door, his back wedged into the corner as I advance. Garret's saying something, but it's all background noise as I press the advantage, pinning this asshole by the wrist. I want to snap his fucking fingers. It'd be so easy, and I have a free hand. All it would take is to reach out and twist. A quick hard turn on each one.

Shit, I probably have a saw, or at least some bolt cutters out in the truck.

He'd never be able to hurt another omega.

He must see some of the thoughts in my eyes, because he goes green and starts swallowing like he's about to be sick, and the rancid scent of urine fills the hallway.

Warm hands wrap around my waist, and a large body presses against me from behind. Teddy's warm cookie scent envelopes me and chases away the rotten stench of spoiled fruit and piss pouring off the alpha in front of me. My free hand drops to trace along the edge of the leather cuffs he always wears, sliding along the surface and over the back of his. His fingers lace with mine at the contact. His face is rubbing side to side on my back, marking me and drawing a deep shuddering breath from my lungs.

Then Garret's there, his hand on my wrist that's still holding the piece of shit. "Sam, you need to let go. The cops'll be here in a moment. The barista called them earlier. They were already on their way when I called."

His voice grows harder. "We don't need to be stuck here all-night answering questions if you damage this piece of shit. If we're detained, who knows how long it'll be before we can get home?"

He's right. I don't want to admit it, but he is. Still, I have to concentrate to remove my hand from the fucker in front of me. He slides down the wall when I finally manage it, crumpling into a heap in front of the 'Staff Only' door. Hopefully, they don't need anything out of there for a while, and maybe they're lucky enough to have a backup mop in the front.

Teddy loosens his arms so I can turn, wrapping my own around him. The faint stench of the asshole behind me comes from his shirt. The collar is stretched and wrinkled where he was being manhandled. It's only my need to comfort my shaking omega that keeps me from turning around and stomping a hole in the piece of shit behind me.

It doesn't stop me from wanting to strip my mate right here and rub all over him to replace the scent with my own. I clearly haven't done that often enough if the fuck on the floor back there approached him.

I need to do better.

He's mine to protect.

They all are.

I have to take care of them.

Since taking off his clothes isn't an option, I tighten my arms around Teddy, rocking him bath and forth. It's hard to force my purr since my body wants to snarl and growl, rail at the alpha who thought for even a moment to take him from me. However, my chest eventually smoothes out into the soft thrum made to soothe an omega, and Teddy melts against me, burying his face in my chest.

Rubbing my jaw along the top of his head, I kiss the crown. Taking a few moments to just breathe him in, I confirm for my inner alpha that Teddy is safe and unharmed. Here with me. A sniff followed by a soft sob loosens my grip enough that I can pull back and raise his chin, look into his red-rimmed eyes.

Rage and shame fill me in equal measure. Rage that Teddy suffered this, and shame that I let it happen. I was so distracted trying to check up on Kelly and Steve that I missed what was happening around me. I missed the possible threat when we walked in, and then I took so long trying to get my stupid sausage fingers to work on my tiny little keyboard.

A commotion in the hallway draws my attention, and I lean back out the door, drawing Teddy with me. A group of two more alphas and a beta are standing at the end of the hallway, glaring at Garret. To his credit, he looks unconcerned with the situation. But the way his fingers twitch around the phone he's holding behind his back is a good tell of how he's really feeling.

Keeping a firm grip on Teddy's hand, I go to stand behind Garret. A loud whimper sounds from the ground as we pass the piece of trash I left there. The boots I wear are heavy duty with steel caps. They're made to protect my feet from falling wood and any random debris on my shop floor, so if I happen to step on and crush his fingers, it probably won't register. No one could hold me responsible for a complete accident. I hope.

Garret's shoulders and arms relax at my approach, and the men standing in front of him tense. Garret isn't small. He's not huge for an alpha—he'd be big for a beta—maybe he can bulk up if he wants to join the fire department, too. My lips tug up at the thought of him and Steven accompanying me on site and ingraining themselves with our community.

The men on his other side don't back off, but they look less outwardly aggressive now, the beta stepping behind one of the alphas. The tall lanky one speaks up. "If we could just get back there, and grab Trail. He's our pack lead. We'll just take him and go. Please, man, we don't need any more trouble." The man behind us whimpers again and just the sound sets my teeth on edge. He's a useless excuse for an alpha and a pack lead.

Before I can reply—or say something that would probably get me into any more trouble with the cops—the electronic bell rings and the front door opens, letting in two large men and a woman, all wearing matching beige uniforms. It takes me a moment to realize that these are police officers.

A small woman in a green apron greets them at the door and leads them back our way. The woman in green waves her hands in our direction, pointing to Teddy and me. The female officer unclips a taser as she eyes us up from across the room. As they get closer, I see tags and badges that mark them as Arizona state troopers.

At their approach, the other pack seems to ratchet up again. The beta cowering behind the alphas, who've turned to keep an eye on my group, as well as the approaching officers. The green apron, a manager going by her name tag, stops in front of us, and I catch the tail end of her conversation. "—had the one in black pinned to the back wall."

I can't stop the growl that slips free at the memory, and all the officers' heads swing towards me. They're all three alphas. It's not unheard of, but it still surprises me, especially the woman. She steps forward, looking around me to speak to Teddy. "Young man, are you in need of assistance? Are you being held against your will?"

Teddy lets out a loud sniff, wiping his face off on the back of my shoulder.

That's gonna be gross.

I think I need to change my shirt now.

"No, ma'am. My alpha was here, he was in the bathroom, and I was waiting for him when...when..." Another broken sob and my body starts purring as I pull him around and into my arms. There's barely enough room in this fucking hallway for it, but I'll be damned if I leave him standing next to that piece of shit back there.

It takes me a moment to realize that the two male officers are speaking with Garret and the trash pack, where they've led them out into a more open area. I see Garret pointing back towards us, and the manager nodding her head. She points to a black dome on the ceiling behind the counter, and it occurs to me that they probably have security cameras here. So hopefully that'll make it a bit easier for us.

"Sir, can you please come with me to answer some questions?" The female alpha reaches for Teddy again and he cringes away. It takes all of my patience to force the words out of my throat instead of a snarl. "Can you please not touch my omega? He's very shaken up." She looks dumbstruck for a moment, looking between Teddy and me as her mind filters out what I just said.

She tries again, not reaching this time, but using a softer voice. "Sir, sir, are you an omega?" Teddy's head nods where it's pressed against me, and I don't think he hears her almost silent "Oh" of surprise. Her voice is louder but gentler as she tries again. "Mr. Omega, can you please confirm for me that this is your alpha?" Again, the silent head nod. She nods like she expected as much. She should have. He said it just a minute ago.

She stands back up, addressing me, as well as Teddy this time. "Sirs, if you could please come over here so we can get a statement from you. I'll also need to see your identification please, Mr..." The question hangs in the air as we walk over to stand beside Garret.

Teddy untangles himself from me and looks down at the officer. "Carpenter. We're Pack Carpenter from Oak Flats, Mississippi. My alphas were driving me back to the omega center in Los Angeles to pick up my nest and get my classes transferred.

We just stopped in for coffee because we've been on the road for a while, and wanted a pick-me-up until we could get to a hotel for the night."

The officer nods along. "Thank you Mr. Carpenter, I *will* still need to see your ID though, as well as any pack registration paperwork on you, if your pack name doesn't match." She looks behind us on the ground before turning to her partners. "We might want to get an ambulance here too, just in case." Her look of annoyance in my direction is clear, but I don't care.

The taller of the two male officers turns around, speaking into a radio on his shoulder, but I'm too busy checking Teddy over again to pay much attention. Then I turn to Garret, who at least takes my confirmation of his safety with a grain of salt, even if it does make him blush.

Once I've made sure my packmates are ok, I trade my keys off to Garret for the drink caddy he's been hauling around, and hand Teddy some sort of whipped cream covered monstrosity. He takes it from me and drinks half of it in the first minute, then bends over and clutches his head. A low muttered, "Fuck," is the only thing I hear before he stands up, tears in his eyes. "Sorry, brain-freeze...but fuck me, I needed something to shock my system."

Garret speaks briefly to the officers before stepping outside to retrieve all of our paperwork and identification. His from their SUV and ours from the glove-box in the truck. Thankfully, it doesn't take long after his return for the police to verify all of our information and give us a brief lecture about updating our licenses and Teddy's omega registration.

While we wait for the medical unit, Garret sits down next to us. At least the coffee he got me is large, if a little sweeter than I'm used to. He asks what was taking so long in the bathroom, and I have to explain to him that I was trying to text Kelly. I was worried since we hadn't heard from them since the night before when she and Steve went out to dinner and then to her parents' house. I had been trying to send a text to check in, but my fingers don't exactly hit the keyboard well, and I was getting frustrated.

We sit in silence for a while before Garret tells us he was able to get in touch with his landlord in Los Angeles. They have a week left of the month that's paid up, but their father did pay out the nose to break their lease. So anything they want, they need to get it moved in the next six days. I'd like to be home before then, so that shouldn't be a problem.

If we *are* going to have to pack everything up, I wonder if we wouldn't be better off hiring a packing company to help us get everything collected and then stuffed in a truck to take home. Garret must have a similar thought, because the next moment he's on his phone, tapping away with speed. I have a brief harsh moment of envy for his delicate hands, but I shouldn't expect anything else from someone who wants to be a doctor. You'd have to be able to do tiny fiddly work in that sort of job.

The shorter male officer comes over to take our statement, and Teddy repeats everything that's already been said, elaborating a bit on some of what the alpha said to him. It makes me want to go back and do more damage than I did. When the paramedics finally arrived, they lead him away. He isn't wearing any sort of brace, but his hand and wrists are starting to turn a nice shade of purple.

The manager takes the lady officer into the office and makes copies of the recordings from the surveillance cameras, and it seems like it should be pretty open and shut. Unfortunately, it turns out it's not quite that easy, and I get a warning lecture about use of excessive force in a given situation. Though she does admit she probably wouldn't be any better if it was her omega it happened to.

The alpha that accosted Teddy isn't a local either, and is taken into custody, with his pack following him to the station. I've almost finished my giant coffee, and the manager brings us all waters while we wait. Teddy and Garret go back for sandwiches out of the case—while a part of me knows I should eat, the nausea that's rolling through my middle says that would be a terrible plan.

The whole situation takes more time than I want to think about, and it's after eight before we finally get released from all the questioning. In truth, we're all exhausted at this point, but the farther along we can get tonight, the better. I check in with Garret before he heads back to his SUV, then I get Teddy settled into the passenger seat of the truck. "Feel free to climb in back and take a nap if you need to. I can make the next couple of hours on my own."

He glares at me, and while he scoffs at the idea, I think a part of it is that he's still shaken up by what happened. Teddy doesn't usually get treated like an omega. And with his heat closing in, he's probably already on edge.

Still, he sinks down into the seat and starts snoring before we've been on the road more than five minutes.

Chapter 20

Garret

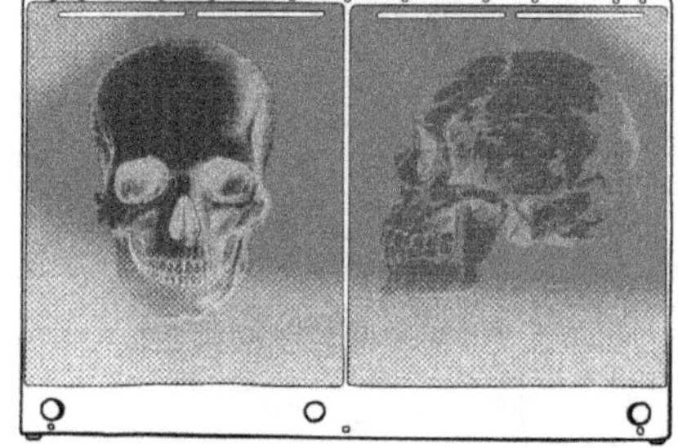

Hitting the call button on my dash, Sam picks up after two rings. I hear snoring in the background and thank my lucky stars that I didn't wake Teddy up. We're about two hours out from our coffee stop, but I can barely keep my eyes open. I don't think I'm going to make it much farther before I become an accident waiting to happen.

"Sup, man?" I can hear Sam trying not to yawn over the speaker, and while I want everyone to be safe, I'm glad that I'm not the only one who feels like passing out.

"Yeah, Sam. I'm sorry. I know we wanted to get farther tonight, but I'm having problems keeping my eyes open right now, and I think we really need to either find another hotel or pull over. I have a couple of bench seats in the back here if you guys need to stretch out on them. Steve and I took turns sleeping on 'em when we were driving to Mississippi. They're not bad, a little cramped, but doable."

I worry I may be babbling in my exhausted state since Sam doesn't say anything, but before I can try again, his voice comes through, sounding defeated. "I'd really hoped to make it a few more hours, but I think you're right. Pull over to the curb so you can check your GPS for the nearest hotel or rest stop. I wanted to get Teddy a hot shower and a warm bed after that bullshit. But I think sleep would be the most beneficial right now."

I nod for a moment before I realize that he can't see me then put on my signal to pull off the road. We haven't seen another car for an hour on this long stretch of highway, so it's probably a moot point, but better to be safe than sorry. He pulls in behind me, his lights turning off and his hazards coming on while I try to maneuver the map to find some place to nap. It mostly looks like one big empty stretch with just the line of the road.

Finally, after what feels like entirely too long, I see a lookout point with a rest stop. It's still about twenty miles away, but I think that's our best option right now. No hotels popped up in the search of the surrounding fifty miles. Relaying all this to Sam, he hums along in agreement, and we pull back out onto the road.

If I can just hang on another twenty minutes, then I can close my fucking eyes. Turning the radio as loud as I can stand it, I roll down my windows, and sing loudly, and probably off-key, until the music cuts off and the car tells me to make a left turn.

I must be sleep deprived, because this is totally giving me KITT from Knight Rider vibes.

Sam's headlights flash in my rearview mirror as I pull into a parking space in front of the stone traveler's center. I turn off the power, and must immediately start to doze, because I startle when he knocks on my window a few minutes later.

Shit, that's dangerous.

"I'm gonna take Teddy in so he can get cleaned up and have a break before we rest. You comin'?" I nod like a bobble head—nearly falling out the door because my legs don't want to work—and follow them into the building. Then pop my head back out and hit the alarm on the car. I don't think anyone would mess with it—and there's no one else here—but it would be just my luck today to come back in a few minutes and find my duffel missing.

Stepping inside, I hear a loud hiss from Teddy. He's trying to pull his shirt off over his head, and my growl echoes Sam's as we see the large hand shaped bruise that's formed over Teddy's shoulder and along the edge of his neck.

The omega makes a mad grab for Sam when his spine snaps straight and he stomps towards the door with purpose. "Seriously, Sam, you're planning to just leave me here to drive two hours back and throttle that fucker? Just help me get some decent fucking photos so I can press charges and then let me sleep. I'm dead on my feet here, Alpha." The last bit comes out with a bit of a whine, and Sam immediately switches targets, heading straight back to the omega and wrapping him up in a hug. His purr is loud enough that it echoes in the small room.

"Garret, can I borrow your phone so I can have a date and time record for these damned things, please?" I bring my phone over. The light in here isn't the best, but we get Teddy standing in front of the mirrors and use the flashlight on his phone to highlight the damage. It takes about twenty minutes before Sam agrees that we have enough from every angle possible, and I'm well past the point of wanting to drive back myself and stab the motherfucker.

I do my business and wash my hands before I leave the two of them alone to finish cleaning up. Teddy is trying to give himself a wipe-down with wet paper towels, paying special attention to the damage on his shoulder. He can probably still smell traces of the alpha from earlier. Omegas usually have the best sense of smell, but alphas are a close second. Still, having it that close to your face can't be good.

I'm sitting in the driver's seat, debating if I want to crawl in the back or just recline the damned thing when Sam knocks on my window again. "Hey, do your seats fold down in the back?" I shrug dumbly, because I never thought to look. He sighs and drops his forehead to the window. "You mind if I check? It might be easier to stretch out that way, plus it would let me hold on to Teddy while we sleep. For both our sakes."

Popping the locks, I scramble out of the driver's door. I open the hatch in the back, looking around for a lever of anything that might lower the seats. Sam opens the rear passenger door, pulls up on a peg on the back of the seat and the whole thing collapses forward.

Oh...that's what that button does.

Well, not that I need it now.

I should probably be glad that Dad didn't report the fucking car as stolen.

Our run in with the cops earlier might have had a very different outcome.

Once he gets both back seats down, there's a large open space in the back. It's big enough for the two of them to stretch out completely. Unfortunately, none of us thought to bring blankets or anything. Sam leads Teddy over and gets him situated while he goes back to the truck and collects clothes out of his bag, rolling them into a tube to give to the omega as a pillow. Then he locks the doors on his truck, crawls in the back with Teddy, and soon they're both snoring heavily.

I want to stretch across the front here, but the console is in the way. After a few minutes of trying to get comfortable in the reclined driver's seat, I give up, grab my own bag, and climb into the back with them. Pushing my back against Teddy's and facing the side of the car. Sam's loud purr vibrates through Teddy and unwinds the tension in my muscles where we're pressed together. Hitting the alarm button, I wrap my arms around my bag—like I want to snuggle in with my beta—and fall asleep.

I don't wake up until someone starts tapping on the glass in the grey light of pre-dawn. Another police officer, in the same matching beige uniform, taps the glass beside my head again. I sit up, rubbing the sleep out of my eyes, and he backs away a step. Lights on a patrol car flash behind him, and a quick glance shows another officer in the driver's seat. I slide down our impromptu bed to raise the hatch so I can get out. Teddy grunts behind me and burrows closer to Sam.

Once I have my feet under me, I turn my attention to the officer who tapped on my window. It's kind of amazing that my voice isn't slurred considering I'm just waking up. "Morning Officer, how can I help you today?" He looks over at me, mildly annoyed, but I don't catch any scent of anger. He's a beta, which seems odd since the three we met yesterday were all alphas. And now I feel like slapping myself for being such a discriminating prick. Why the hell can't a beta be a state trooper?

My hands rub down my face, trying to scrub the sleep out of my eyes. I don't even have my phone on hand to know how long I was out. It must have been a good length of time considering the sky is starting to lighten.

Wait, did he say something?

Shit.

I turn my full attention his way again, taking in the name tag Jenkins on his shirt. "I'm sorry, Officer Jenkins. I'm...can you please repeat that?"

He heaves a sigh as though I'm asking him for his firstborn child instead of asking him to repeat what he just said. "I said, did you know that you aren't allowed to sleep at the rest stop, vagrancy laws?" He points back the way we came, and I can see the back of a sign that we must have passed when pulling in but didn't read.

"I'm sorry again, sir, I didn't see that. We wanted to make it to a hotel last night, however we were all so tired that staying awake became a concern. We thought it better to pull over and rest than to risk an accident." He nods in response, waving as a second patrol car pulls down the ramp and into the lot behind him.

"Well, sir, I appreciate your honesty. But I'm still going to need to see your license and registration, as well as those of your..." He looks past me to where Sam and Teddy are still cuddled together asleep in the car. "...pack. And if possible, I'd like to speak with them as well." I seriously have no idea how the fuck they're still asleep. But Teddy was pretty wiped after yesterday. Still, how the fuck am I the one that woke up? Sam's supposed to be in charge. Why didn't he wake up?

Leaning into the hatch, I touch Sam's leg lightly and he jolts awake with a low growl, hugging Teddy tightly against him. Both of them blink at their surroundings before Sam sits up, his head thumping against the roof of the car. He slides out the back, already looking more awake than I feel. His gaze stares down to meet mine, his eyes asking about the situation without using words. I reply in a normal voice, so the gathered officers don't think I'm trying to be sneaky. "Apparently, it's illegal to sleep at a rest stop due to vagrancy laws."

His reply is a growled and heartfelt, "Shit," as he pulls out his wallet and hands his driver's license over with no further prompting. I agree with the statement, but there's nothing else for it.

Jenkins stares at me, and I realize yes, I have not moved to get my license yet. "Sorry, Sir. It's in the front seat, with my wallet. I believe Teddy's is in the truck, along with our pack registration paperwork." He gives me a brief nod—which I take as an affirmative, and both Sam and I step away—him to the truck, and me just to the front seat for a moment.

My wallet's not in the center console where I left it, where I always leave it—and there's a brief moment of panic before it's located on the driver's side floor. I can only imagine it fell down there in my sleepy scramble last night. Regardless, it takes longer than it should for me to return to Jenkins with my license and registration. By the time I get there, Teddy is standing by the bumper with his shirt off.

What the actual fuck.

I may not be into the omega like the rest of my pack, but that doesn't mean I'm not protective. He was my best friend for years with Steve, and I don't like the idea of anyone harassing him. My own growl rumbles out before I realize what's happening, Teddy leaning down so Jenkins can look over the bruises on his shoulder,

A few moments later, Sam appears at my back, his low growl mimicking mine from a few moments ago. Another officer steps out of the newly arrived patrol car, camera in hand, ready to take pictures to add to the records from last night's event at the coffeehouse.

"So, yeah, I'm really sorry. I was just...really upset after last night, and we did try to find a hotel, but I just needed someone to hold me. So, we pulled over for snuggles, and we must have all fallen asleep. I'm really sorry, officer." Teddy looks at the cop with big, soulful eyes. That must be a trick they teach at the omega center, because I sure as fuck don't remember him doing it before.

Also, it's not quite the story I told, which was the truth. And while I appreciate Teddy trying to keep me out of trouble, I don't like him lying about this sort of thing. I'll own up to it. The officer with the camera starts taking pictures from various angles around Teddy's neck and shoulder, and it frustrates me how much time we wasted doing it last night. Still, better to have and not need than need and not have, I guess. We'll have our own records, just in case.

As I listen to the conversation between Teddy and Jenkins, it becomes clear that they knew who we were before we supplied them with our information. Apparently, there was a notification out to watch for our automobiles along this route, so when they saw us parked, they checked everything over before waking us up to verify the same story.

More delays we don't need, but at least we're all fully awake now. A few minutes later, they wrap everything up. They once again confirm our identities and give me a verbal warning about sleeping at rest stops, especially with an unbonded omega in the car. Then we're on our way again. It's only six thirty, and I'm already mentally exhausted.

Chapter 21

Kelly

A low whimpering sound wakes me up, but it's too damned early. It's still dark outside.

Is Jake ok?

Scrambling off the mattress, I bolt to the door, yanking it open and startling the big dog awake by nearly tripping over him. He looks around bleary-eyed before he drops his snout back onto his front paws, making a low, grumbly noise. Maybe it was just a nightmare? Shaking myself to dislodge any bad dreams, I trudge to the bathroom before trying to reclaim my warm spot on the bed before it gets too cold to snuggle into properly.

My whole body curls around my pillow, taking in the slowly fading scents of Sam, Teddy, and the bundled shirt that smells faintly of Garret. It hasn't been very long, but I miss their warmth already—and having strong arms wrap around me while I sleep. There's just something about being held that makes me feel safe.

Steve has sandwiched himself on the other side of the bed between Teddy and Sam's pillows. His high-pitched whimper comes again, just as sleep starts to pull me under. The bed shakes with his movements, and I reach over, touching his hand that's closest to me, trying to wake him up from whatever nightmare he's trapped in.

At the contact he hugs the pillow tighter, then a second later his hand is wrapped around my wrist. He squeezes hard and pain flares up my arm. His voice cries out. "Wait!" Before he suddenly lets go and curls into himself. His big body hunched and curled. He's gained weight in the last week, but his shoulders are still nearly skeletal as his body is huddled down in the pile of bedding.

The room goes quiet again, only the quiet rustling of sheets as I rub my aching wrist and try to figure out what to do. A loud braying sob interrupts my thoughts, and I give up any chance of being nice and bolt across the room to turn the lights on. Brightness floods the space, but Steve continues to whimper and twitch.

Crud!

My arm hurts.

Do I have a stick or something around here?

I can poke him from a safe distance?

Yeah, it's rude...but ow!

The alpha's body thrashes, trapped in some nightmare. And I do the only thing I can think of to keep us both from getting hurt anymore—I grab Garret's pillow and start smacking him with it until he wakes up. It only takes four good hits before he spasms and uncurls. His eyes slowly blink open, squinting against the light.

I shouldn't have enjoyed that as much as I did.

No help for it now.

"What the fuck, Kelly! Jesus fucking Christ, are you kidding me right now? What the shit happened?" He blinks at me slowly from where he's sprawled on the bed, and I'm still standing over him, pillow raised.

Would it be bad to hit him a couple more times, just because he's being a butt?

Probably...but do I care?

"Ya' got a lotta nerve askin' me that, my dude. It's too danged early...I'm tired, I'm crampy, I wanna cry...and you were flailin' around and hollerin'. Plus, you grabbed me when I was tryin' to wake you up. It hurts." My speech is slurred with sleep as I wave my arm at him. The skin's an angry red that looks like it'll be a hand shaped bruise by morning. It's too bad I don't have something like Teddy's cuffs here to...wait—

My still sleeping mind is tripping over itself. He just wears those as a style thing, right? They aren't actually covering anything up, are they? My train of thought gets derailed when cool hands wrap around my arm, pulling it down so Steve can take a closer look.

"Fuck, Pixie. I didn't mean to...Lemme go see if I can find an ice pack or something like that. What exactly happened?" He wraps his hand gently around my painful wrist and swears again when he sees how perfectly the marks line up with his fingers. His reaction is almost caring until he opens his mouth. "Sam is going to fucking kill me. Shit!"

So I do what any injured woman would do in this case, and my foot comes out, catching him in the stomach and forcing a loud grunt out of him. Clearly, this wasn't well thought out though, since his hand on my wrist tightens, making me scream. Jake starts throwing himself against the door, his voice a loud braying bark as he scrambles against the wood. My eyes water as I untangle Steve's fingers from around my arm and go to open the door.

Jake is on me a moment later, his cold wet nose running over my legs as he homes in on my injured wrist and lets out an almost puppy sounding whine as his head swings from me to Steve and back. The alpha is still on the bed, holding his lower stomach, and looking frustrated when Jake hops back and forth between us.

"Shit...Sorry, again. I didn't mean that...well, I did. I mean, Sam and Teddy are both going to be pissed. But I didn't mean to hurt you, either. Fuck...you kick like a goddamned mule." He's taking deep breaths as he slides off the bed, and I'm envious again of all the damned tall people. Sam built me a small set of stairs for the bed that first weekend, but these guys make it look easy.

Jake prances back and forth between us and I don't know who he's trying to protect as his big wet nose goes from Steve's stomach to my wrist and back. When Steve gets close enough for me to touch, I give up. I can't deal with more drama right now as another cramp makes me lean back against the doorframe.

"Come on, Jake-y, that's enough excitement for one pupper. Let's get you outside for a potty break, and then..." I look over at the old pendulum clock hanging on the wall. "Cripes, let's get back to bed, it's not even four yet." Holding onto Jake's collar, I let him lead me down the stairs, and over to the backdoor. He's more sedate than usual when he wakes up, and I'm clearly not the only one who feels like a zombie.

Standing there for a moment, I wait for him to finish and then trot back to the door. He stops in front of the steps and kicks his feet a few times, flinging grass and dew all over until I pat my leg a few times, and he comes running. Heading back through the kitchen, a startled shriek is forced out of me at seeing Steve standing by the stove.

He looks over at me, and nods to the fridge. "Can you grab out the milk...please. And the whipped cream if you want it." What the heck do I want whipped cream for this early? He has a big canister of hot cocoa sitting out with measuring spoons, and the fire on the stove turned up way too high.

I pass him the milk and watch the kettle for a minute. "Do you think it'd be faster to just nuke a couple of cups of water?"

He blinks at me for a minute before dropping his head to the counter. His reply is a muffled, "Probably," before standing up, turning off the stove, filling two mugs with water, and putting them in the microwave.

He looks at me again and I reach in front of him to press the button for two minutes before stepping back. His voice is low, and I never realized that he doesn't normally have the growl I've come to associate with alphas. "I really am sorry. You may not be my favorite person, but I don't want you hurt, and I especially don't want to be the one to hurt you. It's not about Sam or Teddy or my brother liking you...not *just* about that."

He's quiet as the microwave goes off, and he pulls out the steaming mugs. He reads the side of the cocoa before carefully measuring out three tablespoons for each one, stirring, adding milk, and topping each one with whipped cream. Part of me wishes he would have just let me go back to bed, but this seems important to him, and his meticulous movements just emphasize that.

Instead of handing the finished cup to me, he sits it on the counter by my hip. "Sorry, I didn't know...you're hurt...I didn't want you to get burned."

His stammered explanation seems to embarrass him, and he tips his own drink up, taking a deep swallow before coughing and slamming it down hard on the counter near mine. "Fuck, that's hot!" It takes effort, but I manage to stifle my laugh, and most of my smile before picking up my own drink and taking a small sip. It *is* hot, but cozy.

Steve follows me out to the couch and sits beside me instead of his usual spot on the other end. My stomach twists, waiting to hear whatever spiteful stuff he's going to throw at me. I'm too tired and I don't feel good. The hot chocolate is probably just something to get my guard down.

He takes a sip of his own drink before setting it down on the coffee table. Jake hops up on the end of the couch and leans heavily against the alpha, letting out a grunt before flopping down on the cushion and putting his paw on Steve's leg. If Jake was human, it would look like a gesture of comfort, and Steve scratches him behind the ears before turning back to me.

"Kelly, I'm sorry. Also, just a heads up, I suck at apologies, so let me get this out before you kick me again." A small smile curves the edge of his lips, and he rubs at his stomach.

"It's not your fault. I appreciate you waking me up earlier, and I'm sorry I hurt you. Feel free to hit me with a pillow any time you need to. I...I usually have problems with sleep. The last week with all of you has been the best rest I've had for as long as I can remember."

He stops to take another sip of his drink and looks like he's reorganizing his thoughts. "I don't know what I'm doing. I mean, that's pretty obvious, but...I've been lying to myself for nearly a decade that if I just kept going, if I just did what Dad wanted...if I just did *everything* he wanted, things would be good. Clearly, I'm an idiot, because that was never going to happen."

Rubbing his hands together, he laughs softly to himself. "I can't even believe how fucking stupid I was. Hell, I'm sure Garret knew, but if he tried to tell me, I wouldn't listen. I was so focused on this one thing—work hard, make Dad happy, get Teddy. I never stopped to think that Teddy might move on. I never told him I was coming back, so why wouldn't he? I mean...shit, even if I had told him, I fucking suck, and my life is a complete dumpster fire, why the hell would he want to wait?"

Steve's voice cracks, tears rolling down his face. His voice wobbles, but he keeps going. "I don't hate you...I don't even dislike you. I mean, you're smart, you're kind...that *perky* thing is kind of annoying and your sense of humor is *terrible*, but if I wasn't so fucking jealous, I think you'd be one of my favorite people here. Certainly, the one I can actually talk to. Moreover, I hate that I'm like this. I know I'm being an asshole. I see it happening and I try to stop, but my mouth just keeps fucking going."

He takes a deep, shuddering breath as Jake pokes him in the side with a wet nose. Steve's hand comes down, absently stroking the big dog's ears. "Teddy's not here, Sam's not here...Fuck, not even my brother. There's not one person in this whole fucking house for me to be jealous about right now. And while that seems to have brought back some of the nightmares, it does mean I can actually talk to you without being a raging asshole."

His lopsided smile would be cute if his eyes didn't look so haunted. "I've never had friends, Pixie. I had Garret, and later

Teddy. We weren't allowed to bring friends home very often, and we weren't allowed to go to anyone else's house, not until him. Dad said we'd be enough for each other, and mostly we were, but it means I don't really deal well with anyone else. My social skills are pretty much non-existent and I don't know if it's because of how I grew up, or there's something actually off with my brain, but most people don't feel real to me."

Well, this just went into psycho territory. My fingers wrap around the handle of my almost empty mug as I lean away from the man who just admitted that he thinks like a serial killer. He turns to track my movements, his eyes growing wide as I lift my cup. "What the hell...I'm not going to murder you! God, overreacting much? It's not like that. It's not like this big dramatic thing. 'Oh, people don't seem real, so I kill them.' What the fuck, way to take my opening up and throw it back in my face. Jeez." He slumps on the couch, looking sulky.

Chapter 22

Steve

S he doesn't completely resettle, but out of the corner of my eye, I see her fingers loosen. My hands continue to mindlessly stroke over Jake's ears while I try to explain. "Garret made us talk to a shrink when we moved out. He thought it could help. Now I have all these lovely little abbreviations and descriptions of what's wrong with me." My shoulders shrug automatically. It doesn't exactly bother me to talk about this stuff, but seems to make other people uncomfortable.

"Doc talked a lot about depression and possibly PTSD...but mostly she seemed set on something called DDD, which is ironic considering my cup size." My joke falls almost flat as I make boob grabbing motions at my own chest. Though after a moment, I am rewarded with a little snicker and a half smile.

Picking up my mug, I drain the rest of it. It's barely warm now, but there's no point in wasting it. "Anyway...some days are better than others. Especially this last week, here. Things have color. It feels like I'm actually a fully functioning human, everything is where it's supposed to be. It's freaky really." I chuckle to myself again. "Seriously, for the first five days, I was constantly waiting for the other shoe to drop. Like I'd do...*something* that finally sets Sam off and he'd start screaming at Garret or me. One of us would get hurt again."

Her eyes are huge, her fingers coming up to cover her mouth before she blurts out, "No, not Sam...he's one of the sweetest guys—" Waving my hand, I stop her needless defense of our alpha.

"Trust me, Pixie, I know. Sam is...different. Hell, he's probably the most mellow guy I've ever met. He can be growly, but mostly he's just a big snuggly pup...like this one." Jake looks up at me as I stop rubbing his ears and boop his nose. "But...ok. You're in college right, almost got your degree. You're smart. What are you going for again?"

She stares at me, her big brown eyes blinking owlishly in the dark room. "Kinesiology, but what does...?"

My head nods in response. "Ok, cool, medical field. So, did you ever take any psychology or sociology? Hell, we studied conditioned responses in high school, if you remember Pavlov?" She nods, not saying anything, so I keep going. "It's the same thing, just with people instead of dogs, and getting hurt instead of food. Actually, I think I'd rather be the dog in this case." Jake licks my hand, and I go back to stroking his ears.

"Anyway, I think we came out pretty good. We look fairly well adjusted. But no, I'm not a killer. I may have a pretty fucked up sense of self-worth and the world around me, but I have morals. Also, I don't like seeing people get hurt. The sight of blood makes me vomit. No offense meant to your current...*condition*. And loud noises freak me the fuck out."

My attempt at a self-deprecating laugh is broken and kind of pathetic, but I'm almost done. Then we can go back to bed if she feels like it. I just need to get this out. "So, I'm sorry. I'll try to be better, but I'd appreciate it if you could keep being patient with me. And, if I get outta line, feel free to hit me with some pillows again, yeah?"

It doesn't bother me to admit how fucked up I am or apologize for it. It comes with that whole lack of self-worth—but it seems to have upset Kelly. Her eyes are red and glassy, and she looks like she wants to give me a hug. Which I can appreciate, but we're not there yet.

To distract her from trying to touch me right now—which I know I won't be able to handle—I take her now empty mug from her fingers and carry them both into the kitchen. I rinse them in the sink before putting them on the top rack of the dishwasher. She's already standing by the couch when I return. "Vee?"

I twitch slightly at her use of the name that my bear gave me. "Um, you kept saying 'we' when you were talking. Is Garret ok?" This is his truth to tell, but I don't want to lie to the girl either.

"Garret has his own set of issues. He's not depersonalized...or whatever it was they called me. But he has his own shit going on. I can tell you that Sam's alpha enough—and the pack leader—that neither of us wants to challenge him. Teddy's an omega. There isn't anyone else here that he feels the need to compete with for your affection. Otherwise, you'd have to deal with two batshit crazy alphas living with you."

She stumbles walking up the stairs, and I think we need to work on moving the master bedroom to the first floor before she falls and gets hurt. "Having someone literally obsessed with you isn't necessarily a bad thing, Pixie. Just keep an eye out for red flags, understand he may sometimes be irrationally possessive, and try to help him deal with his own trauma when you can. It really is different for everyone. And let's give credit where credit's due: Garret is a shitload better at masking than I am. Most people would think he's almost normal."

Kelly

We don't get much more sleep before my alarm's going off. With his long legs, Steve beats me to the bathroom again. I'm considering banging on the door just to annoy him, but instead I grab clean clothes and hobble downstairs to that bathroom. Jake is still asleep on the couch, and I scratch his ears to wake him up so he can go do his business before the shower starts going and wakes him up with no way out.

Letting him run loose through the backyard, I hurry to the bathroom and step under the hot spray before Steve can use it all up. It feels so good, but I think part of my next paycheck is going to buy a massaging shower head for my stupid back. Or put it in a jar to start saving up for a bigger water heater. I've mostly rinsed off before it starts getting tepid, but it's still frustrating.

I dry off and get into my work clothes, stopping by my room for some of the pads the guys picked up for me, and a handful of gummy bears. Steve meets me in the kitchen with Jake dancing around his legs and staring intently at the alpha's bowl of cereal. "Did you feed him yet?" I nod my head at the excited dog.

"Shit, I knew I forgot something. I let him in." Steve gives me a lopsided smile and I point to the cabinet that Jake's food is in. Walking into the pantry to pull out the box of chocolate puff cereal I got last night, it's already almost empty. I glare at the back of the alpha's head.

"Seriously, man, I just picked these up...when did you have time to eat them all?" He looks at me, his face flushed with embarrassment.

"Ok, well...I haven't had these in years, I seriously thought they stopped selling them...So I had some for dinner last night...and a snack after my shower...and breakfast."

All I can do is sigh and empty the rest of the box into my bowl. It's a little more than what I normally eat, but not enough to separate into two meals. I splash milk over the top and watch as Steve finishes feeding Jake and inhales the rest of his cereal before picking up the box and giving it a final shake to confirm there's none left. I smile sweetly at him around a mouthful of sugary chocolate goodness, and he snorts a laugh before breaking the box down for the recycle bin.

"Tell you what, Pixie. I'm coming with you today, so I can run down and grab a few more boxes for us while you're at work." I nearly choke on my cereal at the way he says he's going to work with me. No, hello, this is my job, and my school. I have work to do! He must see my confusion, because he quickly explains. "I don't have to hang out inside. I can walk around the block a few times while you work, but I want to look more at the school. Did you know they have a degree for Culinary Nutrition? It's one of their omega suggested degrees, but I want to check it out and find out if alphas are allowed to enroll in the program."

This is the most excited I've seen him about anything that isn't related to Teddy, and I don't want to shoot him down. Besides, maybe having him there will give me a break from Spence for the day. My Thursday class load is pretty low, so I can even see if he wants a tour afterwards.

Finally, nodding my assent, I tell him, "If you're coming with me, you better move your butt, we need to leave for work in less than ten minutes, you ready yet?" He lets out an undignified squawk noise before running back upstairs, and returning with...yes, another one of my shirts.

"You had to pick Demon Slayer? I thought you didn't like cutesy girls." I nod to where a tiny Nezuko is popping out of a box across his chest.

He stops suddenly, looking from me then down the hall and back. "Oh, your delivery. I forgot." Grabbing my arm, he drags me to what will one day be the office. It's located near the nest and is a large open floor area, currently stacked head high with boxes bearing the Nest-n-Stuff logo on the side.

What the heck?

I didn't order...

Oh, that little butthead.

We're gonna be late, but I need to verify this now. Ripping the tape off the nearest box, I pull out a dark, emerald-green pillow with a soft fuzzy fabric. The invoice underneath it says it's a custom order...from our trip last week where that little turd behind the customer service desk refused to take Teddy's information.

Steve stares between me and the pile of boxes and as I bury my face in this super fancy pillow and scream at the top of my lungs. I may or may not be hyperventilating by the time I finish and grab his arm, dragging him out of the house, followed by a bouncy Jake.

While we drive, *slowly*, I explain about our trip to the nesting store, and he growls quietly when I talk about the security guard demanding Teddy's identification. Thankfully, Xan and Gabe are in before me again, and there is a large stack of Jacks's muffins on the table in the breakroom when I go to get coffee started.

They both glare at Steve, until Gabe declares that he's not allowed to sit in the office all day—making him the official office gofer and sending him on no less than four trips to the store to pick up various things throughout the morning. Steve attempts to make conversation and even goes so far as to try to suggest marketing strategies, but neither of the other alphas is interested. Xan says that advertising the only garage in a town this size is like trying to advertise air. "Breathe air! It's the only option you've got!"

Steve is not amused but continues to try until eventually Gabe says he should join the volunteer fire department, and slaps him on the back, almost knocking the smaller man over. They do have a small workout center at the station, so the guys can stay in shape. It'd probably be a good idea for his health anyway, since the only other gym in the area is at the college, and it's only for students and family.

Steve actually looks like he's thinking about it, and a small part of me worries that he might get hurt. Not just because he looks like a strong wind could knock him over, but because, despite everything else, he's part of my pack. It would hurt everyone if something happened to him.

When work's finally over, we head over to the campus for my two afternoon classes. Steve's bemoaning the entire trip about the lack of music in my car. I finally give up and break out my portable Bluetooth speaker, turning the music app on my phone to The Black Parade album. It's one of my favorites since it has such a variety, and he begrudgingly nods at my choice of music before humming along to Famous Last Words.

Thankfully, there's time to get him situated at the registrar's office before I hurry to class. Spence is there, waiting in the parking lot, and scowls at Steve, before following me across campus to 'keep me safe'. It's endearing but also exhausting since I don't feel much like talking to anybody right now. Thankfully, he doesn't take my silence personally, and we have a quiet but comfortable walk until I get to class—where I'm met by the sneers of my classmates after he drops me off.

Both alphas are waiting for me when I come out of class, and there are a few snotty remarks about me being an alpha chaser again. If looks could kill, half the female students in class would be stone dead by Steve.

We walk back to the coffee shop, and Spence has about a million questions for Steve regarding different omegas they've met, and different centers they've visited. Getting a break from the constant inquiries this week is a welcome relief right now, and I tune them out as we all sit down with our drinks. Steve starts talking about growing up with Teddy and how they were all supposed to form a pack together until his designation came in. I've heard this a few times now, and it doesn't *not* make me want to slap him, so I do my best to close my eyes and tune the conversation out.

It's not until Spence's low rumbling growl almost knocks my drink out of my hand that my lids snap open. Spence is standing to his full height, and has Steve lifted off the ground by my danged shirt. The bigger alpha shakes him so hard that Steve's head flops back and forth. His expression mimics my own when Spence growls out, "It was your fault, wasn't it...you left him...and he...Shit!"

Chapter 23

Garret

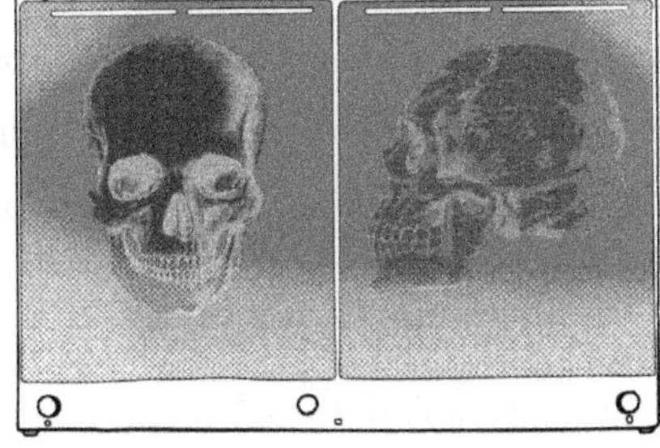

Teddy looks up from the phone where he was just talking to his mom. He's sitting on the bed at our apartment. The moving guys have gotten most everything packed up, but the beds need to be stripped before they can finish that part. Something about bio-hazards.

He looks pale and like he might throw up. Sam rushes around me, wrapping him in his arms and nuzzling against the top of his head, his purr a loud thrum through the room. Teddy sinks into his side, looking like he's about to cry. Sam's big hand rubs down the omega's hair. "It's ok, Love. Tell me what happened. Are your parents ok? Did something happen on their cruise?" He's rocking back and forth, dragging the smaller man with him.

Teddy's voice croaks. He struggles with the words, swallowing a few times before he manages to speak. "No...no, my...my mom's fine. They...they're still on vacation. They get home next week. She said she's taken lots of pictures to send." He swallows again. "It's...it's Brice."

Sam freezes. Not that I blame him. The whole situation with his brother is fucked up. I get the age difference is a bit of a sticking point, but Joseph's reaction seems excessive. Teddy's voice is barely above a whisper when he starts again. "He's sick. He's been sick for a while. Mom says that he didn't even tell Aunt Sandra because they were hoping it was nothing. They didn't want to worry the rest of the family until they knew what it was...or if there was a way to fix it."

We met Brice, years ago, but I couldn't tell you much other than he was sweet to Teddy, petite, even for an omega, with curly brown hair and green eyes. He talked about his pack constantly. It was clear even when we were little how much he loves them all. And the feeling was obviously reciprocated. I remember thinking that was how it should be with alphas and their omega. Even then, I worried that we would never have that because of how different Steve and I are. Of course, that became more apparent later on, but I digress.

Sam starts rocking side to side again, holding Teddy tightly. The omega takes a shaky breath. "It's gotten bad enough that they didn't want to keep it from my aunt...he um...he has leukemia. They're trying to find someone who can donate bone marrow, but it's really difficult. Full siblings have the highest success rate, but even then it's not great—not that he has any. Um...Joseph called Aunt Sandy to see if she could get tested for a match. That's how they found out."

Big tears roll down his face. "A...apparently being a close relative with the same designation and gender, I have the highest chance of matching." Teddy swallows convulsively, looking like he might be sick. "That's why they invited me to stay for my break. Joseph had talked Brice into asking me to get tested to see if I was a match. But then I met Sam the day after I arrived. Mom...um...Mom says that bonded alphas are less likely to let their omegas into what might be a harmful situation, so when they saw me with Sam they...well, Joseph really...he lost it."

Is this why Joseph was so aggressive when we met? Is it just stress or is he worried I'll side with Sam? Teddy's an adult, he can do whatever he wants. I don't want him hurt, but just the initial test is fairly non-invasive—a swab or a blood draw. Even the extraction process for matches has gotten so much easier in the last few decades. It's still entirely his choice. But I don't see why he wouldn't want to help.

Sam's low warning growl provides the perfect backdrop to that thought process. Alpha in protective mode. Shit.

Luckily, our landlord takes that moment to knock loudly on the door and call out. "Mr. Carson?" Sam's head snaps up, his snarl nearly shaking the room as he glares towards the front door of the apartment. He shakes himself for a minute before turning to me.

"Garret, can you go...just...deal with that? I'll get these sheets pulled off and the mattress put up against the wall. Teddy can call the center and make sure they have boxes available for his stuff. Then I'll drive him over while you deal with the movers and the truck. Sound good?" I nod dumbly, relieved that at least one of us is able to think clearly.

Teddy stands up and pulls out his phone, searching through the contacts before pushing the button and lifting it to his ear. Sam starts taking pillowcases off, then stops to grumble about needing a bag. Leaving them to it, I make it to the door just as Mr. Wazowski knocks hard, his voice taking on a slight edge of panic as he calls out again. "Mr. Carson, I really need you to answer the door now, please!"

The apology is already on my lips when I turn the knob and let the door swing open. But it's not Mr. Wazowski's eyes that meet mine. Our father, Marc—Marcus Carson to his business associates—is standing there, an ugly sneer plastered across his smug face. Mr. Wazowski isn't so much *standing* behind him as he is being held by one of my father's security guards. The old man thrashing against the big arms that are lifting him off the ground.

My teeth grind as my gaze drops to the floor, a show of submission I have no control over with the man before me. "Father, I didn't think we'd see you here. We're just cleaning everything out, and then we'll be on our way."

His sneer drops into an ugly frown. "Of course I'm here, you idiot. I live in this fucking city. The real question is, what are you doing here? I told you that I'd cut you off. You'd have nothing unless you came home. Have you decided to crawl back like the worthless piece of shit you are? Find a suitable god-damned omega? Has your useless fucking brother come with you? Steven! Get out here, boy!"

The last is yelled loudly over my head, and I cringe involuntarily. I recognize this tone. He's angry—angry enough to lash out, to cause pain. Even though I know what's coming, I don't cower. That always makes it worse.

"Steven isn't with me, Father. He stayed at home with Kelly, our beta. Sam and Teddy came with me to finish packing up the apartment. Then we'll leave and you won't have to see us again."

Knowing someone is going to hurt you doesn't mean you're always prepared for it, my jaw clenches in anticipation of the hit I know is coming, and the bastard doesn't disappoint. Our father is a large man, bigger than Steve or me. Of course, the way we've lived for the last ten years hasn't exactly encouraged growth, but he's always been solidly built, and the time we've spent away from him hasn't changed that.

His fist slams into my jaw, the rings on his fingers flaying the skin open, and forcing a grunt of pain from me. The cuts will heal quickly, they always do, but I need to try not to crack any teeth since that would require an actual dentist. A lesson we learned at too young of an age, to be sure.

My body slams into the wall, and while my shoulder leaves a deep indent in the drywall, at least it absorbs some of the impact before my head hits a moment later. A sharp searing pain cuts across my temple, and my legs unhinge, dropping me gracelessly to the floor. Thankfully, I don't pass out. Losing consciousness around an enraged alpha is never a good option. And his guards are here to help him, as much as act as eyewitnesses for whatever he does or doesn't want known. They won't step in to keep him from going too far.

Why am I fighting him on this?

Would he stop if I just agreed to his demands, or has it already gone too far?

Is he going to take his frustration with Steve out on me as well this time?

At least my brother won't have to be subjected to this anymore.

The snarl that rips through the room leaves me cowering in a heap. The few times I've heard it before resulted in trips to the hospital, and neither Steve nor Mom are here to take me this time. My hands try to raise to cover my head, but the room is spinning around me, and my arms feel weak and useless.

My eyes squeeze shut, waiting for the inevitable, but it doesn't come. Instead, warm arms wrap around me and help me stand. I still feel unbalanced, but the body pressed against mine holds me upright and half leads/half drags me from the room. I try to open my eyes, to see what's happening around me, but spots dance in front of my vision, and the room spins and tilts.

That's never a good sign.

"Hold on Garret, I've got you. Let's just get you back to the bedroom, and I'll call 911. Your head's bleeding. What the hell happened?" Teddy's voice is an angry buzz in my head.

Each shuffling step ringing in my ears. My skull feels too tight, like it wants to crack open to release some of this godforsaken pressure.

I push against my friend. Dad never let him get too close to this side of things. No witnesses, even a kid. Whenever Dad would get like this, we'd have to stay home for a few days. It was rare enough that it could be explained by the flu or strep or some other childhood sickness. After all, kids get sick all the time. They're little walking germ factories.

But I don't want Teddy to get in his sights now either, especially as an adult. I don't think Dad would hold back on the man he blames for corrupting his son. Which is laughable, I knew Steve was gay before he and Teddy were ever a thing. Our best friend had nothing to do with that, they just happened to fall in love. Correlation doesn't equal causation, but I doubt Dad can see it that way.

Teddy sits me down on the edge of the bed in my room and comes to stand in front of me. He's pale and shaking...it's not a good look on him. "Fuck, Garret. What the actual fuck happened? What the hell did you say to him?"

Ahh, yes, of course.

This is all my fault.

I must have done something to cause this kind of reaction.

I don't remember what it was, but I'm sure there's a reason.

My body sways as the room continues to swim, and Teddy puts his warm hand back on my shoulder to keep me still. The other holds his phone as he puts it up to his ear. It's only a few moments before he starts talking. "Yes, hello. I think I need an ambulance..."

My mind drifts. The loud snarl from earlier is repeated, and I jerk, my mind filled with renewed concern for my friend.

There was someone else here, wasn't there?

Why can't I think properly?

Everything buzzes with static, and something warm tickles down the side of my face. My hand lifts to brush it off, but everything feels loopy and uncoordinated. I finally manage to half slap myself in the face to scratch at the maddening itch and my fingers come away wet with blood.

Oh, that's not good.

Though it might explain some of the spinning and loopiness.

Voices raise in the other room. Yelling, followed by a loud rumbling growl. My stupid wet fingers rub over my eyes, trying to wipe away the spots clouding my vision, but that just makes it worse. Now I'm looking at the world through a film of red. *Shit.*

Finally, one voice is louder. I know it, even though it sounds unhinged, barely human—primal. "I don't care who the hell you think you are. If you ever come near my pack again, I will end you. Do you fucking understand me?" It's not Dad or one of his men. It's not my landlord, but it's familiar...Sam?

Why can't I focus?

My father's voice is low and sinister but still rings through the apartment. "God, save me from country bumpkins. Do you have the slightest idea who you're talking to, young man? Do you think, for one fucking second, you can take my sons from me?" The derisive sneer is back in my father's voice. He likes to make people feel 'less-than'.

"They're worthless to you, but I still have some use for them. Hand them over, I'm sure I can make it worth your while." Sam's low growl is the only reply, and my father huffs in annoyance before his voice turns cajoling.

"At least give me Garret. You'll still have the one your omega wants, and isn't that the important thing? Keeping him happy? You don't need both of them. What are they good for other than taking up space and costing you money?"

My head is still pounding, and my eyes slide shut. I want a few moments of peace before I have to return to that man. No one would be stupid enough to deny my father what he wants. And I'm sure he'll offer a good price. It means that Sam'll have an easier time taking care of the rest of the pack. Steve and Teddy and Kelly.

Shit, Kelly, I'm going to miss her so much. Maybe Teddy will agree to give her a message for me. Tell her I love her. I'll miss her. I know I'm not worth the effort, but maybe she'll think of me sometimes. I wish I had something nice to send her, just a little gift to remember me by.

My vision swims again. There aren't any more voices, just a loud ringing. That stupid tickle is back on the side of my face. Teddy paces back and forth across the room, the phone still held in one hand, and his arm waving with the other. I blink, trying to get rid of all the red, but it seems to be stuck. The room spins, and the floor rushes up to meet me.

My last thought before darkness takes me is that at least Kelly won't have to see the carpet burn on my face.

Chapter 24

Sam

Garret's father is big, but he's also soft. He doesn't look like he's actually worked a day of physical labor in his life. Judging by the way he knocked his son into the wall earlier, there's no denying that he's strong. Still, he looks like he'd crumble at any real pain he had to suffer.

My mind feels almost feral with rage when I see Garret slide down the wall and crumple on the floor, and I can't bite back my snarl of possessive aggression. The kid may not be mine the way the rest of my pack is, but he's still my pack. He's still mine to protect—mine to take care of.

Teddy rushes in, helping Garret stand and hobble to the bedroom—blood is already running down his face from where he hit the wall. His shoulder sunk into the sheetrock, and I thought that would protect his skull somewhat, but that kid has shit for luck by the look of the red streaked down the paint. It looks like his head hit just enough over to connect with one of the studs and one of the fucking drywall nails sticking out of it.

My growl rips through the room again once my omega has gotten to relative safety. It feels like I'm hanging onto my sanity by a thread. Torn between the need to eliminate the threat and check on my packmates, verify that they're alright. My head turns to see Teddy's back. He's standing by the bed, arm outstretched. He's saying something, but I can't make anything out.

My attention swings back to the alpha that started this shit. He's still standing in the doorway. Two larger alphas bracket him from behind. One holding onto an old man, lifting him nearly off the ground. Landlord? Ugh, we don't need this shit right now.

The father schools his features into something placating, but he's not fast enough to hide his sneer of disgust. The beta struggles behind him and when I go to close the door in his face; he reaches out, blocking it.

"I'm so sorry. I think there must have been a misunderstanding here. I came to retrieve my son. I'm so glad you brought him back. His mother has been worried sick." How the hell can he smile so calmly like that with his child's blood dripping off the rings on his hand?

He must take my silence as affirmation. "We'll just retrieve Garret and take him to the hospital. I'm sorry you had to see that. Sometimes children must be brought to heel for their own good." His smile is slimy, and my skin crawls under his attention.

Does he think that anyone believes this bullshit? I'd been stripping the beds, trying to hurry so we could get out of here and pick up Teddy's nest—heard someone yelling for Steve, and when I walked out to check on Garret, I saw everything. My voice is raspy and almost inhuman when I go to speak—my volume control seems jacked up.

He needs to understand that he's not taking any of my people. "I don't care who the hell you think you are. If you ever come near my pack again, I will end you. Do you fucking understand me?"

His smile slips for a moment. The derision back on his features, his tone menacing. "God, save me from country bumpkins. Do you have the slightest idea who you're talking to, young man? Do you think, for one fucking second, you can take my sons from me?"

Ahh, he's one of those people.

I've dealt with the do-you-know-who-I-am clients before.

Fucking hate it.

Yes, clearly you are an entitled asshole.

Thank fuck his kids aren't like that.

Would have left 'em out in that damned snowstorm.

When I don't reply outright, his tone changes. Still aggressive, but less demeaning. "They're worthless to you, but I still have some use for them. Hand them over. I'm sure I can make it worth your while."

I growl involuntarily. He wants to buy his own children? What the ever-loving fuck is wrong with this man? You can't buy people. Did Teddy's parents know just what kind of fucked up situation they were letting their kid around? My instincts say no, they never would have put him in danger. I've only spoken to them once, but they seemed decent—overprotective, but not bad people.

The dickbag in front of me turns placating, his eyes calculating. "At least give me Garret. You'll still have the one your omega wants, and isn't that the important thing? Keeping him happy? You don't need both of them. What are they good for other than taking up space and costing you money?"

He's not wrong. I'm gonna have to figure out how to deal with finances. When it was just me and Jake, I'd been building up a nice little nest egg, but finishing up the house and taking care of four extra mouths isn't gonna be free. I know that there'll be an increase in utilities and food, but that's not important. I can take on more work, advertise more. Whatever needs to be done to support my pack.

Teddy's voice raises behind me—he sounds frantic, calling out Garret's name. Without another word I slam the door, hard—narrowly missing the fucker's fingers in the process unfortunately. Flipping the deadbolt should give me a few minutes to check in on my omega, even if Garret's father wants to push things.

I would hope he's not that stupid, but looking at the alpha laying sprawled on the floor in the bedroom, I have my doubts. I'm pretty sure that man's just an asshole. Quite possibly a dangerous asshole, but an asshole nonetheless.

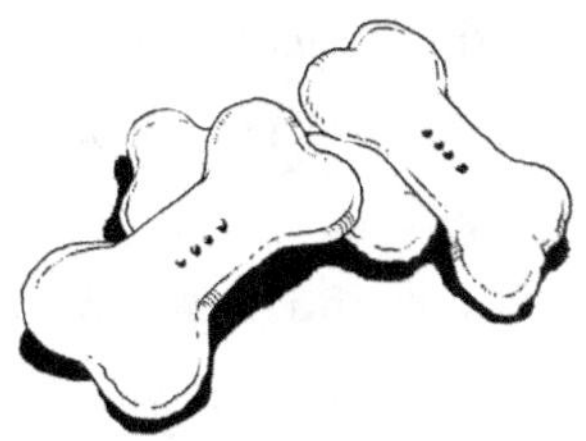

The hospital that the ambulance takes Garret to is some off the wall fucking name, Cedar or Cyanide or Sinai or some shit—and it's fucking huge. They're giving me and Teddy the runaround at the front desk about letting us see him, and I'm about ready to rip someone over the counter until they tell me where he's at.

Totally having a fucking Cheers moment, but I wanna go home where everybody knows who the hell everybody else is. It's annoying as fuck sometimes, but it's rare to have to deal with this kind of shit. Teddy's hand on my arm keeps me from climbing over the desk, but it doesn't stop my snarl at the fucker keeping me from my pack.

I finally let him pull me away, but neither of us is happy about it. "Listen, Sam...I...I can't be here. Ok? It's not...it's not you or

Garret, but I can't be here. This place...it just..." He looks from me to the front desk, his hands twitching up and down those leather bracers he always wears, and my brain catches a random thought before it spins away, and I reach for my omega, but he pulls his arms away, shifting from foot to foot.

"Just...take me to the omega center. I'll be safe there. You won't have to watch me. Then you can bring the pack paperwork back here. They should let you see Garret. I can get my nest packed up and we can get the fuck out of this goddamned city." He finally meets my eyes, and the look he gives me pleads for me not to ask questions, and just do what he needs.

Pulling him into a tight hug, my voice is a rough whisper against the side of his head. "Fuck, Teddy. I need...I need..." But I can't even say it. Words have never been my strong suit. But I need to mark him, make sure he stays safe, make sure I can feel him through a bond so I know if he needs me. But now's not the time.

Knowing it isn't the time doesn't make it any less true, and my jaw rubs against his temple, marking him with my scent, as I hold him tight to my chest. "If that's what you need, Love, I'll take you. Just promise me you'll be safe. Promise me that you'll stay safe, and tomorrow when I come get you, all your stuff will be ready so that we can load up the back of the truck and get the fuck home to Kelly. Yeah? Also, I'm just a phone call away. I don't care what happens. If you need me, you call. Anything, even if you just need me to come sit outside your dorm tonight so you can rest. I'll be there."

He kisses my chin, and we both glare at the beta behind the counter who's been staring at us. Teddy is much more diplomatic than I am as he steps forward. "Sir? Excuse me, sir." The guy's ignoring us now, pointedly not looking our way until I stalk back up in front of them. Then his head tilts back, his eyes staring up at me, face paling.

Teddy raps on the counter a few times to get his attention. "Sir? My alpha's going to take me back to the omega center to finish checking out. He'll be back in a bit to check up on our pack mate, Garret Carpenter. He'll have all our registration paperwork with him, so please, can you just let him see Garret then? We want to make sure he's ok."

I seriously have no idea where Teddy keeps hiding this sweet and polite side that he pulls out for strangers, but it's fucking adorable and makes me want to drag him out to the truck and lock him on my knot for the rest of this godforsaken day. Instead, I take a deep breath, inhaling his addictive cookie scent before leading him out to the parking lot to drop him off for the evening. And it fucking sucks.

The directions he gives me—and writes down for the return trip—are pretty straightforward, and it takes less than twenty minutes, even with city traffic. Walking him in the front door, I'm hit with so many omega scents that it's nearly enough to make me gag. None of them are bad, but none of them are mine either, and Teddy visibly preens when I lean into him to inhale against his hair.

We've brought the paperwork with us, so that they can make a copy for the school and start whatever process he needs to do. I know he'd like to have Kelly here too so she can meet his friend Sarah, but hopefully we can all get together one day when life isn't so crazy. As much as he's talked about her over the last week and a half, it's clear he's gonna miss her like crazy. Good friends can be hard to come by, and harder to keep.

He keeps a tight grip on my hand as we enter the administrative building, almost like he's afraid someone might try to steal me away. He should know well enough by now that he and Kelly are the only ones for me. I like Steve well enough, but if he doesn't stop his shitty attitude towards my beta, we're gonna have words.

Still, Teddy's practically dragging me along by the time we go to the main office. His smile is huge as he greets the lady behind the desk. "Ms. Clarkson, I was about to come looking for you. I need to get my transfer paperwork started. This is my alpha, Sam." He squeezes me in a one arm hug, before turning his face to mine. "Sam, this is Ms. Clarkson, she's my academic advisor. She should be able to help me get my classes moved to online so we can go home." This last part is said with a questioning eyebrow raised as he turns back to the woman at the desk.

Her smile is somewhat brittle, which makes me curious, but maybe she's just having a bad day. "Of course, Teddy. I'm assuming you have all the discharge paperwork filled out for the registrar's office, as well as a notarized copy of your pack registration?"

Teddy's face falls at her tone. "Of course, I submitted it all online a couple days ago...but I also brought paper copies, just in case." He's trying to hold on to his bright smile, but confusion mars his features. "Is something wrong?" His tone is full of concern for the woman who's suddenly giving me a very bad feeling.

She reaches across the counter, patting him on the hand, and it's only his fingers entwined with mine that let me bite back my possessive growl. She takes a deep sigh. "It's just been busy here, coming off spring break, and having to deal with some...unpleasant people all week long. Nothing for you to worry about, dear. I'm very happy for you. Now, let's get you all fixed up."

She sits at the computer and starts typing. "Yes, ok. All your paperwork is here. I *will* need to make an additional copy of your pack registration that shows the notarization, as well as copies of you and your alpha's identification." She looks between us. "I'm assuming you have that, Teddy?"

My omega blushes while we both pull out our wallets and I hand over my license with the paperwork. She steps over to a copier and he looks up at me from under his lashes. "Remember, I said I was resistant to being an omega...well, I kind of set fire to my first few ID cards as a form of not so silent protest."

I hold back my snort of laughter, and pull him against me into a tight hug. "Well, considerin' I work with wood for a livin', I hope you've gotten over your firebug ways."

He just laughs. "Yeah, no, Sarah threatened to beat me senseless with a dumbbell for being...well...a dumbbell."

My body isn't sure if it wants to laugh or growl, and all that comes out is a strangled snicker. I need to meet this girl.

"Is that what happened? Well, remind me to thank Ms. Zhang for her intervention to avoid any further dorm sprinkler mishaps." Ms. Clarkson returns to her seat, handing us back our paperwork and identification.

"Now, Teddy, as for online classes, you should be able to complete everything to finish out your degree in a few months. Is that still your plan?" My omega nods enthusiastically. "I'm glad to hear it. I've already sent emails to your teachers. You will have a new one for Advanced Mathematics, but I don't think that'll be a problem for you. If you could find the time while you're here to stop by their offices and confirm before you leave, I would really appreciate it. Also, Kimberly would like a word with you when you return to the dorm to get packed up."

Teddy's smile is infectious. I was hoping we wouldn't have any problems, and this has been easier than anticipated.

I should'a knocked on wood.

Chapter 25

Of course, the other omegas here are interested in Sam. The man is fucking hot. I growl at a few of the younger ones who come up asking me to introduce them. These girls aren't my friends, they've never been my friends, and trying to poach my fucking alpha is certainly not the way to get on my good side.

I'm practically dragging poor Sam across the lawn to my dorm when Sarah bursts out of the double doors. She runs at me full tilt, throwing her arms around my neck and nearly dragging me to the ground—something of a feat for a girl that I have a foot of height and about a hundred pounds on. Unfortunately for most of the people around her, what she lacks in size, she makes up for in attitude.

As if to emphasize this, she's wrapped around me like a fucking spider monkey and starts screaming at the girls who followed us. "What the hell is wrong with you thirsty bitches? Begone thots! This is Teddy's alpha, and I'm gonna kick all your asses if you don't back the fuck off right now!"

I squeeze her in a quick hug before pulling her off me and setting her on the ground, and her switch flips immediately. "Hi! You must be Sam. I'm so excited to meet you. Thicc, you didn't tell me how fucking hot he is! Why didn't you send me pictures? And you didn't bring Kelly, is she ok? Are you ok?"

She's grabbed me by the elbows and is trying to shake me back and forth until Sam steps up and wraps his arm around me. "Ms. Sarah, it's an honor to finally meet you. Teddy's told us how important you are to him."

She blushes nearly scarlet, and it lights up her olive skin. It's adorable, and I've never seen her blush. Holy shit! But she's doing it at my alpha, and it makes me want to growl. "Sorry, Kelly has work and school. She's trying to graduate this semester. Plus, there's Jake. We didn't want to leave him home alone." At her look of confusion, I take out my phone and pull up a picture I took of Kelly cuddled on the couch with the big dog. He looks like he's in heaven, all four legs in the air.

"Holy fucking shit, Thicc. They're both adorable. You lucky bitch! I want a puppy!" Sam's loud bark of laughter draws both of our attention back to him for a few moments, while he and I contemplate Jake as a puppy.

"I don't know, Shorty. I'm pretty sure Mr. Shaggbutt wouldn't be happy if you got a puppy." I chuckle at her look of consternation.

She stares at me thoughtfully, finally shaking her head. "No, I guess you're right. Shaggy would rip me a new one if I got a dog. Possessive little bastard." She looks up at Sam. "Does Jake like bunnies? I could bring Shaggy and come visit Teddy once you all get settled in. Maybe meet some of your local alphas?" Her eyebrows waggle suggestively.

"Darlin, I'm not sure if the alphas back in Mississippi could handle you. You seem like a spitfire. Gimme a few months to finish up the guest room and build a hutch for Shaggy, and you're welcome any time. You're important to Teddy, so you're always welcome."

She seems to melt listening to Sam's slow southern drawl, her eyes fluttering briefly before turning back to me. "Yeah, Teddy, I think I need one of these. Hook me up."

Sarah jabbers on as we sit in the open common area. Sam's knee bounces, and it's obvious he wants to get back to the hospital. My mind is still spinning with the news about

Brice, but everything that's happened since I talked to Mom has thrown me for a loop. Finally, Sam stands up and takes my hand to pull me into a tight hug.

"Remember what I said; you need anything, you call. I'll be here as quick as I can. I love you. We'll get this shit sorted out and head back as soon as we can. Hopefully, the hospital will let me in to see Garret, and tomorrow we'll stop by to get you and all your nest. Then we can get the hell home."

He pulls my shoulders down so he can kiss the top of my head, then my nose, then capture my lips with his, and I want to melt against him, drag him back to my nest, and do naughty, naughty things to him. But we have a no unbonded alphas in the dorms rule, plus I don't want to invite any more omegas to scent him and get any ideas.

In truth, nobody wants bonded alphas in the dorms, either. It can lead to heat spikes and all kinds of crazy shit. However, it would be nice to have help for packing up all my stuff. I might be able to have Sarah help, since I'm used to her, and I'll need to wash it all when we get home, anyway.

I'm so lost in thought waving to a retreating Sam that I don't notice how still Sarah has gotten. When my attention finally returns to her, her face is red and angry, and she starts talking before I can ask what's wrong. "He said Garret, didn't he? It's not that common of a name, Thicc..." She doesn't finish the sentence, but I see the question glaring at me from her eyes.

Scrubbing my hands down my face, I give her the best answer available. "It's a long fucking story, Shorty. You feel like coming upstairs and watching me pack while I go over the batshit crazy that is currently my life?" She huffs at me, crossing her arms and scowling suspiciously, before finally throwing her hands in the air.

"You don't owe me an explanation, Teddy. But that doesn't mean I'm going to stop worrying about you. Can I at least take your stoic silence to mean that these are the same twins who broke you before we met?"

When I don't answer, she starts cursing profusely, a long and loud combination of English and Spanish words that would probably make my mother faint. She finally tapers off, taking a deep breath, and pointing towards the door of what's been our shared home for the last decade. "Alright, Thicc. But if I'm doing manual labor, I expect gratuitous amounts of pizza and gossip. Not necessarily in that order."

And that's why I love Sarah. She may not agree with all my choices or life decisions, but she still supports me. My palms rub over my leather cuffs again, and her eyes turn stony. "Do they know? Those little bastards, do they know what they did to you?"

I shake my head, not able to answer without either lashing out or crying. Not that I know which one it would be at this point, and neither would be helpful. Her hand lands on my forearm, tracing over the tattoo of the pillar, and the scars hidden underneath. "Do the rest of your pack, Sam or Kelly?"

I shake my head 'no' again, which elicits another round of profanity from my best friend. I didn't realize how much I missed her, how much I'm going to miss her soon. I take a deep breath, wanting to pull her against me and hug her until she stops bitching, but we don't really have a hugging relationship—recent actions to the contrary. I've just spent so much time with Kelly and Sam over the last couple of weeks that I've gotten used to it, and now I want one. Plus, it sounds like Sarah could use one.

She stops her rant, takes a deep breath, and lets it out again. "That's fine...this is fine. Everything's fine." We pass Lily, another omega on our floor, and her eyes flare in concern at the loud sounds of annoyance my best friend makes, but she still gives me a timid smile and a wave as we pass.

Returning her smile with one of my own, I follow Sarah down the hallway. Her suite is across the hall from mine. She opens her door and pulls out a stack of boxes, rolls of tape, and trash bags from her room before following me into mine.

Looking around, I take in the space that's been my home for so long. It hasn't been the full ten years since I saw the guys, but close enough that it doesn't matter. Sarah's the only one who ever comes in here other than me, but I still like to keep the place clean. I go into my nest first and start pulling my blankets and pillows off the bed, stuffing them into the bags to clean when I get home.

Sarah stands in the doorway watching me, her eyes sparkling with unshed tears, and I don't know if it's because she'll miss me or she's worried. After a minute, I give up and wrap her in the hug we both need.

It's awkward, and she pulls away after only a moment. "Thanks, Thicc. Sorry I'm just...I'm gonna miss you." She takes a loud, wet sniff and wipes her eyes with the back of her hand. "Now, spill. What the fuck has been going on that you actually let those fuckers back into your life? Give me a reason not to choke Steve with his own severed dick."

I wince and bring my knees together in sympathy. I would not want this tiny woman mad at me. "Ok. Just hear me out..."

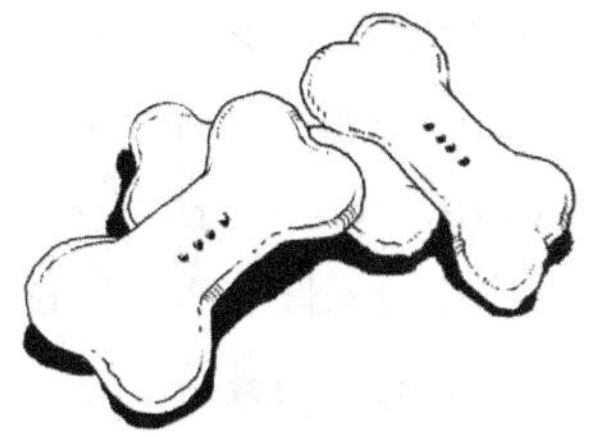

In her defense, she listens to the full story of everything that happened since Brice and Joseph picked me up from the airport. Going full goo-goo eyed over my meeting Kelly and Sam. Scowling when I tell her about Brice calling my mom. Then cheering when it comes to the part about Steve and Garret being stuck in the snow, and booing when I talked Sam into letting them stay with us.

By the time I'm finished stuffing pillows in bags, and stripping all but the basic blankets from my nest—so I still have a place to sleep tonight—we've reached the part about today and our arrival in Los Angeles at their apartment. Her gaze grows darker and darker as she learns about Brice being sick, and then the visit from Garret's dad, and his ensuing hospitalization.

By the time I finish talking, we've moved into the tiny living room, and all my books are boxed up. Sarah watches me intently as I pick Jessie up, running my fingers down her strings before putting her in the hard case with my spare picks.

Sarah hasn't said anything since the story ended, and I wonder what she thinks. Closing the latches on Jessie's case, I turn back to my best friend for the last several years. She's chewing on her thumbnail and staring intently at the carpet.

Finally, her eyes raise to meet mine and she opens her mouth, closes it, and chews on her nail for another minute before wiping her hand on her jeans. "So, you didn't know? You grew up with these assholes, and you had no idea their dad was an abusive fuck?" I shake my head, ashamed that I never realized what was happening to my friends growing up.

"And none of them know about your..." She waves her hands at my cuffs. "...forays into unlicensed body modification?" She doesn't like to say the words, but we both know what she means. I shake my head again. She flops onto the couch. It's not mine—it came with the suite and will get sanitized and de-scented before the next room occupant.

Her big brown eyes look up at me, a darker chocolate color than Kelly's honey brown. "What the hell are you gonna do, T? They should probably know."

Her hand shoots out, forestalling my argument as I sit next to her. "No, I know, I know it's not gonna happen again. You've worked your shit out more. You know you have people to talk to, and outlets. I get that. But...they have a right to know...fuck, you have a right for them to know what they put you through. You sure you don't want me to just break their legs? Just like...a little. One kneecap, I can do a kneecap easy."

Sarah smiles up at me, and fuck, I'll miss her so damned much.

"I'll tell them when I'm ready. It's not like I'm trying to keep secrets, but it's been busy." Her eyebrow goes up, before she asks the question I knew was coming. "Oh, no...you're not hiding it. So...have they seen you without these on?"

Her finger runs over the leather around my right wrist, and I slide it out of her reach with a mumbled, "No."

"Ok, T...well, I'm not gonna nag. But you could tell. That alpha, Sam...you're it for him, man. He looks at you like you hung the fucking moon." I smile at the thought of my big mate. "And he deserves to know the truth about the two guys you've moved into his house."

She holds her hand up again to stop my argument. "No, I know, it's not like they fucking held you down and slashed your wrist themselves. I get that. But they broke you...almost to the point you didn't come back. And I would have been really fucking lonely if you weren't here." She sniffs loudly, big tears rolling down her cheeks. But I don't try to hug her again, just hand her one of the throw pillows from the couch and watch as she wraps herself around it, rocking back and forth.

It takes a few minutes for her to calm down, but eventually the sniffles ease up. Her voice comes muffled from where her face is still pressed against the pillow. "And just...fuck you for leaving me here on my own. What the hell am I gonna do without you?" This declaration is followed by a watery chuckle, and another sniff.

Chapter 26

Sam

The hospital lets me in once I show proof of pack registration. It probably helps that I'm not dragging around an unbonded omega, but fuck them. I miss Teddy already. The beta at the desk finally buzzes me in and gives me directions to the third floor in the north tower. By the time I finally give up and ask for directions, again, I'm all kinds of turned around.

Thankfully, a young woman pushing a cart full of dinner trays takes pity on me and takes me directly to his room. Garret lies in bed, his face pale and washed out, a square bandage taped over his right temple at the edge of his hairline. When I sit down in the chair by his bedside, his eyes crack open.

His voice is a hoarse mumble, and it sounds like he's been under for days instead of just a few hours. "Sam! Wow…I missed you. Is Kelly here? I could use a hug right about now. And she just smells so good. I wanna bury my face against her neck and just sleep. My head hurts…wait why does my head hurt?" His voice takes on an edge of panic. "Sam…Sam, where are we? I…why are you here? I thought…"

Reaching across the flailing alpha, I push the nurse call button. I need to find out what's going on. Or at least figure out why the hell he's losing his shit. Did he smack his head hard enough to lose his memory? I'm holding his hand, trying to calm him down when a nurse comes in a few minutes later. He takes in our joined hands and nods once to himself.

"Hi…Mr…Carson?"

I draw back, affronted. "No, Carpenter. Garret's new pack leader. I know they got copies of the paperwork downstairs."

Do I sound snappy?

Fuck it, it's been a long couple of days.

The nurse looks over his paperwork. "No, no, we have him listed as Garret Carson, brother Steven Carson…"

He stares over the clipboard at the two of us, and I glare back. "Then you need to update his records. I'll be honest, we've only recently been together. I submitted a copy of the notarized paperwork from Monday. We just came back to L.A. to pick up their stuff."

His mouth drops open. "Monday, as in…three days ago, that Monday? Oh, no wonder, sir. Yes, it'll take at least a week to update all of his records. Is his brother here to help verify every-thing?"

I bite back a growl. His brother isn't here, and I'm getting sick of this shit. "No, sir. His brother stayed back in Mississippi with our beta. She had school and work and we weren't comfortable leaving her alone for however long this trip took."

The nurse looks uncomfortable. "I'm sorry, sir, but until Mr. Carson is able to sign off on the release of consent forms, I can't really tell you anything." He shuffles nervously from one foot to the other.

Garret is watching us like a hawk from his bed and looks to be nearly in tears when I turn to him. "Man, can you sign this whatever-the-fuck it is, so they can tell me what the hell's going on and we can get you out of here?" He starts to nod enthusi-astically before hissing in pain and gripping the bandaged side of his head.

I turn back to the nurse. "There you go. Go get whatever forms he needs. He doesn't want to be here." He's just doing his job, but it's still irritating as he scurries off before returning a few minutes later with several sheets of paperwork. He hands me the first one to fill out my contact information and gives Garret the rest to sign so that the doctor will finally be able to talk to me about what the hell's goin' on.

Garret's phone has been ringing on and off since I arrived, and I finally take a moment to answer for him. I don't recognize the number, but the voice on the other end is slightly familiar, as they start rambling an apology for earlier.

Ahh, the landlord, got it.

Quickly growing tired of the man's babbling, I finally cut him off.

"I'm sorry. Garret's still not feeling well enough to talk."

Sam Carpenter, master of the understatement.

Thank you, I'm here till Thursday!

God, I'm so fucking tired.

My pack mate flails his arm at me, and mumbles and I turn my attention back to him. He's saying something, but he points at the phone and makes a 'give' motion with his hand. I don't like it, but it's his choice, so I hand the phone over and watch as he juggles it for a moment, before giving up and putting it on speaker.

"Mr. Wazowski? Mr. Wazowski, are you there?"

The voice through the phone is shaky, the old man sounding both relieved and terrified. "Mr. Garret. I'm so sorry for earlier. I didn't know...I wasn't expecting your father to show up. Please believe me." His voice seems genuinely contrite, and shit, if I'd been manhandled, I'm sure I'd be fucking contrite too.

Garret finally clears enough of his voice to reply, "Mr. Wazowski. It's ok...well, not ok. My head feels like I've been pithed. But listen, I need you to do something for me. I'm going to set up a truck for the movers to load. They can come get all our stuff loaded, then we'll be out of your hair. I'm sorry I caused you problems."

I let loose a low growl, and Garret glares at me. It's not his fucking fault his dad's an asshole. He shouldn't have to fucking apologize for this shit. I miss what he says next, but then he's trying to get his landlord off the phone.

"Sir. Sir, I'm sorry. I really don't feel well. I'll call tonight though and try to get them in as soon as possible. I just need you to unlock our apartment when it happens...Yes, sir, just like before when you let them in to pack. Sam or I will be over first thing in the morning to help. Goodbye, Mr. Wazowski."

He hangs up the phone and lays his hands over his eyes. Before I have a chance to ask how I can help, the nurse comes back in with an older woman in a white coat—her name tag says Dr. Mayhue. She checks over Garret's file and looks at us both before speaking. "So, Garret and Sam...Carpenter?" Garret tries to nod, but cuts off with a hiss of pain. His voice can barely croak out a, "Yes."

Dr. Mayhue gives a quick nod of her own, like she expected this, and turns to me. "Mr. Carpenter, you're lucky Garret's alive right now. I'm only going on the information we have from the EMT, but it looks like his head came down on a nail that was sticking out of the wall...is that right?" She looks over his bruised face, bandaged jaw, and forehead before glaring at me.

Garret starts to reply, but I don't know how comfortable he is throwing his dad under the bus. I'll be happy to do that for him. "That's not exactly true, Dr. Mayhue." She turns her full attention to me, ignoring the glare that my pack mate throws her way.

"I'm from Oak Flats, Mississippi. I met Garret and our omega back home recently, and we agreed to become a pack, along with two others. Garret and I just drove back into town today. We had to come back to pack up their apartment and complete the pack registration transfer for Teddy, our omega, from the omega center. Garret's dad showed up at his apartment, apparently upset that Garret was joining my pack, and knocked the living shit out of his own kid before apparently trying to buy him back from me. Which is fucked up on so many levels."

She looks startled by my use of profanity, but I wanna finish this. Maybe that asshole can be brought up on assault charges. "When he got hit, he slammed into the wall. His shoulder took the brunt of it, but it looks like something sharp got his head. He couldn't stand and our omega had to practically drag him to safety while I tried to reason with his dad. That didn't go as well as I had hoped, and by the time I finished, he had already passed out."

She looks between the two of us before addressing Garret again directly. "Is what Mr. Carpenter says true?" He starts to nod, but then thinks better of it. His voice still isn't much more than a croaky, "Yes."

Her brows draw together. "That's a very serious accusation, sir...is there anyone else who would be willing to act as an eyewitness?" In that moment, I see the problem. We could try to have him charged for assault, but it would be our word against his. Three against three unless the landlord wants to step in, and while he may have apologized, I doubt he wants to put his neck on the line.

The doctor turns to me. "Mr. Carpenter, I would highly recommend you press charges in this matter. I know we can't make you, but it does fall to you as the head of Pack Carpenter to care for and protect your pack. Garret could have died had that nail been any closer to his temple, or any longer. As it is, we will need to keep him overnight for observation."

Her words are like an icepick in my chest and highlight again how useless I am as a leader. How I should have left them all well enough alone, just me and Jake. How Joseph may have lashed out in anger, but maybe he's right and I shouldn't have a pack of my own.

She's looking at Garret now. He holds the side of his head as he tries to shake it back and forth. His words are stronger, but no less rough. "You can't. You don't know our father. He won't stand for charges being brought against him. You don't understand." He's babbling almost hysterically, his whole body shaking.

Wrapping my arm around his shoulders, I purr for the other alpha. It's not normal, but I'm hoping it'll at least calm him down. He starts to settle slowly, his muscles no longer twitching as he leans against me. He lets out a deep sigh. "Sorry, Sam. You remain hot, but I'm still not interested." My low chuckle breaks some of the tension in the room. The doctor's eyes focus on me and I give a quick nod.

Garret's eyes slowly drift shut, and I lower him gently back to the bed. He may not be happy about it, but I'll be damned if I'm going to let their dad beat the shit out of my pack. I take his phone back and use his thumb to unlock it. I scroll through his recent calls to locate the moving company. It's late, but maybe I can leave a message.

To my utter delight, someone picks up on the third ring. I take a moment to introduce myself and ask about getting a cross-country hauling truck sent to the twins' apartment to-morrow, so they can load everything up. I'll need to fill out the forms online—which is going to suck with this tiny fucking keyboard—but then they'll pick it up and start loading it in the morning.

Giving them my debit card information for the payment, I mention that I'll also be renting a trailer to haul my truck home, and they said that shouldn't be a problem. Then I'm off to the truck rental website to tediously attempt to reserve a long-haul box truck with a trailer attachment. Garret's not going to be in any sort of shape to drive for at least a few more days.

And why are these fucking keys so damned tiny?

Chapter 27

Garret

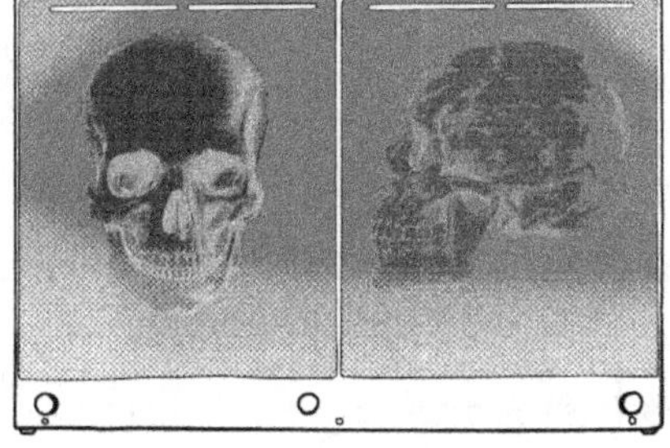

Where the fuck did I fall asleep, and why is it so god-damned bright in here? A better question would probably be what the hell I did last night. My head is pounding like the worst hangover ever, and my mouth feels like I licked a fucking sidewalk.

The room smells stale and sterile, like a hospital, and I cringe at how fucking trashed I must have been to get here. It's been at least a few years since things got that bad, and usually Steve's right here with me, having followed me down the rabbit hole of misery.

Bright, honey-brown eyes swim through my mind, a girl with long dark hair and a laugh that lights up my soul—Kelly! Where the fuck is she? My body jerks hard in the bed, trying to sit up. Cords wrap around my arm, pinching and restricting my movement. My eyes don't want to open. It's too damned bright, but I need to figure out what the hell happened.

The loud, gruff voice of my pack leader cuts through the haze. "Fuckin' hell, Kid. Stop flailing before you hurt yourself." A big hand lands on my chest, not hard enough to pin me in place, but it helps bring reality back into focus. My eyes feel crusted over as I finally manage to pry them open. The room is all white sheets and bright overhead lights, the windows still dark.

Sam scrubs the hand not touching me down his face. "Shit fire, Kid, you had me worried. How're you feeling?" He reaches over and pushes the nurse call button on the side of the bed while my mind spins and tries to make sense of everything. My face fucking hurts, and I strain to remember what happened.

Kelly's not here. She's back at home with Steve, so at least she's safe. There was the coffee shop, the rest stop. Then we got back to the apartment, I talked to the moving company, and we were finishing cleaning the bedroom so they could...Oh...Fuck me sideways. Dad!

Jerking against Sam's hold, my voice is weak and scratchy. "Teddy...Is Teddy ok? What happened?"

He raises his eyebrow. "You don't remember anything? Even wakin' up yesterday evenin' here?"

I think...maybe; I remember Sam and someone else. Sam purred for me, and I made a joke about how hot he is. Fuck, I can't think right now. "Sorry Sam, everything's...fuzzy. I remember going to the apartment, and you guys cleaning, Dad showing up. But after that...nothing clear. Sorry."

The way he gently pats my arm seems so at odds with his size. It's never really been a question of how caring he is as a leader, and the tenderness he shows just screams how different lead alphas can be from how Steve and I grew up. Hell, he openly disliked us a week ago. So much has changed in a short time. I want to thank him for accepting us, because it seems like such a huge thing, but it feels like that would make it awkward.

"Well, after the shitshow with your dad, Teddy called 911. You're in the hospital, and almost got your skull punctured..." He pauses like he's trying to think of how to say the next part, but at least that would explain the horrible ache. He looks intense for a second, opening his mouth to continue, but the sharp knock on the door has him snapping it shut.

A nurse comes in with a clipboard and draws up short when he sees me awake. "Oh, Mr. Carpenter, is everything ok?" I try to nod, but it makes me want to scream, so I croak out a raspy, "Yes," instead.

He nods in understanding. "Alright then, I'll just go see if I can find the doctor for you. Just a moment." He leaves quickly, but it doesn't set any alarm bells off, so I can only assume my father isn't at the hospital with us. He sends everyone scurrying when he's nearby.

Sam watches the door close before turning back to me. "Anyway, after the ambulance brought you here, I took Teddy back to the center to get his stuff. All his paperwork is filled out. I set up a truck rental and the movers to come back to your place to finish picking everything up. Once you're loose, we'll drive over there in my pickup, load it on the trailer, and go get Teddy so we can get the fuck outta this batshit crazy city and go home."

I go to nod again and groan. His hand comes up to stroke my hair, holding it back from my aching forehead and frowning. "Kid, you weren't awake when the doctor came back in. They mentioned some damage, but wanted to wait until you were awake to go into it further. And, well, it's a good thing you got a hard head. It sounds like you're lucky your brain hadn't been completely scrambled already. There anything else you feel like you need to tell me about growing up, anything that might not have come up last week?"

Cringing internally, I don't want to lie to Sam, but there are also some things I'm not comfortable admitting to anyone...at least not yet. He stares at me before heaving a sigh. "Alright, Kid...but it's not just you boys now. You got Teddy, Kelly, and me. We ain't had a proper bonding yet, but it don't matter. We're here if you need us, understand?"

His hand comes down in a gentle pat on my arm before he sits down in the chair by the bed. It has a pillow laying across the seat, and a blanket draped over the back and I wonder how long he's been here, and if I woke him up. Before I can ask, there are two loud raps on the door, and it opens without waiting for an answer.

An older gentleman in a white-coat steps through, his name tag proclaims him as Dr. Baxter. He's obviously been slathered in de-scenter, but I catch the faintest familiar whiff of sandal-wood and sage—it's so rare to see another alpha in the medical field because our strong sense of smell and tendency towards aggression can cause problems in delicate settings. I sit up straighter, wanting to ask him a thousand questions.

Unfortunately, this causes another agonizing throb across my skull, and I double over, retching from the pain. Sam lets out a loud curse, reaching for the pan beside me and holding it under my bowed head—but nothing comes out except drool. There's a scuffling of shoes on tile, and the white coat comes into my line of vision.

"Garret, are you ok? Can you sit up so I can take a look at you, please?" My eyes lift first, and my brain does another one of those little twirls. He could be familiar...I'm back to squinting now, not from the light but trying to figure out if I know this man, and how. Not everyone who knows my name is associated with good memories, and I suddenly feel too vulnerable.

"You need boost, Kid?" Sam's solid hand on my shoulder helps me sit up slowly, and he eyes the doctor like he might start growling at any moment.

To his credit, Dr. Baxter's gaze flicks between me and my open file in his hands, mostly ignoring my pack lead. Thinking hurts and I give up. It'll just be easier to ask. "I'm sorry. Do I know you? You might look familiar, but honestly, everything's kind of a blur right now."

Dr. Baxter's smile is tense as his eyes meet mine. "I'm sorry. We've met a few times, at guest lectures over at UCLA. It's been a few years; you were still an undergraduate. But your teacher spoke fondly about you." His eyes flick down to my chart and back to me. "That being said, is long term memory loss a problem that you've noticed?"

I must be hanging around Kelly too much, because before I can consider an actual answer, my mouth pops open. "Well, if it is, I can't remember it." The doctor looks stunned for a moment. Sam groans and I bury my aching face in my hands.

After a few minutes, I manage to make eye contact again. "I'm so sorry, Doctor, I've spent too much time with my beta recently and she tells the worst jokes. I don't know where that came from." Both of the other alphas smile, and Dr. Baxter nods.

"It's ok, our pack rubs off on us, and not always in the best of ways." He chuckles lightly, like he's thinking of his own mates before suddenly getting serious. "Garret, are you aware of any events that might have resulted in blunt force trauma to your head? There's nothing in your charts, but..." He tapers off, as if unsure how to finish that sentence.

'Sir, do you know you've been hit in the head repeatedly and had multiple concussions?'

'Why yes, Doctor, I am aware. Thank you for asking.'
Fuck my life.

"When we took your x-rays, we noticed several healed fractures—not areas along the growth plates—and we wanted to check for any underlying problems."

His gaze swings from me to Sam and back, causing my alpha to let out a low growl. "Garret, do you feel safe at home? If you need help, we're here for you."

It takes me a moment to realize what he's asking, and I nearly choke trying not to laugh. Which I'm sure would upset Sam more. Once I've gained the ability to speak without snickering, I try again. "I'm sorry, Doctor. I've known Sam for less than two weeks. He's only recently become my alpha because Kelly, my beta I mentioned earlier, was already a part of his pack before we met. She's in a relationship with Sam and my brother's omega, Teddy."

Dr. Baxter looks between us again, momentarily perplexed. "So, am I to understand you have no idea how your skull was fractured, Mr. Carpenter? I find that highly unusual." So much for being on a first name basis, I guess.

Before I can even contemplate whether or not I want to share my father's name, Sam's loud snarl rips through the room. He looks viscous and his voice is rage-filled as he spits out, "Marcus Fucking Carson." Dr. Baxter looks surprised for a moment, but recovers quickly.

"Garret, we'd like to get you in for an MRI to check for any brain trauma or other injuries before further problems occur. It may be nothing, but I'd rather be safe than sorry in this case." I swallow convulsively. It feels like I've been hit by a truck. I just came to get my shit so I can move on to the next phase of my life with my pack.

"Do you think I need one? Ok, stupid question. But Dr. Baxter, it's probably nothing, right?"

The good doctor looks me over for a moment. "Mr. Carpenter, I can only assume you've had one too many knocks to the head to be thinking clearly at this point. Yes, you need the MRI, you studied medicine, you know how this works. Get the damned scan." All good humor is gone from his expression as he stares intently at me.

I look over at Sam, but he won't be any help either, because I'm sure he'll agree with the doctor.

I don't have time for this shit.

Chapter 28

Sam

If I could get my hands around that motherfucker's neck, I would fucking kill him. Rage and vengeance shouldn't be taking priority in my mind right now, but all I can think about is how much these two have had to suffer at his hands for it to be this bad.

If the kid needs an MRI, we'll get one. I mean, that should only take a couple of hours, right? It shouldn't throw us too far off schedule. I can still go get the truck, pick up Teddy, and then come back here to get Garret. No problem.

Garret's loud squawk of, "Two weeks?" drags me out of my planning. "I can't come back in two weeks. I live in Mississippi now. That's not...that's not even an option. Can you get the referral sent to a hospital near Oak Flats, or…Fuck, I don't know?" He's shaking and stressed. This has all been a whirlwind.

Squeezing the back of his neck, I try to offer reassurance where I can. "If they can't send in a referral, we'll get you a flight back or somethin', Kid. Don't sweat it, you're gonna make yourself sick. We'll take care of this shit, aright? Just take some deep breaths. You're not doing anybody any good if you lose your shit."

The doctor looks a bit scandalized at that, but I have neither the time nor inclination to soften my language when my pack needs me. "So, Doc, can we get that referral or schedule done and get the hell outta here? I still need to get the truck loaded, pick up our omega, and then we got a long-damned trip back to Oak Flats."

He looks shocked, and then angry. "Mr. Carpenter, while I may agree, against my better judgement, to discharge Garret today, under no circumstances should he be operating a vehicle. What he needs is bed rest. As for the MRI, I can send a referral to…Oak Flats, you say? But he may need to return here afterwards, depending on the facilities available."

"No sir, that's why I'll be driving. Garret and Teddy will be relaxing as much as possible. But I just wanna get home and get my family back together."

Doc nods, looking somewhat more placated, which isn't a major endorsement, but I'll take what I can get. "Well, there's not much I can do to keep you here if you insist on being discharged, even if I do think you would do well to remain under observation for another day or two."

He turns to Garret, asking silently for him to stay for longer, but the kid just shakes his head before grumbling out, "Sorry, Dr. Baxter, I really want to get home. I'm worried about Kelly and Steve. Moreso about Kelly stabbing Steve because, let's face it, he's kind of a jackass. But he's still my brother, and I prefer him alive and relatively unharmed."

Doc blinks slowly at Garret, like he's trying to figure out whether or not my pack mate's joking. Finally, he throws up his hands. "Fine. Fine. I'll get you discharged!" Then he swings to me. "You, make sure he gets as much rest as possible, plenty of fluids, he is not allowed to drive, and if you can get your omega to purr for him, it should help speed up some of his healing."

He stalks towards the door, but Garret raises his hand to try to get his attention. Dr. Baxter refuses to look over at him, waving his hand in return. "Yes, fine, I'll get that damned referral in, but I'm not happy about this." Then he stomps out the door—it closes slowly on its hydraulic arm.

Garret stares at me, waiting for...I don't know what. This is the reason I don't like talking. Well, that and for the longest time, it was just me and Jake. As long as *he* wasn't replying back, then it seemed like life was doing what it was supposed to. Garret's voice is still raspy when he finally croaks out, "Have you seen my pants? I don't even know where the hell my underwear is."

That, at least, is something I can help with, as I pull out his duffel with a fresh change of clothes. His dirty ones are already packed away in a bag to take care of when we get home. It took forever to get the blood out of his shirt in the damned tiny sink in here.

Teddy

This bed is too fucking cold...and empty. Sure, it would have been better had I not already stripped it, but even last night in the car curled up between Sam and Garret was better than sleeping alone on a soft mattress.

The sun is barely starting to break over the horizon when I give up and finish stripping the bed. Loading the last of my nest into a bag, I text Kimberly to see if there is anyone who can help me load and carry all my stuff up to the main building.

Then I text Sam, telling him I hope he was able to get some rest, and asking how Garret's doing. I want to ask him to come get me, but he already has enough on his plate, and I can wait for however long he needs today.

Kimberly messages me back that she'll send someone down with one of the little Mule trucks to help me get everything up to admissions. They'll have a code to get into a storage room that's used specifically for departing omegas. It's not always easy to clear out a full nest with one omega, and not everyone has betas in their pack to help.

While I wait, I stack boxes and bags next to the entry door so that as soon as the truck gets here, I can load everything quickly. I need to say goodbye to Sarah again. I'm going to really miss her. We already stayed up way too late talking last night, so I'll probably need to knock on her door before I take off.

My phone chimes and I pull it out, expecting it to be someone here to help me get moving. Instead, Sam's picture pops up. He has Garret, and they're about to pick up the truck from the apartment. Hopefully, they'll be here in a couple of hours. Just enough time to move my shit, grab Sarah, and get breakfast together before we head out.

I pace back and forth, waiting for a message about transport, but instead of a message notification, a soft knock sounds on my door. Is Sarah already up? Opening the door, a big beta guard stands outside. He's about as tall as me, but wider, with broad shoulders that fill the doorframe. He looks up from the phone he's holding and checks the door number before turning his eyes to me. "Teddy, right?"

His scent is stronger than Kelly's, an earthy rain smell, not enough like Garret's to throw me for a loop. It lacks that salty ocean flavor. But more like a landlocked storm. Something that comes out of nowhere while you're hiking and blows you away. Kinda like his smile. *Damn.* He introduces himself as Gregory and picks up a couple of boxes.

I'm half tempted to go bang on Sarah's door and wake her up just to come meet this guy to see how flustered she'd get. Of course, I won't be here long enough to enjoy making fun of her, and that thought in itself makes my shoulders slump.

I'm happy I get to go home with my pack, have cuddles with Kelly and Sam and Steve. Pet Jake and fall asleep in the basement watching TV and snuggling. Finish my nest and get ready for my heat. I'll still miss the woman who's been my best friend for the last nine plus years.

A hand waves in front of my face, drawing me out of my thoughts. The big beta smiles uncertainly. "So, these boxes and bags? It'll probably take about four trips to get everything. You feel up to helping me carry?"

It's a pleasant surprise that I don't have to move everything by myself. I was planning on it, but this just makes it easier. It does, in fact, take five trips, because I want to be super careful about Jessie, and the bags of blankets don't exactly stack well.

Gregory was intrigued by Jessie and said it's too bad I wouldn't be around. He sometimes plays and it would have been nice to have someone he could discuss music with. Another point in his favor with Sarah, and I'll have to point him out to her if I get a chance. She took up drums a few years ago—much to Kimberly's dismay—but she's always looking for people to talk music.

By the time we get the last of the boxes into storage and he writes down the key code for me, the sun is well above the horizon. I pull out my phone to check for word from Sam, but so far nothing. I'll take that as a sign that I have time to go grab Sarah for a goodbye meal.

Gregory drops me off at the dorm, and I go make a final sweep of my room, making sure I didn't leave my shampoo or anything in the shower, cleared out the fridge, and the tiny washer and dryer are empty. Sarah's standing outside of her door when I walk out, waiting for me. "So, Shorty, you ready to go grab some breakfast before I head out? One last meal of French toast sticks for the road."

She nods and makes a loud wet sniffing sound before punching me in the arm. "You totally didn't order pizza last night for my help with packing, so you have to buy me breakfast." I don't mention to her that she didn't help pack, she sat on the couch while I packed and talked. It's easier to just agree, especially since I know this is her attempt to lighten the mood.

We're halfway across campus when we see Sam walking towards us. I look at my phone and see that he messaged me a few minutes after nine telling me they were pulling into the parking lot and apologizing for the delays.

Too late, I realize that he wrote 'we' and Sarah is pelting headlong across the grass, death and destruction in her gaze and focused completely on Garret. Her words rush out, a mixture of English and Spanish. I don't know enough to translate, but if her expression is any indicator, then I'm probably glad I can't understand.

Sam catches her mid leap before she can sink her nails into Garret, and she hangs from his arm, spitting and hissing like an enraged cat. I'd probably growl at another omega being so close to my alpha, if she didn't look so much like an enraged kitten who wanted to rip their faces off.

That doesn't mean I'm happy about it either. Lifting my best friend out of my alpha's arms wasn't on my bingo card for this trip, but here we are. Her angry glare turns to me, her voice a loud hiss. "It's not fair, he looks fine. They shouldn't get away with this. If his brother was here, I wouldn't let you stop me, you know that."

I'm once again grateful that she's my friend, because I wouldn't want to be on Sarah's bad side for all the money in the world right now. I hold her back against my chest and take deep breaths until hers sync up. A few minutes later she's calmed down enough that it's probably safe to sit her down without risking Garret's skin.

Sam watches the entire interaction with a thoughtful look before wrapping me in a hug. His purr is a low rumble against my own chest, soothing my frazzled nerves and making my body relax against his. He nuzzles into my hair, his mumbled, "Missed you," making me melt against him further.

An annoyed huff draws my attention. Sarah is still glaring at Garret. "Ok, I'll give you that Sam seems like a good one, but I also think he should know what happened before you let these fucks bond you. That shit's permanent, T." Sam pulls back and looks intently at me again, and Sarah takes her opening. "Sam, have you ever wondered why your omega always wears leather wristbands, even to sleep? Does that seem like normal sleep-wear back home? Doesn't look comfortable to me."

Now Sam's staring intently at my wrist, and I need to escape that scrutinizing gaze. His voice is low when he finally responds to her. "Teddy is free to talk to me about anything he wants to, but I won't force him to do it right now." His gaze turns back to mine. "Not that this conversation is over, but everyone's stressed enough. I don't want you to have to deal with any extra shit right now."

The threat that we'll talk about this later, despite my feelings on the matter, is left unsaid, and I throw Sarah a dirty look. One she responds to with a smug smile.

"Not to completely change the subject." Her voice is saccharine sweet, and I don't trust it. "But Thicc and I were headed to the cafeteria to get some breakfast before you got here. Surely you don't want your omega to be hungry? Why don't you two join us before you head out? Better to have a late breakfast now, so you don't have to stop for lunch in a couple of hours."

She's being entirely too cheerful, and it's putting me on edge. Sam looks between us, not saying anything, but eventually he nods assent. Sam isn't the most talkative guy to start with, but his silence right now is disconcerting. He's like a lion watching his pride, waiting to see what happens and if he needs to step in. Content to let us take care of things ourselves until we can't.

Please, to any gods that are listening. Just let me get through breakfast, get my nest and motorcycle loaded up, and get out of here without any more drama. Is that really too much to ask?

Chapter 29

Kelly

Steve is coming back to campus with me today. After his run in with Spence yesterday, I didn't think he'd want to. Not that the bigger alpha would explain anything to us. He had his outburst, then left. He didn't even say goodbye, just walked out.

Thankfully, it's Friday, and almost everything is caught up at the shop. I get to leave work early, and we head over to school to hit the union and grab our lunch before my first class.

Spence is there again, and while he glares at Steve, he doesn't say anything else. I really want to ask him what he was talking about yesterday, but I don't want him to throttle Steve again, especially since he's once again wearing my clothes. He really needs to start washing them when he's done.

We've barely made it to stand in line for our food when my phone rings—Teddy's picture pops up. It's one I took of him last week asleep on the couch with Jake, and they look adorable together. Answering the phone, my smile is already in place—I've really missed all three of them. It sucks that I got stuck here with the only one I don't want to snuggle. The one who happens to keep cuddling me in his sleep. I don't even mind that so much now that I'm expecting it. I just wish he'd stop freaking out.

"Hey, Pixie. Are you free to talk? I didn't catch you in class or driving, right?" His voice is a deep rumble that I want to cuddle into. I can hear other voices in the background, Sam's gravelly growl, Garret's more cultured accent, and a higher pitch woman.

"No, Steve and I just got to campus. We were gonna grab lunch before class starts." He's quiet for a minute, and I have to hold my hand out to smack at Steve's grabby hands when he tries to snatch the phone from me. Giving up, I step out of line and put the phone on speaker so he can hear too.

"Oh, Vee's there too? Wait, is everything ok? No...Fucking shit! Goddamnit Sarah, give me my fucking phone. Son of a bitch!" The phone cuts out for a moment and I'm glad I don't have it up to my ear anymore because Sarah's loud screech rings echoes through the entire room. "You little son of a bitch! How dare you come close to Teddy again. If I could get my hands on you, I'd wring your fucking neck. He may be sweet enough to let you back in, but he's obviously an idiot for doing so."

There's a sharp intake of breath in the background, along with a low growl that sounds like Sam, then Teddy yelling, "Sarah, goddamnit, give me back my fucking phone."

But Sarah seems to be on a tear, and while I can tell she switched to Spanish, I don't remember enough from high school to actually understand what she's saying. Plus, if I had to guess, they wouldn't teach some of these words in class. "Teo, tal vez yo me haya disculpado que sigues un Hijo de Perra. ¡Si descubro que lo lastimaste, te voy arrancar tu pito y te lo metere en el culo! ¡Si esta lastimado por tu culpa, te voy a matar Desgraciado! Si crees que saldrías con la tuya por lastimar a mis amigos, Yo voy destruir tu puta vida!"

The phone goes silent after a moment, Steve staring at it intently. His skin's gone pale and washed out. Several other people around the room are watching us in slack jawed horror, and I really wish I spoke Spanish right now. Even Spence is back to giving Steve a death glare. Finally, I hear some grunting, and Teddy comes back on the line.

"Sorry about that...um, Sarah says hi. Fucking hell. So yeah. You all good?" He sounds embarrassed and I can hear more yelling in the background as well as Sam's growl getting louder.

I don't even get a chance to think about my answer before Spence is tapping on my shoulder, his voice a loud stage whisper. "Hey, he said her name's Sarah...is she looking for a pack? Her voice is so sweet." I gape at the big alpha next to me, wondering what in that tirade sounded sweet to him, but he's gazing adoringly at my phone.

The yelling in the background has gone quiet, but Teddy rushes out. "I'm sorry, Kelly, Vee...um...Spence, but we need to go. I just wanted to let you know we're about to get on the road to head your way. It's still a long ass drive, and Garret can't take a turn, but hopefully we'll make it back sometime late tomorrow. I miss you both so much. Just another day and we can have lots of snuggles. Love you."

The phone beeps and the call ends before either of us can reply. The yelling in the background had reached a near fever pitch, with even Sam joining in right before it was disconnected. Spence looks between Steve and me. "So, um...Kelly, do you speak Spanish, like...at all? Pretty sure the jackass here does." He throws his thumb over his shoulder at Steve before lumbering off.

Steve has gone from pale to green, and I throw up my hands, dismissing the idea of lunch with everyone gawking at us, anyway. Grabbing his hand, I half drag him out of the union. "Ok, you clearly know what the hell she was saying. Spill or I'm hiding all my clothes," I say, flicking the collar of the shirt he stole today.

He stares down at me, his eyes big and round and full of tears. His throat works and I take a step back, not sure if he's gonna speak or spew, but not wanting to be within range for the latter option. A loud sob breaks from him, and tears run down his face—I give up and lead him away. Looks like no class for me today.

With nothing else to do, I tow Steve back to the car and buckle him in. Spence has disappeared completely and honestly, I can't handle any more alpha crap today, so I'm fine with that. We drive home in relative silence, the only sound the occasional thump of the road and Steve's soft whimpers. I still have no idea what's going on, but hopefully he'll calm down soon and I can get some answers.

Jake's waiting on the porch when we get home, and his head tilts at me when I help Steve out of the car. Whether it's because he's already memorized my schedule, or he's wondering about the crying alpha I'm basically dragging along, there's no way to tell. Regardless, he seems almost subdued when we get to the door, nosing at Steve's hand and pressing his body against the alpha's legs. Their low whines are almost echoes of each other.

Depositing Steve on the couch with Jake trying to crawl into his lap, I head into the kitchen. Hot chocolate with whipped cream is now, apparently, our thing. I put the kettle on and pull down a couple of mugs. I know it'll take longer, but hopefully that'll give me time to think. My brain struggles to remember what Sarah said—also now I'm kicking myself for not paying better attention to school. Teddy was definitely the subject and something about pulling.

BLARGH!
I was never any good at languages.
Most days I'm doing good to English.
What was that movie?
"I only speak two languages, English and Bad-English."

Yup, sounds about right.

My hands fist in my hair, tugging. The pressure feels nice, and honestly between cramps, hormones, lack of snuggles, and now the hysterical alpha on the couch, I really want to just say 'fudge it' and go crawl in bed. But no, I don't get to do that, because I have to be the responsible one.

Crud.

Fine.

Whatever!

The kettle starts puffing out steam, making a halting whistle, and it's as good a time as any to get this stuff sorted out. I roughly measure out the hot cocoa powder into each cup, and pour in water, stirring a bit too vigorously in my frustration so that some splashes over the side. Because why not?

Adding a spray of whipped cream to the top of each one, I carry both cups into the living room and set them on the coffee table. Jake's nose lifts from Steve's lap and he stares longingly at my whipped cream. I don't know if Sam would be ok with him getting a little cup of his own as a treat, so that'll be a question for when they get back.

Steve is hugging himself tightly and rocking back and forth. It's tempting to go get one of the pillows out of the boxes that were delivered, but that just seems like it'd be delaying the inevitable conversation we need to have. He jerks when I touch his knee, his eyes coming up to meet mine.

Honestly, he looks terrible, his face all red and puffy, and I wonder briefly if he's stopped crying at all since the phone conversation. Should I get him some water? He needs to stay hydrated. This is just another delay tactic, though, and I won't let myself do it.

I don't want to have this conversation.

Might as well just rip it off like a Band-Aid.

"Ok, Steve. You're gonna have to explain to me what the heck happened. 'Cause my Spanish stinks. What exactly did she say that got you so upset? And what was up with Spence yesterday? He didn't say anything, and you acted like it didn't happen. I wanna be on your side, but I need to know what's goin' on." There, mostly concise, straightforward, easy.

It's never that easy.

Should I slap him, see if that resets his wonky brain?

It could be fun.

But probably won't help.

Let's set that as a back-up option.

He swallows a few times, and I wonder again if I should have gotten water, but no. Steve's a big boy, even if he is having a meltdown. I want to be supportive, but he needs something to snap him out of being a zombie, even if that just means getting his own water. His eyes glance from me to the cocoa and back again. His hand starts stroking Jake's ears, and the big dog grumbles and settles deeper against the alpha.

When he still doesn't speak, I wave my hand in front of his face. "Steve. Earth to Steve, come in Steve." He blinks at me a few times before he swallows with a dry clicking sound.

Yeah, shoulda got that water.

Oh well, too late now.

Steve shakes out his shoulders. His voice isn't much more than a whisper, a low rasp. "Sorry, Kelly, I got kind of lost there for..." He looks around the room, finally taking everything in. "...awhile, I guess. I...what were you asking?"

Now I really do want to shake him. "I asked what Sarah was talkin' about. I don't speak Spanish, or at least, not as well as you and Spence do, apparently. And what was up with Spence yesterday? You've been acting like it didn't happen ever since we got home last night." His head bobs up and down, and I don't know if that means he's going to answer, or if he's just acknowledging what I said.

The nodding tapers off, but his voice is still croaky. He picks up one of the cocoa mugs and blows across the top before taking a sip and humming to himself. "I'm...still not sure exactly what happened with Spence yesterday, but after what Sarah said, I have a few ideas. My Spanish isn't bad. It's used a lot back in L.A. I don't speak it well, but I can understand, somewhat...if that makes sense."

Nodding along, I make a go-ahead motion. Steve takes another sip before speaking again. "Ok, so the basic gist of what Sarah said was threats. Teddy may be willing to forgive me, but she isn't. If I hurt him again, she'll rip off chunks of my anatomy and shove them up other parts of my anatomy." His eyes finally come up to meet mine.

"But there was also something about him hurting himself, and her killing me. There was a bit at the end about me not escaping...but...the mention of Teddy hurting himself. And yesterday, Spence talking about scars...I'm...it sounds like Teddy did something, but I haven't really noticed any scars. I mean, I haven't gone over him with a fine-tooth comb in the last week, but nothing major stands out. Still, what if I did make him hurt himself? What if..."

I don't hear the rest of what he's saying because my brain is replaying what Billy talked about on Wednesday at the store, about blood and scars. It didn't trigger anything at the time, because, well, I'm bleeding this week, and like Steve, I haven't really seen any big scars on Teddy. The only markings I've really noticed are his tattoos...though come to think of it, Spence mentioned those too and was looking at them. I wish my omega was here so I could look at them again myself.

Nausea rolls through me, and I'm glad I haven't drunk any of the cocoa, because I think I might vomit as I realize what kind of scars are usually on the forearms. Something you might be self-conscious about and want to cover up, especially if you wear a wide band that covers your wrist too.

Nearly tripping over my own feet, I scramble for the bathroom. There's a commotion behind me as Jake jumps off the couch and tries to follow. I hear Steve calling me, but I barely have time to get the toilet lid open before I vomit bile into the bowl. Thank fuck we didn't get lunch yet.

My mostly healed knees throb where I hit the floor. I spit in the toilet before sitting up, reaching for toilet-paper to wipe my mouth with, and flushing. It's suddenly too cold in here, and

Jake sticking his nose in my ear with a low whine doesn't help. I want to comfort my cuddly boy, but my mind is spinning, throwing out images of Teddy, always wearing those bands of leather around his arms. How he rubs at them when he gets nervous or upset.

My mind flashes to the long pillar running behind the card on his left arm, almost like he needed something just a little longer than the other side. My stomach rolls again, and I lean back over the toilet, but nothing comes out but spit. My head weighs a ton, and I just want to lie on the floor in here and stop thinking. Stop putting the stupid puzzle pieces together.

A knock on the doorframe draws my attention. Steve towers over me. His voice is still croaky. "What happened? Are you ok?"

Physically, yes.

Mentally, not sure.

Oh, wait, no, it feels like my knees might be bleeding again.

Physically, mostly.

I need to get a rug for in here.

I sit up, and let him pull me to standing, then limp back out to the couch with Steve and Jake following close behind. Shucking off my work jeans before I try to sit on the couch, I don't think Sam's gonna be mad about me hanging out in my underwear on his furniture, Jake won't care, and Steve can lump it, 'cause my knees frigging hurt.

Hey, look, more blood. At least it's distracting, and it lets me take a couple of deep breaths and focus on the sting rather than the picture that my mind wants me desperately to keep putting together. Steve shuffles around the side of the couch after Jake, and it takes more willpower than I like to admit not to scream when I hear, "Really, Kelly. Why the hell did you take your pants off? I don't need to see that."

In truth, the urge to pick up my still warm drink and chuck it at his face is really strong right now, and I try to tune his voice out to avoid doing just that. He's just so danged...mean. What did I ever do to him? He may have known Teddy first, but he left. He left our omega behind because he was too much of a coward to stand up to his dad. There's probably stuff I don't know about, but that's the gist of it, and now he has the audacity to complain about my taking off my frigging pants so I don't bleed all over my stupid work clothes. After I went through the trouble of making him a hot chocolate and everything.

No, I'm done.

I don't care.

Steve can shove it.

I've tried, I've done everything in my power to help and be friendly.

He's never gonna be happy with me being around, so he can just suck it.

Spinning on my heel, my hand is moving before I even realize what's happening. The loud crack of skin on skin when it connects with his cheek surprises us both, and Jake starts barking. Steve stares at me like I just slapped him, and going by the bright red palm print on his face, I guess I did.

Jake hops back and forth around the coffee table, baying a loud drawn-out howl. He seems to be trying to get close to each of us. As much as I want to comfort him right now, I can't even speak without screaming. So instead, I bend over, pick up my good jeans and carry them up the stairs so I can try to wash the blood out of the knees, and bandage up my aching legs.

Maybe I'll lock the bedroom door and just go to bed early. Steve can sleep down on the couch or in Teddy's room, but I just can't anymore today. I can feel him watching me as I walk up the stairs to the master bedroom, but he's not stupid enough to say anything else. I guess I was an idiot for thinking he might have actually been worried enough about me getting sick that he wouldn't be a critical butthead for five minutes.

Guess I was wrong.

Chapter 30

Steve

My cheek stings. Not badly, because Kelly can't hit for shit, but it was still a hell of a shock. And I knew, as soon as my mouth opened, I knew something shitty was going to come out, but I couldn't seem to stop it.

Maybe if I'd slapped myself, it would have helped.

Probably not.

There's not even anyone else in this house to see, other than the dog, and he doesn't count. I need to apologize, but my feet feel stuck to the floor. For fuck's sake, she got me out of a fucked-up situation, brought me home, made me a goddamned cocoa. I just wanted to make sure she was alright. What the actual fuck did I even open my mouth for?

A loud whine draws my attention, and I look down to see Jake staring up at me. Petting his head absently, I answer the question I can see in his big eyes. "I don't fucking know. I have no idea why I opened my fucking mouth. I was worried about her and maybe I'm lashing out because of everything else. It's not an excuse. I'm just trying to figure this shit out."

He blinks up at me, leaning his face against my leg with a loud huff. "Yeah, I know buddy, I need to go apologize. And find out what happened. People don't spontaneously throw up...Do you think she's pregnant?" My mind blanks for a second before I realize that no, she's having her period, of course she's not pregnant. Maybe it's a hormone thing. I could do an online search to see if that makes women sick.

Jake leans hard against me, and I nearly stumble under his weight. My eyes trace over the drops of blood on the floor leading back to the bathroom. She must have torn open her knees again. She is seriously the most accident-prone woman I've met in my life, and that would explain the taking off her pants.

ARGH!

Fuck it!

Stomping up the stairs, I beeline for the master bedroom, only to find it locked. I knock gently, but when no one answers, I try pounding harder. Still no answer. The doorknob doesn't have a hole in it, so no key...I know there's a way to open doors with a credit card, but I don't think any of mine are usable anymore, and it's not like I know how to do that, anyway. Once again, I could look it up, but, meh. That's too much work, and I'd probably get sidetracked down a video rabbit hole.

I could break it down...if I want Sam to kick my ass, so that's out.

Shit.

Well, I guess the only option is to annoy her until she opens this door.

Is that counterproductive to apologizing?

Yes

But, if I'm already apologizing for several things, what's one more?

My fist pounds on the door loudly. "Kelly! Open up, I need to talk to you!" No sound filters out of the room, so I bang again. "Kelly! I need to apologize. Come on!" Still no response.

"Come on Kelly, I know you're in there. I need to talk to you! Jake needs you. He won't stop crying!" The big dog looks up at me as if calling me out on my bullshit yet again. At least the door unlocks. It barely opens a crack before I grab the edge and force it open. There's a heavy resistance, then a loud 'oof' noise.

I just fucked up again.

I look around the side and Kelly's sitting on the floor, a towel wrapped around her, water dripping down her hair, and blood running down both legs from her scraped knees. The shower is still running in the other room, and I look between her on the floor and the steam billowing out.

Fuck my life.

"That *is* it, Steve! I am so tired of you. I just wanted to come up here, unwind in a hot shower where somebody hasn't used up all the danged water for once this week. Try to relax, rinse the blood off my stupid legs before I have to bandage them again. What?! What do you need that was so important, I couldn't get ten minutes to myself?!"

Standing there, gaping like a fish...I've seen Kelly naked. It doesn't do anything for me. But with her flushed cheeks and angry eyes, I can see why the rest of them find her attractive. It would be better if she didn't look like she wanted to gut me like the aforementioned fish. My mouth opens and words spill out. "You slapped me."

If I thought she looked mad before, it's nothing on the sparks flying from her eyes now. I rush on, trying to avoid her deciding to push me down the stairs and make it look like an accident.

"I completely deserved it, and I'm sorry. I didn't...I keep fucking this up. You got me home; you made me cocoa. I think I have perpetual foot-in-mouth disease around you because I can't seem to say the right thing, and I knew...I knew. I can say that it's because I'm worried about what Sarah said, but..."

Her skin goes pale, all the blood draining from her face, and then Kelly bursts into tears.

Marching into the bathroom, I shut off the hot water—try to save some in case she wants to get back in the shower when she feels better. Then I scoop her up in my arms, thankful that Sam has wood floors instead of carpet since the blood and water on her legs have mixed and drip everywhere. Marching back into the bathroom, I sit on the side of the tub, cradling her in my arms.

Should I try to purr?

Would that help her feel better?

Why do I keep fucking everything up?

Guess Dad was right, and I am fucking useless.

Kelly buries her face in my chest, great sobs wracking her body. My alpha purr rattles to life, but it's nearly a decade out of practice and makes a low wheezing sound instead of the comforting rumble from Sam or Teddy. Shit, I bet Garret could purr if he were here—I suddenly feel even more guilt that she's stuck here with an alpha that can't even purr for her after screwing up so badly.

Her whole body continues to shake, and I rock her back and forth, finally trying to murmur out a lullaby Mom used to sing to us when we were tiny. I can't remember all the words, so it's not very good, but after a while she finally calms down enough that I'm not worried she'll fall right out of my arms.

It's not much more than a whisper when she finally speaks. Her voice is a mumbled rasp against my chest. "Billy told me...I saw him at the store on Wednesday...he mentioned scars, and blood. He was worried about Teddy. Then what you said downstairs...and Spence. I think...I think Teddy tried to kill himself." I almost drop her on the ground, and she makes a gagging sound before she continues. "Remember the tattoos...those things he never takes off his wrists? I think our omega isn't telling us everything."

Her eyes are big when she looks up at me, glassy with tears. "It's his right to tell us. When…if he wants to, but what if I'm right? What if he hurt himself? I don't…I can't lose him Steve. Him and Sam…Heck, even Garret. I love them…I don't…I've been so frazzled with them being gone. I appreciate you staying with me, but there's all these what-ifs swirlin' around in my head. What if I'm not good enough 'cause I'm a beta? What if they get tired of me? What if they decide they want a family later, and I'm not ready?"

Her voice, which was getting stronger, is suddenly no more than a whisper against my shirt, "What if they realize I'm not good enough for 'em. That all I am is a scrawny little girl with no real friends, no life experience, and no idea what the heck I'm doin' with my life?"

I hug the tiny shivering woman in my arms. Fuck, she basically just outlined my own fucking mind. "Well, Pixie, I guess if that's the case they'll get rid of both of us…and we can start a pack together. The 'I have no idea what I'm doing, but at least we have fun and awesome taste in books' pack. Sound good?"

She snorts into my shirt. "Yeah, I don't think Ruth'd appreciate that. Pretty sure she'd kick us out if we tried to file with anything that long."

She's right, the old battleaxe looks like she could kick Sam's ass if she really put her mind to it. "Well then, I guess we better make sure Sam and Teddy know how lucky they are to have us around, and that we'll bring Ruth's wrath down on them if they try to get rid of us." My voice is teasing, and she giggles into my chest.

She shudders again when she sighs. "So, do we straight up ask Teddy, or...do we just leave it alone until he gets back? I feel like we should apologize, but I'm not sure what I'm apologizing for. I only met him a couple of weeks ago."

No, I should be the one apologizing, for having my head too far up my own ass to realize how all this shit would affect him, for being too stupid to reach out, for making assumptions that he would be ok just waiting around. Panic skitters across my mind at the thought that I might have almost lost him forever, and I had no fucking clue.

I can't fix this. There's nothing to fix. Teddy got hurt, and all I can do now is try everything in my power to make sure he's never hurt again. Never give him a reason to question my feelings—alpha up and take care of him like he fucking needs. That's not to say he can't still top me, because I think that's what we both need, but I can take care of him. Fuck, him and whoever else is important to him, this isn't just about my bear.

We sit there quietly, each lost in our own thoughts for a while until Jake appears in the door. He comes over and Kelly lets out a little shriek when he presses his cold wet nose to her hip where the towel has started to fall open. I stand up, waving my fingers at the big goof, and turn the water back on.

"Ok, Pixie, you finish up your hot shower, then I'll help you re-bandage your legs. I can't cook for shit, but maybe we can make some sandwiches or something afterwards, try to get a plan sorted out on this shit. See what we can do to finish the nest up before Teddy gets back. Sound good?"

She nods and lets me set her on her feet, then shoos the dog out of the bathroom before closing the door. I'm glad, we may be working on getting along better, but I'm still not comfortable seeing her naked. Which is probably a 'me' issue I need to deal with now that it seems like Teddy wants to keep us both. I guess I'll jump off that bridge when I get to it.

Chapter 31

Sam

The food over in the union at the omega center is damned good. I'm just opening up my notes app to tell it to remind me to look up some of the recipes they have here to try back home, when Teddy says he's gonna call Kelly and let her know we're headed her way. I don't expect all hell to break loose.

Sarah is walking between him and Garret, giving the alpha a massive case of stink eye. Hell, she's been actin' crazy ever since we got here. She and Teddy don't touch. None of the casual gestures I associate with being friendly with someone. The guys at the station will walk up and slap you on the back in greeting for no reason at all, so maybe lack of casual contact is an omega thing.

I'll ask Teddy later if I remember, but it's just something I noticed in the dining hall, several of the omegas would sit together at a table, but always far enough apart to not touch. They seem friendly enough towards each other, but it seems like that sort of isolation could wear you down after a while. Especially with it being such a problem if one of 'em gets touch starved.

Teddy's voice filters back to me as I speak quietly into my notes app, checking what I said to what it typed out. "Hey, Pixie. Are you free to talk? I didn't catch you in class or driving right?"

It'll be so damned good to get back home. I miss my house, and my bed, and my dog...and Kelly. I didn't realize how fast I got used to having her around, but my chest aches with it.

Sarah is talking quietly to Garret, and I can't make out the conversation, but she still looks angry. Teddy looks at them annoyed when they start getting loud, his voice ringing out above theirs. "Oh, Vee's there too? Wait, is everything ok?" Sarah snatches at his phone, nearly hanging off his arm until she pries it out of his hand. "No...Fucking shit! Goddamnit Sarah give me my fucking phone. Son of a bitch!"

She takes off running across the green—she may be short, but that girl's fast. When she slows down, her voice carries back to us. "You little son of a bitch! How dare you come close to Teddy again. If I could get my hands on you, I'd wring your fucking neck. He may be sweet enough to let you back in, but he's obviously an idiot for doing so."

I snarl and chase after them—we don't need this shit, we need to get on the fucking road. Teddy's almost caught up, but the bigger omega is breathing hard and Garret is flagging behind, holding onto his head. She's lowered the phone, and turns to look back at us, not expecting me to be closing in. I growl again, and she shudders, taking in a quick gasp of breath.

Teddy's voice is loud behind me. "Sarah, goddamnit, give me back my fucking phone." Of course she doesn't.

She tries to dodge around me, raising the phone back to her ear, and yelling in Spanish. "Teo, tal vez yo me haya disculpado que sigues un Hijo de Perra. ¡Si descubro que lo lastimaste, te voy arrancar tu pito y te lo metere en el culo! ¡Si esta lastimado por tu culpa, te voy a matar Desgraciado! Si crees que saldrías con la tuya por lastimar a mis amigos, Yo voy destruir tu puta vida!"

Teddy stumbles, his hand wrapping around her wrist as she ducks under my outstretched arm. Garret's feet stutter to a stop, his eyes wide with shock as they bounce between the two omegas, and then down to Teddy's hand on her arm. All the color drains from his face and he buckles over, heaving into the grass.

Now that Teddy has her, I go back to retrieve our injured pack member. I help Garret stand up. He has drool running down his chin and is sweating like crazy, and I want to throttle Sarah for causing him to run while injured. Teddy's voice is muffled in the background but we finally reach them. "Sorry about that...um, Sarah says hi."

She tries to grab the phone from him again, but he holds it closer to his face where she can't reach it. It doesn't stop her from jumping for it. "Fucking hell. So yeah. You all good?" He sounds embarrassed, and I want to hold him and purr, and tell Sarah her invitation to visit has been revoked if she's going to do this shit. But Garret is making choking noises again.

I growl at the tiny omega who's now walking towards him. She opens her mouth and starts to yell something else at him, but my snarl rips free before she can get more than a couple of words out. It's Spanish, again, and I don't know what the fuck she wants to say, but I am so fucking done with this shit.

Someone must be talking to Teddy, because his hand goes over his eyes, and he looks like he's barely keeping his shit together. Sarah stalks closer to Garret, and he can already barely stand up, his whole body shaking. "That is fucking enough! Back the hell down, Sarah." It's not a bark, despite the temptation. While I enjoy submission, the idea of making someone do it against their will always leaves a foul taste in my mouth.

Her steely gaze turns to me. "You don't know either, but would you like to? I bet you wouldn't be so ready to defend this piece of shit if you knew what happened." Her voice is menacing and even though she's not yelling it carries clearly across the space between us.

Teddy stares over at us, his face a mask of horror, his phone conversation all but forgotten. "I'm sorry, Kelly, Vee...um...Spence, but we need to go. I just wanted to let you know we're about to get on the road to head your way. It's still a long ass drive, and Garret can't take a turn, but hopefully we'll make it back sometime late tomorrow. I miss you both so much. Just another day and we can have lots of snuggles. Love you."

He hangs up the phone, turning and marching towards us across the lawn. Sarah's voice isn't much more than a whisper. "Ask him. Ask him about his tattoos, about his wrist cuffs, ask him what took him so long to come to the omega center after he presented. He won't lie to you, and you need to know the truth." Teddy lets out a choked sob. The look of betrayal on his face as he stares at his friend is heartbreaking.

Sarah has tears in her own eyes as she turns and walks off. Neither of them says goodbye, and it feels wrong. Pulling Teddy under one arm, and holding Garret up under the other, I purr as best I can in this fucked up situation. Eventually, Teddy relaxes enough that he stops shaking, and some of the color returns to Garret's face. I'll need to ask him later, once Teddy falls asleep, if he was sick from running or from what she said. Until then, let's get all our shit loaded and get the fuck out of this crazy ass town.

Teddy still needs to tell me where the fuck he parked his damned motorcycle, because I'm not getting halfway across Texas only for him to realize he forgot the damned thing.

Teddy

I t feels good to be on the road again. That's not something I would have thought three days ago, but now? Now I just want to get home, back to our bed, and Kelly and Vee. Fuck, I hope they haven't burned the goddamned house down or anything while we've been gone. She'll know better than to let him cook, right? Worst-case scenario, they can live on sandwiches for a few more days.

We've been on the road for hours. We have to stop and get gas before we go through the desert, but Sam's trying to push to make it through tonight. Thank fuck this thing has good AC. Garret's asleep on the backseat. I didn't know that they made club cab moving trucks, but apparently that's a thing. He curled up with his duffel bag as a pillow, one of Kelly's sleep shirts pressed close to his face, and drifted off before we'd even left the city.

Sam looks like shit. He probably hasn't had a good night's sleep since we left. I can't blame him, neither have I. Plus I'm sure that driving across the country in an oversized, unfamiliar truck, dragging your truck on a trailer, with a sick alpha and a shaky omega in the cab isn't the most relaxing experience.

I wake up when my phone vibrates in my pocket. It's Kelly texting to ask what size of mattress we need for the nest. It seems like a pretty random question, but I turn to Sam, who's blinking behind the steering wheel. He shakes his head a few times before he notices me looking at him, then gives me a soft smile.

"You doin' ok, Love? Sorry, I didn't want to wake you, but we're gonna have to stop soon for gas, and to give me a rest. Do you need us to find a hotel, or are you good just stretching out in here for the night once we find a truck-stop? I know it's not ideal, but it would get us back on the road quicker after I get some shut-eye, and I figure you're as eager to get home as I am."

He's not wrong. I just wish I could cuddle up with him to sleep. Hell, I'd even take the damned truck bed if there was a camper on it. Let Garret have the backseat here and then snuggle with my alpha. But no, it would feel selfish of me to ask him to find a hotel if he thinks he's ok to just sleep in the cab.

He's silent and I realize he's waiting for me to reply. "Oh, no, um, I'm fine here. If I need to stretch out, I can kick Garret off the bench seat in the back or go stretch out in the back seat of your truck." I'm only half joking, and his low growl lets me know that it wasn't funny.

Heaving a sigh, I try to answer diplomatically. "I want to sleep. If I can do it here, then yes, let's get some rest and get the fuck back home. But first, let's hit the truck stop, wake up Garret for a bathroom and food break, and fuel up. The sooner we can get back on the road, the sooner we get home."

He nods along, but it looks loose and uncoordinated, and I wonder if he'd let me take a turn at driving, just to get a break. Not that I have any experience driving anything bigger than my mom's sedan, but the basics are probably the same.

"So, um...Kelly texted me. She and Vee haven't killed each other yet, so that's something." She's been sending us good-night texts for the last few days, and I kind of want to ask for a selfie just so I can make sure she's actually safe. But at least I got to hear her voice for a minute before we left today, so that's something.

"Anyway, she was asking...they were asking what size mattress we need for the nest. I know you said you wanted to wait to order it, but my heat should be next week, and I think that I should go ahead and let her get it ordered for me, just in case delivery takes a while. Heck, I should probably ask her if my pillows ever came in."

Sam's eyes flick to me. "Well, it was supposed to be a surprise, but that makes sense. It's gonna be a standard pack size bed frame. I got the measurements offline and started building it already. It's out in the shop. Not gonna be super fancy, but lower than the one in our room, in case anybody falls out...Kelly. In case Kelly falls out. I swear that girl is the most accident-prone person I've ever met. Damn...I miss 'er."

Sam sucks in a deep breath, turning his head from side to side until I hear a pop, and then shaking his arms out, one at a time. "After you let her know, can you look up how far it is to the next stop, I'm about to have to roll down this damned window and turn the radio up to keep myself awake, and I'd rather let Garret rest if possible."

I type in a quick reply to Kelly and then pull up the infor-mation he's asked for. "Looks like we're about to run into one here in about sixteen miles, on the right. Are you going to be ok for that long? Do you need me to take over for a bit so you can get some rest?" His low rumble of annoyance is enough of an answer, and I laugh in response. "Ok, no. But let me know if I can do anything. Ok? I hate seeing you push yourself so hard when I'm sitting right here and would be happy to help."

His big hand reaches over the space between us, taking mine and squeezing my fingers gently. "I know it, Love, but I'm the alpha. I'm supposed to be taking care of you, and I've been doin' a piss-poor job of it so far. Thanks for bearin' with me."

I want to scoff at his reply, but Sam's already so hard on himself, I don't want him to ever think he isn't good enough.

Chapter 32

We make it to the truck stop shortly after midnight, and I gently nudge Garret awake. Kelly's shirt is plastered to his cheek with drool—and a little bit of blood where the bandages on his face have leaked through—from where he was cuddled against it in his sleep. Fuck, I want to kill his father. We lucked out and this truck stop actually has short-term sleeping rooms for rent. I lead Garret inside while Sam fills up the tank. We grab some quick sandwiches at the sub shop inside. It's not gourmet, but it's fast.

They only have rooms with single king-sized beds left, so we get one of those, and then go out to help Sam lock up the trucks and give him the second key for our room, telling him I'm going to get Garret settled in and fed. He nods, casting an appraising gaze over our pack mate, who has a bit more color than when we left, but his stomach is growling, and I have a foot-long meatball sandwich with his name on it.

I wave Sam's loaded club sandwich at him, and he tells me he'll eat in the room when he's away from all the diesel fumes. That makes more sense, and I'm thankful that one of us is awake enough to have common sense. Dragging Garret along, we stumble over to room four and let ourselves in.

There's a small round table with two chairs, a bed, and a door to a bathroom. Honestly, that's more than I had hoped for at this point. I settle Garret into a chair and get his sandwich unwrapped for him, wishing I had thought to stop and grab drinks. For a moment, I consider popping back out to find a vending machine, but I already learned my lesson at the coffee shop not to go out without my alphas.

I tense when the door beeps a few minutes later, but Sam lets himself in, carrying several bottles of soda and a couple of energy drinks. Garret must have been hungry, because he finishes his sandwich in record time, and then staggers into the bathroom. The water comes on a moment later, and by the time Sam and I have eaten, Garret stumbles out. His hair's still dry, but I can't blame him with all the bandages he's got going on.

Sam tucks him into the bed and then asks if I want to join him in the shower. Fuck yes! A needy little omega whine slips free at the thought of having Sam all to myself for the first time in weeks, even if we are at a fucking truck stop motel.

It's certainly not the most romantic situation, but since I couldn't even snuggle with him last night, I need the fucking connection. Still, I'm thankful for the sharp disinfectant tang in the air. At least if I'm going to be fucking my alpha in a motel bathroom, it's a clean one. Even the lighting is unnecessarily bright against the stark white tiles.

My poor alpha looks exhausted as he turns on the shower and pulls me against him. His low purr rumbles to life as he holds my jaw and kisses me until I feel like I might melt into a puddle. Part of this is just pre-heat—my hormones are going nuts, and with all the added stress, I need to feel my alpha and have him purr for me. But if I'm being honest with myself, part of it's also just because Sam is fucking hot, and I love him more each day.

He wraps my hair around his fist, tugging my head back firmly and lowering his face to my neck. His inhale against the sensitive skin makes both of us shudder, and a whimpering moan bubbles up from my chest. His voice tickles over my neck, a low growl filled with need. "Fuck, Love. I know you're tired. Hell, we both are. Do you want this? I can just hold you if that's what you need, but I want you. *I* want this."

Sharp teeth rake over my flesh, right where I want him to bite. His beard scratches against me, and I shudder and twitch, caught between being tickled and wanting to grind against his hard body. "Sam, Alpha. Please. I want this, if you feel up to—" He cuts me off, biting hard against the joint where my neck meets my shoulder.

"You questioning my endurance, Omega? Think I can't take care of you properly?" He almost sounds angry, but his low chuckle flits over me. He pulls back, pinching my chin between his thumb and fingers, pulling my face up to meet his eyes. "Oh, Teddy-bear, devils couldn't keep me away if you said you wanted me. I don't give a fuck how tired I am. I'll always be what you need."

Then he's kissing me again, his tongue tracing along the seam of my lips until I open for him. His responding groan is almost feral as he crushes me against his hard chest. I whimper and his grip loosens, a murmured, "Sorry," before he's plundering my mouth again. His teeth and lips scrape against me, leaving me gasping as he trails a hot line of kisses from my lips down my throat.

He grumbles loudly as he peels my shirt over my head and then he's sucking on my skin again, his tongue tracing over my chest. He flicks it over one nipple, lips closing over the sensitive nub. It's almost too much as I writhe against his big body. His hands go lower, skimming along the skin of my soft stomach before unbuttoning my jeans and pushing them down along with my boxer briefs.

I'm already leaking pre-come when he pulls me out. Hard calloused fingers wrap around me, making me gasp and shudder as he strokes up my length—gathering the moisture on the end before pumping back down. "Are you gonna be a good boy for me, Omega? Are you up to taking my knot tonight? Falling asleep while I'm still locked inside you?"

Another needy whimper escapes my lips at the sight of him ripping his shirt off over his head, seams popping in his haste. Then his mouth is on mine again, his hands fumbling with his own pants before dragging me under the steaming water of the shower. He moans into my mouth as the hot water cascades over us.

Our tongues twist together, and he pulls me flush against him. His body is such a contrast to mine. I'm strong because I work for it, but I'm also padded. I'll never have his muscle definition or hard build. Omegas also naturally don't have much body hair, so I live in a forever furless state. Which is fine. I don't need body hair, but I still love the different sensations I get when Sam rubs against me.

He pulls away, spinning me towards the wall, and his mouth comes down on my neck again, his teeth nipping at my shoulder. His low rumbling growl vibrates up my spine as he runs his hands up my back and fists them in my hair. Holding my head to the side so he can suck and lick at my skin.

My perfume is overwhelming in the small space, and I know I have slick dripping down the backs of my thighs. One of his hands stays tangled in my hair while the other slides down my side and circles my waist, tilting my hips back and circling his thick fingers around my cock. I don't recognize the pathetic mewling sounds that I'm making as he fists me and starts pumping up and down my length.

"Sam, please." I'm whining again, and I can't help it.

His teeth press down hard, and for a moment I think he's going to bond me, then his voice is in my ear, a loud rasp. "Open for me, Omega. Raise your leg." His hand stops pumping and holds my hips still, the other coming down to run over my ass and help me lift my left thigh up and out. Soon, I'm sprawled against the shower wall, my hands scrambling against the tile while he presses into me from behind.

His voice is a whisper against the shell of my ear, tension and longing all tangled together. "Say you need me, Teddy. Tell me you need this as much as I do." He nips hard against my lobe, his tongue coming out to soothe the sting that follows.

"Yes...fuck. Yes, Alpha, Sam, please, I need you. I need to feel you. Please." I barely recognize the sound of myself because of the pleading whimpers.

He groans; his breath hot against my skin. "Fuck, yes. Omega!" And then he's pushing against the tight ring of muscles. I'm leaking so much slick that he slides in quickly and we both moan as his slightly swollen knot comes to rest against my stretched opening.

"Fuck. Fuck! Teddy. You feel so fucking good...I can't. I don't think I'm gonna last long right now. Fucking hell!" His beard scrapes against my skin as his head drops back down and his teeth come to rest on the tender flesh of my neck.

His low growl as he slides back down vibrates up my spine, and I melt against him, my muscles loosening further and allowing him to thrust faster. The hand not holding up my leg circles back around and wraps around me again—pumping in time with his thrusts. Each time he bottoms out, he clenches at the base of my shaft, like he's fucking his own hand through me.

A low murmur of words spills from his lips, mumbles and growls of pleasure as he slides in and out of me, his pace growing near frantic. "Fuck, Omega. Teddy. Tell me you're close. I can't hold on. Please, Love. I fucking need you. Wanna sink my knot in you, fucking lock you and keep you forever. Fucking please, please tell me."

His hips stutter and buck against me, and the pressure of his inflating knot pushes against my ass. I twist my head to capture his lips and can see the tendons in his jaw straining as he fights to hold back his release.

Tilting my head up, I lick at his lips. My soft, "Yes," ghosting over them, and then he's kissing me again, and pushing hard against that tight ring. The stretch is amazing, and my balls draw up as my cock kicks in his stroking hand, splattering the stark tile with my come. Pain and pleasure mix as he finally pushes inside and then he's filling me up. I swallow down his guttural moans as he paints my walls with his climax.

We stand together, breathing heavily, the water still steaming around us as he helps me balance while lowering my leg. I have to bend slightly at the waist because of where we're locked, and one of his big hands wraps behind my neck, offering me comfort and security as the other strokes long lines down my back.

His rough whisper washes over me as I stand there panting. It's almost drowned out by the water. "I love you, Teddy. I don't know if I've told you that yet, but I do. You mean everything to me." I shudder under his palms and wish I could turn around and wrap my arms around him. But despite what he said earlier, we can't even easily make it to the bed like this. Thank goodness for unlimited hot water, because we might be here for a while waiting for his knot to go down.

There's a small bar of soap next to an open wrapper on a tile shelf. Fresh bubbles are scattered across the surface, and I'm going to guess that Garret opened it earlier when he was in here. Sam uses it now to scrub my back and shoulders, working out my tight muscles from the last few days until I'm leaning limp and boneless against the wall of the shower. Thankfully, it gives us enough time for his knot to deflate and let him slip free. He turns me around and washes my hair and chest before giving himself a cursory scrub down and shutting off the water.

Wrapping one of the big towels around me, he takes time to gently pat all the water from my skin and blot my hair before drawing my face to his for a quick kiss. He leaves for a moment to get our toothbrushes from the room before coming back and passing mine over.

Once we're both cleaned up, I slip some fresh boxer briefs on and crawl under the covers, placing a pillow between Garret's body and mine. He's wrapped himself around Kelly's shirt again, and I can't imagine that it still smells like her, but if it helps him sleep, who am I to complain?

Sam curls around my body, cuddling in close. Then pulls away and grumbles to himself as he sets a seven-hour timer on his phone before dragging me against him. His voice is rough, already sounding half asleep. "Probably won't sleep that long, but just in case." He buries his face against the side of my neck, kissing softly. Three kisses in, I'm already out like a light.

Chapter 33

KeLLy

We wake snuggled together. Steve still wears his long sleeve sleep shirts and pants, and I wonder briefly how that's gonna work when it gets hot in the summer. His eyes open, and shock flits briefly across his features before he settles. He yawns until his jaw cracks. "So, you think they'll be back this evening?"

I hate to dash his hopes, but one of us should be practical. "Probably not...I mean, it's somewhere around twenty-eight hours to drive, even if they're speeding, they'll still need to stop for food and fuel, so probably closer to thirty. Without stopping at all they'd be home at ten tonight...but it'll probably be some time tomorrow depending on if Garret or Teddy are comfortable driving the truck, and if Sam'll let 'em."

He nods along, like he was expecting this. "I don't like it, but it's just as well. We can start getting the nesting stuff washed now, unpacking all his boxes. I overnighted the new mattress...do you think he'll like it? Shit, should we have waited? I just wanted to get everything ready, so he'd be able to relax when he got here."

Steve looks nervously around the room, and I'm torn on the response. With anyone else, I'd offer them a hug, other than last night we have a pretty solid no touching rule that works for both of us. "Um...Vee." His eyes twitch, and I'm not sure if I'm using Teddy's nickname to get a rise out of him or just as camaraderie at this point. "How did you order a big ol' mattress overnight shipping, wasn't that like crazy expensive?"

His eyes light with mischievous glee, and he smirks at me. "Yeah, it was." His grin is from ear to ear now. "Good thing I used Dad's credit card that was in my online wallet. Plus, since I put a rush on it, hopefully he won't realize it until it's already here." His face has taken on an almost maniacal expression now, and I draw back as he keeps going. "It serves the old fucker right, it's not like he can't fucking afford it anyway. Asshole."

I stretch after I scramble off the side of the bed, and he marches into the bathroom, ready to use up all the danged hot water...again. We gotta talk to Sam about this, try to figure out a solution before I kill Steve. I'm puttering around in the closet trying to find something comfortable to wear. I know Jake needs to go outside, but my knees still sting this morning, and I don't feel quite up to facing the stairs.

Ok, I'll admit it—I'm delaying so that Steve has to do it, so I can then sit on my butt and scoot down the stairs slowly, without Jake jumping on me, or having to bend my stupid legs. Eventually I pick out an older Inuyasha shirt that's badly faded, and a pair of cutoffs. If we're just gonna be working around the house today, there's no point in wasting nice clothes.

Steve's still in the bathroom, so I step out of the closet and pull my pajama top over my head so I can shimmy into a bra. It's easier with more arm room that I don't have in the closet. I get my top swapped out and shuck my sleep pants while sitting on the steps Sam built me, then I pull my shorts on.

Steam billows as the bathroom door opens, and I'm about to ask Steve to turn on the vent fan when he steps out in just a towel. I haven't seen Steve topless yet. He always stays covered, even that time when I was super distracted by Garret, I thought it was strange he was between Teddy and Sam and still wearing a top that looked like long underwear.

He looks even more emaciated without clothes on, his hip-bones jutting prominently and his ribs stark against his skin. But that's all secondary to the tattoos, all black, loops and swirls completely cover from his collarbones down into the top of his towel. I don't see any specific images, just black ink spinning and twisting across every inch of his skin, all the way down his arms and onto the backs of each finger. With his alabaster skin, he almost looks like some sort of tribal zebra.

Then I see it, one small dot of color. I would have missed it if I wasn't staring so intently—I can't help it, the design, or lack thereof is beautiful and chaotic. But one small spot, just over his heart there's a black teddy-bear with a red heart on it.

It's not until I'm stepping in for a better look that I realize Steve's frozen, staring at me with a look of shock and horror. He blinks slowly and then scrambles into the closet and slams the door. There's a loud thump—sounds like he's thrown himself against the door. Not that I planned on invading his space. I'm pretty sure we surprised the heck out of each other.

I try waiting for a few minutes so he can come out, but it isn't long before Jake starts whining at the door. Giving up on my brilliant plan to not injure my knees, I head out into the hallway where my cuddle buddy bounces up and down like he has built in pogo sticks. I take a death grip on the handrail and gingerly lower myself one step at a time until I get to the living room. Jake has run up and back down the stairs at least three times but at least we're both still standing.

Treating my legs gently, I step into the kitchen and let him out the back door. He bounces past me, giving me a doggy smirk, and I wonder briefly if he couldn't hold it earlier and made a mess somewhere in the house. We'll find it soon enough if he did, but Jake is a good boy. So, I think he was just feeling saucy this morning.

Digging out a scoop of dog food for his bowl, I pour it in before grabbing the peanut butter puff cereal out of the pantry—heaving a sigh of relief that Steve hasn't opened it yet, let alone eaten most of it. Jake scrambles at the back door right as I'm pulling down a couple of bowls, and I squeak, almost dropping the stupid things.

I feel lighter after our talk last night, but also on edge for some unknown reason. Maybe just missing my guys, maybe it was the look Steve threw me after his shower. I can ask when he gets downstairs. For now, I settle with running the coffee grinder, getting the pot set up, and pouring myself a bowl of breakfast. Jake watches me eat my cereal while I lean against the kitchen counter.

I put up the milk but leave the cereal and bowl out for Steve before I grab a table knife and go start opening boxes in the room down the hall. We can make a plan from there, if he wants to take 'em to the laundromat to wash all at once or just do several loads at home. My first thought was to get them all done quick, but with how sensitive omegas' noses are, using a public washer and dryer would probably be a terrible idea. And it's not sunny enough outside to hang everything out to dry.

I've grabbed all the still bagged up sheets and blankets in Teddy's room and started making piles in the not-a-nest. Heck, I'm just gonna call this an office. Sam said there was one down here, and it's too big to be a bedroom. Sheets go in one pile, blankets in another, and pillows in an ever increasing third. We can't put those in the washer very easily, so I'll have to ask Steve how to get 'em cleaned...and maybe make him roll around on them like they did all my shirts.

Five boxes in, and no end in sight. Four of them were pillows, though, so at least they weren't heavy. This one, however, weighs a lot, and when I get it open, it's full of additional sheets and mattress protectors, all tightly packed and sealed in together. Each item is tossed into its corresponding pile then the box is broken down and left by the door. Good thing I'm wearing an old shirt. It's already covered in dust and cardboard flakes.

I'm not quite halfway through the stack when Steve walks in. He's carrying his bowl of cereal and looking sheepishly at me, wearing one of his own shirts, with the same overshirt he's worn since I met him. He looks around the room briefly before going to sit on the pile of pillows, but I cast a death glare his way right before his butt touches down.

"Are you seriously gonna be eating a bowl of cereal, with milk, all over these stupidly hard to clean pillows?" He looks from me to the pile before shuffling sideways and plopping himself on the floor, and I fight not to grumble any more as he shoves another spoonful in his mouth.

Ripping through the tape on the next three boxes while his spoon clinks in the bowl is kind of cathartic but doesn't stop me from wanting to throw something at his head when he starts talking. "Um, Kelly, I...I'm sorry." That draws me up short. "Just...people don't see me without a shirt on, and it took me by surprise. I know it's not...it's not attractive. I kind of panicked and didn't know how to react."

He taps the spoon against the stoneware a few times, making a 'tink, tink, tink' sound before he speaks again. "I thought about saying something shitty about how I don't care what you think of me, but I know I'd just be lashing out, and I'm trying really hard not to do that anymore."

I stab my dull knife through a piece of packing tape and turn to look at the big alpha. "I wasn't tryin' to make you self-conscious, Steve. My legs still hurt, and while my cramps are mostly done, I was just kinda killin' time in hopes that you'd go let Jake out and save me the risk of hurtin' myself again today."

His reply is a low, mumbled, "Sorry."

At least he seems to be trying, and while we have a long way to go, I'm glad he's making the effort. "I don't know what you're talking 'bout, anyway. Sure, you're kinda skinny, but your tattoos are beautiful. Sorry if I got too much into your personal space tryin' to look at 'em."

He doesn't say anything, and when I turn back towards him his ears and cheeks are red. His eyes flip up to mine, and he smiles at me. "Thanks Kelly, um...I got the one for Bear, but the others are mostly coverups. I don't like people to see my skin, so tattoos were the easiest option."

This is probably a terrible idea, but I stand up and walk over to the alpha, he starts shivering when my hand reaches out to take his bowl. He whines deep in the back of his throat and it sets my teeth on edge. But he still doesn't stop me when I lift up the front of his shirt. All I can see are swirling patterns of tattoos.

I place my fingers on his stomach, tracing over a spiral pattern, and I can feel where the skin is rough and there's a cratered area under the ink, it's almost perfectly circular—about the size as a pencil eraser. My touch skates over his abdomen and there are several others hidden beneath the black cover—a few long lines that are raised and puckered, more of the small round ones, one larger area that feels almost slippery, like there aren't any pores on the surface.

My mind rebels at what I'm feeling, and my eyes look up to meet his. His whole torso is covered in scars. I gently nudge him away from the wall and pull his shirt up in the back. There are more of them here, lots of the long lines, but some of the circles too, and the first thought in my mind is that there's no way he could have reached to do these himself.

His throat makes a dry clicking sound, and he shudders again, as my fingers run down his arm, confirming the abuse someone must have inflicted on his entire torso. Before I've had a chance to figure out what I'm touching his whole body shivers and he bolts, holding his shirt down as he stares at me from across the room.

His eyes roll, and he looks ready to flee at any moment, so I take the only option left to me at this point. I don't ask. It's his trauma, and while I'd like for him to feel safe enough to share it with me one day, for now, he can keep it. "So, you wanna help me with boxes, or opening sheets up to get those started washing?"

All the air seems to rush out of him in a gust, and he gives me a shaky smile. "Let's open some of the sheets in dark green, that way we can get those started washing while we finish with the boxes."

It's sound logic, and so that's what we do. The rest of the day is spent opening boxes, washing nesting stuff, avoiding talking about sensitive subjects, and waiting for a mattress delivery that doesn't arrive until it's almost dark outside.

Chapter 34

Kelly

Jake's barking wakes me up. I don't know what the big doof is going crazy over. It's been so hard to sleep without Sam, Teddy, and Garret here. I miss cuddles. I get along better with Steve now, but he only cuddles me when he falls asleep.

My eyes are blurry as they open, a flickering glow trickling in. I don't think I overslept. But maybe that's what's upsetting Jake. I need to go let my big cuddle-muffin out. Sitting up completely, something with the light immediately strikes me as wrong. It doesn't look like sunlight. It's coming from the side of the house, and it's...moving?

Scrambling out of bed, I accidentally kick Steve in my attempts to get free from the blankets. When I make it to the window, I see Sam's shop. It's glowing. Flames lick along one side of the door.

Oh god!

My body turns before I can make a conscious decision, scrambling back to the bed to grab my phone. Dialing 911, I can barely hold back my panic as it rings once, twice. It's picked up suddenly and a clear feminine voice answers, "Oak Flats Police Department, what is your emergency?"

Steve shouts from the other side of the room, as he comes fully awake, realizing something's wrong. "Um, yes, ma'am. I...we...there's a fire at my alpha's house. He's not here, I don't...I'm not sure of the address. His shop caught on fire. Sam...Sam works with you but he's not here. He went to Los Angeles to get our omega's stuff and—"

The nice dispatcher cuts off my mad ramble. "Sam? Sam McKinnley? His shop?"

Not wanting to cause confusion, I just give an affirmative, "Uh-huh."

"Ok, miss, we'll be there as soon as possible. Do you know if anyone was in the shop at the time?"

My mind is scattered, and I can't focus. What does she mean? It's a shop in the middle of the night. Why would there be anyone inside? I manage a stuttered response. "No, no, Sam, Teddy, and Garret. They're all gone. They went back to Los Angeles to get Teddy's stuff. It's been almost six days. They were supposed to be back. It's just me and Steve and Jake...Jake's a dog." I don't know why I feel the need to tell her that.

Her reply is cool and crisp. "Ok, miss..." She trails off, and I haven't told her my name. To be fair, this is kind of stressful. "Carpenter...er...Kelly Carpenter, it used to be Parker, but I recently joined Sam's pack, and we wanted a different name from his brother's pack..." Oh god, I'm rambling, why am I rambling. This nice woman doesn't need a history lesson.

"Ok, Ms. Carpenter, please keep the dog in the house unless there is a danger to him. I've already contacted the fire department, and they'll be out shortly. Are you in immediate danger, is the fire spreading to your location?"

"No...no, I don't think so, the shop's not right next to the house, I just woke up." Which makes sense, being the middle of the night, of course I just woke up. I sound like a lunatic. Jake's barking is growing louder. I glance over at Steve who rushes to the door and yanks it open, allowing the big dog to bounce into the room. He's barking like crazy, long drawn-out baying that hurts my ears and makes my eye twitch.

"Can you step outside, Kelly, to make sure the fire isn't getting near the house?" The calm voice on the other end of the phone sounds reasonable, so much more reasonable than I feel right now, and I nod before realizing she can't see me.

"Yes, um...Yes, ma'am. Lemme go check the back door. It's closest to the shop."

Her voice comes through more urgent, now. "No, Kelly. Please exit through the front. If the fire has spread we don't want you to get caught in it, ok? Go to the front of the home, check the knob. If it feels hot, tell me and I'll walk you through trying to find an alternate exit. Ok?"

I manage to grunt out another, "Uh-huh," while Steve is swapping out his sleep pants for jeans and yanking a clean shirt over his head. He grabs Jake's collar and leads him as gently as possible out the door and down to the living room. His hand comes out and quickly pats against the front doorknob before pulling back. He turns to me and shakes his head before grasping the knob and pulling open the door.

Thankfully, he still has a hold of Jake's collar, because as soon as the door opens, my cuddly baby does a one-eighty, barking and snarling, tearing the screen out of the door and almost pulling his alpha handler down the steps as he frantically tries to get to something in our yard. Steve only stops himself from getting pulled over by grabbing onto the railing around the front steps, the dog thrashing like a fish caught on a line as he pulls against Steve's other arm.

Something flares in the driveway, and I let out a little scream before I can catch it. The dispatcher quickly responds. "Kelly, Kelly, what is it? What's wrong?" My hand clutches at my shirt, trying to keep my heart from beating out of my chest. Jake is still snarling, but he's calmed down enough that I don't worry about him hurting Steve while he tries to escape.

I barely recognize my own voice because it's shaking so badly. "I...I don't know. I saw something in the driveway. There aren't any streetlights out there, and the light from the fire doesn't reach because of the house, but Jake's goin' nuts. I think there might be somebody else out here." My voice is high and panicky as my words register in my own mind.

The dispatcher sucks in a sharp breath. "Kelly, get Jake and get back in the house. Can you do that? If the fire is not an immediate danger to you, take the dog, get inside, and lock your doors. We'll have someone out as soon as possible. Do you understand me, Kelly?"

A low menacing laugh carries across the dark space. "Ahh, the beta. Yes, little beta, go inside and hide. We'll be there soon." Jake loses his ever-loving mind, and I scream as another light flickers on in the driveway near my car. It looks like a lighter, someone holding it close to their face, lighting a cigarette maybe.

My playful pupper is gone as Jake jumps and spins, his body twisting and his head sliding free from the collar that Steve is still hanging onto. Steve has gone ghost white, his whole body shaking as he backs slowly up the stairs, now-empty collar still in hand.

Now that Jake's loose, he doesn't attack. He marches back and forth in front of the porch steps—the short hair on his back bristled, and his normally friendly, floppy face is drawn back is a savage snarl. Patting my leg, I try to call his name. While he spares me a quick glance, his attention never fully leaves whoever has invaded his territory. I look down at my phone to see that the call is still active, but the dispatcher hasn't said anything else.

A moment later, my phone rings with an incoming call—Teddy's photo popping up on the screen. I don't want to hang up with dispatch, but it's the middle of the night. Teddy shouldn't be calling unless he's had an emergency. I want to cry and scream. I want my alphas and my omega here so I know that they're alright.

Teddy goes to voicemail before I can figure out what to do. I bring the phone back to my ear, and my voice is surprisingly calm. "I need to go now. My omega just called, and I need to make sure he's ok." A loud crash sounds behind the house, probably something with Sam's shop going up in smoke. The dispatcher tries to tell me to hold on, that someone will be here soon, and to keep her on the line, but I end the call, anyway. I need to make sure they're safe.

My brain feels like it's in a fog as I pull up my missed calls and dial Teddy back. It rings twice before he answers. His voice is frantic on the other end, and it yanks me partway out of my stupor to hear him. He's practically yelling into the phone before I can speak. "Kelly, are you safe? The fire department just called Sam to come in, something about his shop. He's losing his fucking mind because we're still in Texas, and Garret's practically climbing the walls of the truck. What happened?"

My shoulders sag at hearing that they're safe, but then Jake lets out another vicious snarl. He's stopped pacing and stares into the darkness, ready to tear something apart. "Teddy, the shop's on fire. It woke us up."

His breath comes out in a loud hiss. "But you're ok, right? You and Vee, you weren't in the shop, and it's not the house, you're ok? Please, Kelly, tell me yo—" Jake's volley of barks cuts him off.

"There's people here. I can't see who it is, but Jake doesn't know 'em." My voice sounds almost flat as I fight back panic, but Teddy misunderstands.

His breath comes out in a loud whoosh over the receiver. "Oh, wow, they got there fast then. It's ok, Kelly, just...try to keep Jake inside so he doesn't get hurt. Do you see Xan or Gabe?" I can hear other voices yelling in the background. Sam's rough growl and Garret's usually higher, more melodious tones...not that it sounds that way now.

"No...It's not the fire department. It's too dark, and they haven't moved into the light, they're just standing in the shadow by the car watching us." Steve mutters something beside me, but all I can hear is Jake's warning growl and Teddy's panicked voice through the phone.

"Kelly, get in the house. Get in the house now. Take Jake and Vee with you if you can, otherwise, just go. Lock the door. Somebody'll be there soon." I try to stifle my inappropriate giggle because he sounds like the nice dispatcher I was just talking to.

Teddy's voice is barely discernable though a snarl. "Kelly, get your ass in the house now! I'm not fucking kidding here!" I didn't mean to laugh at him, but I think I might be kind of panicky. My brain feels like it's floating away as a huge shadow breaks away from the cluster and starts towards the porch.

My voice is no more than a loud squeak as I spin on my heel, grabbing Steve and trying to drag him back towards the door. My phone slips out of my hand, and I barely register the crunching sound it makes when it hits the porch. There's a loud thump behind us and a muffled whine from Jake, but Steve and I are pulling each other to relative safety. Thundering footsteps sound behind me and a big hand wraps around the back of my neck as my fingers brush the doorhandle.

I'm wrenched back against a hard chest, the scent of burnt rubber choking me. Steve follows me since he hasn't let go of my hand yet. He turns and snarls, sounding a lot like Jake, as he lunges at whoever has their hands on me. A big fist swings out from behind me. There's a wet, meaty thump and then Steve is laying sprawled on the wooden porch, blood leaking from a cut across his eyebrow.

Letting my legs give out, I flop towards the floor. The first thing that comes to mind from what Mom said growing up was don't let anybody take you anywhere, the second was that dead weight is harder to move than someone who's wiggling around. It doesn't seem like this guy got the message though, as the hand around my neck just tightens and he grunts, dragging me down the steps.

Jake whimpers when he sees me. He tries to stand but his front leg buckles. His growl bubbles forth again when I reach for him. The large body behind me lashes out, a heavy boot catching my Jakey in the side of his muzzle—he lets out another pained yelp. "Shut the fuck up, you goddamned mutt. You wanna fuckin' threaten me?" I'm shaken back and forth, but hear a low click noise and a mumbled, "Shoot your stupid ass, dumb fucker."

My body thrashes—because nobody is gonna hurt my dog—and the hand squeezes so hard it takes everything I have just to gasp for breath. A scrambling noise draws my attention back to the porch where Steve is trying to stand up. He leans heavily on the rail, blood dripping over his eye and down his chin.

He lets out a croak as he finally gains his feet before throwing himself off the porch and towards us. His shout is broken and ragged. The long arm swings out one more time, something dark and shiny in his fist. I hear a loud crack as whatever it is lands across Steve's jaw. He crumples again—while I appreciate the help, part of me wishes he'd stay down before he gets hurt worse.

The hand moves and I can finally make out the shape of what it's holding. There's a loud click of the safety coming off and the gun is pointed at Steve's chest. The voice from earlier rings across the yard. "Now, now. He's a pain in the ass, but he's still my son. Don't shoot him unless you have to." The alpha holding me shakes me again and growls before he flicks the safety back on and starts dragging me back across the yard.

I scream and flail, trying to get loose. I need to check on Jake. He hasn't moved. I need to check on Steve.

A moment later, I'm dropped unceremoniously on the ground in front of another man. He sneers down at me while a third large shadow looms behind him. His scent has beachy tones like the twins, but instead of sun and fun or a distant storm, it calls to mind rotting seaweed and dead fish. My stomach turns and I fight the urge to vomit all over his shiny shoes.

My arms shake as I try to push myself up. I need to get away—but he steps forward, his foot heavy as it comes down on my hand and I shriek as the bones grind together under his weight. His voice is a menacing growl when he squats by my head. "So, you're the beta that Garret's claiming, huh? Do you think that worthless piece of shit'll still want you after they're through?" He chuckles darkly, and I try to swallow back the bile burning my throat. "Well, at least you'll be properly broken in for an alpha."

He waves his arm to the two bigger men and takes a step back, freeing my abused hand. My legs kick out, trying to escape, but the hand closes around my throat this time, cutting off my oxygen and lifting me as I scratch and flail at the two figures closing in. Between their bodies I can see Steve still on the ground, trying to stand up—Jake limping over to him and pressing his nose against my pack mate.

The gap closes and a hand tangles in my hair—black spots dance in front of my eyes. I hear a low raspy chuckle, and then nothing.

Chapter 35

Sam

My body screams at me to push through the night and get home, but we need rest. Garret looked better this morning when we left the truck-stop. He and Teddy were sharing Kelly's sleep shirt when I woke up—it was draped over a pillow that they were both hugging. Clearly, I'm not the only one missing our beta. Still, if I push too hard and get us all killed or in the hospital, it won't help anybody.

Teddy offered to take a turn driving, but he looked uncomfortable at the prospect and doesn't have any experience with it, plus he let out a relieved breath when I said no. Garret looks like he's about to drop, but he's refused to spend the day sleeping again. Between twelve hours on the road yesterday, and another twelve today, we should be able to get in tomorrow by noon. We just need to get rest and food.

I pull into a smaller truck stop, the sign out front advertises food and fuel. If I can just stretch out in the truck for a few good hours, then I can push on through. We fill the tank for what I hope is the last time, and Garret and Teddy stumble in to see what options they have to eat. We've avoided anything greasy, but one of those damned burgers is practically screaming my name right now. My mind tells me that I'll have to go out and buy a grill when we get home so Kelly can finally make some. Right now, I just have to choke down another dry granola bar.

Teddy snuggles against me on the bench seat in the back while Garret reclines the passenger seat and is soon snoring lightly. We're almost home, and I can't wait to stretch out on my big bed with them and get some solid shut eye tomorrow once we're home. Sure, we may have to pay some extra fees on the truck for returning it late, but that's a problem for future Sam. For now, rest.

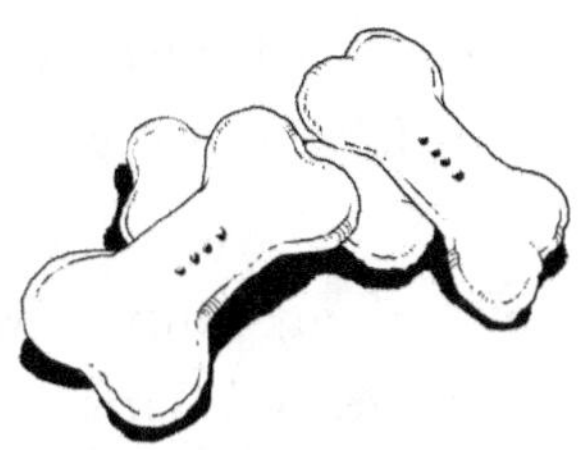

A shrill ringing startles me out of my sleep. There's no light except for the big halogens at the truck stop coming in through the windshield. Garret mumbles and twitches as the ringing sounds again. Pulling up my phone, I notice I've already been asleep about five hours, and it's almost three in the morning. A photo of Joseph and Brice hugging pops up on my screen.

That asshole better not be drunk calling me. I am too fucking tired for this shit.

"Unless someone's dead, dying, or on fire, I'm hanging up." My voice is a rusty croak from just waking up.

In contrast, Joseph sounds wide awake. "Interesting choice of words. Where the fuck are you right now?" His tone has me jerking upright, dislodging Teddy from where he's curled against my chest.

I stare out the windshield, willing my eyes to come into focus. The big yellow and red sign is blurry along with everything else. "A Love's truck stop somewhere in Texas. I don't fucking know exactly. About four hours from home, I think. What the hell, man? What's going on?"

Instead of answering my question, he has his own. "Ok...good, that's good. Is Teddy with you? Kelly? Where are those two others, or Jake? Have you talked to anybody at home?"

I shake myself out of my stupor, watching Teddy. "No...yes...Teddy's with me, and Garret. We're on our way back from Los Angeles with their stuff. I haven't heard from anybody today, we've just been driving. What the hell's going on?"

Again, he ignores my question. "Nothing, nothing's wrong. You guys are fine. Just...It sounds like I woke you up. It's time to get back on the road. Be safe but get home as soon as you can." He hangs up, cutting off any more questions I might have. My hand rubs down my face, attempting to wipe away the exhaustion. Now both packmates are wide awake and staring at me.

Clapping my hands together and shaking out my shoulders I announce, "Ok, sounds like sleep time's over. Bathroom breaks all around, then let's get the fuck home." Garret opens the passenger door to help Teddy down so they can walk over to the restroom area. My phone rings again. They both freeze and quickly look back at me.

It's the fire department dispatch, the number that calls me in when we have an emergency, and the lead weight in my stomach drops to my toes. "Sam. Are you at home? A woman, Kelly, called about your shop being on fire. The guys are already assembled and pulling out, but Joseph told me not to call you again. He said you were probably already on site since it's your place. But if you were, you would have been the one calling. What's going on, man?"

Teddy is staring intently at the phone. The man on the other end isn't trying to be quiet, and our omega is certainly getting part of the conversation. He drops to the ground with Garret and pulls out his own phone, pushing buttons before raising it to his ear. His face grows frantic the longer it rings, and his shoulders sag in relief when it finally clicks over. Then he cusses when he hears Kelly's voicemail prompt. He grabs Garret, dragging him towards the bathroom as his phone starts to ring. He whines, a worried little omega sound, as he puts it up to his ear.

He's yelling into the phone before she has a chance to speak. "Kelly, are you safe? The fire department just called Sam to come in, something about his shop. He's losing his fucking mind because we're still in Texas, and Garret's practically climbing the walls of the truck. What happened?"

Her voice comes stuttering out as he pulls it away and hits the speaker button. "Teddy, the shops on fire. It woke us up."

His breath whooshes out in a loud hiss. "But you're ok, right? You and Vee, you weren't in the shop, and it's not the house, you're ok? Please, Kelly, tell me yo—" The sound of Jake losing his fucking shit stops the words.

There's a brief pause, then Kelly's voice, a low almost whimper. "There's people here. I can't see who it is, but Jake doesn't know 'em."

I see Teddy's shoulders sag in relief. "Oh, wow, they got there fast then. It's ok, Kelly, just...try to keep Jake inside so he doesn't get hurt. Do you see Xan or Gabe?"

But it's too soon. There's no way they could be there yet.

Jumping down, I grab Garret. "I don't care if you have to piss out the fucking window. Get back in the goddamned truck, now!" He looks startled as he croaks out Kelly's name, and then starts clamoring back up into the truck, shoving Teddy in front of him.

Our beta's voice comes through the phone, freezing the blood in my veins. "No...It's not the fire department. It's too dark, and they haven't moved into the light. They're just standing in the shadow by the car watching us."

Jake starts to growl again, and I hear Steve whimper, "Oh, fuck. No."

Teddy's nearly screaming into the phone as I climb behind the wheel, barely giving them time to buckle in on the bench seat behind me. "Kelly, get in the house. Get in the house now. Take Jake and Vee with you if you can, otherwise, just go. Lock the door. Somebody'll be there soon."

She sounds tinny on the other end of the line as she chuckles, but it sounds pained and panicky, and Teddy snarls in response. "Kelly, get your ass in the house now! I'm not fucking kidding here!"

She lets out a loud squeal and there's thumping in the background, possibly running. Then a loud whine from Jake and more thumping. My fingers grip the steering wheel, my knuckles white as I will myself to breathe and focus on driving. More possible running thumps, then rattling, and the call disconnects.

I look over my shoulder while I wait to be able to pull out of the lot. Garret looks like he's about to hyperventilate. Teddy's holding his phone so tight it might break, trying over and over to call her back, but it keeps going to voicemail. The line to get back on the road seems to take hours, but I know it's less than ten minutes.

Chapter 36

Steve

Fucking Fuck, Dad's here.

> *And he brought some of his goons.*
> *Keith, or Kyle, or Kevin, or some fucking thing.*
> *They're all interchangeable assholes, anyway.*
> *He only brings them out for the less legal work.*
> *Stuff he can't drag in front of a board meeting and throw a*
tantrum about to get his way.

I need to stand up, but my head keeps spinning. Something tickles along my cheek, but there's not even enough strength to shoo whatever it is away. Then something cold and wet presses against me, a low whine followed by dog breath right in my face. Thanks Jake.

Shit, Jake. Is he ok?

Fuck!

Kelly, where'd she go?

A choked off cry draws my attention as I attempt to stand up. My head feels like it weighs a ton, and Jake keeps jabbing me with his snout. I can barely sit up enough to see Dad's minions holding Kelly up. She hangs limply from the huge hand that's wrapped around her throat. One of the assholes laughs while the other one smiles and says something, but the ringing in my ears keeps me from hearing anything.

The one holding her up shakes her, and she flops bonelessly. Jake whines and cries beside me, blood dripping off his face. I raise my hand to touch him and he leans into me before turning to face the assholes touching our beta. She's not mine in the same sense that she is with Teddy or Sam, or even Garret's blind obsession. But I think there'll be times when she's the only one I can stand around here. She already knows me better than anyone except my brother, and she's certainly more fun than he is.

Now that he has my attention, Jake's lip lifts. Blood coats his gums and teeth, and our boy here is gonna need a trip to the vet as soon as we get this shit sorted out. He lets out another low snarl and starts limping towards the three alphas who hurt Kelly. He picks up a bit of speed, loosing a loud, baying howl, seconds before he sinks his teeth into the leg of the fucker holding her.

The alpha's mouth opens wide as he screams. I realize the ringing in my head has tapered off when I hear it. Kelly lands in a heap on the ground, and then Jake is standing over her, his stumbling body trying to shield her from the three alphas. I'm trying to stand too, but my balance is off. Everything spins as I stumble forward.

Fucking stupid dog. I can't blame him, but he's never met my father before. The man he bit pulls out a gun, and Jake's head swivels in his direction. The big dog lunges, leaving Kelly unguarded, and clamps down on the asshole alpha's wrist. He screams again, his voice coming in a long wail that just keeps going.

He flings his arm, trying to shake the clinging dog off as his partner slams his fist down over and over against Jake's back. I hear him whimper, but the screaming noise is still going...or...is that a siren? Why the fuck does Sam have a siren at his house? Maybe it's a fire alarm in the shop...why hasn't it melted?

Jake finally releases the man he's holding, his body uncoordinated as he turns towards my father, who's been slowly moving closer to the girl still collapsed on the ground. The alpha he bit is cradling his injured arm to his chest. I guess he's more used to hurting others than to dealing with his own pain.

Jake tries to jump, but his legs don't seem to be moving right. Not that I can blame him. I'm weaving drunkenly over the gravel, staggering and barely able to stop my knees from unhinging. Dad yells as the snarling hound scrambles, tries to reach him. "Don't just fucking stand there! Shoot the goddamned thing!"

He doesn't wait for his men to follow his orders and pulls out a gun of his own—but he's not used to being threatened by anything that can actually hurt him, and the firearm shakes in his hands as he tries to point it.

A loud rumble joins the siren now, and my scrambled brain thinks for a moment that Jake is growling really loud. My steps almost have me within reaching distance when I see the plume of dust on the road. It's hard to see with just the light from Sam's burning shop, but it's there.

The hench-alpha that Jake hasn't bitten finally gets with the program, his own gun coming out. It swings between Jake and Kelly, like he doesn't realize the threat is a 140 pound snarling dog and not a 120 pound unconscious beta girl. My legs push forward, trying to get to our beta.

I collapse, catching myself before my full weight lands on Kelly. Sound and pain rip through me, a thunderous roar and white-hot pain tearing through my shoulder. A loud snarl, and my father screaming, "The goddamned dog, you idiot. What the fuck do I pay you for?"

Another loud bang, and a sharp cry from Jake, before his weight lands against my injured shoulder. I can barely hold myself up, but I don't want to hurt the girl passed out under me. Screeching tires, and then a loud, unfamiliar voice. "Police, hands in the air!" I hear a couple of thumps as two of the alphas drop their weapons. One does not.

"Sir, drop the gun and put your hands in the air. Now!"

Time seems to slow as I look down at Kelly. Her eyes twitch and blink open, her hand reaching up to touch my face. "Steve?

What...?" Her voice is a raspy whisper, her neck already bruising.

Someone's still shouting to put hands in the air, but if I do that I'm gonna fall over. And I may be a little punch drunk, because I giggle when I look down at Kelly, the mental image of me face planting into her chest making me slightly hysterical. There's another alpha snarl and I feel something cold and hard press against my back. "He's my son. I can do whatever the hell I want with him."

My father's voice is like a bucket of cold water washing away any humor. I hear the whispered voices of my father's goons. "This is gonna be so much worse if he kills the kid."

"What the fuck you want me to do about it? That fucking dog damned near tore my goddamned hand off. We're already so fucking fucked."

The gun pressed to my back moves a fraction, as my father hears his henchmen too. "You want to think long and hard before you try to fucking betray me, Kyle." I knew one of them started with a K. Apparently, my dad has a type when it comes to thugs.

The sound of guns cocking is loud even with the sirens surrounding us. I hear what sounds like someone gibbering hysterically. "Not again. I can't...not again."

Then another deeper voice trying to soothe it. The third voice sounds like it should be saying, 'I am Groot.' Instead I hear, "Get the fuck away from Kelly. She's the only one who can get the motherfucking coffee right."

The beta under me snickers and then looks pained as her throat twitches. But the dominance behind that statement is real, and my father's gun twitches a bit farther from my spine.

The second voice, the soothing one, comes back. It's flat now, almost like it's asking how the weather is. "You've gotta be fucking kidding me. Here gimme that." There's a yell from the man who was telling everyone to put their hands up earlier, and Kelly's eyes go wide.

The gun that's been pressed close to me starts to swing away, the loud crack of it being discharged makes my ears burn. Pain rips down the back of my leg from calf to foot and my elbows buckle, crushing Kelly beneath me.

Another bang sounds, muffled through the ringing in my ears and Kelly's scream.

Shouts sound from all around, and my father's body falls to the side, his dead eyes staring into mine with a third right in the center of his forehead. The calm voice still sounds disinterested, but now it's through several layers of ringing cotton. "There you go, problem solved. You can have this back. Now, we need to put out that fucking fire before anything else catches."

Kelly

I t's hard to breathe with Steve lying on me. Warmth pools on my side, and I can hear raised voices and arguing. The world swims out of focus. I can't get enough air, but pushing on Steve doesn't do much good. He may not be as big as any of the rest of my pack, but he's still large and my muscles don't want to work.

Suddenly, there are people all around us. Officer Paul is arguing with Xan. "You can't just take someone's fucking gun and shoot a suspect. There are fucking laws, asshole. Do you have any idea the amount of trouble we could all be in for this shit? Fuck, just the paperwork I'm going to have to file for discharging my firearm."

Xan huffs in response. "There have been several documented instances where if an officer is incapacitated, a bystander is allowed to use their weapon if it allows them to prevent loss of life. Of course, it also depends on training, familiarity, and jurisdiction, but you *were* emotionally incapacitated, and he was about to shoot somebody."

Officer Paul growls, "I know you and your fucking weird ass trivia...do you have that jurisdiction here, Xan? No, I didn't think so. Fucking shit man." The long litany of profanity fades as they move farther away, and I worry about how much trouble Xan just got into.

Leo appears over Steve's shoulder, his eyes wide, and his voice loud. "We need a couple of medics over here. Two civilians, one suspect...and somebody please get in touch with my clinic's emergency line. I think Stephanie's on call tonight. Jake's been shot." There are several loud rumbles in the background before some of the weight lifts off me, and I see Leo carrying my fuzzy friend back towards the firetruck.

Then more faces surround us. People in firefighter or police uniforms. Someone rolls Steve off me and onto a stretcher, and I hear Gabe's growling snarl as he takes in my pajama covered body coated in blood. I want to assure him that none of it's mine, but I need to make sure Steve and Jake are ok first.

A gurney appears and I'm lifted onto it. My throat burns when I try to tell them I'm ok. Only a hoarse croak comes out, and Gabe lets out a long string of expletives, ending in, "Fuckin' asshole." He interrupts Xan and Paul's argument with a loud yell. "Hey, what kinda trouble will I get into if I beat the shit out of a corpse? Like...is that a fine sorta situation or will I go to jail for that shit?"

Xan cackles before coming over and taking a look at me. His eyes run over my body, his face hardening when he gets to my neck. "Shoulda shot him somewhere painful first. You ok, Kelly Girl?" I nod because I can't talk, and he looks nearly murderous. But that ship has already sailed. He nods once before turning and I watch him walk back towards the firetruck.

"Has anybody seen Jacks? It's ok, Love. She's fine. A little bruised, but she'll be ok." Jacks pops out from around the back of the truck, eyes red in the firelight and wraps himself around Xan. The smaller alpha rocks back and forth, rubbing his hands up and down his mate's back, making quiet shushing noises. "It's ok. Everything'll be ok."

I am totally gonna milk this for a batch of chocolate muffins. I giggle at the thought, but all that comes out is an unladylike wheeze that starts a painful coughing fit.

My eyes track the surrounding area. Several of the firefighters have pulled out hoses, but I don't think there's anything left of the shop to save. Hopefully, they can keep it from spreading to the woods or the house. I try to locate Steve, but he's nowhere to be seen. Someone pushes my gurney over to an ambulance, and it's bumpy as they load me in.

I want to protest; he needs to go to the hospital, I'm fine. My throat hurts, but I'll be ok. Then I notice the other bed with Steve on it, and I reach towards him, my fingers brushing over his. He has bandages around his leg and shoulder, and a pad pressed to the side of his face. But his eyes open and he looks at me, the corner of his mouth pulling up as he twines our fingers together.

A man in grey scrubs starts checking my vital signs. Officer Paul's voice raises outside. "Goddamnit Gabe, get him under control now!" I can't imagine what Xan is doing at this moment, but since he hasn't been shot or arrested yet, I'll consider it a win.

There's a loud banging on the side of the ambulance and Joseph steps up into the back. "Miss Kelly...and...I don't know you," he mutters at Steve.

My throat burns but I wave him closer, barely able to whisper, "'s Steve...'s pack."

His eyes flare for a moment, then he nods briefly, looking between us and shaking his head. "The EMTs are gonna get you two to the hospital. Leo'll meet Steph at the clinic with Jake, and I'll give your parents a call once the fire's out. I talked to Sam a bit ago, and he's on his way home. Probably another four hours out, so I'll send him your way when he gets back." He nods to himself like he's done his part and then jumps down, closing the doors behind him. There's another loud thump on the side and then we're moving.

Steve squeezes my fingers as the man in grey scrubs watches the monitors that are attached to my alpha. The low beeping and the rumble of the ambulance make my eyelids heavy, and I drift in and out of sleep all the way to the hospital—not coming fully awake until we pull up in front of the emergency room entrance. Steve still grips my fingers, but his hold is loose now and he looks paler than usual. A feat in and of itself, really.

I blink up at the bright ceiling as they roll us through the doors. Voices are all around, and Steve's hand is pulled from mine as he's taken through a set of swinging doors. My arm reaches out for him, but a nurse steps between us.

"Kelly? Kelly Carpenter, can you hear me?" I nod because my throat hurts and she nods back like she was expecting that. "Ok, honey, we have some questions we need your help with. Do you think you can manage that?" I nod again and she looks at my throat, making an upset tsking noise.

"Ok, Kelly, first let's get you and your mate checked in, and then we can get you something for the pain. How's that sound?" I want to rail against the mate comment, but since I can't, I just nod again. She rolls me over to a counter and hands me a notepad with 'Yes' and 'No' written on it and begins asking questions, having me point out the answer.

Chapter 37

Garret

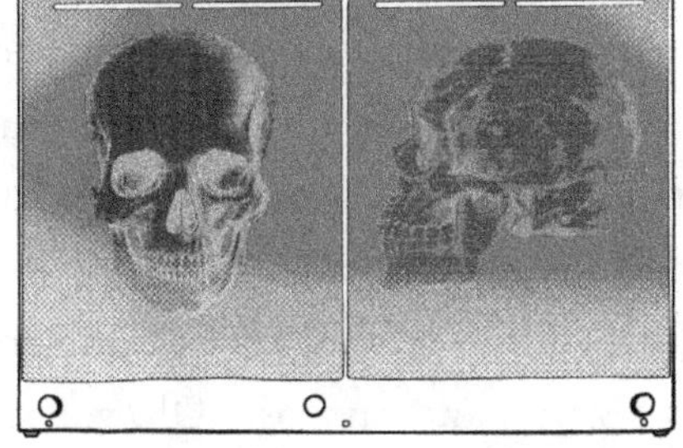

We pull up to the house, and it's chaos. There are police, along with an ambulance and fire truck, still there. Sam scrambles out of the truck, looking around wildly for our pack mates, or anyone who can answer questions—then he takes off running towards the shop. I see two of my father's men sitting in the back of a police car, neither of them looking nearly as injured as I'd like.

My breath seizes in my lungs when I see the bag on the ground. It looks too big to be Kelly, but did they do something to Steve? I can't imagine Dad would be so careless as to let Steve die when he's still considered a valuable genetic donor to the cause. I nearly collapse out of the truck myself, stumbling towards the covered shape, needing to know what happened.

An officer steps in my way. His hair is a shocking, almost carrot orange in the bright morning light. My eyes barely skate over him when his hand lands on my chest, and a snarl rips from me. My eyes are drawn back to the shape in the gravel. The shape with a large russet stain around it.

A warm body steps behind me, too small and soft to be Sam, and I instantly know it's Teddy before his purr starts up. He sounds calm as he addresses the officer, but I can feel the tension radiating off of him, the same as mine. "Officer...Um...Miller?" Teddy squints at the name tag. "I thought Officer Paul's name was Miller."

Officer Miller squints back at us. Looking down and taking in Teddy's wrists and tattoos. "Oh, you must be Teddy...which makes you...Garret? Sorry, Spence just said one of you was pretty and the other looked emo. You look like a bit of both right now with the hair and the circles under your eyes, but if that's what you were going for, hey, you nailed it. My name's Josh...er...Miller, Officer Josh Miller"

Teddy looks at me with his eyebrows raised before turning back to the smiling officer. "Um, yes. I'm Teddy...and Garret's usually the pretty one. But we just drove in from Los Angeles and none of us have slept well. Speaking of Steve, where is he? Sam just took off towards the fire truck to find out, but we're worried about Kelly and Steve...and Jake."

Officer Josh stares at his feet, looking uncomfortable, and I swallow back the bile that rises in my throat. He looks up at me after a moment, discomfort morphing into concern. The hand that's been on my chest drops to my arm.

"Oh, shit. No, sorry. Sorry, they...well, I think they're fine. The EMTs were worried about Steve. Er, your brother, due to blood loss, and Miss Kelly was a bit banged up. But they've been at the hospital for a few hours now, and I haven't heard any word back. I'm taking it as a good sign. Um...Jake, however. Well, none of us have heard from Leo since he took him to the clinic. The big lug was pretty vocal for being shot...er Jake, not Doctor Leo. So, he's probably fine too...er, they're both probably fine...um, Doc wasn't hurt so..."

Is this man an idiot? Why do they allow him to carry a gun? A gun? Wait, shit. "Shot, wait, who shot Jake?"

Teddy has a death grip on my shoulders from behind. The officer turns and nods towards the bag on the ground. "At least, we think it was him. Forensics needs to look into all the weapons, but we know that there were at least two shots fired before we arrived, and then he hit the kid...um, Steve once more before he was subdued." His voice goes quiet, but I don't miss the whispered, "Shoulda' fuckin' shot him myself. What kind of crazy motherfucker shoots a dog?"

He shakes himself out of his low monologue, looking surprised that we're still standing here. "So, um...let's go find Paul, er...the other Officer Miller, and Sam and we can get all your questions answered. I probably wasn't supposed to say any of that, so if you could not tell him, that'd be great." His smile is huge and trusting, and I can only nod, because it'd feel too much like kicking a puppy by telling him no.

There are still a lot of people here, and it unsettles Teddy's omega instincts to have his home in such disarray. He whines behind me, and I grab his hand, trying to offer him the same support he's been giving me. Officer Josh waves us away from the bag on the ground—I still want to ask who it is, but right now I just need to find my brother and my beta. For now, though, we follow Officer Josh around the front of the truck and back towards the smoldering heap that was once Sam's livelihood.

Unfortunately, what we find is a face-off between Sam and Joseph. They're staring at each other, and everyone around them is tense. How long has this been going on? Has our alpha gotten any answers? No one says anything, and I want to scream just to break the tension.

Thank fuck Teddy is the most well-adjusted motherfucker here, and considering what I've suspected since Sarah started screaming at us, that's not fucking saying much. "Hey Joseph. Uh, How's Brice doing?" The alpha flinches at hearing his mate's name, and slowly turns towards Teddy, his face going pale. But our omega continues on. "I...um, I talked to Mom. She's been talking to Aunt Sandra. They told me about him being sick, and that's why you wanted me to come visit."

Joseph swallows, his Adam's apple bobbing up and down. He looks almost as bad as we do on our week of shitty sleep. His eyes have sunken in since I saw him at that fire a couple of weeks ago. He looks pale and sickly, his commanding presence faded. But he nods to Teddy.

"Yeah. Yeah, that's why *I* wanted you here. Brice...well...he's pissed at me because he wanted to have a heart to heart with you before it was too late. Something about the secrets and wonders of being a male omega. I don't fuckin' know. But it seemed important to him to pass on since there aren't many around and you're his cousin. It was important to him."

Teddy's gone pale, his voice verging on hysteria. "What do you mean *was*? Joseph, what happened, is he...?" The words trail off as Joseph meets his eyes, confusion marring the alpha's features.

"What, no, he's fine. Well, not fine, he's sick as shit, but now that you and Sam are together, it's not like he's gonna let you even fucking get tested, let alone donate. The doctors say we're still early enough, but the chances of finding a suitable donor are slim. Still, we're gonna keep looking. The whole pack is sending out feelers trying to find omegas who might be willing to at least get tested."

Sam's boom of laughter surprises his brother—stopping his rambling reply. Joseph spins, marching towards him, his fist raised in the air, until Officer Josh steps between them. The look he gives Sam is admonishing. "Sam, that's just plain mean. You never seemed like an asshole to me."

Our alpha is wiping his eyes, trying to get his chuckle under control as speaks, "Nah. Shit. I'm not laughin' 'cause of Brice. He's Teddy's cousin, and I know my omega's worried about him. I'm laughing at the thought of me tryin' to stop that boy from doing any damned thing he wants to do. Joseph, you and Brice've been together for how long now? What makes you think Teddy's any more compliant than his cousin?"

Joseph blinks, Officer Josh blinks, and Sam starts laughing again at their expressions. It's not until a few moments later when Teddy touches his shoulder and whispers into his ear that Sam's finally able to get himself under control, his voice still has a laughing edge to, "Now, Teddy says if we'd just fucking talked like adults, we could have avoided a lot of this bullshit, as well as making a scene at the mating ceremony. That being said, he probably wouldn't have ended up coming home with me if you hadn't been a fucknugget."

He turns to Teddy. "Fucknugget, really? Isn't that a little old school for you?" Teddy smiles at him and Sam turns back to Joseph. "Ok, I guess we're going with fucknugget. Anyway, he says he's glad you were a fucknugget because now the five of us are together. So, while we're talking about my pack, can anyone tell me what the fuck happened here, and where Kelly and Steve are?"

His easygoing manner from a moment ago has evaporated like mist, and even Teddy takes a step back. Joseph and Josh have gone an ashy sort of pale, both looking startled at the sudden change in Sam. But I don't blame him. I'm tired as fuck, sore, and I want to find my mate and my brother. Plus, have someone tell me who the fuck is in that goddamned bag in our driveway.

Chapter 38

Steve

Where the fuck did I fall asleep, and why is it so god-damned bright in here? A better question would probably be what the hell I did last night. My head is pounding like the worst hangover ever, and my mouth feels like I licked a fucking sidewalk.

The room smells stale and sterile, like a hospital, and I cringe at how fucking trashed I must have been to get here. It's been at least a few years since things got that bad, and usually Garret's right here with me, having chased me down the rabbit hole of misery.

My mind spins towards my twin, and I jerk in the bed as memory slams into me. Was that this morning? How much time has passed? Is he safe? Is Teddy? Oh god, what happened to

Kelly after I fell on her? Raising myself up so I don't pull on any of the tubes or wires attached to me, I peer around the room. There's another bed in here, but the body in it is just a lump, and there aren't nearly as many tubes or wires coming from it. Lucky me.

With no other recourse, I press the call button, hoping to get the answers that my cotton filled brain can't come up with. A few minutes later, an older woman in scrubs comes in. "Oh, hello, Mr. Carpenter, how are you feeling this afternoon?"

Ok...so, it's afternoon, is it the same day?

How long was I asleep?

My throat is dry from the hospital air, and I cough when I try to answer. Nothing comes out but a dry rasp. Her face falls, and she brings me a cup of water to sip so I can speak properly, answering my unspoken questions while I suck down the cold liquid. "I'm so sorry. I thought for sure Kelly would have been awake by now and woken you up." She walks over to the lump and peels down the covers, her face a mask of concern.

"No, bless her heart. It's been a tough day for you two. Even when she wakes up, I don't know how well she'll be able to talk for a while. There's a fair amount of bruising on her throat. I was a bit surprised she was so willing to deal with all the check-in questions, but it does make things so much easier."

She turns back to me. "Oh, her parents are here in the waiting room, as well as three large alphas that say they're the rest of your pack. Would you like me to let them in? Their identification didn't have updated information on it, so we wanted to wait until you were awake."

My thoughts twist at the mention of three large alphas. My father still had two men with him, Kyle and whoever his counterpart is. She wouldn't know their names either. "Um...what do these alphas look like?"

She looks thoughtful for a moment. "Well, the biggest one is very large and muscular, with a short salt and pepper beard, kind of a silver fox vibe going on. The second one has long black hair, a couple of piercings, and looks like he probably wants to scream at people...and the last one looks a bit like you, but prettier...er...Sorry, that came out wrong."

My mad cackle startles Kelly awake, and she raises her head, looking around blearily. The nurse looks taken aback, as if I just yelled at her for saying my brother is prettier. She's not wrong, but that's only because I'm a bit underweight right now. I'm smiling when I finally answer. "No, that sounds like our pack, Sam, Teddy, and Garret. He's my twin, but you're not wrong." She blushes slightly, and I didn't bother to correct her about Teddy's designation. I don't care right now. The only important thing is that they're here and safe.

The nurse smiles at us both and bustles out of the room. A few minutes later, Kelly's family comes in. Her parents rush to her bedside, and her brother flops down in the visitor's chair, his head once again buried in a video game. He raises his face for a moment to nod at me. "'Sup...Steve? Right?" I nod back and get a "Cool" for my efforts.

Kelly's mom reaches over and slaps Tuck on the back of the head, and he scowls at her before standing up and slouching over to say hi. He takes one look at her neck and his eyes flick to mine. "So...did the whole hand necklace thing not work out for you guys or what? Wait, my dude, I thought you weren't into girls. Were you just trying to lure my sister into a false sense of security before you pounced?"

I recoil at the insinuation, and his mother's hand connects with the back of his head again, flipping his hair over his eyes. "Shit Mom, ow!" The short beta woman glares at him. "I mean, shoot...that hurt. Ow! Fine. Sorry Steve, I'm just fu—er, messing with you. The cops told us what happened."

My breath comes out in a loud whoosh and Tuck laughs loudly before dropping against the side of Kelly's bed and getting back to his game. Before his mom can say anything else, his voice pipes up. "Nope, I'm right here, socializing, and being involved. Hey Kelly, how's the throat? Oh, wait, you can't answer. Guess I'll just have to sit here and try not to talk to you, so you don't strain it anymore." His eyes flick up and meet mine over the game in his hands, and he grins before going back to it.

A moment later, the door opens again and Sam comes in, followed by Teddy and Garret. My brother, of course, beelines straight for Kelly. Hopping from foot to foot, trying to figure out how to get around her family so he can touch her. Sam and Teddy stand between our beds, and the space is now officially too damned crowded. I look over at my mates and wave my hand at the other side of the bed, in front of the monitors. "Hey, you two, come stand over here so they have a few minutes, yeah? You'll all get time with Pixie soon enough. But she can't talk much right now."

Sam and Teddy trade looks, but eventually do as I suggest and come to my other side. Teddy looks down at me like he wants to touch me, but isn't sure where I won't hurt. That's a fair question. Everything fucking hurts. Instead, I reach out my not shot arm and take his hand, weaving our fingers together and squeezing. "I missed you, Bear. How was your trip?"

My omega busts out laughing. "Well, we woulda been here sooner, but your brother almost got us arrested going through Marshall, Texas because he was hanging his dick out the window trying to piss. Otherwise, the last leg of the trip was pretty uneventful."

I stare at my brother who is now as red as a tomato, his voice is muffled where it's buried in his hands. "We rushed out before we had a chance to hit the bathrooms. I didn't have a hell of a lot of options, and Sam fucking told me to. How the fuck was I supposed to know he wasn't serious?" Kelly starts laughing, and it's a horrible raspy wheeze that soon sets her off on a coughing fit.

Her mother stares at Garret in horror, and her father looks like he's trying not to laugh himself. Tuck just mutters to himself, "Man, old people are nuts. How the heck did you *not* know he wasn't bein' serious, man? That's some next level lack of thought." A little scoring noise comes from the game in his hand and the kid's grin gets huge, as he sinks deeper into the digital monotony.

Teddy

Fucking stupid ass alphas and their inability to have a normal goddamned discussion. All this shit with Brice because no one could pull their heads out of their asses long enough to actually discuss with me what I might or might not want. Knot-heads, the fucking lot of them.

And then there's Kelly. My poor sweet beta. All I want to do is carry her home, drag her into my room downstairs, lock everyone else out, and purr for her until she's nothing but mush against me. Was I looking forward to having sex with her? Well, I'd be lying if I said no, but right now I just want to cuddle her, and feed her soup until her throat feels better. I bet Sam makes an awesome chicken soup.

Kelly's parents stay for a few hours until finally Tuck is sighing and acting like the most neglected and put upon creature in the world. Shortly after dinner time they take him and go home. Her mother lectures the kid all the way out the door. Watching them interact reminds me that I should probably call Mom soon. I really miss her, and she'll want to know we got home safely. Plus, somebody should give her an update on Brice, and since none of the alphas will volunteer, it falls to me.

Steve needs to stay overnight in the hospital. Thankfully, neither of the bullets hit any vital organs or bones, but he still lost a lot of blood. Garret's going to stay with him and fill him in on our trip. We'll bring them both a change of clothes and some breakfast first thing tomorrow. Sam is in full on caretaking mode and fussing over everything. Kelly's dad's upset that she's coming home tonight with me and Sam, but we're her pack, and it's her choice. But he still glares at me before leaving.

We didn't stay at the house long enough to do more than unload Sam's truck from the trailer so we could drive here. The rental truck sits large in the small parking area, making everything else feel crowded. The russet stain is still on the ground where the coroner finally arrived. None of the police or fire trucks are here, and the smoldering remains of Sam's shop release wisps of smoke or steam into the cool evening air.

Our pack lead groans when he looks over at it. His voice is rough as he lets loose a long string of profanity. Kelly blinks up at him in surprise. "Sorry, Sweetheart. It's been a long few days and I'm just...I didn't expect to come home to this shit. If I'm being honest, my plan was to come home, shower until my skin felt like it was gonna melt off and then drag you and Teddy into bed for cuddles for at least the next thirty-six hours or so. Fucking would have been amazing too, but totally optional."

Kelly cuddles up against his side, her voice is still broken. "I'm sorry about your shop Sam...and Jake. He tried to protect me. Has anybody heard from Leo or Stephanie?"

Our pack lead growls low in his throat. "Not yet, but I'll call Gabe and check on Jake and see how they wanna handle you being hurt. Let them know they'll have to do without you at the shop for a few days while you heal up."

Kelly's giggle turns into a cough. "Only if you agree to take them a thermos of coffee first thing in the morning. Though, after everything else, I should probably just get them a new coffee maker for the office. Pretty sure Xan saved Steve. Though I don't know if it was for the sake of the office caffeine supply or Jacks."

She coughs again and my fingers cover her lips to keep her from trying to say anything else. "Come on, Pixie, your throat'll never heal if you don't stop." Lifting her in my arms, I carry her out of the truck and up the steps to the front porch. Her legs are fine, and she could probably walk with no problem—I just need to be close to her after everything we heard about this morning. We could have fucking lost her because Vee and Garret's dad is batshit crazy...was...was batshit crazy.

Remind me not to piss off the fucking surfer. He is *not* the one I would have thought to be careful of.

Sam checks the lock on the back of the moving truck and then meets us on the porch to unlock the front door. Joseph said he locked it when they took Kelly and Steve to the hospital earlier. Not that anybody around here would do anything, but after everything else, better to be safe than sorry.

The house is too quiet without Jake bouncing around, and I'm not the only one who feels it. As soon as Sam sits his duffel bag down, he pulls out his phone and calls Gabe. The growly alpha picks up on the second ring. "Hey, Sam, is Kelly ok?" It makes me smile a bit that they're protective of my Pixie too. Kelly tries to squeak out a 'Hello' but starts coughing and Gabe's growl rattles through the room.

Eventually the alphas calm down, and Kelly gets down some cool water. Sam brings up the reason we called. "So, is Leo around? We were hoping to check up on Jake." Gabe grumbles something else and then Leo takes the phone.

"Sam, glad you all made it home safe. Yes, Jake's doing fine. He's on some heavy pain medication, so he's a bit loopy. He's staying overnight at the clinic to make sure he doesn't get too active and tear any stitches. That being said, the poor guy took a hell of a beating from those assholes, so he's gonna be sore for a few days. But you're welcome to come by tomorrow any time and get him. He's not gonna be happy about it, but I'd suggest a cone for at least the next week. Stephanie and I will both be in the office all day tomorrow, and either one of us can get him sorted out when you stop by."

Kelly takes a deep shuddering breath, the relief clear on her face that Jake's ok. Tears form in her eyes, and I offer her the water cup again, in case it's from her throat hurting. I assume it has more to do with Jake and everyone else since she keeps insisting that she's ok. But that doesn't mean we're not going to do everything in our power to spoil her, despite any protests that I'm sure she'll have.

Chapter 39

Sam

Being back in my own house is fucking heaven. I turn on the hot water in the bathroom, fully intending to scrub off the travel grime—then wash Kelly from head to foot until she's putty in my hands. But when she takes off her sweats, her knees are bandaged up again. Sometimes I think this girl is trying to kill me with either worry or sexual frustration.

"Sweetheart, what happened? The doctor said that you were only treated for the injury to your neck." Kelly looks at Teddy, her eyes filling with tears before a big sob comes out. Teddy looks baffled and pulls her into his arms. His big body wraps around her in a way that reminds me of when we first met, and he rocks back and forth, making quiet soothing noises.

With a sigh of resignation, I turn the water off and follow them back into the bedroom. His voice is a quiet whisper. "Shh, it's ok, Pixie, I can fix it. Whatever you need. Please don't cry, you're gonna hurt your throat worse. Come on, sweet girl." He carries her to the side of the bed and pulls her into his lap so that her head is resting on his shoulder. I can't make out what she says in his ear, but a cold shiver runs down my spine as Teddy's face drains of color.

Well, fuck.

I guess we're doing this now.

I had hoped to avoid the conversation until Teddy was more comfortable, but after Sarah's little outburst a few days ago, I knew it was coming. Teddy is shaking when I sit next to him, and I wrap my arms around them both, offering what comfort I can at what's sure to be a horrible moment for my omega.

I don't start purring, because I don't want to cause confusion. He can tell me about his wrists, and then I can purr for both of them. If I do it now, it will just cause hormone fluctuations as he relaxes and then tenses up repeatedly. That won't do anybody any good, especially this close to his heat. I hold my pack while Teddy shivers and Kelly cries softly into his neck. They need to get the emotions out. Bottling everything up won't help anybody.

After a while, Teddy's body stills. He takes a few deep breaths before shaking himself and pulling away from me. Then he unwraps Kelly's arms from his neck and passes her over so I can hold her. He's fidgeting and twitchy, and it comes as no surprise when he stands up and starts pacing back and forth.

His voice is cracked as he starts talking, the sentences rambling and disjointed as he walks across the room and back—fingers twisting and curling along the edges of those damnable leather bracers of his.

"Well, I guess...I mean, you've both met Vee and Garret's dad now. He...he was always kind of ass. Not that he ever hurt me like he did them. Heck, I didn't even know about it at the time. It wasn't until recently..."

"Shit, let me start over. Ok, you know Marc was an abusive cunt to his kids? We're all on the same page there?" He stops moving and stares at us, waiting for Kelly and me to nod before he continues his relentless pacing.

"My parents didn't know. I mean, they never said anything, and you've talked to my mom. I'm pretty sure she would have called the cops on him if she knew—and tried to move the guys in with us. She loved both of them dearly. She was completely fine with our planning to mate when we were older. Mom...well, all of them since I presented as an omega—but Mom has always been overprotective. Shit, that's why you talked to them...why the hell am I telling you this? You already know how they can be."

Teddy's shaking again, and Kelly squirms out of my lap to go wrap her arms around him. Her voice is just a whisper. "Breathe." She takes deep breaths against his chest until he starts syncing up with her. Once he calms down, she hops back over and puts her arms up for me to lift her back into my lap.

Teddy's voice is clearer now. "Whew. Ok, so, we know Marc was an asshole. We didn't know that before I presented as an omega. From what the guys said, he made it pretty much impossible for them to talk to me...or they were too fucking afraid of the bastard to try." My omega's expression has taken on a hard edge, and my mind wonders briefly at how he presented as an omega in the first place. Genetic lottery is a bitch.

Teddy's jaw clenches, but he keeps going. "I didn't...I didn't mention this last week when we were talking. It seemed pointless, and until I was sure that they were going to be staying here, there was no reason to bring it up. Um...after my designation came in, Marc reached out to me. He lied to my mom to get me on the phone. Told her that he was worried about his sons. That Garret was ready to go meet new omegas, but that neither of them felt right about it until Vee officially ended things with me."

Kelly's voice interrupts, a little froggy. "But that's not true." Teddy's resulting chuckle is dark, and my stomach rolls when he looks at us.

"No, sweet girl, that's not true. Marc was a lying sack of shit, and I was a newly awakened omega who had grown up thinking like an alpha. I had no problem sneaking out that night to what I thought was a meeting with Vee. Shit, I *wanted* to talk to him. I *needed* to try to understand what was happening, why he wouldn't answer my calls...why they left."

Teddy stops speaking. He's gone kind of green. When he hurries into the bathroom, I'm worried he's about to be sick. Thankfully, the sink turns on, and a few moments later he comes back with water dripping down his face, and his color a bit closer to normal.

"So...Yeah, I got there. I was just told to come to the house. It wasn't anything creepy, like a dark alley, or anything to cause alarm bells to go off. I was a fucking idiot."

"Marc met me at the door. He seemed genuinely contrite about everything, and I followed him back to his office, where he said my friends were. That was a complete lie. Thinking about it, I doubt the guys were even still at the house. It had been about a week, so chances are he'd already sent them off to that private school they graduated from."

He's stalling. Rambling on, like he wants to avoid this next part. While I already have a few strong suspicions, it's his story to tell. I'll be here when he needs me.

"So, Kelly...which ones did you get? Mine were Kase and Kevin?"

Kelly meets his eyes, and a tear slips free and slides down her cheek. "Kyle...I didn't get the name on the other one."

Teddy nods. "Vee explained it to me...his dad has...had some sort of obsession thing with goons whose names started with K. It's fucked up, but in the long run, the names don't really matter, they're all fucking horrible people. Anyway. Kase and Kevin were in the room, not my pack. Marc came in behind me and closed the door."

"He...he said he didn't want to hurt me, at least not in a way people could see. That was sloppy. But his men didn't have the same concerns. The bigger one, Kace, grabbed me by the back of my neck. Told me he'd never had a boy omega before, but that I was cute enough, so it wouldn't be any hardship."

Kelly's crying full out, her breath coming in little wheezy bursts through her injured throat, and my mind turns to murder at the possibility that those two fucks who were taken into custody could have threatened her in the same way.

My omega's voice is stronger when he continues, and I wonder if his thoughts are anywhere near mine. "Marc said he didn't want things to get ugly. He'd rather settle this peacefully, but I had to stop trying to get in touch with his sons. I wasn't worth their time. Male omegas are completely useless...I don't want to go into everything he said, but you've met the guy, so you can probably guess the general tirade."

"The bottom line was that if I kept trying to get in touch with Vee or Garret that he knew where I lived. He knew that Mom was there alone during the day while my dads were at work...and that Kace and Kevin would be happy to pay her a visit one day, or me a visit one night. Kind of the straw that maimed the camel...when they dropped me off at home, you could see Mom through the window, and Kace started talking about how I had her pretty black hair, and maybe he wouldn't wait for word back from Marc."

"I...I scrambled out of the car, making a beeline for the front porch, intent on telling Mom and Murph. If someone was threatening them, they had a right to know. But my phone went off right as I reached the door. A text from a blocked number. If I told my parents, I gave up any protection that was offered. I was a stupid sixteen-year-old kid, and I panicked. I snuck back into the house and never told my parents. With Vee gone, and my being a risk to Mom..."

Teddy trails off. He looks exhausted, but watches the two of us carefully as he unbuckles the leather straps he's kept around his wrists. The skin underneath is lighter from lack of sun, and when he turns his arms over, the tattoos are on full display, along with raised scars running across both wrists. There's a T section as well running from his scars and up his forearm, but those are mostly covered by his tattoos. I can now see how the pattern is done to hide as much of the line as possible, including the additions of the column behind the three of swords.

A loud braying sob draws me out of my intense inspection, and then Kelly's sliding off of me and throwing herself at Teddy. His hands come under her butt and lift her, holding her against his chest. His brow pinches with the new sensation on the sensitive skin that was so recently exposed, but his purr starts up to comfort our beta.

Standing and walking over to them, I wrap my arms around his shoulders, trapping her shaking body between us, and dropping my forehead to his.

Softly, like my breath might break him if I'm too loud, I ask, "Nobody else knows?" It's an assumption, a guess. He was terrified enough to try to take himself out of the equation. He probably kept it inside...all these fucking years. Jesus, our poor boy. If that piece of trash wasn't dead, I'd fucking kill him myself. Teddy's eyes meet mine, our purrs synching up in a cocoon of comfort for all of us.

"Nobody. I mean, after Mom found me, there was all the doctor shit. Even when I started meeting with Dr. Dana. There was already so much to deal with, and part of me was still terrified that if I said anything...I couldn't risk Mom, and I didn't know..." His voice trails off as he sinks against me, Kelly squirms a bit, her hand coming up to stroke his face. Her broken voice rasps as she tries to make soothing noises.

Note to self: order the best fucking coffee maker on the market for Xan and gift wrap that bitch with a fruit basket or cookies or some shit.

Eventually, I'm too exhausted to keep standing. "Ok, everybody strip. Next time, I can show you all the fancy shit I put in the shower. For now, we're gonna get clean and get some sleep. Sweetheart, lemme see your knees. I can tape some plastic wrap or something over 'em if we need to so you can get cleaned up."

Her responding giggle and snort ends with a low murmured, "Ow...Don't make me laugh, it hurts." Teddy sits her on the ground while I kneel and peel away the bandages on her knees. The skin is pink and looks abraded with a few deeper cuts, but mostly healed already. She meets my eyes when I look up at her, and answers my unspoken question. "Steve...he's apparently pretty good at treating injuries, so they don't scar as bad."

After everything else I've learned recently, this is going to require a deeper conversation with Steve, but now's not the time. I'm tired enough that I don't try to hide the grunt that slips out when I stand up. I'm getting too damned old for this much excitement. Thinking back to the frail-looking alpha for a moment, it occurs to me that despite what we've done together; I haven't actually seen him topless. It sends a rush of guilt through me for not being attentive enough to my pack's needs. Only adding to what I'm already feeling about Teddy.

Stepping under the hot water with Teddy and Kelly, helping each other get cleaned up fills me with a relief I didn't know was possible. Despite all the shit that's happened, things will be ok. Caring for my people, and having them return that care, feels better than anything I could have imagined. While it doesn't fix the problem, it does go a bit towards letting me forgive Joseph for his shitty behavior with how worried he's been about his own pack.

Getting clean takes a bit longer for three people than it would if I were just scrubbing myself, but we finally get rinsed and dried off—not bothering with pajamas because it's just an extra step. Crawling into bed, I've missed being able to hold Teddy and Kelly both...as long as she faces Teddy so she can't epilate my damned chest any more than she already has.

It feels amazing to fall asleep with my arms wrapped around her waist, her small soft body pressed against me. Teddy pressed flush against her front, trapping my hands. For this moment, at least, everything is right with the world.

Chapter 40

Kelly

*J**ake is gonna get all the cuddles.*

My poor slobber-muffin.

Leo meets us at the front desk when we walk in. His usual pleasant smile falls when he catches sight of my throat. Still, he shakes it off fairly quickly and walks with us to the kennel area in the back, where we find Jake lying on a cushioned dog bed with a cone around his head. His tail wags slowly when he sees us, but he doesn't try to jump up or go into his usual full-body wiggle.

Even when I open the door and kneel down next to him, he just pushes his big face into my hand, sniffing my palm before licking me a few times. His big brown eyes stare up at me, and

I want to cry again because someone hurt my friend. "Oh, my sweet baby. Are you ready to go home and get all the snuggles?" His tail wag speeds up at my words, but he's still shaky and unsteady when he stands up. Sam grumbles a bit and then squats to pick Jake up, wrapping his arms under my poor pup's legs so he feels more secure.

Sam goes to put him in the front of the cab for the ride home, but Jake whines and wiggles until Sam puts him down. While I'm pretty sure he couldn't make it over the tailgate before he was hurt, it doesn't stop him from trying now. It's not until Sam lifts him into the truck bed that Jake stops struggling. Flopping gracelessly into the corner between the cab and the bed, he looks up at me, a big doggy smile on his face.

After a brief discussion, we head for the hospital to pick up Steve and Garret. We leave Jake to guard the truck, which is code for snoring comfortably, while we step inside. Garret's already talked to the doctors this morning, and it only takes a few minutes before a nurse wheels Steve out. He tries to talk Teddy into giving him a piggyback ride—much to the nurse's dismay—but Sam shuts him down quickly. Steve is still pretty small compared to Sam or Garret, but he's the only one willing to risk further injury to himself if Teddy falls or can't keep him up.

The ride home goes fairly quickly, and when we get there, Sam carries Steve inside and deposits him on the couch before coming back for Jake. Once the two injured parties are situated, because I'm still not counting my stupid throat as being hurt, we take stock of the moving truck. I am totally skipping class and work today, with Gabe's repeated grumbling to stay in bed and rest.

Instead, I spend the next few hours carrying light bags of nesting stuff in while Teddy, Sam, and Garret argue over where to move the furniture and everything else. Sam's water bill is going to be insane after all the laundry we've done this weekend trying to get the nest ready, but with luck, the last load of blankets should be out of the dryer before bedtime tonight.

By late afternoon, Sam and Garret head out to take the truck back to the rental lot in Springfield. Thankfully, Garret's head is feeling better. He keeps brushing off the injuries to his head in favor of hovering over me. Still, Sam insists that they haul his truck on the trailer, so Garret's not driving at all. It seems to take forever, and Steve and I spend the entirety of it cuddling with Teddy wedged between us on the couch.

Tomorrow I need to make it into work and class, despite what my alphas and Teddy keep insisting. I'm almost done with school, and if the needy omega hormone spikes are anything to go by, I'll soon be missing at least a few days of both to help take care of Teddy during his impending heat.

He loves the new mattress that Steve and I ordered. I don't voice my question on whether or not the shipping information was how Marc found us. Steve doesn't need the guilt, and what's past is past, anyway.

Sam is really upset that he hasn't provided a bed frame yet...and that the one he started—along with most of his lumber and power tools—burned up in the shop. It's lucky that he's been storing a lot of the restoration stuff, like sheetrock and insulation, in the house. Still, there's no telling how long it's gonna take insurance to get him sorted out.

Teddy helps Sam make chicken alfredo for dinner, and it smells amazing. Steve wants to help, but he can't stand up for very long yet, so he's relegated to the living room with me and Jake. The easy camaraderie we had when it was just the two of us seems to have disappeared, but none of the jealousy or anger has returned. Which is a bit frustrating, but I'll take what I can get. He may just not be in a very joking mood since he was just shot...twice.

With Garret and Steve's furniture, we finally have a full set of matching chairs, which isn't super important, but right now I'll take the wins we can get, especially when we all sit down to eat. I offer up my chair to Steve so he can have an easier time maneuvering from the smaller area he and Garret usually sit in. He thanks me with a small smile, and then Sam moves the table away from the wall to give me more space anyway, earning a mildly annoyed glare from Garret.

I'm especially glad that Teddy's back. Because while I've been trying to work my way through the stretching toys while they were gone, it's a lot easier if you have an extra hand that can help get the angle right.

Plus, it's a good time to show my omega the strap-on I got for his heat. I haven't tried it on yet, so I save it for after I get out of the shower and come out of the bathroom wearing it over my pajamas. It even has an inflatable knot, and all four of the guys look at me with expressions ranging from horror to humor when I pump it up.

Teddy's the first one to react. "Ok, well, I'm not sure who you think that's going to fit into, because it's not me. Fuck me, Pixie, but please tell me that knot's adjustable, otherwise it ain't happening." I want to tell him that's the point, fucking him—but he looks genuinely concerned, so I make it my mission to read the manual and see how to make it smaller.

Sam snorts, walking to my side and looking down. "You tryin' to make me feel a little inadequate there, Sugar?"

Steve looks angry. "Oh, it wasn't enough that you already have a uterus and tits, now your dick's bigger than mine? Seriously, Pixie?" On that last word, he breaks and starts giggling. "Ok, yeah, no, if Teddy likes it though, I might have to borrow your toy sometimes." He ruffles my hair before hobbling over to Teddy, pulling him under the covers, and wrapping himself around our omega. It doesn't escape my notice that he's still wearing long sleeves and pants. But he can keep that to himself for now.

Garret still stares, slack jawed, for a few moments. "I feel...conflicted." He pauses, looking from my face to my new toy. "On one hand, you're always fucking adorable, and I want to fuck you into the mattress until you're nothing but a little boneless puddle of sweet satisfied beta...on the other, dick...like, really big dick. I...I have no idea what to do with this." He rubs his chin, looking thoughtful.

My voice is raspy, and not much more than a whisper. "Well, my Alpha." I pause, enjoying his low rumbling growl when I call him mine. "Instead of fucking me into the bed, you could always fuck me into Teddy during his heat. That way, I don't get worn out using muscles I'm not used to. You don't get frustrated with all the raging omega hormones trying to throw you into a rut. And we can see if all the stretching I've been trying to do while you guys were gone finally has me ready to take your knot."

The whimper that comes out of him isn't very alpha, and judging by Sam's low chuckle, I'm not the only one who thinks it's cute. But then Garret's trying to get me out of the straps without undoing the buckles and I almost end up face-planting when he gives me a massive harness wedgie.

The startled squawk that comes out of my still healing throat causes his hands to wrap around me and lift me up to the side of the bed. My big ol' dildo is eye level to Sam as I kneel on the mattress. He's doing an admirable job trying really hard not to laugh, watching us as Garret grows more frustrated by the moment. Finally he throws up his hands. "Hold on, I think I saw some medical scissors in the bathroom, gimme a second."

He's so stinkin' cute when he's frustrated, and I think I might have to start cussing more if it drives him this close to the edge. But for the sake of my recent purchase, I grab his hands and lead them to the little black clips on the side and show him how to release them. The entire contraption sags down my thighs, pulled by the weight of the toy. I grab the remote control and deflate the knot so it doesn't stretch out the silicone, and then shimmy the whole thing down my legs, passing it off to Garret to put in the closet...for now.

By the time he gets back, I'm snuggled up against Sam's chest. Garret's breath is hot on my neck as his arms wrap around my waist. "That's not nice, little beta. Do you know what I want to do to you right now?"

I already feel half asleep from Sam's purr, and my voice is mostly a sleepy mumble. "Purr for me and give me cuddles because I'm really sleepy and have to get up early for work. Also, hope that getting more rest tonight means I'll have more energy tomorrow."

He's silent for a moment, before his breath puffs across the back of my neck. "Ok, yeah. That's fair." He rolls me towards him and my body jerks, feeling like I'm falling for a moment. Sam lets out a sharp breath and a loud grumble when my fist tightens in panic. Then I'm settled against Garret's chest, Sam's hand on my hip, Teddy's hand over Sam's. My alphas' purrs surround me, and everything feels right.

Chapter 41

Kelly

Sadly, waking up to my alarm blaring the next morning doesn't feel right. Running into Officer Cedric Ross standing on our front porch with two unknown policemen is even worse, especially when I'm worried about being late.

"Mornin' Miss Kelly, I was wondering if we could speak with you and Mr. Carpenter this morning?" I look at Ross for a moment. He doesn't appear to be any more of a morning person than I am, his grey eyes blinking in the bright morning light.

Sam is two steps behind me. "Kelly, Sweetheart. I know you're an adult, but how can you eat this junk?" He's holding up my box of peanut butter puff cereal and reading the ingredients. It's delicious, but you should never read the ingredients. I can't even pronounce half of that stuff. Sam draws up short when I don't answer, finally noticing the people standing on his porch.

One of the unknown officers takes that moment to include themselves in the conversation. "Sir, are you Mr. Carpenter?"

Sam looks back and forth between the two new cops, and I don't see any recognition in his eyes, either. "I'm one of four Mr. Carpenters who live here. Can you please be more specific?"

The two unknowns confer quietly between themselves while Ross just looks smug. Finally, the first one speaks again. "Is there a Mr. Steven Carpenter here?"

Sam's glare turns hard, but he nods. "I'm sorry. He's not exactly the most mobile at the moment. Can I ask why you need to see him?"

The second officer nods, but it's still the first one talking. "Yes, sir, we're running an internal investigation on recent events where Officer Paul Miller's gun was used with lethal force. And I can only say that much since it pertains directly to the questions we need to ask the both of you."

Letting out a big sigh, I turn to Sam, but he beats me to the plot. "If you'll bring 'em inside, I'll go relocate Steve to the living room, and call your bosses to let 'em know you'll be late." I don't even have to wonder why he didn't mention Xan or Gabe. If this is an investigation on Xan for shooting someone, they should already know I work for the guys. Still, probably better not to bring it up.

Soon, Steve and I are sitting on the old couch in the living room, Jake wedged between us. The two unknown officers—who still haven't given me their names—sit with Ross on Steve and Garret's couch, which is currently wedged into the room. But the guys were running out of space and just trying to shove everything in so they could take the truck back yesterday.

Officer number one sets a small recorder on the coffee table and then starts talking again. "So, Ms. Carpenter. From the information we've been provided, you and Mr. Steve Carpenter were present on the night of the shooting approximately two days ago?"

Steve and I both nod, and the officer nods in response, looking over the file that's open in his lap. "And...Ms. Carpenter, can you tell us, in your own words..." He throws a glare at Ross that I don't understand. "What happened, and what led up to a firearm being discharged at Mr. Carson?"

Steve and I spend the next half an hour or so going over being woken up and then assaulted by his dad. The officers stop us several times to clarify points; specifically, about Mr. Carson's goons and when Steve was shot the first time.

Officer number two finally speaks up. "Mr. Carpenter, please forgive me for a moment, but wasn't your last name Carson up until last week? Are you saying your own father shot you?" The man sounds skeptical at best, derisive at worst.

Steve's eyes are hard when he answers the question. "Yes, I am saying my own father shot me...twice, and it fucking hurt. He also shot our dog and threatened to have his fucking goons rape our beta so that we wouldn't want her anymore. Marc Carson was never a nice man. That didn't miraculously change when he followed us here."

The two unknowns share an indecipherable look, but Ross starts talking. "I'm awful sorry, Miss Kelly. I know you need to get to work, so let's move this on. Sunday morning, when all this shit happened...did you hear officer Paul Miller request the suspect lower his weapon and put his hands in the air?"

The two new officers are trying to talk over him, but Steve and I just nod in reply. Steve adds in, "At least a few times, I wasn't exactly counting, sorry."

Ross nods again. "And did either of you see Officer Paul shoot the suspect?" Steve and I both shake our heads.

Officer two throws up his skeptical look again, while officer one speaks for both of them. "I find it very hard to believe that you were both standing there, and failed to witness who might have shot Mr. Carson."

This time at least I have something to add. I unwrap the floral scarf I'm wearing so they can see the ugly purple bruises still around my neck, and don't bother to keep the rasp out of my voice. "Neither of us was standing anywhere. I was just waking up after being choked into unconsciousness by Mr. Carson's...employees. Jake was lying partly on top of me, blocking my vision, and Steve was doing a funky kind of pushup over us both after he was shot the first time, trying to keep me safe. Oh, by the way, it was really amazing how you managed to hold that for so long. Seriously, I'm impressed." This last part is said as an aside to Steve, who blushes at the compliment.

Ross starts talking again while the two others absorb this. "No, no, that makes sense. I remember that. Um...so, you can't say for certain, but the chances of say...someone walking over, plucking the gun out of Paul's hands, shooting Mr. Carson in the head, and then handing the gun back are pretty slim, right? I mean, what kind of crazy bastard would do something like that?" He meets my eyes with a smirk, because he knows exactly what kind of crazy bastard would do that.

Officer one stands up, his face angry. "Fucking hell, Ross. You're ruining the investigation. We can't get straight answers from anybody if you keep leading the witnesses like that. How the hell do you ever expect us to do our jobs and bring a possible murderer to justice if you keep blurting shit like that out?"

He turns to us, and his partner stands, glaring at Ross now. "Sir, ma'am. Thank you very much for your time and cooperation. We'll be in touch if we have any more questions." They berate Ross all the way out the door and down the steps, asking how no one in his department is able to give them clear answers. Ross smiles and waves as he hops in the backseat of their black SUV before they drive away.

Chapter 42

I can't believe that Vee got so much done in my nest. I mean, Kelly also did a lot with getting the room ready, and helping Sam with the drywall, and then washing all the blankets and linens and airing out my pillows...actually it smells a lot like she and Vee rolled around on them when they were unpacked. Of course, seeing as they left a couple of books in here, they probably just lounged here and read manga together. Even the thought of that makes me smile.

I still haven't had a chance to get curtains ordered, and Sam grumbles when I ask him to help me hang some extra blankets over the windows. Something about damaging his new walls. Well, tough. He also says he needs to go shopping for wood for baseboards, but I don't care about any of that right now. I think it's wonderful just the way it is. I just need to get the blankets and sheets on the bed and it'll be perfect.

Oh, and pillows, lots of pillows. Maybe I should take a few up to the master bedroom so that we can have them to sleep on and get everybody's scent on them...but they can't have them. I need them. They're so cozy and soft, and I just want to drag my Pixie in here and burrow under all the pillows with me, and then kiss her and taste her. Being apart for almost a week was awful. I never want to deal with that again.

I spend the next few hours making and remaking the bed. The mattress they got me is so nice, just the right amount of soft. But I can't get the stupid blankets right. It's all nice and clean, but it just doesn't smell right in here.

And why can't I get the fucking wrinkles out of this god-damned blanket!?

My crying brings Sam into my nest, and just *that* is so much better. His masculine cedar and sawdust makes me warm all over. And I just want to ask him to roll around on the bed for the next few hours until it's saturated with him.

Kelly's at work, otherwise I'd ask her too.

But Vee's here.

I bet he'd help.

Oh, but he's still kind of wobbly.

Well, that means lying down and rolling around should be easy.

Right?

Sam pulls me into his warm chest as we sit on the mattress on the floor. He grumbles an apology out for not making me a bed frame. And I want to throttle the big alpha. He built me a fucking nest, a perfect fucking nest that I love...but I need it to smell like him.

Would it be strange for me to ask him to take off his clothes so I could rub them around the clean sheets?

Shit.

He's gonna think I'm a freak.

"Um...Sam, have we done laundry yet from our trip? I need...something. Maybe everybody's pajamas. It doesn't smell right in here, and I can't...." Sam's face had taken on a small sweet smile while I was trying to figure out how to ask for clothes, but as soon as I start crying, he pulls me into his arms, purring loudly.

I don't fit in his lap as easily as Kelly, but hell, she's not much more than travel sized to start with. His breath is hot on my neck, and when he scrapes his teeth over my skin, I'm pretty sure I just soaked the front of his jeans in slick. Blushing like crazy, I want to crawl into a hole and die, but he won't let go. His voice is a low heated rumble. "Fuck, but you smell good, Omega. I thought we had a few more days before your heat started."

It sends a needy little shudder through me, and then his beard is scraping over the other side of my neck, his lips a soft contrast on the tender skin. "Can't wait to mark you." Kiss. "Bond you." Kiss. "Knot you until you're nothing but a twitching pile of well satiated omega mush."

If this keeps up, that won't be too far away. I dip my head so I can taste his lips, and moan into his mouth when he turns me so I'm straddling his body. He grabs my hips, grinding me down against the hard length trapped in his pants. My mind spins. I need to fix my nest, because it's wrong. But I need my alpha, because he tastes and feels so fucking good that I might spontaneously combust.

He stands up, letting me slide off his lap so that he can unbutton my jeans, and push them down my hips. His hand is big and calloused and when he strokes me, I come undone. I should be embarrassed, but his pleased smile throws me for a loop. "You are such a good fucking omega for me, aren't you?"

His hard kiss leaves my head spinning. "I want you Teddy...so fucking much it's taking everything I have not to fuck you right now and leave my bite on that sexy body of yours. But it feels wrong for it to be just the two of us in here. Unless you want that. We can lock the door, nice and private. But I thought you might want Kelly, at least for that part. If you need me to, I can lock the door now and take you. We can break in your new nest all alone. I just don't want you to regret it later."

His lips capture mine again, demanding and possessive, holding me captive with just a touch. If this keeps up, I'm going to fucking be hard again in a few seconds.

After entirely too short of a time, he pulls away with a long groan. "Fuck...tell me you want me now, tell me you want me to fuck you in your new nest, and screw waiting for everybody else. I'm losing my fucking mind with how goddamned good you taste."

But when I put my hands on his chest and gently push him back, he goes. It's fucking adorable to see my big gruff alpha with a pout like his favorite toy just got taken away, and it just makes me want him more. But he's right, I would feel bad about it later. Because while this nest is wonderful, it's not quite right yet, and the major thing missing is the scents of my pack.

I'm sure having a sexy little beta sprawled in it would help, too.

Sam

Logic tells me you can't actually die from a case of blue balls, but shit. Just because I brought up waiting for the rest of our pack, doesn't mean I'm happy that Teddy agrees. I want Kelly there, definitely, because with the three of us there's no effort, no jealousy. We just fit together.

Those boys have come a long way just in the last few weeks, and shit if I don't consider them mine too...but I have a feeling we still got a long way to go before we can all get along as well as a pack should. Garret only defers to me because Kelly does, but as long as he keeps in his lane, we're good. And Steve could be such a good boy, if he can keep his head out of his ass and learn to share.

Kelly having to go in to work and class today sucked, but I can understand her not wanting to skip. That girl's smart as all get out, and I'm still trying to figure out what she's doing settling for us. That being said, I know it's not really a beta thing, but if she'll let me, I want to bond her too. I want to be able to make sure she's safe no matter what.

Getting that damned call from Joseph this weekend damned near killed me, and if we were bonded, I would've at least been able to check in and make sure she was ok…probably, I don't really know how it works over long distances. Regardless, I just know that she's ours, and I want to make sure she knows that we'll do anything and everything we can to keep her happy if she'll have us.

The cops showing up on my doorstep this morning was a bit of a surprise, but I guess we should have expected it. After all, some guy was killed in my fucking driveway. It'd be strange if they didn't ask questions. I'm still waiting to hear back from my insurance about the shop, but I don't know how the hell I'm gonna work now. Some of those tools were fucking antiques. Things I had picked up and collected from garage sales or the like. There wasn't anything especially sentimental except that they were mine and they helped me start my business.

Sitting at the dining room table—trying to figure out how the hell I can take care of my pack—I wonder briefly where everyone's at. The house is so quiet right now. Teddy was still in the nest when I left. Steve was stretched out on the couch—keeping his healing leg elevated—with Jake. Kelly should be home from class soon. And Garret was upstairs, going through boxes to figure out what needs to be put in a spare room, and what can go in the master closet.

Fisting my hands in my hair, I give a rough tug. It's not like I have a ton of marketable skills. I could have made it pretty easy when it was just me and Jake. Cut back on the takeout and live off instant noodles for a few months until I get back on my feet. But that won't work now. Jake's medical bills, utilities, food...at least the mortgage is paid off, and we have a couple of months before it's gonna be air conditioner weather.

Fuck me hard, what the hell am I gonna do?

I probably shouldn't have spent so much on that fuckin' coffee maker.

Even with Garret going in half.

Especially with no idea of how long their bank card's gonna work.

But fuck it, can't exactly put a price on someone saving our beta.

I bet she lost it when she got to work this morning.

The corners of my lips twitch at the thought of Kelly getting to work and not having to fight the coffee-maker-that-time-forgot. True, I got it for Xan mostly, and Gabe by extension. The fact that she'll also benefit from it is just a bonus. I can just imagine her eyes lighting up. Seriously, I think if it wasn't for that coffee shop at her college, she would have only had drip brew before now.

That girl has the tastebuds of a toddler. It's both cute and infuriating that she refuses to eat anything green unless it's slathered in some sort of canned cheese sauce. An involuntary shudder runs through me. I know I've heard of people hiding veggies and stuff in desserts, not like a carrot cake, but like broccoli and zucchini in brownies. She's not a child, but if that's what I gotta try to make sure she stays healthy, I'll give it a shot. Hell, I'll try anything twice, on the off-hand chance I screwed it up the first time.

I'm still deciding if I want to make tacos tonight, when Kelly gets home. It is Tuesday, and those are usually loaded with onions, lettuce, and tomato, so it might work out. She smiles at me when she walks into the dining room. "Did you see Steve and Jake asleep on the couch? I'm gonna go grab a picture to send to Teddy since he's not in here. And maybe to use as blackmail later."

Her smile is huge, if a bit evil, and I stand up to give her a big hug and ask how her day went. She holds her fingers up to her lips and tiptoes back into the living room for a moment, before sneaking back in and wrapping me in a warm hug. Burying my face in her hair, I spend time just breathing her in. It feels so good to just hold her, like Teddy, and just reaffirms how right I was to suggest we wait—even if it sucked at the time.

When I finally let her go and she draws back, I lean down to kiss the top of her head. I can't seem to stop touching this girl. "So, how was work? Anything interesting happen?" I fully expect to hear about the new coffee machine. Which is why I'm surprised when she says that there was nothing major other than how late she was from having to talk to the officers this morning.

Doesn't it work?

Shit, did I get them something broken?

I mean, it should be under warranty if that's the case.

Still, I'll message Xan later and ask.

I can go get a replacement if they need me to.

She said that Spencer was livid about the bruises on her throat. She had them hidden under her scarf, but apparently Officers Paul and Josh had told him about them. We're both surprised to hear that he and Paul are in a pack together. Not that Paul told him much. But after she didn't go to school yesterday—and the fire—Spence was worried enough to annoy the older alpha until he talked.

Paul finally admitted that Kelly was probably just sore and didn't feel up to dealing with people. After getting that much out of his pack mate, he went to Josh—his best friend and Paul's younger brother—to get more details. Which Josh gave him, under the strict condition that he didn't tell anybody. So Spence was nearly in a panic, waiting in the parking lot for Kelly to get to school today.

"Oh, Sweetheart. How much longer for your birth control shot to start workin'? I'm pretty sure that Teddy's heat's about to start, and I need to know if we should stock the nest with condoms or...?" I let my sentence trail off, groaning when the scent of her arousal spikes the air.

Can we just skip dinner tonight?

I can carry Kelly to the nest, and Teddy and I can take turns feasting on her.

No, if his heat really is about to start, Teddy needs to eat to keep his strength up.

But if I happen to send her into the nest to deliver boxes of condoms, and they just happen to start to have fun, no one could blame me for joining.

I don't know if I can get that lucky.

She snickers at me. "Are you sure this isn't just some ploy to get me and Teddy into the nest together for sex so you can join?" She sees right through my fucking plan. But that's not a no either.

"Well, if you'd rather stay here, I was just about to start on tacos for dinner...but if you do feel like going to check on Teddy, and would like to take some of the condoms with you...just if we're still not sure that your shot is fully in effect. I'd be happy to come check on you in a couple of minutes to make sure everything's working out."

I know I'm probably smiling like an idiot right now, but she doesn't seem to mind. She stands on her toes to kiss me on the chin. "Oh no, whatever shall I do? I guess I better go make sure that the nest has enough rubbers to make it through Teddy's heat. It'd be a shame to run out at a crucial time like that." She nips at my neck and I damn near lose it in my goddamned pants, because seriously, all the two of them have to do is look at me and I'm ready to go.

Chapter 43

Kelly

W ork was long, school was long, Spence completely freaked out about this weekend and growled at several people in class who got even remotely close to me. I love Sam and I love Teddy, but all I want right now is to curl up with them and sleep. I'm just so danged tired. Still, Sam's not wrong about needing some supplies for the nest, probably just not the ones he mentioned.

My throat's still sore, but I don't want to tell anyone, because I'm certainly not complaining after Steve and Jake both got shot trying to protect me. I don't want to seem ungrateful, which deep down I know is ridiculous. We can all be injured, but I feel bad taking attention away from them right now. So I've tried to talk as normally as possible and pretend like nothing hurts. Having anyone dote on me makes me a little squirmy and uncomfortable.

Also, while I'm sure it would cool down their libidos if I mentioned how exhausted I was, I don't want them to feel bad for wanting me. Which sounds stupid even to myself. They missed me and want to be physically close after we were apart. But...I'm...still feeling kind of awkward. I joked last night with the new toy I got for Teddy's heat, but it's still uncomfortable, especially after some of what Marc said. They weren't just planning to choke me. That was just a bonus, I guess.

I retrieve a bottle of lube and some towels from the master bathroom and drag myself to the nest, feeling like if I close my eyes for more than a quick blink, I'll be asleep. The door is closed, so I knock gently. Teddy opens it, but his eyes look red and swollen. The mattress on the floor behind him has stacks of blankets and pillows, and it takes more willpower than I like to admit for me not to crawl under the piles of pillows and close my eyes.

Teddy doesn't look a heck of a lot better than me right now, so I let myself fall against him. We can hold each other up. My hands come up to cup his face and wipe a stray tear from his cheek. I don't even have to ask what's wrong. He nuzzles into my palm before picking me up and folding himself down on the mattress. I still huddle against his warm body, willing my eyes to stay open when his cozy cookie scent surrounds me.

"I missed you, Pixie." he murmurs against the top of my head, squeezing me tightly. "Any chance you feel up to cuddling up in here with me before dinner? I'm so damned tired, and I just want to hold you...plus while the nest smells a little like you, especially on those pillows." He points to the pile Steve and I were flopping on to read after we spent so much time cleaning on Saturday. "It's not enough. Will you be upset with me if I steal your pajamas from the last few days...or can you pick out a few pairs to wear that you're ok with me using for my nest afterwards?"

My poor omega, I forgot how sensitive their noses are. "Sorry, Teddy, I can totally pick out a couple of pairs that you can use, though I've really only got four that I wear and wash, and I threw those in the laundry before I left this morning. When I was living at home, I usually just wore a pair of panties to bed, but I didn't want to make anybody uncomfortable. Would it be any easier if we all sleep down here for a few days?"

He groans against the top of my head. "You mean I could have been cuddled up to an almost naked beta this whole time?" His low chuckle sounds less sad than his voice before. "Maybe we should get you some more pajamas, because I'm pretty sure if you do that here, you'll never get any rest." He takes a deep breath against my hair, and his purr starts, making my body melt into his.

"I'm sorry, Teddy. I'm just so tired today. Cuddles sound amazing...but I gotta warn you that Sam's probably gonna be here soon for more than snuggles. He seemed so excited about breaking in the nest, I didn't tell him I was worn out. And we *can* play, if you both want to...I'm just not gonna be the most enthusiastic participant this evenin'...sorry."

His purr stutters out, and he squeezes me before pulling back enough to look into my eyes. "Oh, Pixie, I would be happy...ok, not happy...but I would accept if I was only ever able to snuggle you and never actually have sex. I want you, so does Sam, but if you don't feel up to it, that's fine. We can always just play together, or make Garret come and give you cuddles while we play with Steve. Though with the way you two were getting along while we were gone, would you rather have cuddles from Steve instead?"

I fake some retching noises, looking up at my grinning omega. "Sorry, but I'm pretty sure Steve and I have come to an understanding. As much as he steals my clothes and books, it's more like an irritating sibling that I have to share my boyfriends with. Heck, I think he even stole my chap-stick last week. Who does that? It was pomegranate flavor and now it's just gone from the bathroom."

He lets out a light laugh at my rambling grumpiness, before stretching us out on the bed, positioning me in front of his big warm body, so he's my big spoon. "Well, as long as you're ok with sharing, and he stops trying to start shit, then we're good. I love you, Pixie. I love that you accept me and Sam despite what you're used to. I love that my best friend growing up has fallen head over heels for you, too. I even love that Vee is now your sassy gay best friend."

My head jerks around, staring at him, and he snorts another laugh. "He told me about the diner. What a bitch. Alpha chaser, really? Couldn't she come up with something better to be snarky about...like blanket thief, or coffee tease...cheese novice?"

He snickers against the back of my head and my eyes slowly drift closed. My mumbled reply of, "Asshole," sets off another burst of laughter as my body finally gives in to the warm comfort he's offering, and my mind drifts off.

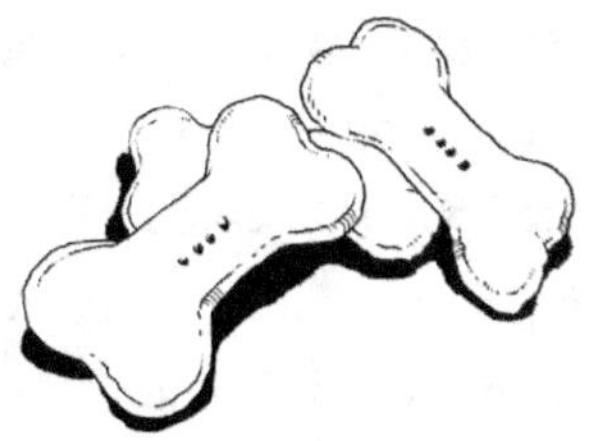

I wake up when the bed shifts, and the body behind me moves away. Mumbled voices filter through my consciousness, and I can't quite make out what they're saying. There's a heated discussion, and I hear Sam's low growl filtering through the room. Teddy's not behind me anymore, but a warm body lies down in front of me. The salty scent of Garret fills my nose as he cuddles close to me.

Burying his face in my hair, all the tension in his body seems to melt, but with all the other grousing, I'm slowly coming fully awake. My stomach lets out a loud rumble, and I can feel his smile against the side of my head. "Are you hungry, Sweetness?

Sam tried to come in earlier, but Teddy growled at him and told him you were asleep."

Sam's fresh cut cedar scent washes over me as big arms come around me from behind and warmth settles against my back. "You know, Sugar, if you'd just told me you just wanted cuddles earlier, I would have listened. You never have to pretend to be ok. I'm sorry I didn't realize how out of it you were. You're just always so upbeat. I didn't think about it. I'm sorry." He rubs his whiskers against the back of my neck, and I nearly come off the bed with a loud, shrieking giggle.

A big hand wraps around my ankle, dragging me to the end of the bed, and then pulling me up and cradling me against a warm cookie scented chest. "Leave Kelly alone. She doesn't feel good. I told you, her neck hurts and she's tired." Teddy's voice is a low growl, and both Sam and Garret curse behind me. I try to push out of my omega's hold, not wanting to be a problem, but he starts to purr and I have to struggle to keep my eyes open.

"Teddy, I'm fine. Seriously, it doesn't hurt that bad. They can snuggle me. I don't want anybody to feel like I don't want 'em around."

Sam growls beside us, but Teddy talks over him. "Pixie, I tried to cuddle you earlier. You whimpered whenever I got close to your neck. Don't lie to me, Love, you're definitely not ok. Now, you can tell me how you're really doing, and what's on your mind, or I can be an overprotective, possessive asshole about it until you decide to."

It surprises me how much the idea of that appeals to me, Teddy being overprotective, *not* telling my guys what's really on my mind. But it's not fair to them. My gaze flips around the room till I find Steve by the door. His eyes meet mine and he gives a small shrug before looking back at the floor. He was with me this week, so he heard what his dad threatened, but he's telling me it's my choice, and I appreciate that.

Still, Teddy told me and Sam something similar happened to him. Maybe we should both come clean and hope like crazy that Garret's head doesn't explode since he's gonna get twice the surprise. I push off Teddy's chest and he sets me down with a muttered grumble.

"This room's a lot bigger than I realized. Even with all five of us in here, it doesn't feel cramped." My voice is overly bright and chipper as I try to change the subject.

True to form, Teddy calls me out. "Yes, my nest is lovely. Thank you for doing so much work on it...all of you. Now, spill Pixie. What's wrong?"

I'm saved from having to answer by my stomach growling again, and then Sam is ushering us all out of the room. He leads us all to the table and insists that I sit down while he fixes me a plate of Spanish rice, refried beans, and tacos...which he loads down with lettuce and tomato. I don't mind the onion so much, but he just laughs at me when I throw a glare his way.

We reconvene to the living room after dinner, and I realize they've rearranged the furniture while I was asleep—I must have missed that when I came through earlier. The old couch is pushed up against the wall directly in front of the coat closet, and the big sectional that Steve and Garret brought from L.A. is wrapped around the coffee table. Jake lies in the corner on his back, his coned head facing me, and his tail making loud thumping noises when I come into the room.

Jake grunts loudly and tries to roll over to scoot next to me, but Sam takes the spot between us, scratching between my fuzzy buddy's ears. Teddy sits on my other side, and Steve and Garret take the other end of the couch. Steve sits next to Jake, gently stroking a hand down the big dog's back. He was never mean to Jake before, but now he goes out of his way to show affection, and Jake is milking his injuries for all they're worth.

My voice starts out shaky, but steadies as I go on. "So, Steve already knows about this, but it kinda relates to Teddy, too. If you feel up to talking afterwards, I think it'd be good. But it's your choice. I'm...I don't want to think about this, so I'm gonna say it once. Then it's done. Please don't ask again, ok?"

My voice cracks a few times as I tell them about waking up and the call to 911. Seeing Marc in the front yard, and then the threats he made about how nobody would want me after they were done, but at least I'd be broken in. Four loud snarls and one whimper from Jake meet that particular revelation. They continue even as I turn to Steve and explain about blacking out, not remembering anything until I woke up under his bleeding body.

Sam nods at the injured alpha, and Garret wraps one arm around Steve, pulling him into a half hug. His whispered,

"Thank you," is almost inaudible. Teddy looks both horrified and relieved as he stares across the couch at the man he has such conflicting feelings towards. After a long pause, Steve picks up the story and explains his and Jake's end of what happened. Including, but not limited to, how they both got shot. I'm a bit surprised it hasn't come up yet. My throat hurts, so I've barely been able to talk, but I thought he would have said something before now to our pack. We talked to the police this morning, so it's just surprising that this is news to all of them.

Once Steve and I are done, I turn to Teddy, and he looks near tears himself. Though if it's from anger or worry, I don't know. "Well, I guess I can see what you mean now. Shit, I didn't want to have this conversation...ever." He looks from Garret to Steve and back, slowly unbuckling the leather around his wrists. When he unwraps them, I'm surprised again by the difference in skin tone.

Both twins gasp as he rolls his wrists over, and a loud sob breaks from Steve. He suspected, we both did. But suspecting and knowing aren't the same thing. Conversely, Garret's mouth is set in a grim line as he stares between the three of us. When he does speak, his voice is a broken croak. "Fuck, Teddy. I'm...I'm so fucking sorry. We...we didn't. Shit. I mean...fucking fuck!" He nearly screams the last part, but Teddy's low chuckle draws him up short.

"At least let me tell you what happened before you try to take all the blame? A month ago, I would have let you...but now...you deserve the truth. Sam and Kelly are the only ones who've heard this, and it was just while you two were at the hospital on Sunday." Steve nods dumbly, eyes fixated on the pale skin, as Teddy tells them the story of the meeting with their dad, and the threat to his family.

By the time Teddy finishes, Sam has pulled me into his lap and tugged our omega directly beside him so he can wrap his arms around us. He's making quiet murmuring noises against the side of Teddy's head as he tries to rock us back and forth. Teddy has gone slightly green, like he's about to lose his tacos. Steve and Garret are both snarling on the other couch, and I hear one of them mutter, "Should have killed the bastard myself." Probably Steve, since Garret wasn't here. Unless they're talking about an earlier time.

Sam looks over at them both. "Which reminds me, you need to call the hospital tomorrow and set up that testing. Also, can you ask about how long it'll take for Teddy to do...whatever he needs to do to get tested to check about matching with Brice?" Teddy jerks and now it's my turn to ask for an explanation.

We're all up until late in the night talking, exchanging stories about what happened to each group over the last week. And by the time we finish, everyone's emotionally exhausted. At Sam's suggestion, we all pile into the nest. He says it's so the nest can smell like all of us before Teddy's heat. Steve jokes about the lack of stairs being a bonus for me and I set my alarm for a half an hour early. There won't be any sunlight coming in here to wake me up, and I am definitely gonna need a shower before I head to work.

Chapter 44

Garret

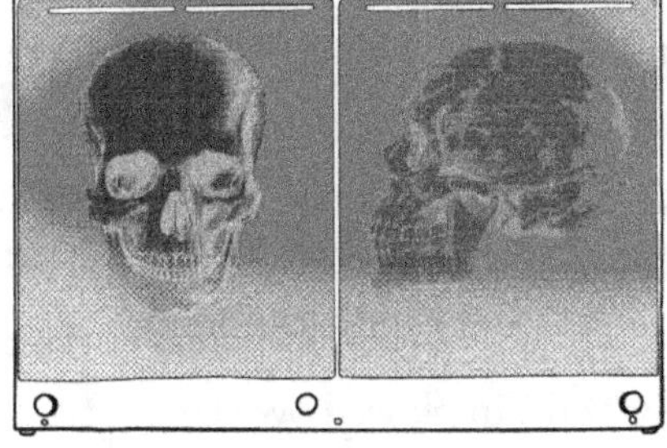

Wednesday is a whirlwind, with Kelly getting up for work early to make sure she's there before the owners to get the ancient coffee maker working. Which is puzzling after we dropped off a new one that she hasn't mentioned.

I *do* call the hospital and schedule my MRI that Dr. Baxter sent in for me. It won't be until next week, but with Teddy's heat on the horizon, that's fine. They also set up Teddy's swab test for the bone marrow matching at the same time. He could go in at any time to do it, but he's really emotional and hormonal right now, and it just makes sense to get it all done in one trip.

I drive her to work and then bring her lunch so I can drive her to school. After what she told us last night regarding my father, I'm in a constant state of near panic about her safety. There's the

375

large alpha that follows her around school, and while I don't like it, he seems protective enough that he can keep her safe while I'm not there. It also gives me someone to talk to while I wait for her. I'll need to find a job soon, because even before Sam lost his shop, I refused to be completely useless. I want to make good enough money that I can give Kelly whatever she might want. My sweet girl deserves to be spoiled.

I walk up to the house behind her, knowing that I'm hovering. I just can't seem to help it. Every instinct I have is screaming at me to keep her safe. She was already attacked here once, and who knows what could be lurking around the corner to take her away from me? The need to bite and claim only intensifies as she opens the door and I'm plowed over by a fucking freight train of pheromones.

Smells like my packmates had an interesting day. Sam and Vee sit on the couch, each with a glass of water and a worn down expression. Kelly rushes over to Sam, hovering and trying to figure out what's wrong. I know she's a beta, but can't she tell from the scent? If Teddy's not already in heat—and going by my pack sitting on the couch instead of being in the nest with him, he's not—then he will be by tonight. So what the hell are these two doing out here?

Steve answers my unspoken question. "My bear kicked us out. He wants to make sure the room's perfect and refuses to let us in until Kelly gets home from school. All because he wants her to be the first one to see all his work." He sneers at my beta, and going by the uncomfortable-looking bulge in his jeans, I can understand a bit of the snark. Shit, I don't even want Teddy, but the fucking omega pheromones that are trying to drown me demand that I take Kelly into the other room and lick her down to the gooey center.

Sam grumbles from the other end of the sectional. "Fine, yes, now, how about instead of bitching out the beta for something she has no control over, we see if she feels up to talking to Teddy before I lose my fucking mind. I'm fine taking matters into my own hand at this point, but if his heat's starting and he needs us, I don't want to be...um...out of juice, so to speak."

Kelly lets out a tired sigh—she's still worn down, even if she doesn't like to admit it—and walks down the hallway to the newly refurbished nest. Her knock is quiet on the door, and it's only a moment later that Teddy answers—like he was just waiting for her. Maybe he was. The big omega opens the door enough to stick his head out. His skin is flushed, his hair a wild tangle around his head, and the scent that bursts forth from the room is gonna leave me with a fucking zipper indent in my raging erection.

I let out a tiny whimper when he takes Kelly's hand and gently pulls her into the room. I can see the look of surprise and awe on her face when she peers inside—before he closes the door, effectively shutting out all the alphas in the house.

The door muffles most of the sound, but I hear Kelly's voice. "Teddy, it's gorgeous. Your nest looks amazing." I imagine the big omega preening at her praise. I've seen catalog displays for nests before, we all have, but each one is unique for its owner.

While many of the store examples are in soft pastels and cream tones, everything Teddy had was dark tones or black. Like some sort of gothic fairytale prince.

Of course, he could probably pull off the goth vibe easily, except he's too broad. I can see why so many people mistake him for an alpha. He looks just like one, and if it weren't for his scent, it'd be impossible to realize he's an omega. Heck, seeing him with my brother, I'd peg Steve for the omega of the pair. But now I'm just trying to distract myself from the sound of Kelly's clear laughter that filters from the room. I'm torn between wanting to retreat to the living room with the guys, or press my ear to the door to hear more of her voice.

I am so fucking wound up for this girl, and I hope like hell she lets me mark her and bond her during this heat. Am I even going to be able to stay in the room, or is it going to get too strange with three other men? My brain is all tangled up between emotion and instincts, and I very nearly scream at being pulled in different directions.

Before my mind can decide which way to go, the door opens again, flooding the hallway with Teddy's fucking perfume. But now it has that subtle touch of lilac that I love so much. Kelly reaches out and takes my hand, looking at Teddy for confirmation before she drags me in.

Sam and Steve are not gonna be happy that I'm coming into the nest before them, but screw it. I look around the room, and while we all slept in here last night, it's nearly unrecognizable now.

The blankets are still over the walls, but they've been secured all the way, so not even a hint of daylight intrudes into Teddy's sanctuary. He's strung small star-shaped lights all across the ceiling, not enough to make the room bright, but you can comfortably see the nest in the dim ambience. All of his pillows and blankets have been spread across the mattress, not a wrinkle in sight as huge mounds of softness curve around a bowl shape in the mattress.

He pulls Kelly into his arms, his whine a high screaming pitch in my head that tells me to do whatever I have to, so he just stops making that sound. Thankfully, as soon as she wraps her arms around his neck and leans up to kiss him, it morphs into a bone melting purr. I need to escape before I'm pulled into something I want no part of. But I'm stuck, wanting my beta, but not wanting to pull her away from someone who makes her happy.

They break apart, and Kelly is panting, her lips red and swollen. She stares up at the omega with a glazed expression of wonder. Despite wanting to be careful about how close I get to him, I'm drawn to her, wrapping my arms around her waist and pulling her back against me. Kelly's hands stay around his neck, and Teddy is tugged along for the cuddles as I bury my face in her neck and scrape my teeth along the tender skin there.

She lets out a soft shuddering moan, and my hips unconsciously jerk against her. I need this woman like I need my next breath. My exhale comes out in a needy moan as she tilts her ass against me, grinding into my length. One hand comes up to cup her breast through the thick fabric of her work shirt, and that doesn't feel right. She shouldn't be in such uncomfortable clothes. Both hands drop to her waist, struggling with the stupid button on her jeans, as my chest rattles in a frustrated growl.

Kelly, my dear, sweet, incredibly ticklish, Kelly lets out a loud shriek of laughter and struggles loose from where she's sandwiched between us. Her breathing is fast, and her cheeks are bright red. My teeth have left pink streaks across her shoulder from where I was tasting her skin. Teddy looses another omega whine, but it doesn't have the same tone of desperation as before. So while I still feel the need to fix whatever's wrong, it's no longer like a storm of needles in my brain.

It doesn't take Kelly long to catch her breath and move closer again, but at least my mind is a bit clearer. I open the door, needing to escape. At least get a few moments of fresh air, but Sam and Steve are both standing on the other side. Sam looks around me, taking in all the work Teddy's done to the room while we were out today, and Steve glares at me. Like I *wanted* to be in here before him.

Then Kelly's there. She wraps her arms around my neck like she did with Teddy earlier, but even standing on her tiptoes, she can't quite reach for a proper kiss. I hear a loud moan from my brother as the omega descends on him, and soon Steve is trapped between Sam and Teddy like Kelly was pinned between us earlier.

Turning back to Kelly, I reach under her hips, lifting her and wrapping her thighs around my waist. I wish I had thought about it before, but we have entirely too many clothes on for this position, and my cock already feels like it's ready to rip through the two layers of denim. One of my hands lets go of her thighs and slides up and over her ass, squeezing tightly before dipping under her shirt and tracing the smooth skin of her back.

I've never had to undo a bra before, and I fear that this may be technology beyond my capabilities as I pull back from Kelly's lips, staring frustratedly over her shoulder. What the hell is this thing closed with, a goddamned combination lock? She laughs again at my fumbling and slides down my front, leaving me gasping and aching for the feel of her in my arms. Reaching behind with both hands, she smiles at me, before peeling her shirt and bra both off at once. Giggling again at my look of shock.

What sorcery is this...Does it require two hands? Sadly, there's no time to contemplate the mysteries of the universe—or women's underclothes—with my beta standing topless before me. I want to fall at her feet, worship her like the goddess she is, spend the rest of my life making sure she knows that she's my life.

Instead, I stare at her, entranced, while she waves her fingers at me. "I think you have on entirely too many clothes for the nest, Alpha. Seriously, you're still wearing shoes. My mother would have a fit." Her smile is huge, eyes twinkling at me.

"Do you really want to be thinking of your mother while you're half dressed in a room with four men, Sweetness?" Her face scrunches in a pout.

"Ew...no...ugh, why'd you make me think like that? Now it's stuck in my head. Strip, Alpha, so I can think of something better." I nod. Her wish is my command, and it's the work of a moment to have my shoes off and set outside the door, followed quickly by my jeans and shirt. When I turn back around, my beta has stripped too. I've seen her naked, of course, even touched her once, but...I'd be lying if I said I wasn't still astonished that she's mine...ours.

My gaze flicks over to the nest. A quick dart of my eyes to see that everyone else is still here, but I'm inexorably drawn back to the sweet woman in front of me.

Chapter 45

Kelly

Garret really is beautiful. I know I said he was a pretty boy, but it wasn't a completely accurate description. He's tall, like most alphas, with long, lean muscles that show no signs of strain as he stalks across the floor, lifting me, and wrapping my thighs back around his narrow hips. His purr starts again, and I melt into him—my body undecided if it wants to be aroused or relaxed.

I know I'll need to be relaxed if I'm going to take his knot. I've been working on stretching almost every evening with the toys Teddy helped me pick out. And while Garret's not small, he's not as big as Sam. That still worries me a bit.

He drops his head to my shoulder and groans against my neck. His breath tickles my skin and makes me squirm against him, which just presses his hard length against my core. His muffled grunt of, "Fuck," and the scrape of his teeth over the column of my throat make me want to do it again. So I do—wiggling my hips until his hands clamp down on them.

"Fuck...Kelly, you feel too good. Please. I need just a second...I've never...Fuck."

Wait.

Hold the phone.

Back up.

Garret's a virgin?

How the heck did that happen?

We've been living together for a few weeks now.

How did I not know this?

I really want to ask, but I don't want to embarrass him either.

It's not like I have a plethora of experience myself.

Even if I've been using toys every night for over two weeks straight.

Jeeze, I must look like some kind of sex maniac next to this guy.

Do I stay here hanging off of him like some sort of deranged lemur?

Should I get down and give him space?

I unwind my legs, but he won't let me go, his hands wrapping around my thighs and holding me close to him. "I didn't say stop, Sweetness, I said give me a second." Instead of the tickle from earlier, his hot breath makes me shiver—especially when his tongue traces down the line of my throat. "Are you going to let me bite you, Kelly? Mark you? Bond you, so I'll always be able to find you?" Each question is punctuated by a small nip of his teeth against my neck, and I can feel how slippery he makes me.

I don't make slick like an omega, but I sure as heck feel like I've got a slip-n-slide situation in my nethers right now. Unfortunately, Garret's stopped moving. Oh, is he waiting for an answer? Shit, I thought that might be an alpha version of dirty talk...Sam said something similar before. Does he really want to bond me?

Do I want that?

The longer I think about it, the more it feels right. Do I need to bite him back? Does it even work for betas? "Please, Garret. I need you. I want your mark." And it's true. I've contemplated it with Sam and Teddy, but as it turns out, I want to bond with Garret, too. I want to always be able to find him and know what he's feeling.

His hands tighten on my hips, pushing me away. I panic for a moment before realizing he's just pulling me back so he can get inside. I'm so wet that he glides in easily, and then he pulls me hard against his body again. His head draws back to look at me, his face flushed as he meets my eyes. "Oh, god...Kelly. You feel so fucking good. I didn't...I had no idea. Just...fuck. What do I...I'm not gonna last, but I need you to feel good. What...er...please gimme some guidance here, Love."

He looks like he might be in pain, and his breath comes in harsh pants as he stares down, meeting my eyes. The friction and stretch already feel amazing, but I arch my back so I can look down between our bodies where we're connected. His gaze follows mine and he lets out another loud groan at seeing himself disappearing inside of me. His knot is already slightly swollen—am I really thinking of trying to fit that inside? Sure, I've been practicing...no time like the present, I guess.

"Take your thumb and trace little circles around my clit." My own voice sounds breathy and lost as I watch his hand lower between us. The first touch is almost too much and my hips spasm and twitch, causing him to grit his teeth. "Now, gently to start. That's it."

He pistons his hips again. The rhythm of his touch along with the slide of his body inside mine, making my mind foggy with pleasure. "Keep going...oh...Garret. Like that, just...oh, right there. Please. Don't stop." He says he's never done this before, but his fingers are long and very talented and soon I can feel myself coming undone around him.

My body twitches, and I can feel him getting thicker as I clench around his length. His thumb freezes. "Holy shit...Kelly. What the...what are you doing?" His hips are bucking against me, his knot pounding against my entrance with every thrust.

I pull my chest closer to him, trapping his hand between us so I can whisper in his ear. "Knot me, please. Garret. I wanna feel all of you when you mark me."

His voice is almost gone, his teeth gritted. "You're sure?" I love that he checks in with me. I nod and he goes almost feral. His voice nothing but a loud snarl as he grabs both my hips and slams me up and down against him. The stretch is there, I can feel it, but it doesn't hurt. Just an urgent pressure. Once, twice, three times, he's hitting that inside spot so good, and suddenly the pressure is too much as he slams me down, his knot slips inside and finishes expanding.

It pushes against my inner walls with the most amazing sensation. Now that he's inside, it's not even uncomfortable, just full...so full. His loud shout echoes around the room, and then he pulls me close, sinking his teeth in my shoulder, right against my neck. Stars burst behind my eyes and I cry out as my muscles tense and twitch, pulling me so tight. His mouth comes loose and I feel his tongue tracing over the slight sting in my skin, kissing his way up my neck and claiming my mouth.

"Your turn, Sweetness. Are you up for claiming me back?" My mouth waters at the thought. I really never considered biting anyone before, but as a warmth blooms in my chest, it feels like him. It's my choice, but I want this. I want him. Always. It's hard to get the leverage, but after a moment of watching me struggle, Garret bends his knees, collapsing into a cross-legged position on the floor. It pulls his knot against me, and makes me wince a little, but brings me into position.

"Um...right here?" I trace my tongue over the area where his shoulder meets his neck. He nods, barely, and his hand comes up to cup the back of my head. A gentle encouragement.

His voice is barely a breath against my skin, "Please, Kelly." I bite down...then bite down harder because this takes a bit more jaw strength than initially anticipated. The salty copper taste of him teases my tongue.

I've bitten hard enough to draw blood, and apparently that's enough as my senses reel from his stormy night ocean scent filling my sinuses. It's oddly refreshing. At the same time my tongue feels like I licked a battery from the lightning in the distance. I pull back, kissing the torn skin and following the column of his throat back to his lips.

He has a soft, sweet smile on his face. And I can feel the love and near obsession levels of devotion deep in my chest. It doesn't feel warm like I expected, it's more like that full-body shudder you get when you slide under a cool blanket on a warm night. Your whole body just relaxes and gives a happy little shiver. Except in that case, you know it won't last. With Garret, I'll always have that happy little shiver.

I rest my forehead against his, just breathing him in, feeling him inside my chest, and the pressure lower down. It doesn't last long before his knot deflates and my hips relax back, letting him slide free. Still, he holds me, his alpha purr soothing my sore muscles before laying sweet gentle kisses down my neck and over the mark he's left. "I love you...I know I said that, but now you can hopefully feel it. Thank you for loving me back." My eyes drift closed as I settle against him, just floating on a cloud of bliss.

Chapter 46

Sam

Watching another alpha mark Kelly first, I'm surprised by how unbothered I am. I expected to be jealous or at least feel a bit aggressive. However, even watching them cuddled up on the floor, waiting for his knot to soften, the only thing I can really think about is how much I wish they had something soft and comfortable to relax against. Still, I refuse to make presumptions about Teddy's nest, so if he wants to invite them in, it's entirely his choice.

I still plan to bond both of them...all four of them. I don't know, but definitely Kelly and Teddy. They're mine. Maybe Steve...Garret...as long as there's no sex involved, maybe. Turning my gaze back to Teddy and Steve, my omega sits on the edge of his nest. His legs opened wide, fingers tangled in the alpha's hair. Steve kneels between his splayed thighs. There's a low moan, but I'm not sure which one it comes from.

Teddy's already peeled off all of his clothing. He wasn't wearing a shirt when we came in, saying it was too itchy. He must have lost his pants while I was creeping on our beta. Steve's still dressed in his long-sleeved shirt. It's now officially out of place. Three people in this room are naked. The omega that he has proclaimed as the love of his life is going into heat. He's going down on said omega, and despite how flushed his face is, he's wearing a long-sleeves and jeans. The only concession he's made is to pull his cock out.

This just feels too off kilter. Still, watching him work Teddy over with his mouth—our omega's head thrown back, eyes squeezed shut—I'd hate to interrupt them. Instead, I take my time, watching them as I peel my own clothes off. Teddy opens his eyes and reaches over, grabbing at my shirt when I remove it. I'm not hugely surprised. He did mention wanting to make sure the nest smelled like us.

I slide my jeans and jockeys down before stepping out of them, handing them to Teddy in case he wants them as well. I'm hard as a fucking rock with all the pheromones in the air. I kneel behind Steve, fist his hair, and yank his head back. We still have to be careful. The clothes cover his bandages, but he's still injured.

Teddy lets out a low groan, his own hands dropping to the side as he watches us, a large drop of pre-come leaking out of his hard dick and running down. I push Steve's head forward and his tongue comes out to catch it.

"You're the only one still dressed, Little Alpha. Don't you want to show our omega how much you need him?" Steve gives a little whimper and I pull his head back and up, close to enough that I can speak quietly, just to him. His body bows towards the bed, his erection straining towards Teddy. Our omega licks his lips, but I shake my head when he looks at me, and he sticks his bottom lip out in an adorable pout.

"Tell me. Why are you still dressed? What exactly are you hiding under your long shirts? I was really hoping that after the last few days we were past secrecy. You seem to know all of ours now. If it's something upsetting, maybe I can help."

After meeting his father and hearing some of what the rest of my pack dealt with at his hands, I'm not surprised to hear his faint whisper of, "Scars." I smile at his trust and nod against him so he can feel it. Then I lean down and gently bite the side of his neck. It's not where I want to leave my mark, but with his shirt on, it'll be impossible to mark him properly.

His whole body shudders as I twist my wrist to pull the hair at the base of his scalp and bite against his neck again, harder. He lets loose a long keening cry as he orgasms, splattering the floor and his pants.

"Well, well. Looks like you made a mess, Little Alpha. Gonna have to get you cleaned up now." I slide my hand up his back, under the long shirt that he wears as armor. His breath comes out in harsher pants as I feel a myriad of bumps and ridges where our skin touches.

If that son of a bitch wasn't dead, I'd fucking kill him myself. Still, if we're going to be a pack, he can't hide the entire time. I look around the room. Teddy is watching us intently. Kelly is sitting cross-legged in Garret's lap now, both staring at us. Neither of them seems as surprised as our omega or myself when I slide the shirt up to reveal a torso swirling in black ink.

I've changed hands so that I only have to release his hair for a moment to get his shirt off—peeling gently down his shoulder—and my breath catches for a moment at the sight. It's too dim in here to see any scars, but I feel them, lurking below the monochromatic canvas of his skin. I wonder briefly if there's a pattern in the tattoos, but now's the time to reassure him. We can talk more later.

"Nobody can see the scars, Vee, it's too dark. Your skin's beautiful. You *will* need to tell me about these later, though." I run my hand around his waist and up and over his chest.

Looking down his torso, the only image I can fully make out is also the only one not made of solid black ink—a tiny teddy bear with a red heart. It's obvious who that's for. He shudders against me again, and I let his body unbow, pulling him into me, and holding tightly while he takes deep gasping breaths.

Still, we just installed this damned floor, so I throw his long-sleeved shirt over the puddle of come he left—we'll need to clean properly later. Teddy meets my eyes, and I nod this time.

He slides off the bed, kneeling in front of us, and goes to wrap his arms around the shivering alpha.

His eyes go wide, and I hear the small, "Oh," escape as he takes in the tiny bear tattoo. Reaching out like he wants to touch it, I grab his hand before he makes contact. I have no doubt that it's covering another scar. The alpha in my arms is broken enough as it is, and I don't want him to panic at the contact. We can give him a bit more time.

Teddy

My mind is fuzzy, stuffed with cotton-y clouds of need. But even through the haze I can tell something's wrong with Vee. Sobbing and twitching isn't the reaction that's expected after you come...at least not in my experience. But Sam has him, and I trust my alpha to take care of us.

Unfortunately for Sam, I need him right now as well. The cramps aren't too bad yet, but they'll get progressively worse without a knot. I want to explore Vee. I want to taste his whole body. Lick my way down his stomach and take him in my mouth like he took me.

I want to taste both my alphas, but if somebody doesn't fuck me soon, it's gonna get really unpleasant. Reaching forward, I capture Vee's face, pulling us together so I can touch him, savor his lips. He twitches when my hands slide behind his neck, and Sam shakes his head at me again. Ignoring my bigger alpha I pull Vee towards me, my mouth capturing his as our bodies press together—and earn myself a low warning growl from Sam in the process.

But I don't care. I need him. Fuck, I've needed him since before my designation came in. Now that my hormones are rolling over me like a freight train, I feel like I might scream if I can't touch him. Sam's growl cuts out when Vee's arms circle my waist, pressing us tighter, and all I feel is bliss at finally having him with me. His mouth opens under mine, surrendering as my tongue dips inside.

He groans into my mouth and I swallow the sound, desperate for more of him. His hands grip my hips, pulling me tight against him. He's already hard again, but the zipper on his jeans chafes my skin, and I push lightly against his chest to help him slide them down. He whines pitifully, his lips trying to reach mine again. He tries to pull me back, then looks surprised when I grit out, "Jeans...stabby...off."

Sam chuckles beside us, and I didn't even realize that our big alpha had moved. "He's gotta point there, Little Alpha. You don't want to risk hurting him, do ya?"

Vee's hands drop as he struggles with the tight denim. It's harder to peel off with his earlier release soaking through the fabric, and he lets out a loud snarl when he nearly destroys the zipper in his rush.

Then he's on me again, pushing me to the floor, nearly feral as he bites and sucks my skin. His breath coming out in a series of tiny whines and whimpers as he bites down against my throat, his teeth scraping over the tender flesh. My body shudders under him at the sensation. I've never seen this side of Vee before. He was always the submissive one when we've been together, but having him on top of me, pinning me, taking what he needs…it's fucking hot.

Not that I can let it continue, at least not for long. Vee stalls out, his kisses turning tender and sweet. His body stutters like he's not sure what to do, and I wrap my fingers in his hair so I can sink my teeth into the delectable skin where his shoulder meets his neck. I don't break the surface, not yet—I need to be fucking him when I claim him. Soon though.

The air shifts around us, and I use my hand to turn his head. Our combined gazes traveling up the long legs and thick thighs of our alpha. It's a long-damned way to look up, and he chuckles when he sees us staring. But holy fucking shit. I've seen Sam naked before, but not from this angle. Scrambling to get off the floor, I drag Vee with me so we're kneeling in front of the head of our pack. I want to lick him like a fucking popsicle.

Clearly, I'm not the only one, since Vee leans forward next to me. Sam shudders as we make contact, my tongue tracing along the thick vein that throbs down his length. Vee seems content to focus on the base, paying extra care and attention to the bigger alpha's knot, licking and sucking the skin. Seeing it makes me want to jump him again. Fuck him hard and fast...maybe while Sam takes me from behind.

My hormones are insane, and a high needy whine slips out, drawing both of the alphas' attention. Sam grabs my hair, pulling me up so I'm standing in front of him. Vee seems to take that as an invitation to stroke me, and I let out a low whimpering moan as Sam drags my mouth to his before pulling away. "Invite us into your nest omega. I need to claim you properly." His voice is a low growl, almost feral with need—I scramble to obey.

My inner omega is careful of all the work I've done, cautiously climbing into the round space I've created on the mattress and looking back at my waiting alphas. My gaze flicks over to Kelly and Garret, and he's still holding her. Even with my hormones going nuts all over the room, he seems content to just sit there forever. His face buried in her neck, rocking her back and forth. She looks up, meeting my eyes—her sweet smile captivates me.

My mind spins, trying to figure out how to get all my mates in the nest together. I hold my hand out to Sam, and the feeling of his big rough fingers wrapping around mine sends a shiver all the way down my spine. Vee is next since he's closest and just follows behind Sam like a lost puppy. Garret can come in. Even if he's not mine, he's Kelly's and I need her. Vee won't like her being here, but he can just suck it because she's mine too.

I hold my hand out to Kelly as well, and while she seems hesitant at first, Garret stands behind her, nudging her gently towards the bed. Her hesitance seems to have less to do with not wanting to come into my nest, and more the fact that she doesn't know what to do. I mentally chide myself for not going over everything beforehand—forgetting that she's a beta. She just melds so seamlessly into my life that I don't think about how different our backgrounds are.

She climbs over the low wall of pillows, and trips. I wonder briefly how she's survived this long, especially with her childhood bedroom being upstairs. Garret and Sam both throw their arms out to catch her, but she slams into my chest, anyway. It's not until I look down that I notice the new bite mark on the tender skin of her shoulder, and while part of me is a little jealous, the other part is just glad she has so many other people to help me take care of her.

Placing a gentle kiss on her lips, I turn her back towards Garret and gently pass her over. They were snuggly and adorable earlier, and she needs to keep her energy up. She'll probably be the only coherent one of us before this is all over with. Then I turn to my two alphas. I don't miss the smug look on Steve's face before Sam grips his hair again, tilting his head back to meet his eyes. His voice is a low growl. "You're not gonna start that shit here, Little Alpha. It's Teddy's nest. He decides who's welcome. Understand?"

Steve's reply is a low, "Yes, sir." Which makes Sam's chest even more rumbly as he snarls and yanks Vee lower into a deep kiss.

Plundering his mouth and making me more than a little jealous. Not wanting to be left out, I drop in front of Vee's prone body, licking a long line up his erection, before taking the head in between my lips. He jumps like he's been electrocuted, and a tiny voice inside me says it serves them right for not including me.

This is gonna be a long fucking heat if my mind is already so damned scrambled.

Chapter 47

Steve

I'm trapped in the best way possible and I'm not sure if I'll survive to enjoy it. Sam and Teddy overwhelm me. I wasn't trying to smirk at Kelly earlier. I'm just happy for Garret that they bonded. It must have come off wrong, though. Not that I'm complaining about the punishment.

Sam dominates me wonderfully. He's not overly aggressive, but he's firm in his demands, not giving my self-sabotaging thoughts a chance to intrude. It's freeing to let him take control, let him take care of me, let both of them take care of me. It hasn't been long, but I already trust him implicitly. True, he doesn't tolerate me snarking at Kelly, but I like to think that the two of us have worked our way past that.

Ok, I've worked my way past that. I got to know her, and while I'll never be interested in her in the way they are, I can appreciate her for her own brand of wild and crazy. Honestly, hanging out with her is the most fun I can have here while not having sex. So, she better let my mates bond her, too. That way, she's stuck with me by default. Though now that she's bonded to Garret, I guess she really is my beta-in-law.

My thoughts scatter again when Sam pulls away from me. "Are we boring you, Little Alpha?" His gravelly voice makes me melt and I don't try to stop the little whimper that comes out. Teddy sucks me down harder and I nearly levitate off the fucking nest before he releases me with a loud popping noise.

Sam tugs on my hair again. "What's going on in your head, Vee? We're trying to help you out of it, but I need you to be honest with me for that." It's embarrassing to admit that I was thinking about my brother's beta, their beta. So I backtrack my train of thought to before then.

"Just thinking that I trust you, both of you. You make me feel so good and push all my destructive thoughts to drain away. That I love you. It just feels strange to say it out loud." My alpha's eyebrow quirks up like he's not sure he believes me or not, so I admit a little more. "And that I'm glad that Kelly let Garret bond her. I like my brother being happy." I can feel the slight pout on my face at admitting that, but my mates' smiles are worth it.

"Ok, Little Alpha, just so long as you remember that if she bonds to Teddy and me, you'll be getting it indirectly." Teddy smirks up at me from where his chin is resting on my stomach.

"Well...shit." My voice is petulant, but they understand that it doesn't really bother me now.

"Now, if you're done being a brat, I'm pretty certain our omega wants to fuck you while I knot him. Are you ok with that?" I try to swallow, but my mouth suddenly feels like a desert, so I just nod dumbly, my head swinging between them.

"Will you let him bite you, bond you while he's deep inside? Making you both feel so good?" I nod again, mesmerized by my alpha's eyes. They're so pretty...how did I not realize they're so pretty? A stormy greenish grey.

I feel a little stab of jealousy when Sam releases my hair and stretches over me to kiss Kelly. It's just a small peck on the lips before he stands up and steps out of the nest. My arms flail as I'm suddenly picked up by my omega.

Shit, I keep forgetting how strong he is. Not that I'm back up to my full weight, but come on. He steps over the edge of his nest and places me on the mattress, pulling pillows down from his creation to prop up under my hips.

Sam's voice is a low rumble behind him. "Sorry, Teddy. I'll get a frame built soon. I know being this close to the ground is awkward." Our alpha hands him something, and before I know it, I'm being tipped up, more pillows stuffed under my lower back.

Oh, I guess that's how this is going to work.

Fucking cold!

There's a click as Teddy closes the bottle of lube he just poured over me. Then my loud groan when he wraps his hand around my length, stroking me quick and hard, taking me right to the edge before stopping and dropping his hand down to my ass. I'm a needy panting mess as he circles his lubricated fingers around my puckered entrance.

What the fucking hell was that?

He's trying to kill me.

Slowly, giving me plenty of time to adjust, he presses inside with one finger, thrusting gently back and forth and spreading the lube around. I stare down my body as Sam kneels behind Teddy and tilts his head to the side, dipping his lips to the soft skin of our omega's throat. Teddy looses a shuddering moan, his finger faltering. Sam whispers against his neck, loudly enough that I can hear. "Move, Omega. He needs you."

Teddy's whole body shudders, and there's that click again when he adds more lube and an additional finger. My hips are flexing on their own now, needing to feel him inside me, needing his hands back on my cock.

Forcing my eyes open, I watch as Sam pets our omega's hair, his lips moving against Teddy's throat, but I can't hear what he's saying. I'm so fucking close. I just need a little more. My voice is a breathless whimper as I reach for my mates. "Please. Bear...I'm ready. I need you." His eyes flip up to mine, then back down to watch his hands. He raises up on his knees, kneeling over me.

"Do you want this, Vee? We do this and you're stuck with us. No going back, no running away. Are you ready for that?" His eyes plead with me to say yes, and I'm always surprised that he wants me the way I want him. I don't know how I ever got so lucky. Licking my lips, I nod, and he leans forward, kissing me hard before he presses against me. It's the same burn from before. Not bad, but an intense feeling of being stretched as his head breaches the tight ring of muscle.

His moan flows past my lips while he rocks his hips. Bringing us closer together, until he's fully seated, his stomach pressed into the back of my thighs. Sam rises behind him, and I can sense the tension in Teddy's body as our alpha slides inside him. I'm slightly jealous that my bear makes his own lube and is made to take knots. What would that feel like? My body twitches and shudders as Teddy's hand wraps around my leaking cock.

My voice breaks in a high cry as Sam starts to move, shuttling Teddy's body back and forth. I bite down, gritting my teeth to keep from coming so soon. But I can't hold on. They feel so fucking good. Teddy kneels above me, one hand beside my neck. His long hair's a swaying curtain around us as he's rocked back and forth, stroking me in time with the movement. His eyes are glazed in pleasure, and he moans as he lowers his face to my throat, trapping his hand between us.

It's too much. My skin feels too tight when he squeezes down on my knot. My release barrels through me, coating my stomach and Teddy's hand as his teeth sink into my skin. Every nerve in my body lights up as I feel him, like a light shining inside my chest. It's warm and comforting and despite the uncontrollable twitching of my body, it makes me feel relaxed, like a warm blanket in front of a cozy fire.

His lips kiss the mark he's left, his tongue coming out to trace over the broken skin that now joins our souls. His head raises, eyes meeting mine and pleading. My arms feel like I'm lifting lead weights. They're so fucking heavy as I wrap them around his shoulders. My own injured shoulder giving a brief twinge of pain...but I need this, I need them.

Sam still moves behind him, and the sound of slapping skin seems a sharp juxtaposition to the tender moment I'm sharing with my omega. I pull Teddy closer and Sam lets out a loud snarl. When my eyes meet his, he looks lost to his own pleasure.

Teddy whimpers against me as I bring his face closer, trailing sweet kisses down his neck. His voice is a stuttering moan against my skin as I bite down, tasting salty copper and sweet skin. The bond between us glows brighter as it locks fully into place. I want to hold him against me, melt under him, never let him go.

Instead, I gently lift his head away, tending to my bite and allowing Sam to pull him upright. The big alpha's arms wrap around Teddy's chest, pulling back. Making me shudder and moan again as he slides out of me. Sam stares into my eyes over our omega's shoulder and his whole body convulses, his hips slamming flush against Teddy. His knot locks them together as he strikes, sinking his teeth into our omega's neck, opposite of where I marked him.

Teddy twitches and moans as he reaches his own release. And if Sam was grumpy about me making a mess, I hate to think of how he'll react to this one. Still, his arms stay wrapped around Teddy, gently rocking them both back and forth as he kisses his bonding mark. It almost feels like I'm intruding, but that's probably just my own issues acting up since a few moments later Sam reaches down and strokes my hair as well.

He's still nuzzling against Teddy's throat, but his eyes are soft when they meet mine. His big, calloused hand slipping around my jaw and gently guiding me to sit up. Teddy's arms are languid as they stretch towards me, pulling me closer before he gently guides me closer to our lead alpha. He twitches and lets out another ragged moan as Sam's rough voice vibrates against his freshly bonded skin.

"Do you want my bond too, Little Alpha? It might hurt a bit, since it's not quite the height of passion. But if you want it, and Teddy's ok with it, I'll be happy to have you too." Teddy's head nods numbly up and down as Sam pulls me closer. His tongue branding my flesh in a hot swipe before his teeth fasten against my neck. There's a long pause, almost as if he's asking for assurance.

My hands fist in his hair, pulling him closer, demanding the promise he's offered. Sharp pain slides into my neck. A hot mix of agony and euphoria as I come again. My mind whites out, flicking briefly between the sudden feeling of solid strength that's now anchored in my chest next to Teddy, and the random need to go get some towels to clean up the huge mess we've made.

Sam's tongue swipes over my skin, sending sparks dancing under the surface before his low, growling chuckle makes me shiver. "Little Alpha, I'm 'bout to start worrying that you and our beta are gonna yank me bald. You wanna ease up there a tiny bit so you can mark me back?"

The idea of leaving my mark on this big dominant alpha fills me with both elation and terror, momentarily stunning me into silence at how unworthy I am of bonding either of these two amazing men. But before panic has a chance to dig its claws in, two sets of arms wrap around me.

Teddy twists his torso, and his fingers slide up my chest, finally coming to rest over the teddy bear tattoo I had done so long ago. The catalyst for all the other marks now covering my body. Sam pulls back, his eyes tracing over my face but feeling the certainty that settles into my chest as I realize where I need to mark him. It doesn't stop his grunt of surprise as I lean over and sink my teeth into the skin directly over his heart. My bond to him now matching where I first bonded myself to Teddy in ink.

Chapter 48

Kelly

Garret's arms are warm around me, and I'm pretty sure I could fall asleep curled up in his lap. His erection is totally poking me in the butt—which is odd, because I thought guys usually had more of a resting period required between rounds of sex. Maybe it's because the room is full of Teddy's scent, or it's an alpha thing. I sort of understand that. It makes me all tingly and breathless, but I'm just so tired.

And hungry, apparently. My stomach lets out a loud rumble, and I want to curl into a tiny ball and hide from embarrassment. Three sets of eyes snap to me. Even Garret raises his face from where it's buried in my neck, leaving soft little butterfly kisses over his bonding mark. When my stomach decides to protest again, his arms dip under my legs and he stands abruptly, holding me like a princess. The surprised shriek I make doesn't sound princessy at all.

Sam and Teddy watch us leave as Garret carries me out into the hall and down to the living room. He wraps me in a blanket before settling me on the couch and heading towards the kitchen. I remember a few minutes later about the unfortunate soup incident of their first night here, but then he's coming out of the kitchen with a plate and a glass of water.

"Sorry, I...I don't really cook. But I can make peanut butter and jelly...on wheat." His smile is both nervous and adorable. Also, I happen to like PB&J.

"Thank you," I say, taking a huge bite. And I can feel his pleasure as it thrums through our new bond. "Oh, but what about you? You need to eat, too. And don't tell me you don't. I've been with you all day."

He blushes and nods, scurrying back to the kitchen and returning a short time later with his own sandwich and water. He snuggles against my side for a moment as Jake creeps ever closer along the cushions. My big fuzzy protector is staring intently at my sandwich, and while I know that peanut butter is one of Rufus's favorites, I haven't really talked about that with Sam. I need to make a note to ask about what kinds of treats Jake can get for being such a good boy.

He notices me staring at him and starts to wag his tail. While he still has to wear the cone when he's unsupervised, he's tolerating it much better now. He snuffles at my fingers when I reach over to scratch his ear, grumbling quietly when he doesn't find any treats, but enjoying the attention anyway. Garret finishes his sandwich and pats his thigh as he stands up. "Come on, you great floppy beast, let's get you a bathroom break and a treat, then you can rest while I take Kelly back to the nest."

Treat is apparently the magic word as Jake flops off the couch and follows my alpha into the kitchen. The back door opens and closes and then I hear, "Kelly...what kind of dog treats do we have?" It's a good thing I just put down my water, otherwise I'd probably spray it out my nose. As it is, I choke, trying not to laugh, because I don't know how he expects me to know. It makes me wonder if they ever had pets growing up, or since then. Probably not.

I make it into the kitchen with my now empty plate and glass right as Jake scratches at the back door. Garret rifles through the pantry, a worried expression on his face. "Isn't he supposed to have...like, dog biscuits or something? I promised him a treat, and he's going to hate me if I can't find anything."

I doubt Jake could hate anyone, but I'm not opposed to cheating to ease some of the panic filtering through our new bond. Grabbing a handful of kibble from the tote Sam keeps it in, I pass it off to Garret, who eyes me skeptically. "This is just his normal food. He's not stupid enough to think this is a treat."

Of course, when I let the big dog in, he runs straight to Garret, prancing back and forth in front of the alpha. Garret holds his hand out and Jake gobbles up the bits of kibble without a chance to taste them. "See." I wrap my arms around his waist when he comes over to wash his hands. "It wasn't time for a meal, so any food is a treat. I've seen him hoover up his food in under a minute, but we can't be sure if he even knows what it tastes like."

Garret dries his hands, spinning in my arms, before leaning down to kiss me sweetly for a moment. "Should we get back to the nest, maybe bring some bottles of water? I hope they ate already, but I can make more sandwiches if anybody's hungry." He waits for my answer, but I can't help smiling and laying my head against his chest. Just breathing him in for a few minutes. From what I've heard, heats can get super intense, so the guys will probably need at least a reminder to eat and drink for the rest of this week. I'll also need to call work and email my teachers since I have to miss Thursday and Friday.

He purrs into my hair, and I just want to melt against him. Finally, I sigh. "We can take in some bottles of water. I don't think anybody's gonna be up for a sandwich right now, maybe in a bit." He nods and takes my hand, following me back down the hallway. He's carrying three bottles to my two, but the nest is quiet when we get there. Do we knock? Just walk in? There must be heat etiquette I'm not aware of.

After a moment, Garret reaches around me and turns the knob. All three of the guys are still near the end of the mattress, though they look like they've scooted up a bit. They're also all asleep, with Sam still plastered to Teddy's back, while the omega uses Steve as a pillow. Garret takes the water bottles from me and sets them by the door before picking me back up and carrying me to the other end of the bed. He steps lightly up onto the bedding, carefully watching the rest of our pack, before laying me down and cuddling up behind me. Now that I have some food in my stomach, and a warm purring body wrapped around me, it only takes a moment for my eyes to drift closed and sleep to claim me again.

Chapter 49

Teddy

It's so hot, and it feels like I'm sandwiched between furnaces. Oh...wait, that's my new mates. My face tries to stick to Vee's stomach when I sit up, and my heat hazed brain isn't sure if it's due to sweat or other fluids. Normally that would gross me out completely, now it's just kind of whatever. I slide away from Sam, feeling him slip free and moisture coat the back of my thighs. My neck is tender, but I don't care. It's amazing feeling my pack in my chest.

Steve's a warm, comforting sensation, like being wrapped in a soft cozy blanket and held. Sam is almost overwhelming, less a warm embrace and more a raging inferno burning away any doubts I have, keeping me safe and protected from anything that might hurt me. He's more confident than I give him credit for. The concern is still there, but it all seems to be for others.

I can't wait to find out what Kelly feels like when we're bonded. Something tells me sweet and sparky will be the internal flavor of my firecracker beta. It's still too hot, and I make my way towards the door, needing water. I'll need to look at getting a mini fridge or something in here before my next heat. A place to keep drinks where they won't get hot from all the body heat in the room.

I'm almost to the door when I see five water bottles sitting on the floor. Kelly and Garret must have brought them back for us. I quickly guzzle one down, scanning the room and finding them passed out near the wall at the top of my nest. I know my sweet girl is tired, but I want to remember bonding her, not have it happen when I'm so far down the rabbit hole that I'm mindless with need.

My cock thickens at the thought of her using her new toy on me too...as long as it's not at the highest setting. She was so adorably excited about getting to try a strap-on. Part of me hopes she enjoys it. Another part of me feels sorry for Garret if she does, because my once-best-friend would do anything to make her happy. Even take it up the ass. It probably wouldn't be as enjoyable to him, but who knows, maybe he'll learn something new about himself.

For the moment though, I make my way across my nest, carefully climbing over the mounds of pillows, and settling into place directly in front of my Pixie. She snores softly, and

I wonder how long she's slept. The water isn't cold, but it was probably a bit less than room temperature. What time is it? Not like any of us are wearing a watch, and a clock in the nest is just anxiety inducing.

Brushing her hair back from her face, I lean in to kiss her—Garret's eyes pop open behind her, shiny in the dim lighting. A low warning growl rattles out and he pulls her closer to his chest. After a moment he seems to realize who I am, and his growl fades to a low thrumming purr while he nuzzles the back of her head. He kisses her hair gently, unwinds his arms, and allows me to pull her into mine. Then he stands up and mouths the word "bathroom" before sneaking out of the nest.

My own purr starts up as I pull her close. Something about this girl makes me feel like I need to be sweet and gentle. Sam makes me feel safe and special, like he'll take care of everything. Vee makes me feel dominant, like I need to make him submit. But Kelly, being with her makes me feel ten feet tall, like she's this tiny, fragile person that I need to protect and take care of.

Of course, as clumsy as she is, she's obviously not fragile. She's a feisty little pixie who would probably take on an ogre for those she cares about. My head drops, pressing my lips to her forehead. The rational part of me wants to let her sleep because she's been through so much. Unfortunately, the needy screaming omega part of me wants her to wake up so we can fuck, bite, and bond my sweet little beta.

Luckily, the answer is taken out of my hands when her eyes blink open. Kelly gazes up at me. Her voice is hoarse but happy, and she smiles. "Teddy, are you feeling any better? Want me to make you a sandwich?" It seems like a pretty random thing to ask an omega in heat, but at least she cares.

Leaning forward, I nibble on her ear, causing her to giggle. "I'd rather make a pixie sandwich with Sam. What do you think?"

Her sharp intake of breath makes me worried that I've fucked this all up, but when she meets my eyes again, her cheeks have gone that beautiful pink color—I can't help but tease her. "Hmm, you like the idea of that, sweet girl? Sam and I at the same time?"

Her tongue comes out to wet her lips and I have to bite back a groan at the thoughts that are swirling in my head. My hand moves, cupping that blushing cheek and running my thumb along her plush bottom lip. "So, would you want me here?" I gently push against her mouth, and she opens, letting my thumb inside. When she sucks on it, I damn near lose myself right there.

Then she smiles at me, scraping her teeth over the pad of my thumb, and I'm done, gone, lost forever to a tiny beta girl who tells dad jokes, trips on flat surfaces, and thinks blue cheese is fancy. Sliding my thumb free, I pounce, pushing her flat against the mattress and capturing her lips. I swallow her tiny squeak of surprise and keep going. Coaxing her tongue out with mine, I suck lightly and she moans into me, her small body trapped under me, squirming and writhing. Driving me harder than I thought possible.

I love Sam, I love Steve, but there's something about Kelly. The best word I can come up with is obsession. I would give up everything else in my life to have her, and the biggest reason for that is that she would never ask me to. She'd never want me to sacrifice anything for her. She wants me to be happy and feel amazing, just like I want that for her. Which is why I can have her and Steve and she can have Garret...and we can share Sam together or apart. He's good either way.

Thinking about the big alpha seems to summon him, and a heavy hand lands on my back. Gasping, I pull away to look up at Sam. His voice is a low rumble. "Did I hear something about a pixie sandwich?" Kelly lets out another little gasp and moan, her body shivering where it's pinned under mine. It makes my heat hormones surge, and I'm half tempted to tell Sam to go away so I can hold her down and lick her until I look like a glazed donut.

Sam's big hand comes around the back of my neck, possibly sensing my train of thought, possibly just feeling possessive. But instead of saying anything to me, he looks at Kelly. "You ready to try out all that training you've been doin', Sugar? I saw you with Garret earlier. Can't say I wasn't a bit jealous."

She tenses under me, her big, honey-colored eyes staring up at Sam. "No, Sugar, I'm not mad. That doesn't mean I wouldn't fucking kill to be buried inside you and trading bonding marks, though." His voice is rough with desire, but he doesn't push, waiting to see both of our reactions. Her eyes flick quickly from my face to his before she gives a tiny nod, and that's all the encouragement I need.

Sliding down her body, I capture her hips, spread her thighs open, and swipe my tongue up her slit. She's already so fucking wet for us. Muffled moans sound from above me, and I flick my eyes up to see that Sam has captured her lips, stealing her sounds of pleasure. My fingers glide up her thighs, sliding through the moisture I find there and using it to slide inside. Her hips jerk against me and I raise my head, checking that she's ok after taking Garret earlier. I'll do anything to keep from hurting my sweet pixie.

Her eyes are closed, head tilted back. I can't see more of her face because Sam's still kissing her. Her hands are tangled in his hair, holding him close, so hopefully that means it was a good hip movement. I go back to my feast, flicking my tongue over her clit before sucking it into my mouth, pumping two fingers into her. She twists and writhes between us, her body trying to arch away from the pleasure. I add an extra finger, because Sam is bigger than Garret, and none of us want her to have any discomfort, let alone pain.

I suck her clit again, and she clamps down on my thrusting fingers as her whole body bucks and shakes. I'm hit with even more wetness—glazed donut look achieved.

Sliding one finger down, I circle her back entrance. She shudders and makes little mewling noises. If we're making a pixie sandwich instead of a spit-roast, then she'll need to be comfortable back here as well.

She wiggles and moans as I gather more of her wetness and bring it back there, slowly working my way past the tight ring of muscle. I'll stop if she wants me to, but honestly, I want to have this girl in any and every way she'll let me.

Her sweet sounds drive me out of my mind, but when I try to lick her again, her hand comes down, gently stopping me. She pulls away from Sam with a gasp. "Sorry...'s too much...sensitive. Oh...god Teddy..." Her hand touches my cheek as my fingers continue their pressure. Sam sits up so he can see what I'm doing and his resulting chuckle is dark, sending a shiver down my spine.

"You like that, Sugar?" His mouth comes down, capturing her nipple and she jerks and mewls again.

Her voice is a broken rasp. "Please, oh...oh, Sam...Teddy. I...oh fuck, please, I'm so close. Please." Sam chuckles again, his cheeks hollow, sucking harder—his free hand coming up, fingers pinching and tugging on her other nipple. He smiles, and I can see his teeth as he bites down. Not hard enough to break the skin. Not hard enough to bond her. But she screams and comes again, more of her wetness soaking the finger I still have buried in her heat. Her muscles finally loosen enough for me to breach her ass.

"Where do you want my mark, Sugar? Here?" Sam gently bites down on the top of her right breast. "Or here?" He takes her hand, laying deceptively gentle kisses down her wrist. "Personally, I'd choose here." He licks his way back up to her neck, right over the vein pulsing near the surface, biting down hard enough to leave teeth marks. She spasms against me again with a long, keening cry. Huh, I wouldn't have guessed that my little pixie likes a bit of pain.

Chapter 50

Kelly

My body feels limp and wrung out and so, so good. Teddy pulls me up and turns me on my side so my back is against his stomach. One big hand brushes my hair back from my forehead while the other comes up and rubs down his jaw, wiping my juices off before sucking on his fingers. "I need you, Pixie, want to feel you here." The hand he was licking moves down over his heart, and I know just what he means. I can feel Garret deep inside me, cool and calm, relaxed.

Sam passes him a small bottle and I have a brief moment of panic before Teddy pulls me higher, kissing my neck. His soft lips trailing over the indents left by Sam's teeth. My body moves automatically, wiggling against him until one hand tangles in my hair and the other grabs my hip to pin me to his chest.

"Please, Kelly." His voice is barely a whisper in my ear, and with his grip on my hair, I can't even nod.

My own voice rasps out a, "Yes," and then Sam claims my lips again. Teddy releases my hair, his hands gripping my shoulder and hip as he grinds against me. Sam runs his fingers over my breasts, down to tweak my nipples while he plunders my mouth. All I can do is open to them while bolts of pleasure rocket through me. Sam's fingers drop lower to dip inside, Teddy behind me, thrusting against me before the click of the bottle has him pushing his well lubricated fingers against my back passage again.

Gotta say, that's not a thing I ever thought I'd be dealing with. Pegging him, sure he suggested it. Anything near my behind, it's a bit of a shock. Not bad, though, not at all. Little zings of pleasure ripple up my spine with every movement. Between both of their attention, I come again. I already feel like a floppy wet noodle, my body having seized and relaxed so many times that my muscles are worn out. How the heck do omegas do this for a few days? Teddy still seems pretty coherent, so maybe it's less intense for boy omegas?

My consciousness is floating down from somewhere in the stratosphere when I feel Teddy again, but it's thicker than the two fingers he already had inside me. I fight the need to tense up, and he grunts behind me as the head of his cock breaches me. I let out a shocked squeak and they both freeze, Sam's thumb stops circling my clit, his fingers pause their thrusting and scissoring inside me. The only movement is the up and down of Teddy's chest and his harsh panting against the back of my neck.

It sounds like he's speaking through clenched teeth. "You ok there, Kelly? Did I hurt you, Love? Fuck, you're so goddamned tight." His hands are shaking where they grip me, but it takes a moment for me to be able to catch my breath to answer.

"Yeah...yes, I'm ok. Just...a bit of a shock. Can we...can we go slow, please?" Sam's purr rumbles to life from where he's pressed against my front, and it only takes a second for my body to start relaxing. Almost immediately Teddy starts purring too, and that is a completely different sensation since it sends tiny vibrations through his whole body. I repeat...his whole body. I'm now impaled...in my butt...with a purring vibrator, and I have to bite back a laugh before they think I've lost my mind.

They continue to purr for me, as their movements start back up, first Sam's hands, the one that's not partially inside me coming up to cup my cheek, watching my face for any signs of distress as his fingers go back to pumping in and out. His eyes flick over my shoulder, lightning quick, and he nods his head before turning his attention back to me. Teddy starts to move, his fingers contracting and twitching as he slowly sinks inside of me.

Teddy stops when his hips come to rest against my butt. His breathing is heavy, and he peppers soft kisses all over the back of my neck and shoulders. If it weren't for the initial shock of stretch, I don't think there would have been any problems. I can't say it feels good exactly, but I'm definitely full. Sam's eyes go over my shoulder again, and I kinda feel like smacking these guys for having silent conversations around me.

Sam pulls away, his hands leaving me, and I want to snatch them back. They felt so good. Instead, I let out another little whimper as Teddy rolls onto his back, taking me with him. His hands slide down under my thighs to lift them and spread me open.

Sam is left kneeling in front of me. He stares at us both, his eyes gleaming in the dim lights that Teddy strung across the ceiling. He does a quick check-in. "Teddy, you ok under there?" My omega only answers with a pained groan, but his purr gets louder, the vibrations making me moan and gush more wetness.

"Fuck, Sugar...You're killing me here." Sam's voice sounds pained as he crawls closer, bracing himself against my splayed thighs. His eyes are dark when his gaze trails over my body, and I shiver a bit, despite how warm the room is. Teddy's fingers flex under my thighs as he raises me like an offering to our alpha, and I can see Sam's Adam's apple bob up and down. He reaches out, trailing his fingers from my throat all the way down to my weeping core.

It's too tense in here, and I want to beg him to take, stop, go, do something before I explode. I must let out a whimper or something, because Sam jerks like he got goosed.

Then he's moving with a purpose. One hand comes down, brushing over Teddy's fingers to hold my thighs open. He brings the other up, holding himself, stroking the fat head of his cock against me. Spreading my moisture around before dipping inside. The stretch is intense in this position. Everything feels tight, and I'm sure having Teddy shoved in there doesn't help that. Sam tries to be gentle, sinking in slowly. His breath comes in short gasps with several muttered utterances of, "Fuck!"

By the time his knot brushes against my entrance, I can barely breathe, I'm stuffed so full. Sam leans over me, eyes intent on my face, looking for signs of pain. "You still with us, Sugar?" I reach for him, my fingers tracing over his face, running across his short beard. He closes his eyes for a moment, savoring the sensation before he captures my fingers and brings them to his lips, kissing the tips.

"Gonna move now, Kelly. You sure you're alright?" I manage to nod this time, and his resulting smile tears at my heart. He leans up, back straight, and hands gripping my thighs as he swivels his hips. Teddy lifts me a bit higher and then his stomach flexes under my back, thrusting into me.

My breath comes out in harsh pants as they find a rhythm that works. Pushing and pulling against me, it feels like my whole body is about to explode. So many sensations. Teddy's breath is a gasping pant against my ear. Jumbled words, a mix of devotion and profanity, praise and degradation, spill from his lips as his grip gets tighter and he slams his hips against me.

In front of me, Sam looks almost stoic in his intensity as he stares down at where we're joined. His hips pumping, he moves his hand and then his thumb is circling my clit. He lets out a deep, shuddering gasp. His rhythm stutters as I'm pitched over the edge. I fall into an abyss where fireworks skate across my skin.

Teddy's fingers dig into me, almost painfully, then teeth sink into the back of my neck, right above my spine, and I cry out, arching against the pain and pleasure all mixed together. There's more pain, though not as sharp, but an ache as Sam thrusts hard into me, his knot already almost too big to fit. I gasp against the stretch, the sensation of being too full.

Another set of teeth takes the side of my throat, this one sharp enough to set off more fireworks. I can't tell where one orgasm ends and the next begins as they roll through me. Each twitch setting off fresh waves of sparks under my skin until I feel like I'm going to pass out. My chest swells, my heart feeling like it might give out as I'm hit with a swirling bedlam of feelings and sensations. The overwhelming sense of devotion leaves me gasping for breath.

I don't even realize my eyes are squeezed shut until a warm hand caresses my jaw. Sam's voice is quiet, barely heard over the loud panting behind me. "Mark me back, sweet girl. Please. I want you deep inside. Always." My head is tilted and firm flesh meets my lips. I open automatically, but biting down is still difficult. Breaking through skin isn't something I'm used to. Then salty copper and warm cedar caress my senses—the intense feelings in my chest growing, swirling and settling, love, devotion, joy.

Sam jerks inside of me, his knot throbbing as he comes again. He raises me up, wrapping me in his arms. Teddy and I both gasp as he slides out of me. Sam pulls Teddy up so he's kneeling beside me. His face is flushed, eyes glazed. "Now, Teddy's turn. Do you have the energy, Kelly? We can wait, but the memory won't be as good once his heat hits fully." I nod dumbly. This is important. Teddy's mine, and I need to make sure everyone knows.

I twist my torso, opening my arms, and Teddy slides towards me. Not a full collapse, but he nuzzles into my neck, licking and kissing over the mark Sam made, and causing our alpha to shiver, his cock twitching inside me again. "Where do you want it, Sugar?" Leaning forward, I pick my spot, just next to Sam's slightly towards the front. Last one, I bite.

Teddy is softer, and no stubble. My teeth break the skin but I don't get the heavy copper flavor that came with my alphas, just sweet cookies. It's probably because my omega is releasing so many pheromones, but I'm grateful, regardless. His sweet, comforting warmth spreads through my chest. Like sinking into his arms. I feel safe and protected.

I kiss the damaged skin when I pull away, but don't have another moment before he lunges at Sam. His own bonding mark suddenly overlapping mine on the side of Sam's neck. My legs twitch, and another wave of pleasure rolls through me. Sam cries out, "Fuck!" One hand tightens around me and he groans, bringing the other up and holding Teddy against him.

Teddy nuzzles between us. His mouth tracing both new marks. His arms circle my waist, sandwiching me between them again, while he quietly whispers, "Mine," over and over against my skin. It feels safe and warm, and I hate the thought of the real world ever intruding again, but eventually his arms go slack and he lets out a soft snore.

I'm still trapped on Sam, but he manages to maneuver us all to stretch out. His hand reaching out, brushing Teddy's tangle of hair away from his face. "Mine too," is all he says before he buries his face in my hair, his breathing evening out to join Teddy's. Well, crap, now I'm stuck. Might as well try to grab my own nap, I guess.

Chapter 51

Garret

Steve settles next to me on the couch. He looks the most relaxed I've seen him in years, completely blissed out now that he's tied himself to Sam and Teddy. Not that I blame him. The joy and pleasure I feel coming through my bond with Kelly has me grinning like a lunatic, even if I'm not the one giving it to her.

He gives me a side-eye as he sprawls on one of the towels I spread across the couch. He's managed to pull on some sweat-pants, but his chest and back are fully exposed. I can't even remember the last time that happened.

"Hiding out while your mate gets railed by other guys?" Considering those 'other guys' are his mates, and he looks about as laid-back as I feel, it can't be a serious question.

"Nope, just checking up on Jake and getting water and snacks. You? Jealous that your other half...halves...guys are in there with Kelly and not you?" He looks over at the big dog asleep on the other end of the couch and seems to seriously consider this for a minute.

"I was worried I would be...But I'm not. I'm theirs now, no matter what. So is she—she's also yours. I can feel how much they need both of us. Besides, what kind of asshole would I be if I kept stealing her clothes and books and shit while also being jealous of our shared relationship?" My only reply is the raised eyebrow that his statement so rightfully deserves.

His laugh is fast and easy in response. "Oh, yeah, I deserve that. Seriously, I don't know. Maybe it was all the talking while you guys were gone. Maybe it's the bond, or you three just rubbing off on me. But I can see liking Kelly, one day...sort of."

When my eyebrow quirks higher, he slaps me on the arm. "Not like that. Fucking hell, gross. She's fucking my brother, for Christ's sakes. Also, vagina, *so* totally not my thing. Ick!" I rub my arm where he hit me.

"She didn't seem surprised by your tattoos." It's not a question, and he doesn't answer it, just nods. Reaching over, I ruffle his hair. We haven't had this easy affection in too many years, and I'm going to enjoy it while it lasts. I hope it lasts forever. I've missed my brother *and* best friends. He just ducks his head but doesn't pull away.

"Is it too late for dinner? Too early for breakfast?" We both turn towards the window, but it's still pitch-black outside. And he doesn't wait for an answer before getting up and limping into the kitchen. After a few minutes, Jake rolls off the couch and we follow Steve. The clock on the microwave says it's 3:38 in the morning and I groan internally.

My brother shuffles around the room, pulling leftover taco stuff out of the fridge and reheating the meat before assembling a couple and rolling them up. He passes me one while Jake looks on, licking his chops and hoping we drop something. Steve finishes all but the last bite in silence, looking thoughtful.

"She saw them. I came out of the bathroom in a towel, thinking she was already downstairs. It was shit timing...but she said they were beautiful. Then I freaked out and hid in the closet for a few hours." My brother's cheeks blush pink. He rarely gets compliments.

Not that I'm going to give them to him, but he's been so closed off. "I thought she was going to scream at me or hit me...or something. She was so tense when she touched me, felt the scars...but she didn't say anything. There was no yelling, none of that shit we grew up with."

He pops the last bite in his mouth, chewing thoughtfully, while I stand there gaping at him, my arms hanging loosely at my sides in shock. Jake takes the opportunity to come steal the last few bites of my taco right out of my hand. He loses a few chunks of tomato to the floor, then looks up at me and licks his lips again before hoovering up the floor food. He stares between my brother and me for a moment before going and scratching at the back door and looking at us again.

My mind still reeling, I let the big dog loose and he lopes down the steps, still sore, but doing so much better than when we first got him home. I'm glad we'll all be sleeping in the nest for the next few days, because getting bombarded by taco dog farts first thing in the morning is not something I want to have to explain to Kelly or Sam.

Steve rattles around behind me in the cabinets and I turn to find him pulling a large lidded water jug out and filling it and a couple of glasses with tap water. Once he's done, he hands me one, guzzling his own glass in the process while we wait for Jake. The big guy's a bit slower right now, but Dr. Leo said he'll be fine soon.

He comes limping back across the yard soon enough, and doesn't even acknowledge me as I hold the door open for him. Poor guy is probably already sore again. He ignores both of us as he hobbles through the kitchen, and there's a loud grunt when he hops back up on the couch. I can't even begrudge him my taco since he got hurt protecting Kelly.

I help Steve carry more water back to the nest—Sam can come out later and grab food if he feels up to it. My plans of carrying Kelly to the bathroom to get her cleaned up are derailed when we find all three of them fast asleep in the nest. It's probably going to be a long few days and they need their rest. Even if what I read about male omegas having lighter heats due to less intense hormones is true, it'll probably be at least three days of marathon sex. Not that I'm complaining.

Steve looks back and forth, surly that Kelly's lying where he wants to be. Then he cuddles up behind Teddy, wrapping his arms around the big omega and purring. That in itself is jarring, since I haven't heard him do it in a decade.

It's slightly more difficult for me to find a cuddle spot. Circling to the side of the nest closest to Kelly's head and pressing my spine against the curved wall of pillows, I reach out to touch her hair. Her fingers loosen their grip on Sam's chest and slide up to meet mine, twining together. Closing my eyes, the sound of my pack's breathing and the touch of my mate soothe me into a deep, dreamless sleep.

Chapter 52

Teddy's heat breaks on Saturday afternoon, but they're all so exhausted that they're still asleep in the nest. Kelly did have to step in on Thursday evening and Friday afternoon as Steve and I started to wear down. After a little trial and error with the inflation, her new toy really helped with Teddy's hormones. Of course, she said it's a great workout, and she'll have abs of steel if she does this very often. Garret gave a worried little groan that he may get volunteered for her to practice on.

We were able to keep a good system of breaks going to make sure Teddy ate—even when he didn't want to—and stayed hydrated. Kelly said we need to invest in camelbacks before his next heat, but I think our girl needs to do a bit more research since the availability of water is less of a problem than a stubborn omega. I do agree with her on the mini-fridge suggestion, as well as installing some shelves and cabinets for storage.

Not that I can build anything. I've been checking my phone daily, and my email now that I've stepped away to make dinner. There's still no word back from my insurance about the shop. I know it was under its own business policy, so that may take some extra time, but I'll still be calling them again first thing Monday morning.

Jake's following me around the kitchen, not quite begging, but sniffing every time my hand moves down. I'm half tempted to let him snarf up a chunk of one of the peppers I'm slicing so he'll remember not to eat food he finds lying around on the ground. But he's just now feeling back to his old self. I'll just have to remind everybody else not to feed him any sort of people food in the kitchen.

When the chili is finally in the slow cooker, I head upstairs to get a shower. I haven't exactly missed my bedroom with everybody in the nest, but my legs have been hating me for trying to get up off the floor each morning. The mattress is super plush. Kelly and Steve picked out a great one—but a new bed frame will be high on my priority list as soon as the shop's back up and running.

The hot water feels fucking amazing, but I am gonna need to upgrade that soon too, since a twenty-five-gallon tank only worked out well for one guy. With five of us in the house, it's already problematic. Just one more thing to add to the list of shit I need to take care of, and how I'm still not good enough. Sighing, I scrub my face and hair, the soap stinging the still raw bonding marks around my neck and making me hiss.

My mind is running in circles again, so there's no point in wasting water while I try to figure shit out. Shutting the shower off, I step out and wipe the fog from the mirror. Kelly's bite is the most noticeable just because it's so much smaller than the ones Steve and Teddy left. Teddy's is, surprisingly, the biggest, intersecting Kelly's. He was a bit of a shock, but fuck, I wouldn't trade it for anything.

Debating briefly if I should shave off my scraggly beard so they're more visible, I rub the warm spaces on my chest. Teddy and Steve are barely there, probably still asleep. My eyebrows lower. Kelly feels...worried? Well, shit. I run the towel over my hair and chest before stepping out into the bedroom. Kelly's lying there on the bed, staring at the bathroom door.

I stride forward, as she sits up. "You ok, Sugar, what's wrong?"

She hums in thought. "I could ask you the same thing. I woke up, and you felt really frustrated and frazzled...I was worried about you."

Shit.

Dumbass, of course it works both ways.

It's ok, stay positive.

"Sorry, Sugar, I was just stuck in my own head." The look she gives me is skeptical. "Ok, fine, I was thinking again that I'm failing y'all. My shop's been burned down. I haven't gotten the bed made for the nest. I'm worried about money, and I need to replace the water heater." She slides off the bed—almost stumbling when her feet hit the floor—and wraps her arms around my chest.

"You know you're not alone anymore, right? I mean…I get that you wanna take care of everybody, but we're in this together. I only work part time now, but I'll be out of college soon, and I'll find something full time. And I'm sure Garret and Steve don't just plan on sitting around all day. I don't know what Teddy might want to do, but he doesn't seem like the type to not contribute."

My heart rips and chest rumbles a low growl at the thought of my omega or beta having to work since I should be good enough. But she's right, and I have no problems whatsoever about any of them working if they want to. I just want to take care of them. That being said, the twins better plan on helping out. Is that a double standard? Probably. But I can't bring myself to care. I'm happy to have them here since they make Kelly and Teddy happy, but we gotta have more than one income going on.

Kelly cuddles against my chest, and my breath comes out in a deep sigh, shoulders relaxing. Just knowing someone else cares makes shit easier. After a bit, I untangle her arms and step back so I can cup her jaw and make eye contact. "Sorry, Sugar, you keep doin' that and I'm gonna want back inside you…but I'm thinkin' you might already be a bit sore from the last few days."

Even after seeing her naked for the last three days straight—and nearly walking bow-legged myself—I want to drag her into the bed and claim her again when she blushes like that. Instead, I lean down to kiss her on the tip of her nose, making her giggle.

"So, can I fix you up somethin' to eat? I know it's not breakfast time, but an omelet might help with your energy. I just put a pot of chili on for dinner, so it'll be at least a few more hours." She smiles and steps into me again, kissing the hollow of my throat, and making a purr rumble to life in my chest.

"That would be so good...but what about you? Did you already eat?" I nod and hum an affirmation as I pull on some briefs and jeans. If I was home alone, I'd probably skip the shirt. Then I realize again that they all live here now, so fuck it, shirtless it is.

Not gonna lie, the way she bites her lip when I walk outta the closet in just the jeans is fucking addictive.

It's still quiet downstairs with just the two of us as she follows me into the kitchen. I make a mental note to add a bar top to the far side of the island so I can bring in some stools. Garret comes out about an hour later, immediately latching on to Kelly and snuggling her on the couch before going to grab a bowl of that god-awful cereal she brought into the house. I won't say anything to her, but I'll try to make sure we have some things on hand for mornings that aren't 75% sugar.

Teddy and Steve roll out of the nest shortly before the chili is finished up. I've made up cornbread and baked potatoes to go with it. Hopefully, it'll help everybody recover from the last few days. Plus, the weather is warming up, and we won't have many more days where it's a good meal option.

The rest of the day is relaxed enough, though Kelly and Steve do outvote the rest of us on what movie to watch. I get the feeling there'll be a lot more animated or subtitled movies in my future.

Teddy and Steve have just pulled the sheets off the nest to toss in the washer when my phone rings. It was too much to hope that the rest of the world could give us one more day to relax before life goes back to normal. Unfortunately, it's also not a call I can just ignore.

The dispatcher starts speaking before I can even say hello.

"Sam, sorry. Gabe told me not to call because you were on heat leave, but Pack Asher is all on probation because of last weekend, Pack Garcia has the stomach flu, and Pack Allen is out of town. I really hate to ask, but we need you here if possible. I'm hoping it's a false alarm and won't take long, but is there any way you can make it to the station?"

She sounds nearly panicked when she finally stops speaking. While I'd rather stay here and rest, I signed up for this shit so I could help people. Besides, Xan and the rest of them are on probation for that shit with Steve and Garret's dad, so I can't flake out now.

Actually, that's a good idea.

Stuffing my phone back in my pocket, I point to the twins. "You two, get dressed. That was dispatch. You're going to join the volunteer fire department starting today." Garret actually looks excited, but Steve turns a little green, standing there and gaping at me like a fish.

"I don't know anything about fighting fires, and look at me, I'm too scrawny." He's not wrong, he is scrawny, and underfed. But we can fix that. Right now, he needs to step up. Plus, he just sounds whiny, and he's clinging to Teddy like he wants to hide behind our omega. I'm pretty sure Teddy would jump at the chance, but there's no way in hell I'm letting him anywhere dangerous.

"Boy, get your pants on and get in that truck now." I don't like having to exert authority this way, but I will if I have to.

Thankfully Teddy has my back in this, pulling Steve around, kissing him hard and shoving him towards the stairs. "Go, get clothes on. Snuggles when you get home." Steve blinks at him but mopes off as Garret is coming back down the stairs, carrying a pair of socks. He's developed Kelly's habit of no shoes or socks in the house. While it's cute, it means I'll have to be extra careful about tracking in any debris from the shop.

By the time Steve gets back downstairs, he looks less petulant—his brother and I are waiting in the truck as he scurries across the yard. I throw Garret a questioning look, but he just nods. "Don't worry about it. This is the happiest I've seen him in years. It'll be good for him to get a little physical activity. I need to find out where the closest gym is around here, otherwise you'll be rolling us out of your house with how well you cook."

Steve climbs into the cab while I think about it and get turned around. "Sorry, Kid, the old gym burned up a few years ago, though it was already shut down. I think most people head over to the college. Students and families get covered by tuition costs, otherwise you gotta pay. It's not a bad price if you need it." I may or may not flex a bit since working on the house so much leaves me no time to go to the gym, but it's left me in pretty good shape.

Chapter 53

Kelly

Thankfully, the fire was a false alarm. The diner wasn't really on fire. Hope had hit the alarm by leaning on it while making out with her boyfriend when he stopped by—ironically, he's an alpha. To top it off, instead of admitting it, she tried to shove him out the back door, which also has a fire alarm, and sent the whole place into a panic.

Luckily, no one was hurt, but I don't know if she still works there. Regardless, I don't plan on making any trips for takeout without at least a few of my pack mates. Garret actually looked sulky when they got home a couple of hours later, and while Steve still had an attitude, Teddy says that he could feel how disappointed his mate was.

I'm glad everyone is ok, and I need to check up on Gabe and Xan when I get to the shop this morning. It can't be easy for them to sit around not doing anything if somebody needs help. Pulling on my jeans and a fresh polo shirt, I make my way downstairs, where Sam hands me a breakfast sandwich and a to-go mug of coffee.

"Just in case the one at work's being janky," he said, kissing me on the forehead and holding on to Jake's collar so I can escape. Sam has an appointment today to have my slobber muffin's stitches taken out, and while I'd love to be there, I can't miss any more school.

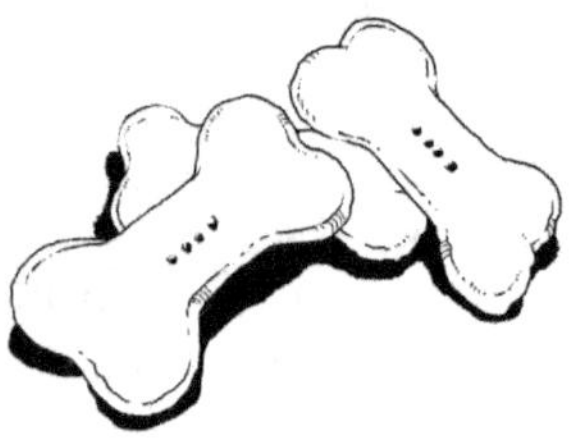

Gabe spits coffee across the front counter when I walk in. Which is made even more awkward when he pulls a greasy rag out of his coveralls and starts trying to wipe it up. Now my desk is wet *and* oily. *Fun*. Also, I thought they couldn't get the coffee maker to work. Maybe Jacks made to-go mugs for them like Sam did for me.

Gabe knocks on the window to the shop and Xan walks in, says, "Shit!" really loudly and scrambles into the break room before slamming the door and locking it from the inside. What did I walk into? Gabe continues to wipe ineffectively at the counter while several more curse words and some loud banging comes from behind the door.

Eventually he looks down at the mess he's made and gives up, grumbling about needing paper towels. All the cleaning supplies are in the break room. It's the only room in the shop other than the bathroom that has a separate space and a lock. He looks from me to the mess and finally slams his fist down a few times on the door. "Give it up, man. It's too late."

Another resounding, "Shit," can be heard just before the locks turn. Coffee beans and grinds are scattered all over the floor. The beat-to-heck old coffee maker is sitting on one of the couches while a shiny new machine is half crammed under the cabinet. The countertop where everything normally sits is empty, and the two alphas stare at me guiltily.

"Ok...so...Lemme just get some cleaner and towels...then you two can get back to whatever you were doin'." There's not really a question there. Because while these guys are my bosses, they're also my friends, and I don't want to make them uncomfortable.

I step over to the area that acts as a broom closet and pass the broom and dustpan back to a guilty-looking Xan while taking the spray bottle of orange cleaner and roll of paper towels for myself. No one says anything while I clean the front desk. Since Xan hasn't done the floor either, I take the broom from him afterwards and sweep that up too.

They both continue to stare at me expectantly, so I finally ask, "Did you, um, need me to get the coffee started this morning or...?" They both glare at the floor while I walk back to the desk and pull up work orders.

Eventually Xan says, "Shit," for the third time since I've been here.

He gently pushes me towards the breakroom and pulls the large silver box out from under the cabinet where it was partially hidden. "Sam and Garret got us a new coffee maker last week after everything went nuts at y'all's place. We didn't want you to think we didn't need you, so we've been having you make coffee in the old one in the mornings and using the new one in the afternoons after you head to school. Also, while you were out for Teddy's heat. We didn't think you'd be back for a couple more days. Sorry." This last is said while still staring at the floor.

Gabe talks loudly from behind me. "Of course, we still need you here to do paperwork and shit, so it's not like we're firing you or anything. Don't think that."

Stepping to the side, I look back and forth between my bosses before walking over to get a better look at the stupidly fancy new coffee maker on the counter. It has a hopper full of beans attached to the top, and a digital screen that's off right now since it's not plugged in. But I'm guessing this thing costs more than my car and makes really good drinks.

"This does explain some of the funny looks Sam's been giving me, and why he was so interested in how work was going this week." I shrug it off, plugging the fancy coffee box into the wall, only to be met with a full color display and a rotating carousel of coffee choices. Not gonna lie, it makes me feel a bit obsolete.

"You should have told me about this before. I could have been getting an extra twenty minutes of sleep every day if I didn't need to come in and get the coffee maker started before you got here."

The two alphas shuffle and grumble behind me, and I hear a mumbled, "Sorry."

Once I finish my to-go cup, I'm totally gonna try this thing out though—it looks high tech and fancy, something I've come to expect with Sam and food.

Chapter 54

Garret

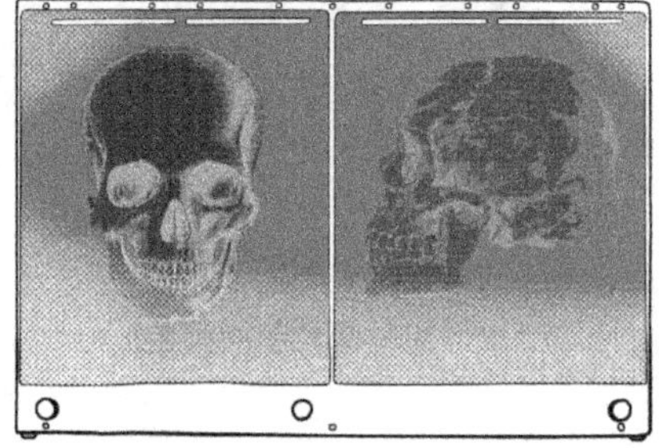

One Week Later

Waiting sucks. Teddy and I both went in last week for our appointments, and while his results from the genetic matching only took a couple of days, I'm about to lose my fucking mind.

Which is fine...my mind I mean, not the waiting.

There is absolutely no damage to my brain.

Sure, Dad was a horrible person, and there may have been some fractures, but the tissue should be fine.

I've never had any problems before.

Kelly wraps her arms around my neck, snuggling against me in the flimsy plastic chair. We're sitting in the college common area between classes. Steve needed to come up to turn in paper-work registering for next semester, and I wanted to check out the gym area that Sam mentioned, so I tagged along.

"You're spiraling. Gimme a hug. Tell me what's on your mind." She looks up at me and my chest eases. It's not that I forget about the bond, I just don't think about it. She knows what's wrong, but she's right that maybe getting it out instead of bottling it all up might make it easier.

She has all kinds of cute and sometimes really strange southern sayings that I've never heard before. They don't always make sense.

Nervous as a long-tailed cat in a room full of rockin' chairs.

Rainin' like a cow pissin' on a flat rock.

Can't carry a tune in a bucket.

Dumber than a sack of hammers.

That last one was used to describe our mom and dads when they called last week to tell us that Steve and I had been written out of Grandpa's will. Mom said she was worried about us being "out there in the country with all those hillbillies." She'd asked if we'd ever watched Deliverance, and said that those types of people can't be trusted. Apparently, it's an old movie from the 70s, which Sam assured us was supposed to take place in Georgia, not Mississippi. Also, something about banjo music, but by then Kelly was giggling so hard that I couldn't focus on anything but her.

I let my forehead lower to rest against hers. "Sorry, Sweetness. My mind's just all wrapped up, worried about...well, my mind.

I've never noticed any problems. But if there is some kind of damage, what effect could that have for finding work? I mean, I got my degree. I just need to find another place to do my residency before I can use it."

Her arms tighten around my shoulders. "Garret, you are one of the smartest guys I know. If something happened to your big sexy brain, we'll see what options there are. We'll cross that bridge when we come to it, y'know?"

I pull back. "So, wait, you do know how that saying goes?"

Her big brown eyes meet mine, and her smile is mischievous. "Of course I know, I'm not stupid...but let's be honest, crossing the bridge isn't always the best option. Sometimes I'd rather jump over the side than cross. Or set fire to it and watch the flames dance merrily in the dark."

Fuck, I love this woman.

She's such an adorable fucking weirdo.

My adorable fucking weirdo.

That I happen to share with my brother's mates.

I can think of worse things.

Like not having her at all.

My phone rings, and I tense until I see the photo of Teddy and Kelly pop up on my screen. So what if all my contact photos include my mate? I'd rather look at her than anyone else. I slide my finger over the button to answer, and Teddy's nervous voice breaks over the line before I can speak.

"Hey, Garret. Sorry. Um...Apparently there was some confusion at the hospital about me being your omega. They called me to schedule my bone marrow harvesting for the end of May so that Brice has time to finish chemo and get ready...Shit. So, anyway, since they thought I was your omega they were trying to give me all your MRI results, and I told them that they needed to talk to you, so...you're supposed to go to the hospital in an hour and a half to get the results, sorry. I just thought you'd want the earliest appointment so you could finally get answers."

All the air seeps from my lungs as my mind processes what he just said. Hour and a half, appointment, thank fuck it's in the same town as the college and I don't have to head over to Springfield. I can do this. My mouth feels numb as I reply, "Thanks, Teddy. I really appreciate it. I'll probably send Steve home with the truck if Kelly feels up to taking me to the appointment."

My beta nods against my chest where she's hugging me. "Ok, I'll let Sam know you two'll be late. Can you remind Steve to go by the store and pick up some milk and a couple boxes of cereal? He finished the last of Kelly's s'mores and I don't want her to kill him." Kelly's head pops up off my chest, glaring at the phone, but she doesn't say anything to alert him that she heard.

"Sure thing, man. Call if you need anything else." We say our goodbyes and I hang up, looking at the time on my watch. "Looks like you need to get to class, Sweetness. I'll hang out here till you're done, then we can head over?" She nods, biting her lip before kissing me softly and sliding out of my lap, to hurry away. I spend the next hour searching online forums about treatment and therapy for long-term damage and brain injury.

Kelly places her palm on my leg, stopping it from tap-ping up and down. We're sitting in the waiting room at the hospital and her hands haven't stopped touching me since she joined me after class. Each little pat or caress helping to fortify my mental armor against the chaos whirling through my brain. I didn't expect to show up to my appointment and just walk in, but come on. We've been here for almost an hour.

Finally, a nurse opens the door. She's staring at a clipboard as she asks, "Mr. Carpenter?"

Kelly nods, and I stand up and walk over to the door the nurse emerged from so she can confirm, "Mr. Carpenter? Garret?"

Kelly nods again and I say, "Yes."

She looks at Kelly. "And this is your...?"

I say, "Mate," and at the same time Kelly says, "Beta," then starts giggling. I think my girl laughs when nervous. The nurse just nods and leads us to the back, explaining what the MRI was looking for, and a quick and dirty rundown of what it does. All of this is information I already know, so I try to take in as much detail from my surroundings as possible. If I ever want to do my residency, I'll need to find a hospital, and this one might work. If they'll have me, considering the drama Dad caused.

She puts us in an exam room and asks several questions before telling us that the doctor will be with us soon. Thankfully, it doesn't take long before an older beta in a white coat arrives carrying a laptop. She looks at me and verifies, "Mr. Carpenter?" before sitting down.

I nod again, and she smiles and opens her laptop, her eyes moving over the screen. "I'm Doctor Hanby. It's so nice to finally meet you. I've been talking to Dr. Baxter because he sent over the referral and wanted to confer. He sent me a copy of your x-rays so I'd know what I was looking for."

She pauses for a moment to look between Kelly and me. "Now, first off, the MRI didn't show anything unusual. That doesn't mean everything's fine. Some things can take longer to show up. Though based on the appearance of the fractures, they all seem to be older."

I nod. "Yes, ma'am, at least a decade."

Her breathing sounds in a sharp intake. "Well then, young man, I'm glad you're still with us. This sort of thing...well. I'm assuming you didn't get them playing football in school?" She looks at me hopefully.

"No, ma'am, sorry." She nods once more, her lips tight.

"Well, regardless. I'm glad you're in a better situation." Her eyes flick from me to Kelly. "You know, if you ever feel unsafe at home, either of you, we're here to help." She closes her laptop with a snap and nods at us both.

Kelly gives a little, mumbled, "Thank you." I just nod.

"As I said, I'd like to monitor this for a while. If you can talk to reception, they can get you scheduled for a follow up in about six months." I nod again, my mind too relieved to form many sentences.

Neither of us really talk on the way home. After being tense for the last week, all my muscles are exhausted. Kelly keeps her hand on my thigh unless she needs to take a corner. I finally get a taste of what Steve mentioned when we were gone, but we're late for dinner, and I know better than to get between Kelly and food.

Strangely, Sam isn't in the kitchen when we walk inside. Jake comes bouncing over to greet us while we go looking for our pack. Teddy stands in front of the stove, flipping chicken breasts and stirring a pot. He smiles when Kelly steps up behind him, kissing him between the shoulder blades.

Turning around, Teddy says, "Thank you for not trying to hug me. I don't want you getting burned." Then he leans down and kisses her on the forehead before straightening and nodding at me. "Sam and Vee are out back taking measurements for the new shop. Insurance finally came through and he wanted to get started on figuring out if he'd be able to do the rebuild, or if it made more sense to hire a crew. Apparently, he hates dealing with concrete, but he said it's as good a time to upgrade as any, and having a slab floor would help."

I step towards the stove, intent on asking if he needs anything, but he just glares at me and says, "You do remember the soup, yeah? I don't want to piss Sam off. He's in a good mood. Speaking of which, sit the fuck down and tell me what the doctor said." He smiles before turning back to the stove and nods along while Kelly and I pass the story back and forth, occasionally filling in parts the other missed.

A short time later Vee and Sam come in the back door, heading straight for the shower to rinse off the soot and dirt. When they get back and we sit down to dinner, Steve talks excitedly about the classes he's signing up to take in the fall semester.

Kelly and I again recount my visit to the hospital. Sam smiles at each of us, looking content with life. Or as Kelly would say, "Happier than a pig in poop." Somehow, I don't think the original saying uses the term poop. Still, I can certainly get behind being happy again.

Chapter 55

Kelly

One Year Later

"I told you, we'll be fine with just one bedroom. It's just gonna be her and her bunny. They don't need that much space. Besides, I doubt she'll even spend much time at the house. Sarah can't hold still for very long." Teddy's following Sam's pacing form across the living room, trying to get our alpha to relax. He's been in a constant state of near panic, trying to make sure the guest bedroom is ready for when Sarah gets here.

"I'm telling you, Love. She won't want a big fuss. She's dealing with some stuff right now, and she just needs to get away. The best thing we can do is give her a nice cozy room to rest in, let her have full access at the gym to work out her energy, and just be there for her if she needs us...um, me more than you, probably."

Sam is shaking his head. "I'm sorry, Bear. I'm just worried about embarrassin' you in front of your friend. Shit's been hectic lately. I've had to take on more at the station since Joseph's pack officially resigned. Not that I blame 'em. After everything with Brice, they want to spend as much time together as possible, just in case of a relapse. But nobody else was up to takin' charge."

Our alpha tugs on his hair as we bookend his big body. Teddy nuzzles the back of his neck, while I bury my face in his chest. He starts purring, one hand running over my hair, the other petting Teddy's arms that circle us.

Tilting my head up, I meet his eyes. "Besides, I'll totally volunteer Garret for extra duties. He needs to get out more than just the gym. I know starting a new business means long hours, but it's been almost a year. If he keeps this up, he's gonna look all swole and lumpy. I like him streamlined."

Teddy chuckles against Sam's back, and my alpha meets my eyes. He's more sensitive to my moods, and I squirm uncomfortably. "Besides, you know I worry about him. He gets obsessed with stuff and doesn't take care of himself, case in point." I move my hand up and down my body, and Sam hugs me tighter.

"Well, Sugar, you're worth obsessing over. Besides, I kind of get feedback from him through you, and this feels different than before. I think he's just really passionate about helping people, and wants to make this a success. Don't worry, I'll talk to him if it looks like he's startin' to push himself too hard."

My arms squeeze tighter around his middle—not that I can squeeze hard enough to hurt him. Still, I want to make sure he knows how much I appreciate him. As much as I love Garret, he tends to neglect his own needs in favor of those around him. It turns out when you bond with someone and can feel their emotions; you have a good window into their mental health. He still needs help, but we're working on it, slowly but surely.

Jake comes scrambling in from the kitchen, looking excited and running straight for the front door. It opens a moment later and Steve walks in, followed by Garret. They both look tired, but otherwise good. Steve has filled out considerably over the last several months. And while he still wears mostly long-sleeved shirts when he's around other people, he's slowly stretching out my danged T-shirts too with his now wide shoulders.

Maybe I should order him some of his own shirts for their birthday in a couple of months. Try to keep mine from being destroyed. Steve points over his shoulder. "Hey, I found this one at work again. Thought I'd bring him home to help get everything ready for Sarah to visit. Really hope she doesn't try to make good on her threats." He squeezes his thighs together and I realize I never did get a good translation.

They both kick off their shoes and hang them on the shoe rack by the front door that Sam made, before sliding on the slippers that are his concession to my habit to not wear shoes in the house. He said he can only clean his work boots off so well from the shop and doesn't want to risk any damage with how clumsy I already am.

Garret crosses the room in long strides to plaster himself to my back. He's dressed in his usual work clothes for the gym, which is just a tight T-shirt and shorts. Technically, it's a uniform since it has the company logo on it—Carpenter's Gym: Building Better Bodies—but it's still hot on him. Yeah, the slogan's cheezy as heck, but Teddy funded the thing, so he got to name it. He blames the slogan on me since I came up with our pack name, and they like to accuse me of having a dad sense of humor.

As much as I enjoy being the meat in an alpha sandwich, I'm gonna choke to death between Sam's stress pheromones and Garret's work sweat funk. Plus, having a slightly swollen knot grinding against my butt doesn't help the situation. Still, when I tip my head back to look at Garret, he's grinning at me, and I enjoy how much he shivers when I wiggle against him.

Steve heads straight towards Teddy, but since he's behind Sam, I can only guess he's giving a similar hug. A few minutes later, his head pops around the side. "Oh, Xan asked me to tell you that JJ said her first word this weekend and while Lexi apparently isn't interested in talking, he's had to baby proof everything that's not nailed down now that she's walking."

I extricate myself from the alphas, hopping up and down as I circle around to talk to Steve, so I'm not yelling over bodies. "Wait, aren't they only about ten months old, isn't it a little early for that?" Sam heaves a sigh and the group hug dissolves. The guys know by now that once we start talking about Candice's kids, we're gonna be busy for a while.

They were about a month premature, but they've caught up really well. Everything was crazy at work for the first four months or so. Doctor Leo was the only one who wasn't freaking out, though I still wouldn't exactly say he was calm, either.

"Oh, Officer Josh also stopped by today for an oil change." Steve's rapid change of subject grabs my attention back. He obviously brought it up for a reason.

"Oh, how's he doing? Haven't seen him since Spence brought him to the gym around Christmas." Josh is pack adjacent to Spence. They're the same age and best friends, and he's also Paul's younger brother. Paul and Spence are in a pack together with another alpha that I've only met a few times since Spence started working for Steve and Garret at the gym late last year.

Steve may hate all the business classes he took, but he still learned how to run one. Teddy's our gym rat from hanging out with Sarah for almost ten years. My kinesiology and Garret's medical degree aren't as useful, other than in trying to keep people from injuring themselves.

I may go back to school in a few years to be a physical therapist, and Garret may look into residency at some point, but for now, we're focusing on the present. Being together, building something new, and dealing with our issues.

Steve nods. "Yeah, no. He's good. He wanted to tell me and Xan that all the charges against Paul have been dropped. You know, Dad's...Marc's goons got extradited pretty quick since they had warrants out for assault back in California." I nod my reply, bending down to give Jake a good scratch behind his floppy ears.

"Well, I guess there was some sort of issue with them testifying after so long and from out of state, so it took a while. But yeah, everything's clear now. He was setting up a celebration for this weekend at the diner and said we were welcome if we wanted to stop by."

Officer Josh is, apparently, also a fan of One Punch Man, so when he stops by the gym and Steve's there, neither of them gets anything done. Spence banned him from coming in unless it's an emergency or a holiday, saying he's worried he's going to lose his job for his family monopolizing one of his bosses' time.

Steve only really works weekends at the gym now, anyway. He's taking morning classes at the college and works in the afternoons at the garage since I moved full time to administrative stuff at the gym. It's not what my degree's in, but I know paperwork and none of these guys seem to be able to multitask worth a darn.

The gym is co-owned by the whole pack, kind of like Gabe's Garage. So we all work there as needed. Lots of the high school girls like to come in and ogle my alphas, but I haven't slapped anybody yet, so that's a win.

Sam's head pops out of the kitchen. "Hey, it's Tuesday. Are we doing tacos, enchilada casserole, burritos? Somebody make a choice."

"Tacos!" yells Teddy.

"Burritos," I shout simultaneously.

"You guys suck, I want quesadillas," pouts Steve. "Oh, we learned a new recipe at school today, for chicken quesadillas." He jogs towards the kitchen.

Garret walks up behind me and wraps his arms around my shoulders. He trails his tongue over the shell of my ear before grinding against me again. His voice is a breathy whisper against my neck. "I could go for a taco right about now."

It wasn't very quiet though, as Teddy bursts out laughing. "Fuck man, it's a good thing you two are already mated. Nobody else would fall for that bad of a pickup line." He cackles all the way into the kitchen after Sam and Steve.

Garret nuzzles me again. "I told you it was a terrible joke."

Giggling, I turn in his arms to face him. "It was, yeah...but you love me anyway, even with my terrible jokes."

His smile is bright enough to light up the room. "Of course I do, you're mine."

Kelly's Calendar

May 13
Sam
Books – Mystery
Gift card to Cooking store
Tools??
Jockey shorts

November 19
Teddy
Guitar Picks
Books – Horror
Gift card to music store
Dumbells Sexy boxers!

June 14
Garret
Fancy Tea Set
Books – Romantic comedy?
New Boxer Briefs
Gym Clothes or cute
panties

June 14
Steve
Cookbooks or Manga
Shirts!!!!
Gift card for video
games or music?

August 8
Kelly
Manga
Snuggle coupons?
Stuffed critters
lingerie Yes!!
Bookcases
Shoes? (non slip)

December 15
Jake
Rawhide bone?
New bed? New stuffy
Replacement collar
or harness for walks

<u>*Acknowledgements:*</u>

Huge thanks to My Tallest/ Husband/ Father-of-my-spawn/ Most-Support-ive-Man-I've-Ever-Met. Without you to encourage me and help me make time, I don't think the first book would have happened, let alone the rest of my madness spilling out of my mind.

This story wouldn't have made it this far without the amazing support of my Alpha and Beta readers: Alice, Amanda, Debora, Jennifer, Catherine, Susan, Michelle, Jessica, Nicole, Crystalizelle, and Gabrielle. You all are amazing, and I can't thank you enough for all the support and encouragement you give me, as well as finding my obnoxiously bad spelling errors and overly enthusiastic/incorrect use of commas.

More thanks to the wonderful people in the writing community, especially the OV writing groups. A.R. Lines is awesome and if you like fantasy omegaverse stuff you should totally check her out.

My great gandma/mammie who had a tiny red bloodhound statue that I loved when I was a kid, and I realized halfway through this book that it's were Jake came from, at least to start. Jake, for his part is a mutt with bloodhound and great dane and who knows what else thrown in.

Thanks to everyone who stuck around for the second half. Yeah. Steve's still an asshole. Steve will always be an asshole to those people he doesn't think of as his. Steve and Garret are basically cats. Black and orange respectively. IYKYK

In other news, I finally got my website set up, so be sure to check out www.Galadrealsimmons.com where I'll be posting bonus content and updates as they happen. I should put in a blog section or something. I'm also still around on Facebook at Galadreal's Book Case, or find me on LinkTree to see where else I hang out.

So, thanks for hanging out. I'm hoping to get back to work on Sarah's story. Yes, Spence will be one of the MMC's along with Officer Paul, an unmet alpha (Alistair), and the sexy beta guard from the omega center (Gregory/Greg). I'm not sure who's gonna have their hands full more, Pack Miller or Sarah.

Galadreal Simmons was born at a very early age. She doesn't remember much of it, as she was tiny and squishy. Regardless, after 45 years...she's still short and squishy.

She was named after an elf proving that nerd genes run in her family. It is spelled differently, because try teaching a five year old how to spell something that long. When she was of an adult age, she had it legally changed to include the misspelling.

She lives in a not overly remote location in the southern United States with her husband, two small creatures that share her genetic material, and a cat named Nyx.

She enjoys reading, avoiding human interaction, and feeding crows in the hopes that they will form a crow army and do her bidding. So far, that hasn't worked out, but she continues to do it anyway—because they might be hungry.

www.ingramcontent.com/pod-product-compliance
Lightning Source LLC
Chambersburg PA
CBHW071730110726
47908CB00006B/1558